PRETTY BROKEN WINGS

ALINA MAY

Ebook ISBN: 978-1-964979-08-3

Paperback ISBN: 978-1-964979-09-0

Hardcover ISBN: 978-1-964979-10-6

Book Cover by Occult Goddess

Formatting by Deliciously Dark Editing

Illustrations by Lulybot

Editing by Deliciously Dark Editing

Hardcover Page Edges by Painted Wings Publishing

This content only suitable for 18+

❀ Formatted with Vellum

For all those who've said: men ain't shit.
This one's for you.

AUTHOR'S NOTE

There's a lot of man-hating in this book. If that's not your vibe, I'll see you on the next one.

The FMC begins as angry, aggressive, and mean. In dark romance, we see this characteristic a lot in MMCs but not a lot in FMCs. I think it's super important to remember that women can and do respond to trauma with anger and aggression. Coping is not 'one size fits all.' If you've been through trauma, please remember never to hate yourself for the way that you had to survive.

While there is always consent between the main characters in this book, there have been times in their past when they have not given consent. This also happens for one character as a child. Please also note that these characters are unhealed, and their relationships begin as toxic. There are also harsh realities in this book. There is domestic violence, characters unable to afford food, and highly illegal behaviors for which there is no consequence.

Please take this as your warning. For a more detailed list, please see my website www.alinamaybooks.com

Also note that this story is set in the 90s and can be read with stories from Harleigh Beck, Kat Blackthorne, and Kinsley Kincaid in the Hollows Grove series.

If you enjoy a good trauma dump because it makes you feel less alone, I see you. If you're here for just entertainment, I see you also. Have fun with the pegging.

Xoxo
    Alina

CHAPTER ONE

RAVEN

There's nothing better than making a grown man cry.

I love the little sounds they make—the little whimpers and quick puffs of breath, wet sniffles, and tiny hiccups. The way their body shudders when they want to do something that I won't let them do. It's like playing with a chained lion—dangerous, stupid, and a little thrilling.

The man currently under me is definitely crying. I feel his body jerking, my stiletto pinned to his shoulder, and his silk tie wrapped around my fist. I wish they'd turn the club music down so I could hear those pitiful sounds better.

I lean down, careful not to touch the stall walls. We're in the men's bathroom, and I know there's urine all over them. The man is bent forward, kneeling at my feet, one hand rubbing his cock from outside his dress pants.

"You're pathetic," I say loudly to make sure he hears me over the music. "You think you're good enough to get a taste of me?"

The man looks up at me slowly, his eyes trailing up my fishnet stockings and locking on my tits. I know he can see my pussy, but he won't look at it. His cheek is still red from where I slapped him for that earlier. Then I told him he was an embarrassment and a shame to his family and mankind.

I don't know him, but I made a guess. I met the man at the bar tonight, and he just screamed, *'I need a mommy.'* He was too eager. He tried to play it cool, but when I slid in next to him and told him his suit made him look fat, his pupils dilated.

Was it stupid? Yes.

Was I drunk, and did it feel good? Also yes.

The alcohol gives me courage.

"Lick it," I demand, staring down at the man under me. He barely fits between the toilet and me. There's a brief flicker of fear in his gaze when he looks up at me, which only makes me stab my shoe into him harder.

The man is big. Easily six feet and packed with muscles. He's in his forties, but he's kept up with himself. He could get up at any point. But he chooses not to. Because secretly, he likes this. Which both arouses me and pisses me off.

"You think I'd let your small dick get anywhere near me? Lick my shoe." The demand fills me with a rush of adrenaline. Licking the pissy bottoms of my shoes may be where he draws the line. Might be where he gets up, slams me against the door, and calls me a crazy bitch. Might be where I get my ass handed to me.

Fucking hurt me. If a man isn't hurting me, it makes me jumpy. I don't like men who wait for me to let my guard down before they strike.

As the man drops his head to lick my shoe, I get a whiff of something. I pull in a breath, sorting around the smell of urine and disinfectant.

Cologne. And not just any cologne. The kind *he* used to wear. The kind I always thought smelled like cassette tapes right after you opened them. This man is wearing it.

Immediately, my body locks up, and I feel hot.

"Get off me," I say, my blood heating. My whole body is on fire, and before I realize it, I've backed into the stall door with a bang. My other foot comes down to steady myself. The man is moaning, rubbing himself through his pants, and all I can smell is that damn cologne.

Fuck. I gotta get out of here.

Scrambling for the lock, I realize that the door opens inward, and it won't open with both of us here. I'd have to step into the man.

Gotta get out. Gotta get away.

"Get up!" I demand, trying to kick the man out of the way.

He just continues to moan, jerking himself.

"Move!" I shove him back, the world blurring. Somehow, I burst out of the stall, stumbling into the bathroom. The air surrounds me like a blanket of cologne and ammonia.

It's not him. It's not fucking him.

I have to get out. I stumble to the counter where I left my purse.

Only I'm not alone. There's another man in here blocking my way. He's tall, over six feet, and heavily muscled, with thick-rimmed black glasses and a ball cap on his head. But something seems... off.

"Wow." The man slowly starts clapping his hands.

Fear skitters down my back like ice shavings. He's not only blocking the door, but he's blocking my access to my purse, which is sitting on the counter. My purse, which has my wallet and the only cash I have left to cover me for the next few days.

I can't leave that.

"Excuse me." I step around the man, and he moves, only he backs up into the counter, further blocking me.

I don't let him stop me. I dart my hand back, my fingers brushing the leather of my purse, when the man's hand snaps down, grabbing my arm.

"Hey!" His voice is startled.

I jerk back, managing to free my arm. "Fuck off!" Stumbling

back, I stare at the man with wide eyes. And as I take him in, I realize why he looks so different—he has no eyebrows. Or eyelashes. Or hair.

Only he does. But they're white. And behind his glasses, his eyes are...pale. It's almost like the features that would normally have pigment are covered in frost. He has a haunted look about him.

"Didn't mean to scare you." The man holds up his hands, palms out. "Thought you were grabbing me." He flashes me a Playboy smile.

There's a loud bang, and I flinch, turning around. The door to the stall I was just in is moving back, only it looks like it's happening in slow motion. Then, slowly, the man I was messing with comes stumbling out.

"Sorry." There's a touch on my arm, and I jump again. The frosty man is grabbing my arm, smiling at me like he knows he's attractive.

"Hands off, asshole," I spit, and suddenly, I'm hit by the scent of mint, and it breaks me slightly out of my daze. The man with the icy hair chews absently, squinting his eyes at me.

"He bothering you?" Behind his glasses, his eyes narrow.

I suck in a breath, getting a whiff of that mint again, and it overpowers the smell of cologne. I straighten, sucking another breath into my lungs. Because, like fuck am I going to have a panic attack right here and now.

"Fine. I'm fine."

The man turns and grabs my purse, then hands it over to me.

Embarrassment heats my cheeks. I needed him to give me my purse. I was just weak. So fucking weak. And if there's one thing I'll never be again, it's weak in front of a man.

I snatch my purse from him and waltz out of the bathroom. I should be running. I don't like the unnerving intensity the man with glasses looked at me with. Like he was soaking in every tiny detail to use against me.

And I'll be fucked if I give him that.

It takes about ten minutes to walk home in the shockingly cold fall air. It gives me a chance to clear the alcohol from my brain.

Stupid. I'm so fucking stupid. Can't help getting myself in trouble, and for what? I didn't even get to ruin that man's orgasm.

Fuck.

I check to make sure no one is following me. The street is empty, lit up by the street lamps and yellow Halloween lights strung up in the bushes outside the gas station. I have a car, but gas is expensive, and almost everything in this stupid town is close together. All the shops and department stores are in one small area. Everyone here knows everyone. I've only lived here a few months, but this town is odd. Lots of people like to say it's haunted, but I don't believe in that bullshit.

By the time I make it to my studio apartment, my nose is running. It takes me three tries to get the key in the front door, and it's not just because my hands are numb. I check again to make sure no one followed me.

Fuck, I'm being paranoid.

Finally, the key slides in, and I step inside, shivering in the warmth that floods over me. I can only afford to keep the place at sixty-five, but it still feels far better than outside.

Flipping on the main light, I wince. It's bright and harsh, lighting up the sparse apartment. There isn't much. Just a small kitchen built into the side wall, and beyond it, my bed, baseball bat, my meager collection of childhood books stacked on the floor, and my plastic drawers full of clothes. It looks so bleak with the fluorescent light. I think this place used to be a shop, but the owner turned it into three narrow studios.

I'm the only sucker who saw the old creepy department store and said 'Sign me up!' I keep meaning to find a lamp at the secondhand shop, preferably one with a yellow bulb. Easier to read with the soft light. Not that I have the energy to read much anymore.

I can feel the buzz leaving my body, leaving me numb and hungry. I shouldn't eat this late, but I open the fridge anyway. Inside is my container of rice and beans from earlier.

I shut the door.

I shouldn't eat it. That's lunch for tomorrow.

Pacing to the bed, I strip my clothes off. It feels like the urine and cologne are sticking to my skin. I need a shower. A scalding one.

During my shower, I can't keep the anxiety away. I don't like the way the minty guy looked at me. And the way he had his hands all over my purse.

My purse. I didn't check it. I just grabbed it and ran.

My stomach twists, and I turn off the water, ripping the towel from the rack that never stays up.

Paranoid. I'm being paranoid. No reason to rush.

But I do. I towel off quickly, my hair still dripping wet, and jump into my old sweats and oversized T. Then I dart to the kitchen, snatching up my purse from the counter. I rip it open, feeling around inside, my hand meeting nothing.

No. No, it's gotta be in the corner. I feel around frantically, but it's not there.

My wallet is gone.

CHAPTER TWO

RAVEN

I feel like my brain has been unraveled roughly and shoved back together. I'm fucking exhausted.

By the time I realized my wallet was missing, the bar was already closed. Still, I walked all the way back and banged on the door with no luck. When I got back to my place, I was too jacked to sleep for more than an hour or two.

So, now I'm out of the last bit of my paycheck that was supposed to go for food. But worse, my wallet had my driver's license in it.

With my real name.

Panic surges through my body again, making the tips of my fingers go numb.

I came to this middle-of-nowhere town and started using my middle name to try and disappear, and I've already lost it?

The man in the bathroom took it, the tall playboy who was listening to us in the stall like a fucking pervert. There's no way it fell out.

I pace my studio apartment—sixteen paces down and twelve across.

Why in the fuck did I keep my license in my wallet? I spin on my heel.

Because I told myself that most of the people here don't care. To them, I'm the side character in their story. The most they'll do is give me a pity look and move on.

But that's not what the man from the bathroom did. He looked at me like he could see me, which is unacceptable. No one sees me.

I pace back and forth, back and forth. When people see me, I always end up getting hurt.

A sharp knock at the door makes me jump. I whirl on my heel, staring at the door.

Who the fuck is that? Could it be the man from the bar?

Then, my thoughts get darker. It's my ex. He found me after all these months.

My legs tingle. I could run. I could slip out the back door, get in my car, and go.

But as soon as I think that, I shoot it down. I don't even know who's at the door.

The knock comes again, and I straighten. If he's here, I will not hide.

Marching to the door, I grab my pink aluminum bat. Then, I check the peephole.

It's the hot man from the bar. The wallet thief.

Fuck.

A mix of relief and shame rushes through me. Of course, I was being dramatic. My ex isn't here. This is ridiculous.

I rip the door open.

Pretty Boy's face lights up. "Hey!"

In the daylight, he looks different. Taller, if that's possible.

His cheekbones are defined, and his lips are the lightest shade of pink. He doesn't have the hat on today, and his hair is icy white. He looks ethereal.

The man's face is stretched into an easy grin as he stares at me. "You gonna hit me with that?"

I blink, looking down. The bat is still in my hand.

My first impulse is to laugh it off, to make him feel comfortable even though I have no obligation to. And I hate that reaction.

I don't let go of the bat. "You have something of mine?"

"I'm Axel."

I blink.

He grins. "My name."

I glare at him.

"Oh, right." Axel laughs, reaching into his pocket. "You left this in the bathroom last night."

He holds out my wallet, and I stare at it for a second. He thinks I'm going to believe that bullshit lie?

I snatch the wallet out of his hand.

The corner of his mouth twitches, but as soon as I look at him, it's gone.

"Sorry it took me so long to get it back to you." Axel tucks both his hands in his pockets as a blast of cold air rushes past us. I smell mint again, and I spot him chewing gum.

"It's okay." The words are out automatically before I can stop them. Immediately, I hate myself. It's *not* okay. So, I adjust. "I mean, you took it, so I wouldn't expect you to get it back on time."

Axel's grin doesn't falter. If anything, it stretches wider. "Ouch. Okay."

Okay, picking a fight with a man I don't know is arguably very stupid. I've never been very good at balancing my hatred with common sense.

Axel peeks behind me. "Nice what they did with the place, huh?"

I move to block his view. He's looking at my home. My safe space. "I, uh, I have to work."

"Sorry, yeah." He raises his hands again. "It just sat empty for years. Weird to see it as a studio."

I didn't realize how much everyone was in everyone else's business till I moved here. Fucking small towns.

I glance around. There's a car parked out front with someone in the front seat.

"Hitched a ride, so I'll let you go. Catch you later, *Raven*." Axel glides off my front step, climbs into the car, and they take off.

Raven. Why did he say it like that?

Because he saw your license, you idiot.

Fuck. As panic surges in me, I shut the front door and lock it.

Axel took my wallet. He stole from me. Then showed up at my door.

Fuck him for that. I'd like to hurt him for that. Make him cry. Make him beg me to stop.

My skin crawls. This is the exact opposite of laying low.

I place the bat beside my bed, then check the time on my microwave. Fuck. It's almost two, and I have to get to work. I'm working the second shift as a cashier at a mom-and-pop grocery store called Newmans. I'm basically starting my career over, and all because of a fucking man.

I've considered stripping. Are you even a woman in crisis if you haven't considered stripping? There's a strip joint around the block from the grocery store called Trick or Treat. It's obviously a play on the weird name of the town itself, Hollows Grove. The club sits there, mocking me every night when I walk home from work. I just don't think I can keep my boiling hatred down enough to make any money.

I'm fuming the whole time I get ready. The brisk walk to work cools me off for a bit, but after about an hour of checking people out, it starts again. The anger is like a fucking shot glass filled to the brim. Anytime it gets bumped, the rage starts again.

After a man in scrubs rudely shoves his cash at me, I count to ten. Men should be required to take a lie detector test to be employed. Hurt anyone? Jail. Stolen something? Jail. Existing? Fucking jail. In fact, all men should start off in jail. The only way they can get out is if a woman vouches for them.

Scratch that. At least three women.

I try to focus on the cadence of the beeps as I swipe the products across the scanner. My boss, Mrs. Todd, an older lady who wears pantyhose every day, has been walking between her office and the back a lot tonight. So, as much as it hurts, I keep my customer service voice on.

"Long time no see."

That voice is familiar.

I snap my gaze up, looking straight into the light-colored eyes of the man I thought I had left at my apartment.

Axel.

"What the hell?" The words slip quietly from me.

Axel just grins, his teeth straight and white. "Small world, huh?" There's a knowing glint in his eye, and he adjusts his glasses.

He's following me. First my apartment, now this?

"Leave me alone," I whisper.

Axel waves at a loaf of bread on the belt. "Ran out."

I stare at it, then back up at him, the flush spreading across my face. So he grabbed an item just to harass me?

"Stop," I say softly. Way softer than I wanted to, which just makes me angry. This isn't who I am now. I don't take shit from men.

I clear my throat and say it again, louder, "Stop following me."

Axel chuckles. "Damn, a man can't get hungry 'round here?" The way he flicks his gaze up and down my body makes me livid.

"Leave. Me. Alone." My voice is louder now, and I feel every limb trembling. I'm not sure who this man thinks he is, but we're done here. Vaguely, I notice people turning to look at us.

Axel's voice gets softer. "Didn't know you worked here, little bird."

Little... what? Did this man just call me *little bird*?

The energy inside me explodes, and I see an image of me punching the hell out of his face fill my head. I almost do, but at the last second, I snatch the loaf of bread and sling it at his face as hard as I can. Which isn't hard, considering he's only a foot and a half away, and it's fucking bread.

Axel doesn't move, but the bread knocks his glasses to the side. Slowly, he fixes them, his grin growing.

"Get. Out," I hiss, my heart pounding.

"What seems to be the issue here?" Mrs. Todd's voice says behind me. I startle, only to see her and her fake smile push up next to me.

"This man is following me," I say, my cheeks heated. It's all I can get out; the anger and hatred are mixing so potently that I'm lost for words.

There's a tense moment where I feel like I just tattled to the principal. I glare at Axel, watching his face. He looks right back at me, those light eyes looking through my soul. I can't tell if they're blue or a sort of colorless purple, but as he stares, I get the odd impression that he sees everything and nothing at the same time.

Then, his face shifts, and he snaps into a charming grin. "Not following, Mrs. Todd. She must have mistaken me for someone else."

He just lied. In front of my boss. Of course, he did. Blood rushes in my ears, but Axel just continues to grin like he doesn't see me.

"I'm sorry, Mr. Newman. You have a nice night." Mrs. Todd waves her hands in a soothing motion. "So sorry. I'm so sorry."

"Don't worry about it, Jane."

I stare between the two of them, realization slowly sinking in. They know each other. Because, of course, they do.

"Have a nice night, Miss *Raven*." Axel throws me a wink, then takes off, leaving without paying.

CHAPTER THREE

AXEL

As a general rule, I don't fuck with women. Well, I *fuck* them. Then I cut them loose. Sometimes, I have to peel them off me if they try to crawl back. Sex means nothing other than a good time and a nut-draining orgasm.

Women, I find, don't agree with me. I'm more of a let-me-use-your-body-then-let-me-go kind of guy, and that's why I have one big rule: never fuck the same woman twice.

The grilled cheese sputters on the stove, a butter bubble popping and snapping me out of my thoughts.

Celeste—or Raven—was pissed tonight. So pissed that I could see the way her pale skin blotched red as she yelled at me. I wonder if she would have treated me the same way as that man in the stall? That night, when I heard the smack, I thought that whoever was in there was hitting her, and I almost booted the door down. But then I heard her sexy, rough voice tell the other man exactly what was going to happen if he looked at her pussy again.

And I froze. Because fuck me. I love it when a woman talks like that.

Fuck. My groin feels tight. I glance down at myself, and sure enough, my dick is pressing against my pants.

The sweet butter smell takes on a charred scent, and I snap out of it, ripping my pan off the stove.

Jesus. Since when have I ever been this distracted by a pussy?

I flip my sandwich onto a paper towel and immediately take a bite, the burn ripping through my mouth as I chew anyway. The pain amplifies my headache. It was bright out today. I stepped out on my lunch to return Raven's wallet, and the sun hurt my eyes the whole time.

But I don't care. Because I noticed that Raven's first name is Celeste, and she's not from here. The address on her license was an old one. I only found her through a slip of paper tucked in the billfold that showed she had turned on the trash service to her little studio.

She's not from here, which is kinda perfect. I love playing with women who don't know a thing about me.

Another throb runs through my head.

Will Raven be at the bar tonight?

A thrill rushes under my skin, and I lick the butter from my fingers. Raven, Raven, *Raven*. There's something captivating about this girl. The way her body lined with a mixture of attraction and tension when she leaned across the bar to chat up that old guy. The tiny flinch her hand made when he set his drink down too hard. The way her lip curled down just slightly the whole time they were talking.

Stupid fucker didn't even notice.

But I did. It doesn't take a fully-sighted person to see that Raven is angry at the world. And broken. So very broken.

She's someone I could fuck with my glasses on. I usually take them off. Every hookup is a 10/10 when you can make up how they look in your head.

I tell people I'm legally blind for the shock value. But I actually can't see. Not well, anyway. On my best days with my glasses, I can see the gist of things across the room without any details. I can even read with a magnifying glass. Without my glasses, I'm fucked. I've been told it's similar to looking through a foggy shower door with little to no detail and vague shapes. I'd be able to tell you if that was true if I hadn't been born like this.

I'm glad I chose to see last night because Raven is fascinating, and I want to know more about her. Because I'm fucking *bored*.

I've fucked most of the women in this town and the surrounding ones, too. It's probably partially that I'm a charmer and partially that people like the novelty. Everyone wants to fuck the blind guy with the white hair. The novelty wears off, though. The amount of times I've been called a ghost in this haunted town makes me want to vomit. It's not even hard anymore. Women crawl over themselves trying to get to me.

But you know who wouldn't come crawling?

Raven. Or should I say, *Celeste*? The woman with hate in her eyes.

In fact, she'd run. As far as those broken wings will allow.

A slow smile breaks across my face.

Oh, this'll be fun.

CHAPTER FOUR

RAVEN

8 Years Old

"Siloh, please be quiet; we're getting to the good part." I shoot Siloh a look. She's my stuffed cat, and she's always causing problems. All of my stuffed animals are lined up in a semicircle around me as I read, and Siloh is tipped over. Again.

I sigh, fixing her as I get back to my book. We're just getting to the part where the girl jumps on the back of the bad guy and hits him until he runs away. Onyx, my dog, is quiet in my arms. She's such a good dog.

I wish she were real. I'd take care of her if she were real. I got every book on dogs that the library had. I'd be her best friend. I am her best friend, but I'd be her *real* best friend.

Suddenly, the garage door grinds. For a second, I just stare at my book, then I realize what that means.

Dad's home.

I dart to my feet. He's back, and I forgot to take the chicken out of the freezer.

I race to the kitchen, turn on the hot water, and shove the pack of chicken thighs under it. Dad asked me to do this a few times before he left, but I got distracted with my book. It was a book my old friend Kimmy gave me before my dad said I couldn't go to the homeschool group anymore.

I should have remembered to take the chicken out. Mom leaves every week for her Bunco game, and every week, I'm in charge of dinner.

I hiss as I test the water, which is now hot, and I put the chicken under the stream. Dad is going to be so mad, which makes me want to both run and punch something at the same time, but instead of doing that, I freeze.

It's never good when Dad's mad.

Poking the chicken, I feel how frozen it still is when Dad's steps sound right outside the door. I turn, darting to the living room and sitting on the couch. At the last minute, I realize that I left the water on. But there's no time.

Dad comes in, carrying his lunch bag and coat. His cheeks are pink, and immediately, I know he's happy. His cheeks are always pink when he's happy.

Dad just dumps his stuff, moving to the bathroom.

As soon as the bathroom door shuts, I feel an odd pause. Did he... forget? Sometimes Dad forgets when he's drinking his adult coffee. He says it makes him want to throw himself off a bridge less, and he needs it every day. But I don't like it. He's not as nice when he's drinking it, even though he says it helps.

Darting up, I turn off the water and hesitate, unsure where to put the chicken. I can't put it back in the freezer, or he'll really know. Or will he know if I leave it out?

I hear the toilet flush, and I dart past the bathroom to the stairs. Maybe if Dad doesn't see me, he won't remember.

I'm in the safety of my room for what feels like forever

before I hear a bang and Dad says a bad word. Immediately, my whole body locks up.

I hope he doesn't come up here. Please don't come up here...

I hear the sound of him moving around, listening for the creak that the wood floor makes right by the bottom of the stairs.

Then, I hear it. The creak, and then the loud stomping and muttering.

I dart to my feet, unsure what to do or where to go. I feel stuck. Frozen.

Dad barges into my room, making the door slam into the wall and bounce back again, hitting him. Dad's face is red. "You can't do one thing?" The way he's looking at me, I know he's not all the way happy. His eyes don't look like marbles, and he still looks tired.

I wish he were all the way happy.

But I'm a brave girl. I messed up.

I straighten, looking him in the eye. "I forgot."

Dad blinks at me, then his fists clench, and he moves a step closer. "So you're just disobeying, yeah?"

He looks so big, and some of my courage goes away. I'm angry and scared, and I don't know what to do. I want to run, but I can't make myself. "Sorry, I was reading and—"

The arm snaps out of nowhere. I forgot how fast Dad is. He snatches my shoulder up, gripping me so hard I let out a cry. I feel every one of his fingers digging into my shoulder.

"Why are you so disobedient, huh?" He shakes me, and my head snaps forward. I'm washed in sudden embarrassment at how weak I look. I'm not being strong. The girl in my book wouldn't look like this.

"Please sto—"

Crack. I hear it before I feel it. Suddenly, there's a warm wash over my eye, and behind it is an explosion of pain.

"... defy me... " Dad is saying something, but I can't hear it.

My ear is ringing. Why is my ear ringing? And my face hurts so bad, I think I need to throw up.

"Please stop." The tone is mocking, and my dad's in my face, sneering. I blink, trying to see straight again.

"All day, all you do is sass me. I try to teach you how to obey. How to be a productive member of society. How do you ever expect to succeed if you're like this?"

The pain that felt like when I stuck my hand on the stove now boils down to a throb, and I gasp at the relief between pulses.

"Please stop," Dad laughs. "You did this to yourself. Now, what do you say?"

"S-s-sorry." I realize that I'm crying. Why am I crying? But it's only from one side. The side where the pain is coming from. My nose is leaking, too.

Then suddenly, Dad lets me go with a snort. I drop back on the bed, gripping the sheets, trying to keep the real tears in.

I'm wrapped up in that horrible feeling between staying strong and crying while Dad paces in front of me. I spot Onyx lying on her side, and with a rush, I realize she's probably sad. She never likes it when Dad and I fight. I just want to give her a hug. I don't want her to be sad.

Then, Dad stops. He takes a breath in, and in that silence, I try to breathe. Only, the breath comes in so loud, and it sounds like I'm hiccuping.

"Son of a bitch."

I tense, and then Dad is there, sitting on the bed next to me. "Fuck, I try so hard to help you." Suddenly, his arms are around me, and he wraps me in a tight hug. We sit there for a long time, me angry and stiff, and him just holding me. But as time passes, my back bends over, and my fingers on the bedspread let go.

"Come here." Dad pulls me in closer, and I don't fight him. I'm so tired. So, so tired. It feels like that one time I stayed up all night.

"We'll get through this," Dad says, squeezing me once. "I do this because I love you."

I swallow. What if he left marks on me? What if someone sees them?

"This is what love is. Forgiving each other and moving on."

He squeezes tighter. "I love you, Celeste."

I'm mad, but it feels like a distant haze. Dad still loves me. He may have been mad, but he still loves me. He's going to be happy again.

"I forgive you. Okay?" Dad seems to wait for my response.

I don't want to talk. My face still hurts, and I just want to sleep.

"Okay?" Dad asks again, a little louder.

"Okay," I whisper.

"And?"

I stare at my pants, picking at a spot on them.

"Celeste." There's a note of warning in his voice.

"And I forgive you, too."

"Good girl." He kisses the top of my head. "Love you, baby bird."

CHAPTER FIVE

RAVEN

I got fired.

I stand outside the grocery store, staring at the cars that come and go, the rattle of the carts filling the air.

I got fucking *fired*.

Do you even know who Mr. Newman is? Mrs. Todd had asked, her face red. *Do you have any idea?*

Turns out, 'Mr. Newman' is a fucking executive with the company. As in, his family *started* the store.

Fuck my life. *Fuck my life.*

My anger got me fired. I know I have a problem. I get angry over things that normal people would just let go. But I can't let them go. I burn up inside, and I can't fucking *stop*.

I didn't use to be like this. I was lovable. Back in the day. Back before...everything.

What the hell am I going to do?

I spin in a circle, running a hand along the top of my head.

I can't go back. I can't. My next paycheck isn't for another week, and rent is due at the end of the week.

At this point, panic is becoming a familiar friend.

So I do the only thing I can do. I start walking home.

It's weird going home during the early evening. There's so much traffic out. As I'm moving past the next strip of stores, a car honks. I jerk my head up as tires squeal and two cars narrowly miss crashing into each other.

I glance around. No one seems to have noticed or cared. Then, the glowing sign of the strip club catches my eye. It's neon pink with a skimpily clad witch on it, and the parking lot is full.

Which means there are customers there.

Paying women money.

I need money.

Before I can think twice, I cross the street. My heart races, and once I get in front of the doors, I stop.

I can do this, right? Waltz in and ask for a job? In my sports bra and grocery store polo?

I'm stuck there, staring at the one-way glass. There are cut-out skeletons placed across it that shiver in the wind.

I can do it. Who needs to twerk anyway? You can dance without twerking. I tried tossing it back once in the bathroom and horrified myself so much that I never tried again. But I can do other things.

"You going in?"

I jump and turn. There's an older man behind me, rubbing his hands in the cold. He has an expensive coat on and shifts impatiently.

My lip curls. He's probably been handed everything in his life, yet still can't wait two seconds to go inside? What's his rush? He doesn't worry about bills. He comes here to throw money away while other people starve.

Ah, see? There's that anger again. It's threatening to smother me alive.

I shake myself out of it. The man asked me if I was going inside.

"Yep." I grab the handles and step in.

I think about asking for a job right there, but in a last-minute bout of critical thought, I realize I know nothing and have brought no clothes or shoes. So I pay for my entry with the last of the bills in my wallet in the hopes that I can at least watch a girl dance, memorize it, and then come back more prepared. I might be a little impulsive, but when I set my sights on something, I plan on getting it.

The club is dark, with multicolored lights flashing all around, and the music pounds. The base settles deep in my chest, thumping away until it's all I can feel. It's peaceful in an overwhelming way.

There are a few guys here, so I settle into a seat on the other side of the room. There's a dancer on stage in a bright pink bikini. She twists and turns in a way that makes my gaze lock onto her in fascination. The way she moves is... liquid. Can I do that?

The song switches, and the dance she does is slower. I watch her closely, trying to get down the moves she's doing, but even the slow stuff is complicated.

Then, someone sits down next to me. I stiffen, immediately moving to the edge of my chair, then blink. It's the guy from the bar's bathroom. The one I had on his knees and then ran from.

Immediately, my mood sours.

"Hey." The bathroom man gives me a bashful smile.

I stare at him. He looks even older and more worn in here.

Fucking nasty.

He slides a drink my way. "Sorry about the other night. I was pretty drunk."

I just stare at the drink, then back at him.

He adjusts his tie. "I just thought... I don't know..." His pupils are blown.

"Yeah, I don't care." I stare at the stage again, and out of the corner of my eye, I see him smile wider.

So he's come back for more.

Pitiful.

However... I currently give zero fucks about anything. Degrading a shitty ass man might actually make me feel better.

I make Bathroom Man get me a new drink. He jumps to do my bidding, and I watch him closely the whole time. The way I see it, Satan has given me this chump in the form of a sorry-I-fucked-up-your-life-at-least-get-drunk sort of gift. And then, at the end of the night, I plan on pinching the change from his wallet. It's the least he can do.

I down drink after drink, becoming more and more confident in the space. I could absolutely work here. Mr. Bathroom keeps pushing me to go to the bathroom with him, and I keep turning him down, partially because I want to keep watching the dancers and partially because it's fun to watch his disappointment.

When he tries for a third time, the lights are spinning in circles in front of me, and I'm not sure if it's from the alcohol or if they're programmed to do that. I wave the annoying pest off.

I blame the alcohol for missing the way his gaze tightens with anger. Suddenly, his hand is on my arm, and he's yanking me up roughly.

"You're such a flirt."

I'm falling into his body, and then we're moving. Ah, there it is. He's going to hurt me. He's so predictable that it makes me want to laugh.

Are we moving? I'm drunk, and the world is spinning. He smells like sweat and yeast and beer.

"Fuck you."

"I know you want this."

I reel back, trying to yank myself out of his grip. "I'll cut your nuts off, you disgusting fuck."

We're already almost off the main floor, and I pull away again, but the man's grip is digging into my flesh.

"No." But the word even sounds hollow to me. He won't listen. Since when do men ever listen?

A bitter laugh makes its way through my chest. Anger wars with helplessness inside my chest.

Suddenly, the man dragging me stumbles. I fall partially forward with him; his grip loosens on my arm, and I yank away.

"Don't think she wants to go with you," a deep voice grumbles.

There's a leg outstretched into our path, and I look up to see the one and only Axel Newman sans glasses.

For a second, my mouth drops open, and all I can do is stare. He looks just as handsome as before. Maybe more so in the low light with his sharp cheekbones and light eyes. What is he doing here?

Axel just flicks a bored gaze at the man who had been dragging me.

"Fuck off, John."

The man sneers at Axel. "We were just going to the bathroom."

"No, you were just leaving." Axel waves his hand at him.

When John doesn't do anything, Axel's voice lowers, and the menacing depth of it makes me shiver. "Get out."

"You mother..." John falters on his words, then turns on his heel and walks away.

I watch him start down the hall, then turn on his heel and stalk out of the club, but my vision is twisty, and for a second, he looks like he's walking on the wall.

There's movement, and I see Axel lean back in his seat, throwing me a *look*.

And that look ignites the quick fire of anger again. This motherfucker just got me fired, and he's what, here kicking back like he didn't just fuck up my life? The heat roars through my body, fueled by the alcohol.

"I didn't ask for your help."

Axel barely looks at me. Just turns his gaze back toward the stage. I see that he's left his glasses on the table beside his hand, where his finger taps against the tabletop.

My life just fell apart, and all he can do is tap that damn finger on the table. I'm so hot I feel lightheaded.

"You know, stalking is illegal," I spit.

There's a pause. Then Axel says, "I know."

"I could call the cops." I hate the bored look he's giving.

Of course, he doesn't care. Why would he?

I see his glasses sitting there, and in an impulsive move, I snatch them up.

"Fuck you, Axel fucking Newman." I know I shouldn't, but the anger is fully in control now, and I can't stop it. I throw the glasses on the ground and stomp on them, crushing them under my foot.

Axel looks at the ground, then up at me, squinting. Then, there are black spots in the shadows of his cheekbones. I blink, but they get bigger.

Is he... is something happening to him? Is he turning into Satan in front of my eyes? Or maybe I'm Satan, and I'm getting yanked back to hell. It would almost be fitting. Hell would feel safer, with all that fire to protect me. You wanna hurt me, you gotta get hurt too.

But instead of fire, everything feels fuzzy. I have to lean on a chair for support. At least, I think it's a chair.

And then, things go black.

CHAPTER SIX

GAGE

Right after the woman snatches my glasses, I hear the snap of plastic, then the crystal crunch of glass. For a moment, I'm frozen.

Did she just... break my glasses?

Then, I catch a vague movement. I think the woman is grabbing her face, then she crumples to the ground.

Christ! Reaching out, I try to break her fall, but all I can get is her clothes. She hits the ground with a puff of air.

Fucking drunk dancers, man.

Rolling the woman over, I check for injuries, but I can't fucking see, thanks to her. All I see are blobs of light and dark contrast. I rub my hands along the lighter patch where I assume her face is, and my fingers meet soft skin.

I don't feel anything wet. I pull in a breath and don't smell copper.

I let the air puff from my lungs as a confusing mix of relief and annoyance flashes through me.

Fucking hell. She thinks I'm stalking her?

My brother did it again. Fucking Axel for the motherfucking win. I can always count on him to crash out and take everyone else with him.

I'm actually gonna kill him.

I feel down the woman's body, trying to find her legs to hold them over her head. From what I can feel, she has cargo pants on and sneakers. What the hell? Is this a new thing? She's also light as a feather.

I get her legs up and then look around. I try to wave at the vague blur of people on the other end of the club. At least, I think it's people. The dim light doesn't help.

Ironically, I come here for the dim light. I stop by when I want to shut everything else out, feel the music, and watch the fuzzy lights flash across my vision. It's also the place no one will think to look for me, so when I need to feel like I've disappeared, I come here.

And now, instead of feeling better, I have Axel's current baggage passed out on the floor.

No one is coming over to help, and I dig in my pocket for my cell phone, flip it open, then dial my brother. I listen to the tones and pray I hit the right numbers. Dialing my brother is something I try not to do on a regular basis.

No one picks up the first time. Because, of *course* not. Then, on the second dial, the line connects.

"What's up, prude?"

I grind my teeth. I'm only a few minutes older than him, but Axel thinks that because I don't fuck every woman who crosses my path, I'm against fun.

"Come get your girl."

"Huh?" I hear music in the background. Is he... at the bar?

"Come get your fucking girl," I snarl into the phone. Said girl is starting to stir, making a pitiful little moan.

"Which girl?"

Of course he doesn't know which one this is because it's a new one every day. And yet, he's never slut shamed. Everyone looks at him like the golden standard. They praise him for his charisma and pat him on the back.

Except me. I'm over it. "Well, I can't tell you what she looks like 'cause she broke my fucking glasses."

There's a pause on the other end of the line.

"She... what?"

"You're blind, not deaf. Now get the fuck over here."

The woman groans, rolling over, so I stand up. Clearly, she's fine. Well, if not fine, she'll *be* fine when she sleeps it off.

Axel laughs. The fucker *laughs*. "Oh my god!"

I hang up. I don't have time for this. Almost immediately, my phone rings again. I let it go to voicemail. My glasses are special prescriptions. It will take weeks to get new ones in. How the hell am I going to work?

Finally, when Axel calls back the third time, I pick the phone up and growl, "What?"

"Where are you, bro?"

My face heats. I don't tell him I come here. And now, I have no choice.

"Trick or Treat. Your girl had too much to drink and passed out."

"What?" Axel's voice sobers.

"John from the bank may have given her something, too." I stare at the vague outline of the woman, who is still on the floor.

"I'm on my way. Fuck, is she okay?"

"How should I know?" I flip the phone shut.

Why should I care? Now that I know she's breathing, I feel around for the pieces of my glasses. Fragments of glass brush against my fingers, and a helpless wave washes over me. Helplessness, then anger. What did I think I was going to do, glue them back together?

I stand, stalking over to the bar, bumping into what sounds like a chair on the way over.

Axel is going on about something; I'm not sure what. I don't really care. My brother has made his bed; now he needs to lie in it.

The phone rings again, and I flip it open just to hang up. Again.

CHAPTER SEVEN

AXEL

I'm drunk. The kind of drunk I usually reserve for Halloween to keep the memories at bay. But waiting for Raven to show up at the bar, I can't stop thinking... so I keep taking shots.

Gage's call sobers me just enough to realize how drunk I probably am. What the hell is Raven doing at the club? Is she okay?

I make my coworker and drinking buddy, Dave, drive me the short distance to the club. He's become my go-to driver, always brown-nosing as a way to advance in the ranks. I think he also thinks he'll get more pussy if he hangs out around me. That part might be true. Dave can get insufferable, but if enduring him gets me a driver, then I'll endure it.

As we drive, the lights from the streetlights are all blending into one and spinning like bubbles in a tub. I pop a piece of gum in to try and cut through the blur.

As the car slows and we pull up, I can make out shapes outside, but it's dark and my head is swimming in alcohol. Gage must already be waiting for us. It's blurry, but I think it's Raven leaning on the building. Gage gestures at the car.

I get out, saying, "I see you found my—"

Gage just shoves something at me, and I blink down at it. It's a purse.

"Brother, you shouldn't have—"

"And give me these."

I see his hand coming, and it feels like I dodge him in slow motion. Gage's hand knocks my glasses loose.

"Those are mine!" I reach up to fix them.

Gage is mad. His whole face is red, even his eyebrows. Both of us get red eyebrows when we get pissed. Comes with having very little melanin. Usually, we look fairy-like. Now, he looks like an angry red fairy.

It makes me laugh.

"Flavor of the day broke mine, so I'll be taking these until I get a replacement pair." He tries again for my glasses, and I dodge faster this time. One of the downsides of being identical twins is that our prescriptions are the same.

"Hell no," I grin. "I have to get my *fucktoy* home." I can't help but needle him more. Gage never gets pussy, so he's always so mad when I do.

Gage freezes, then looks at me, narrowing his eyes. I see his nostrils move as he pulls in a breath. "Are you... drunk?"

He looks from me to Dave in the driver's seat. Gage's breaths are coming in pants, and I laugh because getting my brother wound up is my favorite thing in the world. It breathes life into my soul.

"Fuck no." I smile at him, even though I'm sure he can't see it, although I know he can probably hear the smile anyway. "But Dave might be." He's not, but I know it'll piss Gage off.

I see the movement, but this time, I don't want to dodge it. There's a blow to the side of my head that whips my face around. A buzzing fills my head. A delicious buzzing that drowns out the thoughts.

"You let him drive you over here drunk?"

Oh, he's *mad*. The buzzing feels warm, and there's a dull throb, like I should be feeling pain.

"I'm not drunk," Dave's voice comes from inside the car. It's high and a little panicked. He knows my brother's a lawyer. "I only had one beer."

Suddenly, I'm slammed against the hood of the car. Gage is in my face, his breath hot. "You need to get it together." He smells like cinnamon.

I chuckle. "You need to—"

The glasses are whipped off my face. Before I realize it, I'm sliding along the hood of the car. I try to catch myself, but there's no handhold, and I fall, grinding my palms into the asphalt.

I hear Dave protesting from inside the car. But he doesn't bother to step out.

Smart fucker. Everyone knows not to get between my brother and me..

"Did you hear me, fucker?" Gage rages.

The throbbing is turning into a baseline now, squeezing pressure in my head. Gage must have hit me again. I don't care. 'Cause I made the mighty Gage Newman swing.

It's funny.

"Where does your bitch live?"

My bitch? The words make delicious pleasure roll through me.

I'm pretty sure I must have been sitting there, grinning, 'cause Gage's foot boots me in the ass.

Okay. That's a little much. I stagger to my feet, but Gage is pushing a feminine form into the passenger seat. Then he climbs in the back and slams the door. I hear the window roll down.

"Call Mom to come pick you up. Or sleep here, for all I care."

Then Dave and Gage leave with the car, my glasses, and my fucking girl.

My fucking girl.

That fucker better not touch her.

You know what? Fuck no. I stumble over to the building to call a ride. One of my buddies was still at the bar. He picks up and says he'll be on his way over.

As I wait, something sounds like it's skittering to my right. I look over to squint at the club door. Getting so close up that I almost bump into the door, I can vaguely see it's lined with Halloween decorations. Among the skeletons are little creepy ravens with their heads turned over their shoulders.

They look just like the ravens that we used to set up every Halloween.

Suddenly, I'm hit with a memory.

"Axel, get that one, will you?" Rich, my stepdad, motions at me from the attic ladder. I shuffle over the plywood to the Halloween decorations and slide them over to him.

"Thanks, bud!" He grins, and it makes warmth move through me. No one can tell Gage and me apart except for Mom and Dad, and sometimes they still call us by the wrong names. That is, until Rich came along. He can always tell us apart.

Shuffling back down the ladder, I trot along behind him. We open up the decor, pulling out orange and purple lights, ghosts, and witches. It's always been my favorite.

"Got you something." Rich pulls a plastic bag off the counter. Excitement rushes through me. Mom didn't get us a lot of stuff after she and Dad split up.

Inside the bag are little birds. They look like crows with real feathers.

"Smartest birds in the world." Rich pulls one out and hands it to me.

I take it, the soft belly feathers brushing the pads of my fingers while the longer feathers rasp against my palms.

"You want to know the scariest thing about this town?"

I narrow my eyes, skeptical. Growing up in a haunted town means I've heard it all.

"It's not the ghosts or the witches or the scarecrows." His voice lowers. "It's the birds."

I stare at Rich. That seems dumb.

Rich's voice stays quiet, not quiet like he's trying to be scary, but quiet like he is scared. And that makes goosebumps run down my arms.

"All the other things in this town are pretty easy to deal with," Rich says. "You ignore them. The raven?" He cocks an eyebrow at me. "Smarter than cats. If they don't like you, they'll organize their whole family to peck your eyes out."

Suddenly, Rich lunges at me.

I jump back, and Rich laughs. "Birds are weird animals, son. Stay away from them."

I blink, suddenly back in the windy, cold parking lot.

Fuck. I have to keep a handle on this shit. Memories keep popping up more and more frequently now. It's always this time of year.

I open my phone, trying to squint to see the time. The screen is so small that I can't tell, but my friend isn't here yet. I try him again.

"Yeah, man, I'm coming!" I hear the sounds of the bar in the background. Meaning he hasn't left yet.

Fucker.

I can't believe Gage stole my fucking car.

I consider calling the cops on him just for fun. See what the lawyer does to get out of that one. But I don't feel like explaining how the car got here.

My drunk brain rolls. He's in the car with Raven.

Annoyance skitters through me. He's going to her house. Is he going to go inside? Will she let him?

I start pacing back and forth. I don't like the idea of my brother alone with my plaything. What if he tries to mess with her before I have?

Oh *fuck* no.

I check the time on my phone again, but it doesn't get any clearer despite my squinting.

I don't want Gage alone with Raven. She's fucking mine.

Where the hell is my ride?

After waiting a bit longer, I realize Raven's apartment is just around the corner. Around the corner in a car, but still. Surely it wouldn't take long to walk?

As soon as I have the idea, it sticks with me. I start off at a brisk pace, walking in the darkness. But it doesn't scare me. Lack of sight isn't as important as sighted people make it out to be. There are other ways to connect with the world around you.

Suddenly, the air is punched out of my lungs as I run into something hard. I stagger back, coughing. Nothing comes at me, so I feel around.

A telephone pole.

Fuck me. I'm so drunk.

After I right myself, I keep walking. Above me, I hear a raven caw. Suddenly, I hear Rich's breathless voice in my ear. *"This is what all men do."*

Fuck.

I speed up, walking faster. Walking faster will let me outwalk the memories.

"It's okay. Hey bud, it's okay! It doesn't mean anything."

I walk faster.

I close my eyes to pretend he's not here. But that doesn't work. It *hurts*. It feels like I'm on fire.

"I love you, buddy. This'll be our little secret, yeah? Don't tell your mom."

The bed squeaks. My cotton sheets are damp under my hands. And his breath... It smells bad. It smells like the underside of a muddy rock. One with rotten mushrooms.

Mom always says to brush your teeth in the mornings.

Rich never does.

His breath ghosts over me again. "This is what people who love each other do. Everyone does it, so they don't tell their friends about it. It's nothing special."

It's worse than muddy mushrooms. It's like when I accidentally left spaghetti in my lunchbox for two days. Like when the sink clogged up, and mom had to get a stranger to come and fix it.

I never want to smell like that.

After it's over and I cry the night away, I spend the rest of my allowance on a pack of mint gum.

My eyes prick with heat. Why the fuck can't I just put this behind me? It didn't mean anything then, and it's over now. Done. Why the fuck does it haunt me every year?

It takes too long to get to Raven's apartment, but when I do, my car isn't there. I sigh in relief, then realize that maybe he parked in the back.

No. No, Gage isn't going to ruin this for me.

I stumble to the back lot, but all the cars are in shadows, and I can't tell for sure if they're my car or not. Why isn't there a fucking light back here? I stumble past each one, keeping enough of my head not to set the alarms off, feeling to see if they're hot.

None are.

Relief rushes through me, and I fall back against the car and face her apartment.

What is she doing?

Not that I care. She doesn't mean anything. She's just a distraction. Just a fun little toy.

This doesn't mean anything.

Nothing at all.

CHAPTER EIGHT

GAGE

8 Years Old

The smell of melted cheese makes my mouth water. I suck in a breath, catching a whiff of savory pepperoni. *So good*.

"Move." Axel pushes past me to get to the table, putting the steaming pizza down. It makes his glasses fog up.

"Happy birthday, boys." Mom puts down a box of something else, and my eyes widen when I open the lid. Monkey bread. She got us monkey bread!

Today is Friday, which is usually our 'secret meal' night. It is the night when we use whatever is in the fridge to try to make a five-star meal. We have a whole ranking system, including ratings for taste, texture, and quantity. Some weeks are better than others, but it's so much fun. Afterward, Mom makes us toast with cinnamon sugar for dessert.

Fridays are the best.

But today, we got to pick whatever we wanted to eat, and of *course*, we chose pizza. Who wouldn't pick pizza? It's frozen pizza, but it's the good stuff.

"So, tell me about school." Mom sits at the table, smiling at us. Axel immediately starts rambling around mouthfuls of food, telling her about how his friends surprised him for his birthday by pieing him in the face.

I was right next to him when it happened and got bits of whipped cream on me. I'm happy for Ax, but my tummy also starts to twist despite the pizza being so, so good. It's my birthday too, and I didn't get pied. After lunch, one of Ax's friends slid me a bag of chocolate candy and said happy birthday, which was nice, because they're more his friends than mine. Not that I blame them. Axel is happy and funny and all around everything I should be, especially because we're identical.

Mom is laughing at Ax's story, which he's now animating in exaggerated motions. She laughs so hard that tears run down her cheeks.

I like seeing Mom happy. Ax's stories always help. He only tells Mom the good ones. He likes to leave out that he also has a successful business where he trades little personalized poems for pieces of gum. The love-sick boys at our school eat it up, writing their crush's names in and leaving them in their lockers. Ax pays me in an endless supply of cinnamon gum to not only write the poems but to keep my mouth shut about it.

Ax continues talking, and Mom continues laughing, but the pizza feels heavy in my hand.

Mom has been better since she left Dad. She doesn't fall down the stairs as much, and I like seeing her smile. But recently, she's been so tired, and her face looks different. She says she's so cold all the time. I'm saving my money to get her fuzzy socks, a sweater, and more pants. She said the other day her pants don't fit anymore.

I take another bite of my pizza despite not being hungry

anymore. I wonder if I had friends who did stupid stuff like Axel's friends do, would it also make Mom as happy?

As I sit there chewing, I realize that Mom hasn't had any herself.

"Have some." I push a paper towel at her.

"Oh, it's okay, honey." She wipes her eyes, then takes the paper towel to blow her nose. "I only like the crust, you know that."

I stare at her, and for some reason, sadness fills me. There are a lot of things Mom doesn't like.

I wish she'd eat with us.

I finish my piece but leave some sauce and pepperoni around the crust, and Mom eats it quickly. I get a second piece and leave almost half of it, pushing it across the table. Mom just sits back, looking tired again. "I'm sure you'll be hungry later. We get to have this for lunch tomorrow, too."

"Yes!" Axel pumps a fist in the air.

Mom smiles at Axel, looking less tired. I wish I could make my mom smile more.

Why can't I be more like Axel?

CHAPTER NINE

GAGE

Buddy woofs gently right before there's a knock at my door. My pitbull jogs up to the door, tail straight up, while I heave myself off the couch.

It's seven AM. Who the hell is here?

As soon as I crack the door, Buddy takes a huge sniff, then her body relaxes, which can only mean one thing.

"You gonna let me in, asshole?" the muffled voice comes from outside.

Axel.

I groan, opening the door all the way. My brother stands there with dark circles under his eyes, looking like he got run over by a bus. But he still has that signature air about him—the cocky confidence that gets him all the girls, dark circles or not.

Buddy gets excited, the traitor that she is. She has a particular distaste for every single person who isn't Axel or me, which may be because he smells like me. I'm not sure. I can only guess what her life was like before to make her even hate women. She's not aggressive, but she is protective. She thinks everyone who comes through my door is trying to hurt me, sans Axel. I even have to pen her when Mom comes over.

"Move." Axel shoves the door open. And, because I'm a glutton for punishment, I let him. I shouldn't. He got drunk and pissed off some woman so much that she broke my glasses. But when someone needs help, I can't seem to stop myself, particularly when that someone is Axel.

"Took you long enough." Axel shoves past me and shuffles right to the kitchen, Buddy following.

"What do you want?" My voice is gruff.

"Do you still get that sourdough?"

I stalk to the kitchen, where I see him rummaging through my shelves.

"Ah hah!" He pulls the bread out and throws a wink back at me. "Great minds."

Jesus.

"You know I have that trial, and I was up last night cleaning up someone's mess." I cross my arms.

Axel snorts, then mimics my voice, "I'm Gage; I'm out here saving damsels in distress. I can be an asshole 'cause I'm a hero."

I ball my hands into fists and take a step forward before I force myself to stop. Axel always likes picking at me. I work in civil law, mostly with divorce cases, and the one I'm working on now is nasty. Not that I can even say that now.

"Get the hell out of my house."

"Chill, bro. I'm hungry." Axel shuffles things around on my burner now, feeling by hand. "And I came for my glasses."

"No." The word is out without a second thought.

"Yes?" Axel turns the gas burner on with a tk-tk-tk, and then the whoosh of the flame. "They're mine. You taking them is theft. You should know that, Mr. *Don't-Break-The-Law*."

I glare at him. "Your girl broke them thinking I was you. Therefore, she broke your glasses. These are mine."

Axel laughs, throwing a slice of bread onto the pan, then one at Buddy, who wolfs it down in two bites. "That's bullshit, and you know it."

"Don't feed Buddy. I have a big case this week. I need to be able to read."

"And I have a fuck ton of meetings." Axel turns around to face me, sucking his finger while he slips another piece of food to my dog. "I need them. Just order another set."

I grind my teeth. "They won't come for weeks."

"Then hire a personal assistant." Axel shrugs and moves to the fridge, grabbing the butter. Buddy follows him, panting happily.

"No." I glare harder at my brother. Every time I've hired a personal assistant, they've sucked. They've either been no help at all, gotten mad at me for the extra help I need, or tried to get in my pants. The last one was one of Axel's flings, who thought she could get more of Axel by getting me.

She was very wrong.

By the sniff of a smirk Axel makes, I think he's remembering it, too.

"Get out of my house. And for the love of god, I don't want any more of your women on my doorstep."

"Glasses, asshole." Axel shoves his hand out like he's waiting.

"Go to hell." I whirl and move to go down the hallway. I'm over this. Why did I even let him in in the first place?

Axel's voice follows me, "If I miss these meetings, we could miss out on some great brand opportunities. You know how badly Mom has been wanting that particular pizza."

I stop cold. Mom keeps bragging about how proud she is of Axel for taking over the business. Tells all her friends at their book club about the new gossip at the store. She also tells me about it and the joy that fills her face whenever she talks about what Axel has done, especially now that he's apparently bagged her favorite pizza company.

My chest hurts. I want Mom to talk about me that way, but she doesn't. She's always gotten stiff about my job. The most she does is pat my back and say she's proud of me.

For a brief second, I think about walking away. Letting Axel battle the consequences of his own behavior. But then I think about my mom's disappointment.

So I turn back around.

And once again, I enable my brother to be the star of the family at my expense.

CHAPTER TEN

GAGE

This fucking light. I throw my highlighter down, and it skitters across the desk and clatters between it and the wall. The light over my desk keeps wavering, making the page under my large magnifier look like it's underwater. It's so fucking dim in here, and I've been at it for hours. My head is pounding, and I've only made it through part of what I have to do.

Buddy whines, getting up from her spot on her couch and walking over to me. She's blind, but she can still navigate the house really well. I always keep everything in the same spot for her. And let's be honest, it's for me too. Buddy has Progressive Retinal Atrophy, a genetic condition that's left her blind in her old age. I found her in the paper. I don't normally read the paper —it's a lot of work with a magnifying glass, and I prefer to use that energy to work. But I always comb the section about the animal shelter, and Buddy was in the paper for weeks. No one wanted a fully blind dog. I named her Buddy after the first seeing-eye dog because I thought it was ironic. The blind leading the blind.

I pull off my old pair of glasses. It has a similar frame to the ones that were broken, but the prescription is old, and it almost makes things worse.

This is never going to work. My head hurts so bad from squinting at the blurry, dim words that I want to hurl. I absently scratch Buddy's head. The case I'm working on is a domestic violence case, and it's pissing me off more than it should.

I hate these cases.

Why did I ever take this job? For the thousandth time, I think about how it won't reverse time.

And yet, here I am.

For two days, I've fought the suggestion to get help. Two days of pure misery, and I don't even get natural light for long because it's October, and the sun goes down so fucking early.

I hem and haw about the potential of asking someone for help. I don't even have an office. I had an office before, but I find it's just easier to meet clients in coffee shops or even the goddamn library and then bring the paperwork back to my place. All of my magnifiers are here, and when I have the right glasses, it's not that big of a deal.

When I stand up, I get dizzy.

This is not working.

"No one's gonna apply," I mutter, untucking my piece of gum from between my teeth and cheek, chewing in a nervous habit.

It's a short-term position, literally only two or three weeks, just to be my fucking eyes. I refuse to ask my mom. She hates my job, and I don't want her to see the details of this case. She's lived it once; it's not fair to ask her to live it again.

So the next morning, I put an ad in the paper. Personal Assistant Needed for Gage and Co. Start Date: Immediately.

CHAPTER ELEVEN

RAVEN

It's cold, and the wind from the coffee shop door blows up my skirt.

Fuck. I uncross, then recross my legs, trying to get the warm parts of my thighs to warm up the rest of my icy skin. The shop is cute, with maximalist decor, dark lighting, and a bunch of framed photos and collector's items all over any spare wall space.

I'm here for an interview.

The stripper job didn't work out. It couldn't be because I got black-out drunk and then passed out in their facility. At least, that's what they told me I did. I'm not convinced I wasn't drugged because I don't remember much, but I do remember Axel was there. And I think he brought me home.

I seem to collect men who hate me like it's a sport. They're drawn to me like I'm a wounded animal, and they're fucking starving. I must have been a horrible person in a past life because I seem to have the absolute worst luck.

Just when I was thinking of begging for my job back at the grocery store, I came across an ad in the paper. The opening is immediate, and the pay is good. Almost too good to be true. I'm not sure it isn't a setup because I was told to wait at a specific table in the shop, but I don't have the money or energy to care all that much. I'm fucking hungry, and I'm fucking tired. I'm starting to question if it's worth it to keep running.

Don't get me wrong, I'll cut off my ex's balls before I go back to him, but how long will his death buy me? Two weeks before the cops come knocking? My parents have the money, but they hate that I got with a man without marrying him. Hate, as in, cut me out. Said I was living in sin. I'll die before I go begging at their doorstep.

With the past two days of no food in the fridge, that's looking like a potential. I'm not gonna lie; I swung by the dumpster at the grocery store and picked out some produce that wasn't half bad. The food waste that goes on there makes me livid. Of course, Axel would run a wasteful business.

The bell on the door tinkles, and I turn, taking in the entrance of the coffee shop. A huge man steps through the doorway in a jewel-toned blue suit, with hair white as ice, and cheekbones cutting icy shadows on his smooth skin. Axel fucking Newman strides into the coffee shop. Only today, he doesn't have glasses on, and he strides straight to my table.

He's stalking me. He's actually stalking me. The realization moves through me like syrup. It takes until he's standing at the other end of the table for me to click all the pieces together.

I stand up, grabbing my purse. "You just can't leave me alone, can you?"

Axel squints at me. Then, he steps around the table, getting closer to me and staring at me.

"Fuck off!" My heart is racing now. I try to back up, but I

bump into the chairs behind me. Axel's getting closer and closer, and I'm fucking trapped.

Before I can move, he darts his hand out to grasp my wrist, yanking me closer. His breath puffs over me with the smell of cinnamon. "You?"

I struggle to rip my hand from his grip. He's fucking strong. "Get away from me! Fuck off!"

Axel doesn't let go. His grip is firm, but it doesn't hurt. His eyebrows are twisted in surprise.

The people around us are starting to look. But no one does anything. They just stand there, watching.

"Christ above," Axel groans, looking at me closer. Then, he lets go of me.

I scramble back, waving at the baristas who are paying no attention. "I'm calling the cops."

"Do what you want. I won't work with you."

I get a table between us, and then his words hit me. He won't work with me? *He* won't work with *me*? I whirl on him, a sneer on my face.

At that moment, the door opens, and someone else enters the shop. Only, it's not someone else. It's also Axel.

Everything stops, and I stare at the man who just walked into the shop. He's a carbon copy of the one at the table. Only the one who just walked in has glasses and a deep red suit.

What the hell?

The glasses copy spots me, and his face lights up with a grin. "Raven!"

Okay, I'm still drugged from the other night. There's no way I'm seeing doubles right now.

As the copy gets closer, he glances at the double to his right. Immediately, he frowns. He looks between the copy and me, looking me and my skirt up and down. Then, he turns to face the copy, his face dropping into a sneer. "Brother. What are you doing here?"

The copy without the glasses crosses his arms. "Axel."

What in the actual hell is going on? I take a step back, grabbing onto the chair behind me. How can I wake up? Surely, there can't be two of them.

But neither one disappears. There's some sort of tense standoff between the two of them, both of them standing straight up, their necks stiff.

"Is the Ice King going on a date?" There's a mocking tone to the newcomer's voice. "Thought you swore off that."

"It's not a date."

"No?" He motions at me. "Sure looks like it."

"Not a date. But it would be none of your business if it were."

Someone gets up from a table nearby and skirts around the Axel without glasses, then avoids the one with glasses. Slowly, I realize that this is real. I'm not drunk. Other people can see both of them.

They're twins.

Fuck. I've been fighting with twins.

"So what is it, then?" Glasses Axel glances at me again. The edges of his eyes are tight, but they soften when he looks at me. "What are you doing here, little bird?"

"I'm doing what you said." The other one ignores his question to me, throwing his hand in my direction. "Getting a PA."

There's a tense silence where they look like bulls standing off with each other.

God, they're fighting over my job application? Which one is Axel? No. I need to get out of here.

I inch toward the bathrooms. Maybe if I stay in there long enough, I can sneak out. Sneak out and leave this town for good.

My foot gets caught on the edge of a chair, and I trip. I catch myself with a clatter, turning around to face them.

Both men are looking at me. "Where are you going?" the one without glasses asks.

Now, I really do need to go to the bathroom because I think I might hurl. My first instinct is to cower, but I straighten and force myself to think. There are other people here. Neither of them can truly hurt me. "Going to the bathroom, not that it's any of your business." When neither of them responds, I feel my anger rise. "Who the hell are you?"

"Axel," Glasses says slowly, like I'm stupid. Then, he grins, motioning at the one without glasses. "Gage."

I stare stupidly.

"Badass." Glasses—the real Axel—wiggles his eyebrows. "Breaking a lawyer's glasses."

Oh shit. Oh *shit*? I look at the one Axel called Gage. He just glares at me.

He's a lawyer? Of course, he is. That's the position I'm interviewing for—a lawyer's office. My heart starts racing.

I'm fucked. This is so bad. I can't pay for those glasses.

Gage just glares at me. "Go to the bathroom, then meet me back here. We have to talk about the terms of your employment." He pulls the chair out and then sits down.

My mouth drops open. He wants to... continue the interview? After all this? Oh fuck no. He probably just wants to fucking sue me, and this is how he'll get my information.

But before I can say anything, Axel frowns, turning to his brother. "She can't work for you."

"And why the hell not?" Gage glares at him.

"Because she's—she can't."

"I need help since you won't give me those glasses."

Axel's face is getting red. "You know damn well I need them."

"Then stop throwing a hissy fit."

Axel looks like he's going to say something, but then he stops. His hand clenches into a fist, and he laughs. "You know what? Fine. Fuck this one, too, for all I care."

Then he turns on his heel and stalks out.

The red creeps up Gage's neck, but he just sits in the chair, waiting.

I could walk out. I could leave right now. Maybe move towns. Surely, there will be better options somewhere else.

But then my stomach grumbles. I haven't eaten at all today. I have one more half-rotten apple, and I don't have anything in my account. The rent is due, and I'm fucking hungry.

Gage speaks, "You owe me. Let's talk."

Oh, this asshole. Just as dickish as his brother.

I stand up tall, straightening out my blazer. I won't let another Newman take advantage of me. I'm here to get his money and get out.

I march up to the table, slamming my purse down. "I want an advance."

CHAPTER TWELVE

GAGE

Working with Raven will be about as easy as chewing fingernails to the cuticle. She's pissy and hostile and fucking awful. That, plus all the extra noise in the coffee shop, is giving me a royal headache. I'm pretty sure stabbing kitchen knives through my eyes would be more pleasant than this.

If I didn't hear the jealous tone in Axel's voice, I would have walked straight out. But I heard it. It was there. He doesn't want me to work with his... whatever the hell she is to him. For once, I finally have an opportunity to have something Ax wants. And *that* is an opportunity that I can't pass up.

Though I'm beginning to question why the hell he wants it.

"Chattel?" Raven asks, and I can hear the frustration in her voice. She spits the word out like it tastes bad in her mouth.

"It means—you know what? Let's take a break." I pull the

documents from her. We've spent hours going over the legal documents for this case, with Raven reading to me while I try to keep track of all the information. The woman filing the divorce went through a bunch of shit, and we haven't even gotten to the years' worth of police reports.

"I don't need a break." I can barely see Raven's blurry form on the other end of the booth. When I have my glasses on, I can see things that are close. But any farther than across the room, shit starts to get hazy. Without my glasses? I just see movements and color.

I know from dropping Raven off the other night that she's hot. Probably why Axel wants her. She has delicate features, plump red lips, and long silky black hair. Today, she smells... unusual. Almost like she's wearing men's deodorant with a Fiji or tropical hint. At first, it pissed me off, thinking she was using something Axel had given her. But I've never smelled that smell on him, so I relaxed. Raven's voice is also low and raspy. She'd be walking sex on legs if she weren't so damn aggressive.

"Well, I do." I push up. My stomach growls. "Get lunch. We'll start again after."

I've been smelling all the baked goods in the shop, and people keep unwrapping what I'm guessing are sandwiches around us. The paper crinkles, and then the crust crunches when they bite into it.

My mouth is watering, and my head is pounding. Food usually helps.

I take a few minutes to order, expecting Raven to either follow suit or go out somewhere else, but she's still in the booth when I get back.

"Did you get something?" I drop my chicken bacon ranch sandwich down on the table, but I misjudge the distance a bit, and it drops harder than I mean to.

"Oh, uh... yeah," Raven says, her tone different.

My cheeks heat, and I rescue the sandwich, finding that the

bread has fallen off the inside. I hate when people act differently because of my vision difference. I'm just as fucking capable.

I start eating so I don't murder everyone in the store. I don't even taste the first few bites, I'm eating so fast. As I eat, I don't see her moving or eating anything.

"I can wait while you get something," I say.

"Uh, not hungry."

Something uncomfortable skitters across my skin. It's lunchtime. Is she trying to be obstinate?

But I try to focus on my sandwich. What a woman eats or doesn't eat isn't any of my business.

"So this guy is a real piece of shit, huh?" I see and hear Raven messing with the papers.

"Yeah."

"So, what do you do?" Her voice is less aggressive and more hesitant.

"What do you mean?" I glare in her direction. Can't she see I'm trying to eat? I fucking hate people who talk shop on lunch break.

"Like, is this lady going to get the house? Half of his money?"

"That's the plan," I bite back. If she doesn't get half of everything, then I've done a shitty job.

Raven is silent for a bit.

Once I finish eating, I feel a little better. Raven is also less hostile. She reads me the notes with less of a tone and even remembers details that I forget.

My phone goes off a few times in my pocket, but I ignore it. I know who it is. It's Axel. And the knowledge that he's pissed that Raven is with me, even for these few hours, brings me way more satisfaction than it should. It almost erases the throbbing headache behind my temples.

CHAPTER THIRTEEN

RAVEN

22 Years Old

"You're awfully short." Max, the man training me, throws a look over his shoulder. I just met him today, and I was struck at first by his presence. He seemed chill and like nothing bothered him. So different than anyone I grew up around.

I stride to keep up with him. The manufacturing plant is still loud, even though it's midnight.

"Yeah, well. So are you."

Max laughs and throws a look back. For a second, I'm afraid I've pissed him off. But then, I catch the teasing glint in his eye. "Real original there, short stack."

I snort. I just got this job. I graduated with an English degree, but jobs in that field are few and far between. I was offered a job as a personal assistant at this manufacturing plant, but I didn't want to get stuck there, jumping to do the bidding of lazy men who couldn't do it themselves. So when I saw a security guard opening pop up in the same company, I jumped at it. And shockingly, I got it. I'm sure they had a diversity quota to meet, but still, I'm here.

Max shows me all around the plant. It's a fucking maze, and I know without a doubt I'll get lost a few times before I can get everything down. He keeps up the light banter the whole time, and despite the fact that it's my first day, I feel at ease. Max is easy to talk to. Like my childhood friend, Kimmy was.

On lunch break, Max takes me to the large front office. It's nothing but floor-to-ceiling windows that look out onto a pond with a fountain. It's surprisingly bright in here.

"I usually keep the lights off." Max waves at the space. "I don't know, it's kinda peaceful."

I sit on the end of a couch, opening up my lunchbox.

"So. You Amish or something?"

I glance up at Max. He raises an eyebrow from under his security ballcap. He's cute, and I find myself feeling a weird fluttering in my stomach, which I immediately stomp down. I didn't date much in college. Secretly, I wanted to, but... I don't know. Hard to meet a guy when you spend every spare minute in a book.

"No?" I furrow my brows at him.

"Oh. Well, you just didn't know what movie I was talking about, and it's like... a fucking classic." Max takes a sip of his coffee.

I flush. Mom and Dad didn't let me watch much TV. They thought it was sinful and would rot my brain.

I mutter, "I didn't see it."

"Okay. Amish girl," Max mutters, grabbing a cookie from his bag. But it's not said with the same biting tone my dad uses. It's more of a tease.

It's been lonely since college. I kept to myself and focused on my classes, and now that I've graduated, I try to keep as far away from my parents as possible. When I was a kid, I told Mom about Dad hitting me, and she just laughed and said she hoped it taught me some sense. She never seemed happy, even though she claimed she loved homeschooling me. Every day was tense.

But that's not how I feel around Max. He has an oddly relaxing presence, like deep down, he doesn't give a shit what I do or say.

"Whatever, Magdaline. Martha. Mary?" Max peers at me with squinted eyes.

"Celeste." I take a bite of my sandwich.

"No, I could have sworn the Amish don't use names like that." He pauses.

I smile around my bite of food. It feels awkward, and I stop immediately.

"Oh, she does smile!" Max grins widely now. "Okay, tell me what movies you have seen."

I hesitate. I don't watch much.

"I uh... mostly read books."

There's a pause, and then Max clasps his chest in mock horror. "Christ, woman! You're not helping yourself here."

This time, I smile fully.

He interrogates me about what I've done, which isn't a lot. Max is horrified that I went to a religious college, that I haven't drank yet, and that I am a nerd. I keep the fact that I've only dated one person to myself. I especially keep it quiet that all we did was hold hands. I'm getting the picture that non-religious people don't understand. Not that I'm religious anymore. Not really. It's hard to stick with a god who demands kids get beaten and laughs about it.

"Just one shot. Please. I want to be there when you take it." Max is actually begging with the praying hands. "You can choose the alcohol."

"Okay, fine," I laugh. What can it hurt? Just one won't make me like my dad.

"Fuck yeah!" Max pumps the air.

As we get up to get back to work, Max elbows me in the side. "Just saying. You'd be a cute Amish girl."

I laugh, then catch the glint of the moonlight against his wedding band. Wait, he's married?

Instantly, I sober.

"What's wrong?" Max asks.

"Nothing." I straighten. Why is he acting like this if he's married?

Maybe he's just being friendly. Right? Is this how people make friends?

Over the next few months, I learn the plant forwards and backwards. I could walk it in my sleep, and I'm pretty sure I did a few times. Max is on shift with me a lot, and he leaves little sticky notes around the building, giving me movie suggestions. After ignoring the first few, I started writing a book suggestion underneath it, and eventually, he started buying the books. He updates me on which chapter he's in, and then I start watching his movies.

They're crass. Not the kind of movies my dad or my church would have approved of, but I feel an odd thrill watching them. Like I'm doing something I shouldn't.

Max always seems to know when I have a bad day, and he leaves stupid jokes in my lunchbox. Even though they make me cringe, they also make me laugh. I learn that he is, in fact, bald. A fact I give him endless shit for.

The day after my probation ends, Max and my other coworkers invite me to a pool party, where I take a shot of tequila at Max's request.

It's nasty. But everyone cheers, and that makes me feel warm.

I finally have friends.

I tell myself I can just have a few drinks, and then I'll stop.

I look around the pool at the coworkers I've come to know over the past few months. Two of them are in the water, trying to drown each other in a drunken, sloppy way, and the rest are standing around the fire with me, cheeks flushed. I smell the scent of alcohol, and it makes my knee bounce. But then Max throws me a covert wink from across the fire, and immediately, everything feels okay again.

It'll be fine. Right? For sure. I'm not my dad.

I lean into the party, the alcohol making me loose. I take a few more shots, riding the high of the buzz. Who knew drinking could be this fun? I feel relaxed… happy.

Eventually, people start leaving. I'm not sure why since I'm still having fun. At some point, Max drags me into the water. The crisp water crashes over my head, and as soon as I pop back up, I gasp. Max is beside me, sucking in a breath, and I splash him. "Hey!"

He throws his head back and laughs.

"Okay, lovebirds." One of my older coworkers is suddenly at the edge of the pool. "We're going inside. Don't drown, yeah?"

I frown. Lovebirds? But the world is spinning, and Max just laughs. "Leaving already, ya old fuck?"

"Yeah, yeah."

I grip the side of the pool, enjoying the way the water washes over me.

Max hangs on beside me, grinning at me. "You're drunk."

"No, I'm not!" Am I acting drunk? Sure, maybe I'm happier than normal, but I thought I was handling it well.

Max just laughs. "Okay, whatever you say, Magdalene."

I splash him again.

For a while, we just sit there, listening to the thud of the music inside. The lapping of the water and the moving of the lights on the pool edges are mesmerizing, and I just stand at the edge of the pool, watching them. Everything feels so peaceful. I had no idea that alcohol could make things so… warm.

Suddenly, Max is in front of me. He is so close that his skin brushes up against my hand that's gripping the edge of the pool. For a second, I'm frozen, staring at where we're touching.

"You're fun."

I lift my gaze to Max, and he's smiling, but it looks... different.

Confusion mixes in my gut.

"I'm so glad I got to train you." Suddenly, Max moves and presses me against the wall of the pool.

I suck in a breath, feeling his hot skin all over mine.

"What–"

His hand lifts, dripping water down, and he traces it along my jaw.

I'm frozen again. This doesn't feel right. The spark of the physical touch feels stolen.

I try to squeeze away, my back grinding against the pool's edge. Max stops me, his arm blocking my movement, which makes me freeze up more.

He says nothing; he just looks into my eyes. His pupils are blown, and I hate the jump of attraction that I feel. He's married. Why is he doing this?

I realize that his free hand has moved, and he's tracing it down my neck.

"Max..." I try to push away again, but he just sticks to me, the water making it easy for him to glide with me.

"Raven." His lips are so close I can feel his hot breath. Actually, my whole body feels hot, and I feel like the pool is floating along with me. I'm floating in the pool that's floating, on the world that's floating. And spinning. And it's so, so hot.

There's pressure moving down my collarbone. Then, something brushes my nipple. "You're so fucking smart and funny. I wish I had met you a long time ago."

I suck in a gasp. "Max!" But my body feels stuck. I like the words he's saying, but fear also laces me. He's so much bigger than I am. Suddenly, it feels like I'm a kid again, and I can't fight back. I'm not strong enough. He'll push me underwater and drown me.

Suddenly, Max's hand is on my pussy, and I let out a strangled cry. I thrash, trying to get out of the space.

"Shit!"

My back grinds against the edge of the pool. Then, Max is gone.

"Raven, are you okay?"

I'm ripping myself away, my whole body hot and the world spinning. "Your wife," is all I can say. Why is he doing this? He has a wife.

I get to the stairs. Max doesn't follow me, and the rush of relief fills me.

I got away.

Max just grabs the edge of the pool, hanging his head.

All my muscles tremble, and I have no control over them. Max is my friend. Why is he putting me in this position?

He just stays in his spot, head down.

With a rush of fear, I realize that he's mad at me. I scramble to grab a towel, terrified he'll grab me and drag me back in.

But he doesn't.

The next day, Max lets me know he'll have to stop talking to me and that he has some things to work out with his wife.

The next few months are a shitshow. I lost the only friend I have, and rightfully so. I'm angry at him, and I hate him for what he did. Why couldn't it just stay like it was?

Unfortunately, Max still works the same job as me. The same shift as me. Every now and again, he still leaves me notes. In those notes, he talks about how much he misses me. How amazing I am, and how much he wants to keep me.

I throw every single one away. They make me sad and so, so angry. Then, after I throw them away, I go back to my apartment, completely alone. The silence is stifling, and the guilt is even worse. I should have known better.

Eventually, Max separates from his wife, and I see him every day. Every damn day, he's apologizing. Telling me how much I had led him on. And I believe him. Because I did. I wanted friendship more than I cared about anyone else.

And on a bad day, I find a note with a movie recommendation. I snarl, writing a book recommendation under it where the woman kills her cheating husband.

The next day, I find another. And I give another similar recommendation.

Then it happens again and again and again until I'm less mad and more lonely. We start taking our lunch breaks together. I don't say a word, and I make sure he knows just how mad at him I am.

Max always accepts the silence and gives me his pack of animal crackers after.

I hang out with my other coworkers with him there. I make sure he sees just how much fun I'm having without him.

Only I'm not. I'm not fucking happy. I'm miserable. I'm miserable and alone, and I have no friends, and my days are full of empty hallways and machine rooms all day, every day. Birthday? Hallway. Couldn't sleep all night? Machine room. Almost lit my kitchen on fire? Bathroom.

And Max is always there. One day, I can't take it any longer. I run into Max in the boiler room.

"Oh, hey, Martha." His voice is quiet and sad.

"That's not my name, and you know it," I snap.

"Sorry." He twists his hands.

I turn to go, and Max says, "Hey, I liked the end of that book."

I freeze, hand on the door.

"The main character was badass. Killing him with his own house keys."

I should go. There are more hallways to walk. But just hearing someone else's voice instead of the thoughts that circle my own over and over feels like a balm. Slowly, I turn back around.

"Listen, you have every reason to hate me. It's fine. But you haven't given me a new book in weeks. I've reread your others like twice."

I glare at him. He gives me a shy look. Tension fills the air. It feels like so much rides on this one thing, and I see the lines at the corners of his eyes tighten.

"Sorry, I shouldn't have asked." He starts to turn, and against every instinct, I want him to stop. I want to talk to him about books. I don't care that it's him; I just want *someone* to talk to.

After that night, we start talking again and then form an on-again, off-again relationship.

Eventually, one night, we get hammered, and he takes my virginity on my couch. He leaves me at 3am, bleeding, drunk, and scared.

I hold onto my career like a lifeline. It's the one thing I built for myself, and I'll be damned if I lose it. I try to get different shifts, but he always ends up working around me. And I'm always alone. And every time, he sits with me in the loneliness.

Never once does Max hit me.

CHAPTER FOURTEEN

RAVEN

By the end of the day, I'm exhausted. I feel like *I'm* the one who can't see, and everything feels blurry. I'm caught up in names, dates, and terms that I have no idea what they mean. My years of reading didn't help prepare me for the legal jargon, and it pisses me off to have Gage listen to me struggle. Despite that, we got a lot of work done, and even better, Gage handed me enough cash for at least five days' worth of food if I stretched it.

For the first time in days, I feel lighter.

I climb into my car and drive home. I didn't want to burn the gas to get here, but this coffee shop is on the edge of town, closer to the richer homes.

I stop by the grocery store, glowering the whole time. I hope against hope that I don't see Axel here. But this is the only place in town where I know I can find the cheapest food.

While I'm checking out with food, my phone rings. I traded numbers with Gage before I left. Maybe he needs something? I flip it open.

"Survived your first day with my brother, hmmm?"

I spin on my heel, checking around me. Fuck, is Axel here? Becky, my old coworker, gives me a look as she checks me out.

"He's a bit unbearable," Axel goes on. "But I could have told you that earlier."

I don't see him. I flip the phone closed, hanging up. Immediately, it rings again. I grab my groceries and scurry out.

This is just embarrassing. Absolutely the worst possible day. I need to go home and eat my food and fucking forget.

Axel calls a few more times, so I turn my phone off. When I get back home, the apartment is empty and dark and smells like plaster. But it's home. I flip the lights on and lean back against the door, letting out a breath.

Fuck.

I have this vague sense that I'm being chased by a fucking bear. I'm exhausted, and I have no idea how to live my life safely while Axel openly licks his fucking chops. And I know Max is hovering in the background somewhere, just trying to track me down.

It feels like it takes forever to cook the rice, but I'm actually just starving. When it's finally done, I burn my mouth wolfing the first bites down.

I'm finishing my first bowl when there's a knock at the front door.

I jump, gaze immediately flicking to the door. No one ever comes here. Well, no one except Axel.

My mood immediately jumps all over the place. It better not be fucking Axel.

I haven't had time to really process my feelings about him. I'm pissed and angry, and fuck, I wish he and his brother weren't so goddamn hot. It was like staring at a marble statue of a god all day, if that god had veiny hands and a deep voice that made shivers run across my skin.

I shake myself. Yeah. Max was cute, too, and look where that got me.

Except these men are *hot*. Max was nothing compared to them. I wonder if they're married, too? I haven't noticed a ring on either of them. And I checked. Because my brain is apparently super fucked up. I'd rather fuck my bat than let either of them touch me.

The person knocks again.

Snatching up my pink bat, I suck in a breath. No more. I'm taking my power back.

I stride to the door and swing it open.

Standing on my doorstep is Axel.

He grins at me. "Hey, little b—"

I shut the door in his face. Not fast enough to miss the way he tries to look past me.

My hands shake, and I shake them aggressively. Why am I afraid? I have no reason to be afraid. I'll brain Axel if he tries anything.

There's more knocking, and I just stand there, staring at the door. Obsession is never good. It can only mean one thing: pain.

The knocking continues, rattling around inside my already tired brain, making me buzz. Will he stop? Leave? Forget my number?

But if he stops, will he actually leave? Or will he just wait for me to check and ambush me later?

No. I don't want to leave that option open.

My body feels trapped in that frozen state until Axel knocks again.

Fuck it. I'm done with this. I yank the door open again, my bat still in my hands. "What—"

"I'm sorry." Axel holds his hands up like he's calming a wild animal. "I'm sorry, just hear me out."

Narrowing my eyes, I focus on the feeling of the bat handle in my hands. The thin rubber is cool, and the bat is heavy. One swing and it's lights out for Axel. He's standing on the bottom step, so he's eye to eye with me instead of being taller. It would be easy to hit him.

I glance around. Axel's driver is waiting about a block away, giving us a semblance of privacy.

"What do you want?" I ask.

"I should have told you about Gage. I'm sorry, I just didn't think you'd run into him."

Axel's in that red suit, and it's molded to his body. His thick body. Good god, why are they both so big? Attraction rolls through me, and disgust follows quickly after. Why am I cursed to find men attractive? Why the fuck can't I like women?

"Yes, you should have." I pull my gaze back up to Axel's face, staring at him. Despite the fact that I spent all day with Gage, I seriously can't tell them apart besides the glasses. Their eyes are the same blueish purple, their eyebrows have the same arch, and their lips are the same biteable pink.

He sees me staring and gentles his voice. "I'm sorry I didn't tell you."

"How do I tell you apart?"

Axel laughs softly. "Uh, I'm the hotter one?"

I move to slam the door again, and Axel holds out his hand, stopping it. "Wait, I came to offer you your job back."

I freeze.

"I didn't know you got fired that night. Mrs. Todd told me later."

There's a weird surge of relief, followed very closely by suspicion. He didn't care until now. Why does he suddenly care?

"What's in it for you?" I trace the tip of the bat along the floor, and Axel's gaze snaps down to it.

He thinks I'm gonna hit him with it.

That makes me smile.

Axel looks back up at me. "Well, you clearly need a job."

The statement makes me angry. "I already have a job."

A flush creeps across Axel's face. I watch it bloom on his skin.

Axel genuinely doesn't like that I'm working with Gage. A thrill mixes in with the anger. I have control over something that Axel hates.

"I just thought you'd want a stable job." Axel adjusts his suit jacket. "My brother only needs help until his glasses come in, so he won't pay you for long."

I rip my gaze from Axel's veiny, strong hands on his jacket. Why the hell does he care how long Gage pays me?

He's jealous. He's totally jealous. Jealous of the girl he stole from and then got fired from her job.

And now I have power over him. And that thought makes me happier than I've been in a long time. I'm not sure if it's the exhaustion or the delirium from not eating for a while, but I can't stop the next words from coming out of my mouth. "Beg."

Axel's gaze snaps to mine. "What?"

"You heard me. Beg me to take it back." I stare at him. Anger flickers in his eyes.

Fear shoots into my muscles, and I tense. Immediately after that, a rush of excitement follows.

If Axel tries to hurt me, I'll splatter his brains across the ground.

But, instead of trying to hurt me, Axel locks eyes with me and then slowly sinks to his knees. He grits his teeth, the word coming out tense. "Please."

I stare at him, watching the way his pupils dilate. He's on his knees in front of the whole street. Begging me.

My blood feels like it's full of tiny firecrackers.

I like this. I like it a lot.

But instead of letting him see that, I say with a bored expression, "I've heard men beg much better than that."

Axel makes the tiniest flinch my way and my entire body tenses. Then Axel holds himself still. There's a beat where I'm not sure if I'm going to actually have to hit him. But then his chest heaves, and his pupils widen so much there's barely any color on the edges. He gives a tense laugh. "Goddamn, woman. I'm trying my best here."

"No, you're not." My heart is racing, and I can't tell if it's fear or arousal. Or maybe both. "If you were, you'd be crawling for me."

There's a beat of silence, and a challenge flashes in his eyes. The cold air whips around us, going up my skirt and making me shiver.

Am I really doing this? I'm playing with fire right now, and I feel like I'm either about to die or about to truly live.

Then, Axel drops his giant frame over, bending to put his hands on the threshold. He looks up at me from under wispy, white hair, his tone mocking. "Please?"

I can't help the tiny grin that stretches across my face as I look down at him. The muscles under his suit jacket are bunched and coiled like he's uncomfortable, and that goes straight to my pussy.

I lift the bat, tracing it gently up Axel's arm. "What a good boy, doing what you're told."

Axel gives a heavy huff of air, and his whole body shivers. He hates it, yet here he is, still on his knees.

I trace the bat up along his collarbone until it's at his sternum. Axel watches me closely.

I bend down so I'm closer to his face. "Now. What was it you wanted?"

His eyes bounce between mine, and there's a glint of a smirk before he says, "Work for me."

It's that smirk. That Playboy smirk. He thinks he has me. Just like he thinks he can get any woman, either through money or sex. And *that* pisses me off.

I hold his look, my entire body buzzing, thinking about everything before this point. The longer I take, the more the side of Axel's mouth quirks up in a confident smirk.

I smirk back. "Go bother one of your toys, slut. I don't have time for you."

Then, I use the bat to push him back and slam the door.

CHAPTER FIFTEEN

AXEL

I'm down bad. I'm down motherfucking *bad*.

That look in Raven's eye when she told me no and slammed the door? Fuck me sideways, she looked feral. Wild and angry and so, so fucking hot.

She also called me a slut. And *that* fucking pisses me off.

At that moment, I almost jumped up and slammed her into the apartment. Almost pinned her against the wall to make her see just how much a 'slut' could rock the fucking stick out of her ass.

I buzzed about it all night, even fucking my fist until I came over and over. But nothing helped. I want it from her. I want her mouth wrapped around my dick. I want to punish her mouth until she cries, then force her to come over and over until she screams.

My dick throbs, and I have to adjust myself.

I made Dave park across the street from Raven's apartment. He was oddly quiet when I asked, and it pisses me off. It's not stalking. I just want to know where Raven and my brother will be today.

My blood runs hot even thinking about it. Gage doesn't deserve her attention. He wouldn't know what to do with someone like her anyway. The man hasn't seen pussy since Jessica, and she was a boring lay.

Suddenly, I see movement in the alley. Raven's car makes an appearance, and I catch a glimpse of her pretty face behind the wheel. At least, I know it's pretty. Stunning, actually, but she's fuzzy from here. She drives toward town.

I direct Dave to follow her, secretly hoping she stops at the coffee shop again. I can stop there for lunch and see her sans bat.

Or, you know what? Maybe keep the bat. I like a little bit of danger. It makes my heart pump, and I feel *alive*.

But Raven doesn't stop at the coffee shop. My skin gets hotter and hotter as we drive toward the other end of town.

Toward Gage's house.

Sure enough, she pulls in front of his house, then gets out of the car, flouncing around in that dark, pleated skirt of hers. The one that I wish I could see up last night after I dropped to my knees in front of her. Raven looks stunning today, with her dark hair streaming down her back. I can't see her face, but I know her features are fucking sharp and soft at the same time, her cheekbones cutting out of her face, covered in soft, dewy skin.

She looks good.

She's playing a game with me.

I clench my hands so hard my nails bite into the creases of my palms.

Raven wants to play hard to get with the fucking *slut*.

Okay, little bird. Let's play.

GAGE

18 Years Old

"Pretty boyyyy," Jess whines, grabbing my shirt. We're at a Halloween party, and I'm dressed as an elf. I wanted to go as a pirate, but Jess wanted me to go as an elf. Said it makes her hot, and I'm not gonna lie, it feels good to have a girl falling all over me. And not just any girl—Axel's ex.

Axel ignores us from across the room. He's actually been ignoring us all night, but this is on him. He cheated on Jess. She came to me with a broken heart, and there was something about the tears on her pretty face that I couldn't say no to.

Jess sways into me, and I stumble back. The music is loud and disorienting, and my head is spinning. I don't normally drink at these—that's Axel's gig—but tonight, I have a pretty girl on my arm, and it's Halloween.

I'm pretty sure I'm drunk.

"Wanna get out of here?" Jess looks up at me. She's so close I'd normally be able to see her, but everything looks more fuzzy than usual.

Yeah, I do.

I grab her arm, and we stumble back into the hallway. This place is dark, and I don't know my way around. My toes run into something hard, and I feel around to find a dark staircase away from the noise and pull Jess up. I bump into the handrail, and Jess bumps into me. She giggles. I feel like I'm floating, like everything I was stressed about is suddenly gone. Why don't I drink more often?

I can feel the rational side of me creeping in, trying to say that Axel always drinks so much on Halloween that he makes himself sick. That he needs someone to take care of him.

I frown. Not this time. I'm not my brother's keeper. For once, I'm just going to be me—Gage. Not a twin to Axel. Just me.

At the top of the stairs, Jess pulls me toward a doorway. I realize it's a bedroom in time for her to fall backwards on the bed.

"Should we..." I look around. Are we allowed to be up here?

"Pretty boy," Jess whines again, opening her arms.

The room is spinning, so I fall onto the bed next to her. The bed bounces up and down, and I fight to gain stability.

I look at the girl beside me. She's stunning. She has beautiful chocolate hair and skin that is so smooth, I just want to touch it. Not only is she pretty, she's nice. She listened to me talk about my animals and the fox I've been trying to rehabilitate, and even told me about a new book at the library about wild animals that she thought may have a section about foxes. I was always jealous of Axel when he was dating her. I can't understand why he'd cheat.

Jess looks over at me and smiles. "Hey."

"Hey." I grin.

She smiles wider, although I can still feel sadness in her. She's been sad since Axel, and I just want to fix it.

She's close. So close that I can see her gaze bounce between my eyes and back down to my mouth. She says it again, slower, "Hey." Then her tongue darts out, and she licks her lips.

Fuck, is she going to kiss me? God, I want her to kiss me.

Suddenly, nerves dance to light in my stomach.

"Kiss me," Jess whispers.

Those nerves turn into firecrackers, and that, along with the alcohol, makes me feel hot. I trace my hand along her jaw, feeling the softness of her skin. I watch her eyes, slowly pulling my head closer. I want to soak in this moment. Wipe any last trace of sadness from her eyes. Want to kiss her and for her to kiss me back so hard we can't pull away. Want to remember it forever.

"Kiss me," Jess says with more power behind it.

So I do. I press my lips to hers and kiss her. Jess immediately melts back, moaning. She doesn't kiss me back. She just lies there, her lips flaccid.

I pull away. "You okay?"

"Too hot. Take these clothes off." Jess is thrashing, trying to pull at her clothes.

I frown. Is she uncomfortable?

"Please, A—" she stops, and I freeze.

Was she about to say Axel?

"Actually, I'm just hot. Please, help." Jess has pulled her shirt off and is wrestling with her bra. And I'm momentarily distracted looking at her breasts. They're medium-sized but full, two perfect handfuls, and I desperately want her to let me touch them. Want her to shove them in my mouth as she rides me. Maybe shove something else in my mouth, too...

"There." Jess pulls the bra off, and suddenly, I can see her nipples. The soft brown patches with hardened little nubs. Then, she's yanking at her pants.

My mouth goes completely dry. Is this happening? Is it really happening?

"Condom." She pulls a foil packet out of her pocket and shoves it at me.

Okay, so this is happening.

Suddenly, I'm full of nerves. I've never done this before. Am I going to be enough for her?

Then, Jess is lying on the bed, completely naked. My eyes snap to her like they're magnets.

She's stunning in every sense of the word, and all I want is to be inside of her.

"Big boy," she moans. "Take your pants off."

I realize I've just been lying there, staring at her. Then, something digs at the back of my mind. Big boy? Isn't that what she used to call Axel?

Then she's on me, kissing me and pressing me back into the bed. Suddenly, everything flares to life. She's everywhere, touching everything, her sweet smell invading my senses. Her hands are fumbling at my pants and brushing my dick, sending shockwaves through me. Fuck, it feels so good.

I feel a rush of cool air over my dick and realize she's gotten my pants off.

"Give that to me."

The packet is snatched from my hands, then her hot hands are on my dick, gripping it. I groan, bucking up into her hands. I want her to keep doing that, to keep doing whatever she wants to me.

Then, I feel the roll of rubber over my dick, and I can't feel her warm hands as well. That thought immediately goes out the window when she rolls onto the bed beside me, tracing her hands down to her pussy.

"Please," she whines.

I roll over Jess so I'm lying on top of her. She responds by throwing her head back and baring her neck to me. Does that mean I can kiss it?

I do, peppering little kisses up and down her neck. I can feel my dick pressing against her pussy, and it makes me throb so much I almost want to come.

No. Not yet. I can't come yet.

"Please." Jess bucks her hips.

I grab her chin, wanting to look at her and see what she's feeling. Jess's eyes are squeezed shut, and she's breathing heavily. There are little furrows between her brows.

"You want me inside you?" I say, lips so close to hers they're almost touching.

"Yes!" She bucks again.

Anything to please her. If I come, I come. I'll just try to stay hard long enough that she can get off.

I have to look down, trying to position myself just right. It's dark, the world is spinning, and my dick has gotten less hard.

Jess groans, and her hand snakes between us. She grips my dick, shifting me so that suddenly, the head is surrounded by tight heat.

I grunt, involuntarily grinding into the sensation.

"Yes, fuck me." Jess lifts her hips, making more of my dick slide into her. The sensation is earth-shattering. Pleasure lights up all along my groin, and I push so that I'm seated in her as far as I can go.

She lets out a breath of air that sounds happy, and it makes goosebumps run across my arms. She likes it. It feels good.

"More."

So I do. I pull out of her, almost to the tip, then push back inside. The movement sends pleasure shooting up my spine, and I groan. I want to bottle this feeling up and feel it forever. Does Jess feel it, too? I want her to feel it.

I look at her, but her eyes are still closed.

I slow, hoping she's okay. She just whines.

So I go back to pumping in and out of her. It feels like heaven, and I trace my fingertips along her collarbone, feathering them down to where her breasts are trapped beneath me. I wonder if she wants me to go further? To play with her clit.

But she doesn't say anything, and she doesn't direct me. She lies there, eyes closed. I already feel close to coming.

I draw up so I can reach her pussy. I've read enough magazines to know girls like their clit played with. Jess mews, writhing against me. I'm not sure if I'm doing it right, how hard to press, or how fast to go. I try different pressures and tempos, but Jess doesn't change up her moans. They're all the same.

"Fuck me," she demands again.

I prop myself up on my hands over her and pound into her. Immediately, her moans increase. It feels harsh and impersonal, and she still won't look at me.

"Yes." Jess wraps her legs around my waist and yanks me to her. I can barely move anymore, but the feeling is electrifying, being buried so deep in her pussy that I can't escape. Already, I'm throbbing like I'm a stroke away from coming.

Then, Jess opens her eyes and looks at me. "Yes, fuck me, Axel."

It takes a second for me to process what she said, but Jess has lifted her hips up, and she's slamming into me, holding me close with her legs and squeezing my dick so hard I come. I grunt, erupting into the condom while she pulls me in further. The orgasm takes me without my permission, and the pleasure is harsh and quick. I feel her pulsing around me, and when I come back down, the world is spinning even more.

Axel. She called me Axel.

Jess doesn't seem to notice. She's limp again, her legs letting go of me, and her eyes are still closed.

I pull out of her, confused. The high I just felt is crashing, and suddenly, things don't feel so good anymore.

She called me my brother.

I pull the condom off and yank my pants back up, turning to check on Jess. She's patting around for her clothes, and she peeks at me. "You okay?"

"I…"

She stares at me.

I feel the high tumbling further and further out of reach. Why did I think this was a good idea? She can't even tell us apart? My thoughts spiral, and I wonder if she is only with me because I look like my brother.

"Was that good for you?" she asks.

I swallow.

"You know you can go harder." She pulls her shirt over her head. "He always—I like to be thrown around."

My face heats. She wants to be thrown around? And was she talking about Axel? Axel threw her around, and she wants me to do that, too?

I don't even think I want to. I wouldn't know where to start, and I don't want to hurt her.

Where there once was a rush of euphoria, I now feel sadness sinking in, and in a horrifying turn of events, I feel like crying. Heat pricks at my eyes, and I straighten.

No. I will not be weak. No one can see me cry.

There's an awkward silence, then Jess says, "I'm just gonna... go back downstairs."

I don't argue with her. She used me because of my brother. She didn't like me for me. I was a fool to even think that.

It makes me angry, and I want to scream and yell. Throw things. Purge the feelings that are bubbling up in my chest.

A week later, she's back with Axel, and I learned that even though I may see the best in someone, it doesn't mean they see the best in me.

CHAPTER SEVENTEEN

GAGE

My head still hurts from the other day. I almost called Raven to cancel, but I'm not nearly prepared enough for this case. All I know is that I can't sit in that coffee shop again with all the noise. And I don't want to ask Mom to drive me. She'll ask questions that I don't want to answer. For where Mom is concerned, my life is fine, I have no complications, and there is absolutely no woman.

Fuck. I don't want Raven here.

I go to the cabinet, grabbing some pain relievers that I always keep on the top shelf immediately closest to the right edge of the cabinet. I toss a handful back. My clock chimes, telling me it's almost nine. If I'm going to change venues, I have to do it now.

Fucking Christ above.

I grab my phone, angrily stabbing in Raven's number.

I hate her. I hate all of this.

Buddy ambles over to me, poking me with her cold nose. It makes me take a breath.

I can do this. I have to prepare for this case, and Raven is just a means to an end. Literally just that.

Raven agrees to the switch, and I move to the couch to wait, absently scratching Buddy's ears as she pants her stinky dog breath in my face. I've tried brushing her teeth, but it's like wrestling an alligator. I pet her behind the ears, sinking my fingers into her soft texture. I know she's a pretty gray, not that I can see it right now. I don't think I could ever handle fully losing my sight because then I'd lose seeing her.

After a bit, there's a knock at the door, and Buddy stiffens. Before I can grab her, she's running to the door, barking. The noise makes my head pound, which reminds me that there's no way I can handle anything crazy today. I need those painkillers to kick in, goddamn it.

"Buddy." I follow her to the door and try to pull her away, but she scrabbles on the tile, trying to stick her nose through the door.

"Just a minute!" I drag Buddy to my room, apologizing to her as I go. Once inside, she gives a huff, but I see her fuzzy form jump on my bed, where she knows she isn't supposed to be.

Whatever.

I shut the door gently, then move to the front door, opening it. Raven's standing right in front of me, backlit by the sun. I imagine her like a hazy, dark-haired demon.

I just stand there. Why am I doing this?

"Gonna invite me in?" Raven's voice is dry.

I just stare.

"Probably easier to whack me inside without the whole street seeing it."

I blink. Whack her? Does she think... Did she just accuse me of being a murderer? And of not knowing how to commit a crime in one breath?

Nope. I'm not doing this. I go to shut the door when Raven says, "I have a knife on me." She sounds bored. "It's pink."

That throws me for a loop for a painfully long second.

"Figured you'd want to know what it looks like 'cause if you try something, you won't see it coming."

I'm pulled back to the present, and my mouth drops open. She just insulted my blindness and threatened me at the same time. For a moment, all I can do is watch Raven's fuzzy form while an electric buzz races across my skin. It's both hatred and... something else. Something that makes me feel alive.

It's then that I realize I'm hard. Really fucking hard.

No. My face burns. *No, no, no,* Gage! This is not how things are going to go. What the hell is my problem?

"What's your brother's problem with you?"

"What?" My heart races and my skin feels hot. I can smell Raven again, and of course, she smells fucking good.

"He literally came to my door and begged me not to work for you."

The words cut through my haze. What happened?

I hear the rustle of fabric and vaguely see Raven cross her arms. All I can do is stare in her general direction.

Axel begged her not to work for me? The thought makes me angry, but I just say, "He doesn't have a problem with me." Well, other than brotherly animosity. I was always the one compared to him. He has everything. There's never any reason for him to mess with me.

"That's not how it sounded."

Raven's voice is like smoke, curling around me and sending shivers up my arms. Goddamn it, Gage, wake up!

I shake myself. "My brother doesn't care what his hookups do. Never has, never will. So why are you making shit up?"

There's a sharp intake of breath, then a loaded silence. Then, Raven's voice is more coal and hot smoke. "I'm not his hookup, and I'm not his whore. I won't fuck Axel, and while we're on the topic, I won't fuck you. So let's put that to rest."

I'm simultaneously laser-focused on her while the rest of the world feels like it's floating. Fuck me? I never asked her to fuck me. But also, it pisses me off that she's telling me she won't. I haven't even asked.

Not that I would.

"Shall we get to work?" Raven's words are clipped.

Absolutely not. And yet, Axel *does* seem extra focused on this girl. Even if she's lying, I've heard the jealousy in his voice. For some reason, he wants her. Unless this is some elaborate prank to get another woman in my bed so he can laugh at me about it later?

To be fair, Axel never laughed at me about Jess. Actually, he never even brought it up.

I'd like to keep it that way.

Right now, I have a goddamn trial to prep for. I'm not sure where I got distracted in all that.

I straighten. My prefrontal cortex is developed now. I won't let another of Axel's whores fuck up my life. She's here to do a job, and I'm here to get the job done.

So, I step back and let Raven inside.

CHAPTER EIGHTEEN

RAVEN

Gage and I work for a few hours, both of us acting like the conversation on the porch didn't happen, which it most certainly did. I'm setting up boundaries. I don't care if I need a knife in my hand to do it; I'm fucking doing it. I'll stab a man before he can take advantage of me again.

The work is detailed and slow, but there's something satisfying about digging through this piece of shit's life, stacking up the cards so he loses as much as possible. The atmosphere here is also so much better than the shop, despite the hulking glower from across the table.

We only have two more days before the first trial on Gage's schedule, and I get caught up in the details, only breaking when Gage rubs his temples and stands up. He mutters something about letting the dog out, then disappears down the hall.

I perk up. I heard the dog barking when I got here. Animals are always better than people.

I take a minute to really take in Gage's living room. I don't want to look like I am spying, not that he can see me doing it. Well, he might be able to. I'm not sure how much he can see, and I'll be damned if I ask. The living room is sunken, lined with flower print couches on one side and floor-to-ceiling windows on the other. It looks out into a small yard and woods beyond, the leaves brilliant oranges and reds.

I hate to admit that it's pretty. Homey, even.

Gage comes back into the living room, guiding a pitbull by its collar. The dog is panting, mouth open in a smile. Once he lets the dog outside, it stands there, wagging its tail. Gage moves to the kitchen, and I hear the fridge open.

Well fuck. I realize I got distracted by the sudden location change and forgot to pack lunch.

I watch as the dog moves into the yard, squats to pee, and dances back up to the back door. It stands there, tail wagging and tongue out. Fuck, it's cute. Sucks that it's stuck with a grumpy asshole.

The dog digs at the door where there are streak marks on the glass.

Gage doesn't come to let the dog in. Instead, I hear the microwave going. Maybe he can't hear it.

I shrug, getting up and going to the door. I at least want to say hi. As I crack the door open, the dog shoves past me and barges into the house. I freeze, and so does the dog. Its whole body is frozen, and its tail is stuck up in the air.

Fuck, is it scared?

"It's okay, baby," I keep my voice low. Immediately, I notice the dog's cloudy eyes.

Oh shit. Can it not see?

"Sorry, bud." I step back. "Not your owner."

The dog sniffs a few times, then unfreezes. It skirts past me, running for the living room with its tail between its legs.

Oh my god, the dog is scared of me. Fuck. I feel like a horrible human being.

"Did you pack lunch?" Gage's voice floats into the room over the sounds of the microwave.

Cool. Can this get any more uncomfortable? I shut the door and glance at the dog again, who's taken up residency where Gage was sitting on the couch.

The money. Just think about the money.

"I'm good." I sneak back over to where I was on the couch while still giving the dog some space.

The fridge door slams and I jump.

"I didn't ask if you were good; I asked if you packed lunch." Gage sounds pissed, and for a second, I freeze.

I drop my hand to the knife in my purse, and I flip out the blade.

I will not let any man bully me. Not anymore. If Gage tries anything, I'll turn him into a pincushion for Halloween.

There's the sound of plates clattering, then silence. I don't like the silence. Dad was never silent before stomping up the stairs. So what is Gage doing?

Suddenly, there's a warm tongue on my hand, and I jump, looking down. The dog has moved over to me with its back to the couch. It licks me again, tail thumping slightly.

Poor thing's just as scared as I am.

Wait, why is it scared?

I have a horrifying thought. If I find out Gage is abusing it, I'll slit his throat right here and now. I pull my knife hand back so I don't cut the dog, and pet it with my other hand.

Then, Gage rounds the corner, and I stand up. Only, instead of squaring up with me, he has two plates of food in his hands.

I'm gripping the knife so firmly that the handle is pressing into my hand, and the dog just backs into my legs, pressing against me.

Gage maneuvers around the couch and then drops the food

in front of me. It's spaghetti. Then, he moves to the end of the couch, sits down, and starts eating.

I'm stuck there, staring at him. For a second, he doesn't do anything. Then, he freezes, looking up.

"Buddy?"

The dog's tail thumps, but it doesn't move from my side.

"You let Buddy in?" The anger rises in Gage's voice, and I tense, readying my knife.

But Gage doesn't come after me. He just runs his hand through his white hair. "She didn't bite you, did she?" He sounds stressed.

"What?" I look down at the dog, who looks just as scared as I feel. It's a she?

"Did she bite you?" Gage asks, his eyes moving from me to the dog. "Buddy, come here."

Her tail thumps more, but she still doesn't move.

"Are you holding her?" The anger is back.

"No!" I glare at him. "She seems scared of *you*."

Gage laughs, and it's bitter. He laughs and laughs, slapping his knee like it's the funniest thing in the world. I just stare at him like he's crazy. Because I think he is.

Finally, he wipes his eyes. "Buddy is scared of women. Always has been."

I stare at the dog, then back up at Gage, still skeptical.

He squints like he's trying to see. "Did you feed her something?"

"No."

Gage doesn't look mad anymore, and slowly, I release my death grip on the knife. It's then that Buddy perks up, staring at the extra plate of food on the coffee table.

"Don't let her eat that." Gage waves at the food.

"Why?" I glare at him, still unsure why the dog acted the way she did. Is he starving her?

"Do you want to be up at 2 AM cleaning up the diarrhea?" He arches an eyebrow.

I just frown. Buddy is inching her head toward the food. Reluctantly, I pull the plate of food onto the side arm of the couch. Buddy just repositions, facing me with her tongue out, looking up at me with those milky eyes.

"Is she blind?" I ask.

There's a silence, and then Gage answers, "Yeah."

The silence continues, and I look up to see Gage watching me with the most intense look in his eyes. He's watching me like he's cataloging every single feature and every movement I make, which he can't be because he can't see me. Right?

It's unsettling. It makes me feel like I have something on my face. I shift, tucking a piece of hair behind my ear. What is he looking at?

Finally, Gage grunts, looking down at his plate. "Eat."

I brush over my face, making sure everything is fine. Nothing seems wrong. He's not even going to say why he was staring? I want to ask him about it, but I stop myself. You can't ask a blind person why they were staring.

I glance at the food, but I don't eat it. First, he invites me over to his house, acts all weird about his dog, and now he's feeding me some mystery food?

"Eat," Gage demands as he continues to eat.

"Don't like spaghetti," I spit. I do like spaghetti, but he's being bossy, and it scares me a bit.

It's clear Buddy likes spaghetti 'cause she's started drooling on my leg. Suddenly, I worry that he told me not to let Buddy eat it because he drugged it.

Gage sighs, then gets up. I tense, but Buddy doesn't. And that's the only reason I don't stab Gage. He stops a foot away, handing me his plate. "The food is fine. Switch me."

I stare at him.

"Listen," annoyance floods his tone, "I'm paying you to do a job for me. You can't work if you're starving. So eat the goddamn spaghetti." He hands me the plate. Reluctantly, I take it and switch for the one he gave me.

Gage sits back down. The smell of tomato sauce and noodles wafts up and makes my mouth water. I am hungry.

Another drool spot hits my leg.

I send an apologetic look to Buddy, then quietly stick my fork in a meatball. Silently, I bring it to my mouth and chew, and fuck if flavors of tomato sauce, meat, and Italian seasoning don't explode across my tongue. I think I let out a small sound of appreciation, then sneak a glance at Gage to see if he's caught me. For a second, I think I see the lines between his brows smooth, but then I blink, and he's back to angry, and I wonder if I even saw it.

CHAPTER NINETEEN

RAVEN

I go home exhausted. The next morning, right before I leave for his house, I get a call from a restricted number. When I pick up, it's Gage, saying we have another case to prep for and asking to meet at the library today. I'm slightly disappointed I won't get to see Buddy, but I tell myself it doesn't matter. This is a job, and I'm just there to get paid.

I've never been to the library, but once I get there, it's nice inside. It's an old brick building, and the inside is warm and inviting and smells like books. Immediately, I feel comfortable.

There's a big 'no phones' sign as I go further in. I find Gage in one of the private rooms near the back, with papers strewn across the table. His hair looks messed up like he's already run his fingers through it.

"What's the case?" I put my purse down and slide in across

from him. I packed a small lunch of rice today, if only to keep Gage off my ass.

"Don't know much. Some divorce case, I think. I'll need you to read the reports for me."

I frown. Tomorrow is the trial for the big case we've been working on, but who knows how lawyers do things. I sit down to get started.

"Oh, turn your phone off. They get pissy about that in here."

I shut it down and then get started with the reports. They're confusing, and this case seems much more complex than the last, with all kinds of different people. As I read, Gage glares up at me, and I can feel it smoldering across my face.

Finally, I put the papers down. "Are you okay?" I thought we made some progress yesterday, being able to work without fighting. Clearly not.

There's a tiny spark in Gage's eye, then he goes back to his normal look. "No problem."

"Right. And I'm the Queen of England." I wave at the papers.

Gage snorts. "Far from it."

The way he says it makes it sound like he thinks I'm worse than the gum on the bottom of his shoe. I narrow my eyes. "What's that supposed to mean?"

"I mean, she's polite and doesn't carry weapons around to hurt people with."

"Not people. Only men." I smile at him. Gage's eyes seem to track the movement on my face, and he grins back.

The look makes me consider grabbing the knife that's sitting in my purse just to remind him that I have years' worth of anger that would love to turn him into a pincushion.

"I don't think you would." He's sorting the papers.

I arch an eyebrow. "What?"

"Hurt me." Gage leans in, putting his arms on the table and getting so close I smell mint on his breath. "I think you're too scared."

My heart races, and I realize again just how big of a person he is and how secluded we are. He didn't seem this threatening yesterday.

"Wanna bet?" I hiss, ready to fight again. I'm always ready to fight. It's fucking exhausting.

"Scared little Raven, always so angry." Gage tilts his head. "Want to know what I think? I think you're running from something."

The way he looks at me is all-knowing. Like he looked into me and knew everything about me. Fear hits my body in a rush of adrenaline. He can tell? No, surely he has no idea.

I shove up from the table, legs shaking. Gage also stands, rounding the table toward me.

I grab my knife, fumbling to get the blade open, and then Gage is right there.

"What is your *problem*?" I jerk the knife up so it's sitting on his chest. He stops, and I know he feels it because it's cut through his button-up shirt. "Get off me."

Gage stiffens for a second, glancing down. Then, he smiles, raising his hands to show me they're not touching me. "Jumpy, aren't you?"

"You came up on me!" The adrenaline is coursing through me, and I want to scream and fight.

"You looked like you were having a panic attack. I came to help." Another grin. He doesn't seem the least bit concerned that I have a knife to his chest.

"Back off." I shove, earning a hiss from him when the knife meets his resistance. He doesn't move.

Something isn't right.

I stare up at him, watching every movement. "Why the new case all of a sudden?"

Gage just smirks. "Don't change the subject. You're running from something, Raven. And I want to know what."

"What did we talk about yesterday?" My body is shaking.

Gage leans his head closer to me, then pulls in a deep breath.

"You know, it's a shame I can't see you right now. I'm sure you look so pretty with those lips trembling and tears in your eyes."

"Axel," I breathe.

He grins. "Hey, little bird."

Confusion rocks my world for a second. Then, I register the mint and the slightly manic glint in Axel's eyes. The confusion morphs into rage. How fucking dare he?

I try to shove at him again, and all I feel is warmth on my pinky. Warmth? No, liquid.

Blood.

"Back off!" The panic is a mix between him not letting me go and me cutting him. There isn't a ton of blood, but it's enough to coat my pinky.

"Why?"

"Because!" It's all I can get out. I'm so afraid, and I fucking hate it. I hate being afraid. And I'm scared of what it'll make me do. "I'll hurt you."

"Yeah, no shit." Axel's laugh is gravelly.

My back is pinned to the wall, and there isn't enough space to get around him without getting closer to him.

"Help!"

"Tell me what you're running from, and I'll let you go."

I peer around Axel. No one is coming. The library is empty.

"Why?"

"Because I'm curious, that's why." Axel puts his hands on the wall beside me, caging me in further.

Suddenly, I can't breathe. He doesn't care that I have a knife.

My hand shakes.

"I'm curious why you come into town, limping around, trying to blend in like you belong here." His breath puffs across my face. "I'm curious why you act like you're so much better than everyone else." His lips are so close that they brush my forehead. "And I'm curious why you put men in bathroom stalls and make them beg?"

All cohesive thoughts leave my head. All I can think about is the last thing he asked, and a bitter laugh escapes me. "Why?" I sputter. "Can't imagine that there's a woman who doesn't fall at your feet and worship you?"

Axel laughs, the sound gentle and restrained. "Are you afraid I'm going to hurt you, little bird?"

"I'd kill you first," I hiss, shoving at the knife to emphasize the control I have.

"Ah, the bird has claws." He licks his lips. "I wouldn't hurt you unless you begged for it."

"Right." I laugh, but there's no humor in it. "Like I begged for you to take my job."

"I offered it back." He's so close that I feel his body heat. The copper from the blood is so strong I can almost taste it.

Before I can stop him, Axel darts his hand down, grabbing the wrist that has the knife. I startle, trying to pull away.

"Shhhh." He pulls my hand and the blade up to his face, pulling in a deep breath. His nostrils flare, then he sticks his tongue out, licking the blood off the blade.

"Axel," I breathe, staring at him, and I stop moving. He could cut his tongue off.

Axel groans, the arm still braced on the wall, shaking.

Then, he pulls away from me. "You and I could have a lot of fun together. Much more fun than my brother." He lets go of my hand. "I'll figure you out, Celeste. Whether you want me to or not."

Then he turns and strides out of the room.

CHAPTER TWENTY

RAVEN

I'm not even sure how I got home from the library, but when I zone back in, I'm in my car behind my apartment. The car is still running. I shut it off to keep from burning gas.

This is fucked. This is so fucked.

I want to get out of the car, but my body won't move. It's like I'm in a fog.

How can I work like this? I can't work like this. I don't *want* to work like this.

This town is fucked. I need to go. My hands shake as I count the cash in my wallet. I don't have enough to move. I have enough for gas and a hotel room for maybe... two nights?

I let my head fall back on the headrest. That's not enough. I need more. I need at least enough for a rent deposit somewhere else. At the thought, tears fill my eyes.

I need more money. I can do a few more days, right? Maybe I can convince Gage to pay me at the end of every day.

That is, if he keeps me on after today. I power my phone back on. Sure enough, there are two missed calls and a text asking where I am.

I groan. What do I tell him? His asshole brother tricked me into thinking he was him? And what will I do when Axel lies his ass off about it? Because he will. Who's Gage going to believe? The girl who broke his glasses and clearly can't stand his guts? Or his literal twin brother?

Right. I'll just keep my head down and earn as much as I can, then leave town.

I check the clock. It's only ten thirty. I'll just tell him I slept in and pray that he keeps me on.

I hit redial and bring the phone to my ear. I feel my hand shaking.

Gage picks up on the first ring. "Raven?"

"Sorry, I overslept. I'm on my way." I crank the car on.

"Christ, woman."

There's silence, and I worry he's going to fire me right then, so I start talking, "I won't take a break, and I'll work late; I'm so sorry. I'm coming."

Silence again, then a deep sigh. "Whatever. Just get here."

I drive to the front before realizing I don't have any lunch with me. And I'll be damned if I eat his food again after all this. So I pull my car up to the front of my place and jump out to grab the extra rice I had from the night before. As I do, I notice there's a piece of mail in the small mailbox attached to the front of my house.

I grab it and shiver as I unlock the door. Fuck, it's gotten really cold here really fast. I grab the food, toss the letter on the front seat beside me, and then fly across town.

CHAPTER TWENTY-ONE

GAGE

This girl, I swear to *god*.

I've gone through a pack of gum while pacing and waiting for her. Does she think the whole world revolves around her? The trial is *tomorrow*. Axel told me I could use the glasses for the trial itself, but today, I still need to prepare.

My grandfather clock chimes again, and the song plays halfway through. It's ten thirty.

I run a hand through my hair again when there's a hasty knock at the door, and Buddy jumps up. I stride over as Buddy races with me, then yank the door open.

There's movement, and a wash of Fiji scent pushes past me. "Sorry."

Buddy's jumping around, yipping in excitement, which just

pisses me off more. Buddy doesn't even greet me like that; what is her deal?

I brace myself for Raven's attitude, but she just greets Buddy when she goes to the couch.

"Do you want to get started on the reports from two months ago?" Her voice is tense.

I stalk to the couch and grunt, "Yeah."

Papers rustle, and then she starts reading. It's not until the clock chimes again and the bells start going off that I realize I haven't paid attention to anything she's been saying. I'm just sitting tense, waiting for her to yell or pull her damn knife again. A little tingle runs across my skin at the thought.

"Is that a clock?" Raven asks.

"What?" I clear my throat, shaking out my arms.

"The chiming."

I frown, glancing in the clock's direction. "Yeah?"

"Ohhhh," Raven says. I realize then that the clock is around the corner, and Raven probably can't see it. Fucking sighted people.

"I've never seen one in real life."

I blink, then clear my throat. "It's on the desk by the hallway."

Raven gets up, and I see the movement as she goes to check it out. After a minute, she asks, "How does it work?"

I glare in her direction. "You wind it."

There's a pause. "So, how does it stay accurate?"

I blink. What the hell does she mean?

"Like, what if you don't wind it and it gets behind? It won't be accurate."

I see movement as she comes back to the couch.

"You don't have to like the clock." Automatically, I reach my hand down to pet Buddy, but she isn't there. She's next to Raven. I clench my hand.

"It's not that I don't like it! I'm just curious."

"Buddy, come here." I pat the couch. I need my dog by me.

For a second, I don't think she'll come, and my heart drops. But then I hear the click of her toenails, and then her warm body is at my knees. I bury my hands in her fur, instantly feeling better.

Raven's voice softens. "I've only read about them in books."

I struggle to remember what she's talking about. "The clock?"

"Yeah."

Papers rustle, and then she starts working again. I try my best to focus, but for some reason, I can't.

Raven likes to read? I fucking love reading. I wish I could read physical books more easily, but I have audiobooks on disks. It reminds me of when Mom used to read books to us before we went to bed every night. I loved it.

I try to shake myself out of it. Who cares that Raven likes to read? I sure don't. She's toxic, and I don't want anything to do with her.

After lunch, Raven gets up, and I hear the swish of her clothes and the clink of dishes. Then she's in front of me, and her soft smell washes over me like a rough embrace. Despite myself, I suck in a breath.

"You done with this?"

I blink to focus. She must be talking about the plate I have balanced on the side of the couch.

I clear my throat, "I'll get it."

"I'm already going to the kitchen." There's movement, and then her hand brushes against mine. It's a soft movement, and her skin is both warm and dry. She's not tugging or yanking. Her fingers just rest on mine as she grabs the plate, and for that brief second, all my hairs stand on end, and electricity runs through me.

Then, she takes the plate and leaves.

My whole body trembles, and I want to follow her. To feel her softness again. To touch more of her.

Fuck.

Fuck, fuck, fuck.

We work late into the night, and while I try to focus, I wonder if Raven meant to touch me. If she felt the same connection I did. I wonder what she'd feel like under me. Or, fuck, on top of me. Raven doesn't seem to be the kind of woman who likes to be told what to do in the bedroom.

Or does she?

Fuck, I can't focus. I need to focus. I fell for a pretty woman who was my brother's once before. Never again.

So why the fuck can't I stop wondering what books she likes to read?

CHAPTER TWENTY-TWO

RAVEN

There's some sort of weird energy between Gage and me, and I can't figure it out. He stares at me with such unnerving intensity that it makes my legs tremble, and heat creeps up my face. It's like he's trying to see into my soul, which is dumb because he's mostly blind, but I feel like he sees in ways other than just sight.

Then I remind myself that it's just how he looks. Gage doesn't care about me. He's just another man who'd hurt me if given the chance, and that sobers me up.

We wrap up the prep, and I move to the front door, saying gruffly, "Well. Good luck with tomorrow."

I wince. Good luck? Why the fuck didn't I say: go fuck yourself?

Gage just grunts.

I take off before I can embarrass myself more and walk to my car. It's even colder than this morning. It's the kind of cold that needles into your bones and makes your skin ache with how dry it is.

I arrive back at my apartment hungry, freezing, and fucking pissed off. Snatching up my things, I bring in the mail I forgot about this morning in my rush to get to Gage's.

As soon as I get inside, something doesn't feel right. I flip the lights on and realize it's cold in my place. Like, icebox cold.

What the fuck?

I rush to the temperature panel. It's set normally at sixty-five. It now shows just slightly warmer than outside.

What the hell? I search for the hot water heater, or whatever the hell they have here, and realize that I can't find it.

Fucking hell. It must be in one of the other units since this place was converted.

Shivering, I move to the stove to heat up some dinner. There's no wind in here, but it's cold. Just what I fucking needed. I'm mad, I'm tired, and I'm fucking cold.

I don't want to call the landlord. I don't want to give him any reason to kick me out.

For a brief second, I think about calling Gage. Immediately, I shove that thought away. What the hell is wrong with me?

I have to call my landlord. This isn't annoying; it is a legitimate issue.

I go back and forth on it for a minute, then dial my landlord. The phone rings and rings until I get his voicemail. Cussing, I leave him a message, flipping my phone shut again.

I eat dinner, and the house is cold enough that my food steams visibly. Wrapping myself in a blanket, I check the mail I brought in from earlier. Maybe I didn't pay a bill?

Immediately, I see it's not a bill. It's a letter addressed to me by hand. Only it's addressed to Celeste, not Raven. The handwriting is messy, and my stomach drops.

No.

I rip the envelope open and pull out a letter, scanning to the bottom.

It's signed by Max

Fuck.

I drop the letter like it's poisoned. He found me? How the hell did he find me? I did everything I could to hide from him.

My heart races, and suddenly, I feel sick.

I need to leave much earlier than expected. I need to leave *now*.

I count the money in my wallet, my fingers barely able to move, but not because of the cold anymore. Now, my whole body is thrumming.

It's not enough. It's not fucking enough.

It's fine. I'll just live out of my car. Right? It can't be any colder than it is in here.

I glance at the letter. What did he say? Is he angry? I left him in the middle of the night. Just took what few things I had and left without a word.

Whatever it is, it's just a letter. The letter can't hurt me.

Right?

I look at it.

Celeste,

My girl, my beautiful woman. I don't know where to start. I miss you every day. It took me so long to find you. I'm sorry for what happened, but you have to know I didn't mean to hurt you. I love you. Why didn't you call? Write? At least explain? I feel we have so much to fight for. I love you. You're my best friend and the best thing that ever happened to me.

I'm at a loss for words.

Please, Celeste. I fucking miss you. I'll go to the ends of the earth to get you back.

You can't hide from me.

Max

. . .

At the bottom, he scribbled his phone number.

I stare at the letter, a horrible mix of emotions rolling through me at once. Then, a snort breaks through.

Max never loved me. That's not what love looks like.

Then, pain follows quickly after. I *wish* Max loved me. I *wish* I knew what love looks like. All the pain I've been holding in rushes through me, and I choke back a sob. I'm so goddamn tired of being angry. So goddamn tired of hurting.

Will I ever feel what real love is like?

There's a knock at my back door, and I startle.

Is it Max? Fuck. Fear rushes through me, and I grab my baseball bat. There's no peephole, so I can't see who's there. I crack the door just a smidge.

Axel stands there. "Oh hey, little bird!" He takes one look at my face, then sobers. "Raven. You okay?"

Horror rushes through me slowly. It's Axel. The man who taunted me earlier. The man who's seeing my red eyes. Oh my god. He caught me crying.

I try to slam the door, but Axel steps in, looking around. "Are you okay?" He looks angry, searching the apartment.

I jerk back. "I'm fine." I school my face and clear my throat. "I'm fine. Get out."

Axel looks around again. "Why are you crying?"

Fuck, of course he noticed.

"I'm not!" I raise the bat. "Now get out!"

Axel eyes me for a calculating second. Then, he shuts the door, cutting off the cold wind. "Not until I know you're safe." His features smooth over, and he rubs his arms. "Kinda cold in here."

"Axel." My body starts to shake, and I can't do anything about it. "Get out." Axel isn't listening to me. He isn't listening, just like Max didn't listen. I raise the bat.

Axel raises his hands. "Don't hit me; it'll get me off. And your landlord asked me to take a look at your heat."

No way in hell. I don't lower the bat. I'm so fucking over being treated like a doormat. I'm getting in my car, and I'm leaving. To where, I don't know, but I'm going.

"Nice guy, Kevin is. Drunk as fuck tonight, though." Axel starts wandering through my place.

"Hey." I chase after him.

"Where's the boiler?" He stalks to the kitchen, poking around.

"It's not here, asshole. Don't you think I looked?"

Axel spins, hands on his hips. "Damn it."

For a second, I wonder if hitting him will make things worse. If he'll pull it out of my hands and beat *me* with it.

I find myself stuck in the same nightmare I've been in since a child: rollover. Play dead. Don't anger the man, and he won't hurt you.

Suddenly, Axel is right in front of me, hands caging me in on either side. "You can come to my place," he says. The look he's giving me. It's the same look Max gave me after... he did what he did. It's a placating look. A gentle look. It makes me feel sick.

"C'mon." Axel's smiling now. His eyes are all soft, but it's not real. I know it's not real; I just can't put my finger on what's wrong.

Axel grabs my hand. "We'll go to my place."

His place. He's going to move me to a different location. He's taking me somewhere else so he can do what he wants to me. My entire body feels locked up.

Axel pulls me gently along behind him. I don't want to follow, but instinct screams that I do. That I just appease him.

The steps I take are in slow motion, and my gaze locks on the book beside my bed. The book I used to read as a kid where the main character jumped on the back of the bad guy and beat him over the head. I always wanted to be her.

You might not ever have a chance to be her if you let him take you.

I stop. I dig my weight into my heels, and Axel stops, turning back around with raised eyebrows.

Fight. And don't stop fighting till you make it out.

Fuck, I'm scared. I scan Axel's face, looking to see if he's mad at me. To see if he's going to hit me.

He'll do worse than hit you. Fucking fight.

"You okay?" The space between Axel's brows bunch. But it's all wrong. The furrows are too deep, like he's trying too hard to look concerned.

"Yeah." The fear sneaks out before I can stop it, and I give Axel a tiny smile.

"Okay." He smiles back, grabs my keys off the counter, then pulls me toward the door.

I've been hit before. I survived.

Another step.

I've been assaulted before. I survived.

One more step.

I can feel that book's presence burning into my awareness.

No. No more cowering. It's time to fight.

Then, I yank my arm from Axel's grip, and with a scream, attack him from behind.

AXEL

14 Years Old

"What is it?" I creep up to the dead bird on our back porch. It's big, with glistening black feathers and a long beak.

"Ew, it's a crow." A shiver skitters down my spine. "Get back, it'll claw your eyes out."

"It's a raven." Gage pushes me out of the way, kneeling down.

"Don't touch it!"

But Gage ignores me, gently moving the bird's wing. With a snap, the wings are flapping, and I jump back, glasses slipping down my nose. It's still alive!

"Its wing is broken." Gage doesn't seem flustered at all; instead, he gently reaches his hands out again and grabs the bird's body.

"Gage, don't."

The bird flaps again, but Gage just murmurs to it. The bird weakly struggles.

"Get some water," Gage tells me.

"What?"

"Get water."

"Why?" I look around. "What are you going to do?"

Gage snaps, "Just do it, Garret."

"Don't call me that!" Gage loves calling me by my first name. I hate it.

Gage ignores me, still murmuring to the bird, stroking his thumb down its back.

I huff, going inside. Mom would kill Gage if he brought anything else inside. He's like a magnet for broken animals. A damn Snow White, if you will. And yet, none of his animals respond the same way to me. They run right up to him but skirt past me. It's annoying. How can they tell who is who? I tried for a while to steal Gage's clothes, thinking it was that. Still, they ignored me. And that pissed me off. It's extra annoying because everyone else loves the animals. All my friends want to know what kind of pet Gage has next. Lola the raccoon has been their favorite.

Still, I get the water and go back outside. As soon as I put the dish down by the bird's head, it freaks out again.

"Slowly," Gage says.

"Yeah, whatever." I throw my hands in the air. I'll never be Gage. I'll never have the touch. But whatever, I don't need it. When could I ever need to tame an animal?

Fucking never.

CHAPTER TWENTY-FOUR

AXEL

Suddenly, a weight crashes into my back, and I stumble forward. I almost fall, but Raven slides to the ground, and I'm able to recover. Just as I do, she's jumping on me again, beating on my head. She screams, the sound ear-splitting as she rips at my ears.

"Fuck!" Adrenaline and pain fill me. "Goddamn!"

I whirl, ducking my head and driving myself into her body.

Raven screams, staring up at me with absolute hatred, her eyes tight with fury. Fighting me. Always fucking fighting me.

She doesn't fight Gage!

I steady my feet, then take a breath. Be cool, Axel.

I swallow and say, "It's too cold here. Stay with me."

"Get out!" Raven screams.

Okay, fuck me. When I turned off her heat, I thought things

would go smoother than this. I can get every girl I want, but not Raven?

I'm basically Gage. At least, in looks. The fucker is way nicer than I am. I am, in fact, a horrible human being, which should be impossible since we're identical.

"Raven." I gentle my voice. "I'm not going to hurt you." Then, I duck down, tossing the woman over my shoulder.

"Axel!" Raven screeches, the sound startled. I turn, marching out of the kitchen, both her thighs clasped under my arm. Fuck, she's light.

I'll have to feed her more.

"Put me down!" Raven fights, attempting to kick her legs, and raining light hits down on my back.

Okay. I'll have to teach her to fight, too. Once I'm sure she won't fight *me*.

I duck through her door

"Axel!" Her cry switches from anger to fear.

"Not safe for you to stay here. Too cold."

They're band-aid words. Gage words. What I want to say is, *'Shut the fuck up. You're mine, and I'm going to make you love it.'*

"What are you doing? Put me down!"

I hit what I hope is the unlock button on her keys. The car beeps, and the lights flash.

Damn it. I hit the other one, hearing the locks slide up.

This will be the tricky part. Flinging the door open, I throw Raven off my shoulder into the driver's seat. She tries to bolt, but I drop my arm across her chest and wedge my knee against her thighs, pinning her to the center console.

"Easy, wild thing."

Raven does not take it easy. She snaps her head forward, nearly colliding with mine. I don't jerk back in time, and pain lances across my skull. Groaning, I pull her right hand toward the steering wheel while fishing a pair of cuffs out of my back pocket. As soon as she realizes what I'm doing, she screeches.

"Axel, no! What are you doing?"

"Hold still, little bird." I struggle to keep her wrist close enough to snap the cuff around her without hurting her. I'll hurt her later. When she asks for it.

Raven's not strong, but god, she's panicked. Finally, when she's reaching her other hand back to hit me, I hold her still long enough to fasten it without grabbing her delicate skin. Then, I clasp the cuff to the wheel.

"What the fuck?" Raven yanks back, and I step out of the car, softly shutting the door. Inside the car, she screams, the car muffling the sound. A mixture of feelings runs through me: excitement, adrenaline, and a hint of annoyance. That fucking hurt.

Raven screams again, and a thrill runs through me. She's so fucking feisty.

I get in on the passenger side.

"Axel." Raven flexes her hand, leaning as I turn the wheel. She has a pretty hand. So small and delicate.

"Yes?"

"Let me go. Right now."

"Nah," I reach across her to put the keys in the ignition. "You're gonna drive us to my place."

There's a stunned silence where I can almost hear Raven's brain trying to process what I just said. And processing is not what I want her to do right now. Obeying is.

Snapping the knife out of my pocket, I revel in the snick it makes as the blade opens.

There's a moment where I can almost taste the fear that rolls off Raven, and it goes straight to my head, filling me with adrenaline.

I'd only hurt Raven to keep her safe. And safe, in this instance, means obedience. I need the fear to overwhelm her free will because she may just use that free will to run us both off the road. Although, a fireball wreck caused by the hottest, angriest woman around wouldn't be such a bad way to go.

Adrenaline pumps into me so hard I feel like I'm floating. I trace the knife down her thigh. Nowhere vital. I don't want her to feel like I'm going to kill her. Crashing would hurt more.

Raven lets out a breath that snaps me back down to earth.

"Drive," I warn in a low breath.

And, miracle of miracles, the firebird listens to me. Slowly, she starts driving, reversing from the spot and making our way out to the street.

I'm floating again. We're driving together. Our first time. It's so thrilling. She's being gentle too. I assume that's to keep the knife out of her kneecap where it's currently resting, but I like to think it's 'cause deep down, she wants to do what I asked.

I give her directions to my place, and all the while, my hand shakes with energy. The more she's silent but can't get away, the higher I get.

She can't run. She's *mine*.

I feel like I'm flying above the car, and I've never been more excited.

"Faster," I say. I want to get her home where she can be comfortable and won't hurt herself trying to get away. Then, she can fight me all she wants, but she'll be safe while she does it.

It doesn't take long to get home. I live in a small house downtown. It's a modest two-story, three-bedroom house, but it's all I need. I can tell we're back by the rumbling of the car over the gravel driveway.

"Home sweet home," I say right as Raven violently throws the car into park.

I'm slammed into the dashboard, pain shocking through my system. I can't resist a bubble of glee as I move around to her side of the car, uncuff her, and grab her around the middle to throw her over my shoulder.

"Put me down!" Her voice is higher and more panicked now. "Police, help!"

"Begging just turns me on, brat."

Her response is an attempt to claw my eyes out, which almost makes me fall while trying to unlock the door.

"Fuck," I cuss, catching myself before I can land on Raven and crush her.

"Fuck you! I fucking hate you!" She's ripping at clumps of my hair now. I feel it snapping as I scramble to get the door unlocked. I'm alive. I'm so fucking alive. I almost want to keep this moment frozen in time.

But I get the door unlocked, and then I dart up the stairs, my woman bouncing at my back. Once there, I move to the back room that I've prepared for her. It's simple, with a queen-size bed, a dresser, and a bathroom attached.

Kicking the door shut behind me, I put Raven down on the bed. She bounces up, and immediately, I back away, holding up my hands. "Easy."

Raven launches at me, screaming and kicking and clawing.

I shove her back just enough that she catches herself on the bed. Although she's smart not to trust me. I'm not a good man.

Raven screams, immediately backing up and looking around the room, her eyes wide. She darts to the bathroom, and I hear her wrestling with the window.

I'm buzzing. I did it. I fucking did it.

I want to rush through the rest of the steps. I think back to what Gage always did with his animals. They'd fight him at first, but he'd be gentle. He was so gentle. He'd take care of their needs, then spend time with them so they'd get used to him. So they'd trust him.

I rest my back against the door. Raven won't be able to open the windows. I made sure all of them were nailed shut so she couldn't open them.

Raven goes from window to window, trying to get out, searching for a weapon.

"Raven, it's okay—"

"It's okay?" She whirls on me. "It's *okay*? You just kidnapped me! Let me go right fucking now." She's shaking. I lock in on her hands, which are quivering. Just like they did the first time I saw her at the bar. When the man scared her.

"Raven..." I sink down against the door, sliding so I'm lower than her. I hold my hands out in a soothing way.

"No, fuck you!" Spit flies from her mouth, and she points at me. "Let me go! Now!"

"I'll make sure you won't miss work."

She heaves in a breath, her face snapping back to fear. She backs up, putting the bed between us.

Good. I want her to make herself comfortable.

"I'm calling the cops! You'll go to prison!" She digs in the bedside drawer and then paces between the bed and the wall. "Call Gage!"

I keep my mouth shut.

"Call Gage!" she screams, throwing pillows at me. They don't hit hard, and that seems to make her even more mad. She rips all the bedding off the bed, screaming and screaming.

Raven is so afraid. I close my eyes, dropping my head against the door. Every creature Gage saved was afraid. They fought him, even bit and scratched. But they came around.

Just like Raven will.

My little bird with the broken wings.

All mine.

CHAPTER TWENTY-FIVE

RAVEN

6 Months Ago

Something wakes me up. I moan, blinking in the darkness of the room. I'm warm and comfortable, and I almost fall back asleep before the movement starts again.

It's Max's hand between my legs.

Slowly, disappointment and dread creep into my tired brain. I told Max a while ago that he could mess with me while I slept. I thought it would be hot until he started doing it multiple times a week, mostly on days that I said I was tired or didn't want to fuck him before bed. And he'd never get me off.

Max is still, and I wonder if he went back to sleep. Maybe he did. Maybe he could feel the stiffness in my body. Slowly, the exhaustion pulls me under until, again, his hand moves. Up and down, up and down, waking me up.

I roll over, exhaustion muddling my brain. I can't think clearly. I can't even think when I'm awake. I'm just tired. So fucking tired. Work has been a lot. I've tried to tell Max that. Tried to let him see the depression in my eyes. All I want is to sleep.

Max stays still long enough that I start to drift off again, and then again, his hand moves between my legs. He's rubbing.

I groan and flip over aggressively. Why won't he let me sleep?

About five minutes later, Max starts again. I shove his hand away.

Another five minutes later, it starts again. This time, I just let him. I know he won't stop until he gets off, and I'm tired. I feel the bed shake rhythmically, and his breathing starts to pick up. Finally, it stops. He rolls out of bed to go to the bathroom, and I hear the faucet turn on. Then, he comes back, and his breathing evens out almost immediately.

I can't fall back asleep, but I don't open my eyes. If I do, it means I'm admitting defeat. Why is it so hot in here? I toss, hoping my movement wakes him up. Max's snores soften for a second, then pick back up.

I toss for hours, sweaty and angry, planning my fight with Max for the morning.

The next day, I'm exhausted. Exhausted and pissed off. I've had a bad feeling all day. As I rage clean the dishes, I drop the soap bottle into the water a second time.

"Fucking stupid fucking soap."

The garage door opens, and I know Max is home. I stiffen, the feeling of dread not going away. One of two things is gonna happen. He's gonna brush me off or get angry. I slam the soap bottle back on the counter.

I dare him to try and beat my ass. Fucking dare him. I have years of pent-up rage, and it may as well go somewhere.

The door opens, and he steps inside with a swish of his clothes. "Hey."

I ignore him, continuing to wash dishes. There's a beat of

silence, and then he continues inside, putting his stuff on the dining room table. He doesn't say anything else; he just moves around, putting things away, and then goes upstairs to change. When he comes back down, I hear him put the TV on.

Oh, so he's gonna pretend like everything is fine.

I whirl on him, keeping the kitchen island between us.

He glances at me briefly and then does a double-take. One of his hands twitches.

I glare.

"You... okay?" he asks.

My skin gets hot. "Oh yeah, I'm okay. Totally fine."

Max evaluates me, then blinks once. "Ookay..." Then, slowly, he reaches for his controller.

Which makes adrenaline rush through my veins. "Because of course I'd be okay. I get great sleep every night. Not like someone's waking me up then keeping me up for hours." My whole body is thrumming, waiting for him to unplug the controller and throw it at me. If he does, there's a butter knife right by my hand. I'll teach him to hit me.

But he doesn't. "Oh, fuck. Sorry."

I stare at him.

He raises both hands. "Didn't know I was keeping you up."

"Well, you gotta stop. I can't sleep."

"Sure, okay. Yeah, no problem." He looks at me like he thinks I'm crazy.

Maybe I am crazy. I feel crazy, standing there stiffly, waiting for him to attack me. When he doesn't, the energy still doesn't go away. "Is that it?" I ask.

"That was my bad." Max eyes me, then the TV.

Still, no effort to get up and hand my ass to me.

"Is that all?" He clearly wants to play his game. As if this meant nothing to him.

I guess it is.

Slowly, I go back to the dishes, but my entire body still feels stiff. That's not how easy life is. If he's not gonna beat my ass, he's gonna do something.

Why the hell couldn't he just beat my ass and get it over with? At least then, I'd know what to expect.

Two weeks later, I've had a long day at work pulling overtime, and all I want to do is sleep for the foreseeable future. I fall into bed, passing out almost immediately.

The next day, I'm horny. The house looks weird, but there's a hot guy here, and all I want to do is climb him like a tree. So I do, hugging him to me. His thigh brushes my clit, and it sends a thrill through me.

Suddenly, the guy fades, and I'm looking at the edge of my pillow. The horny feeling doesn't stop, though. What is going on?

Something licks at my opening. Slowly, I realize I'm waking up. Someone's head is between my legs, licking between my vagina and my asshole. I blink awake. It's Max. He has my cheeks spread so he can tongue my ass.

I'm so confused. Was I dreaming? Max continues assaulting my hole. My body is already wired, pleasure running through me, and I'm not fully awake. I think this is wrong. I think it's wrong, but I'm on the edge of coming.

You weren't ready. You should have seen this coming.

I squeeze my eyes shut, wanting to go back to that pleasant fog. No. I don't want to wake up. I want to stay asleep. Because something tells me that around the corner of consciousness, there's a monster of bad feelings waiting. I know it's there. I can sense it.

Instead, I focus on the feeling of my body. The feelings that I didn't ask for but are there anyway. They feel warm and inviting.

Warmer than the monster. These feelings won't hurt me. These feelings want me to come.

So, I flit my hand down to massage my clit. The warmth seeps into me more, and I squeeze my eyes shut, chasing it harder.

You're not safe.

Fuck. I circle my fingers, pushing myself harder in the way I know feels good. I feel a shift behind me, and then a groan follows. I focus on nothing other than that safe feeling that's creeping away faster than I can chase it down. Then, I push myself over the edge, coming on my fingers. There's more shifting, and then something's at the entrance of my pussy. It's Max. He shoves his dick inside my pussy. He pumps a few times before coming.

As soon as he rolls out of me, he goes back to the bathroom. I'm squeezing my eyes shut, but I can still tell he came inside me. My legs are sticky. The monster is screaming that I'll have to get up. I'll have to pee so I don't get a UTI.

But I don't want to listen. I don't want to wake up 'cause I can feel the shame burning against my skin.

You're a coward. You let this happen. This is your fault.

I bury my head under my pillow and focus on the wetness between my legs. The pleasure. Anything but reality.

I put the book down for the third time today. I can't focus anymore. Usually, I read, but I haven't been able to get through this book at all, and I've been trying all week, which pisses me off 'cause the book is right up my alley. It's about a badass woman who takes control of her dad's mafia empire.

I stare at the cover, trying to find a reason to blame the book. Maybe it's the writing style? The chapters are too long?

But deep down, I know it's because I'm tired. Max hasn't

stopped waking me up. The thought makes nausea run through me.

Where's all the courage I had when I told him to stop? Was ready to fight him? Instead, at night, I'm just a scared little girl. A coward. I can't make him stop. It's like I'm frozen. Because if I freeze, he'll eventually finish and leave me alone.

I know some part of me should be angry. Should be deeply, irreparably angry. But for some reason, it's like the anger is sitting behind a glass wall, and all I can do is look at it. Right now, all I want to do is pretend like I don't exist. Maybe if I wear my clothes to bed, he won't want to do it. Maybe if I don't say anything, he won't continue.

I stare at the book cover. It has a fierce-looking woman on the front, her hair blowing in front of her face. I have a sudden, intrusive thought: she wouldn't allow this kind of behavior.

Shame washes over me, and with it, a lick of anger.

Fuck it. Saying something can't make things any worse.

I grab my phone and send Max a text.

> Me: Hey. Can you fall asleep with your hand on my back or legs? Just not on my kitty; I can't sleep. Thanks!

I drop the phone, my heart beating quickly for the first time in a week. A response comes back quickly.

> Max: Oh, sure! My bad, no problem.

A week later, I'm woken up again with his hand between my legs. And this time, I don't sink back into that welcoming numbness. The woman on the cover of my book stares at me from my nightstand, daring me to stand up for myself. Daring me to be what she is.

And that's where my anger was finally born. Like a shield, it rose up around me, burning so hot no one could come near me. So no one could hurt me. Not even the people who say they love me.

Especially the people who say they love me.

I leave Max that night. Screaming and throwing things around, embracing the anger that's been building for my entire life.

It's time for a new Celeste. A new me.

Raven.

CHAPTER TWENTY-SIX

RAVEN

I've lost it. Full-on lost control of my actions, ripping at the bedding, throwing the bedside lamp, and banging on the windows. Nothing fucking helps. It doesn't fucking do anything except to spark a tiny bit of something in Axel's eyes before it's soothed over again.

Fighting with Max got me away for a few months, and now he's stalking me. What will fighting with Axel do?

But there's no stopping now. No stopping until I get away. Until I find a place where there are no people and hide there for eternity.

I shake, looking around the room again. It's sparse, with a dresser, a bed, and a closet. Almost like he planned this.

Fuck, he planned this.

Axel just sits against the door, eyes partially closed. Every time I move, he glances at me out of the corner of his eye. Otherwise, he just sits there. Doing nothing.

My heart is going so fast that I feel nauseous. I don't have my knife. I don't have my purse. I don't have *anything*. He took it from me. Just like he took my freedom. Just like he'll take what he wants from me, and I won't be able to stop him.

The monster is creeping around the corner again.

I force myself to breathe. I suck in a breath, trying to lower my heart rate so my voice comes out as serious as I mean it. It takes me a good few breaths. I watch Axel's chest move up and down slowly as I fight for control. When I finally get there, I breathe out, "I'll never forgive you, Axel Newman."

When I say those words, something breaks free in my chest, and I realize I'm talking to more than just him.

Axel's eyes close, and we sit there in silence for what feels like forever. Then, Axel lets out a breath. "Get some sleep." He opens his eyes, looking straight at me, then away again.

He's ignoring me. Ignoring my voice. A mixture of helplessness and rage bubbles up in me. Trapped in this room with him with no weapons, there's nothing I can do. All of that energy races through me, and I feel like exploding. Then, to my horror, tears well up in my eyes. I'm scared and angry, and I can't keep the tears in. I start to cry. The sobs push through me, the terror from Axel and Max blending together into something I can't control. I sob and sob while Axel just winces and stares at the dresser in front of him.

I cry for a while until I'm spent. My knees shake, and I want to sit down. I need to, but I refuse to get on the bed.

I squat with my back to the wall so I can still see Axel. He doesn't move. Exhaustion overwhelms me, and every limb feels heavy.

I stare at him, feeling empty. "Get out."

"Not going anywhere, little bird."

"That's not my name."

There's a tiny smirk.

"I hate you."

"Good."

I sit in silence, but I'm not done fighting. My eyelids feel heavy, but I refuse to fall asleep. I'll wait till he does, then strangle him to death.

It feels like it takes forever for Axel's breathing to even out. His whole body relaxes against the door, and his head tilts to the side.

I eye the lamp I tossed at him earlier. It's sitting right beside him. Maybe I could bash his brains out with it?

I wait for what feels like so long to make sure he's really asleep. It feels like so long that I catch myself nodding off, but when I do, I feel hands on my pussy, and I snap awake, looking around in a panic.

Axel is nowhere near me. Hasn't even twitched.

Fuck. The adrenaline is rushing through my veins. Slowly, inch by inch, I ease myself up. My muscles tremble as I try to maintain slow movement. Finally, I straighten, and Axel doesn't move. Then, slowly, I take one soft step.

"Don't even think about it."

I jump, eyes wide. Axel doesn't even open his, but he's smirking.

I was so quiet. Does he have superpower hearing? Rage fills me.

"I promise I'm not going to hurt you." Axel's eyes open, and he focuses on me through his glasses. "I'm trying to help you."

"Kidnapping counts as hurting."

"No, it doesn't."

"Yes, it does!" I wave my hands at him.

He arches an eyebrow. "Where are you hurt?"

I stop, stumped for a second. My hand aches slightly from yanking on the cuffs. I snap, "My wrist."

Axel straightens, a look of concern filling his eyes as his gaze locks onto my wrist. He moves like he's going to get up.

"No!" I jerk my hand behind me, backing up. "It's fine. It's totally fine."

"Let me see." Axel gets up slowly, putting his hands out in a placating manner.

"Get away from me." I skitter back along the bedside.

"If you're hurt, I'm going to make it right."

"I'm not! I lied."

Axel stops prowling closer.

"I lied, it's totally fine."

He frowns, then shakes his head and turns back around. I relax slightly.

"Christ woman..." He lets out a breath. "You're going to let me look at it in the morning."

Fine. That's fine. As long as he gets the fuck away from me.

Axel hesitates for a second longer, then returns to his spot at the door. After a while, my legs shake from standing, and I go back to my spot on the floor, once again locked in a stalemate.

Fighting didn't work. There's a rush of emotions—disappointment, anger, fear. And then, numbness starts to creep in.

So that kind of fighting didn't work. There are other kinds of fighting.

I have to be smart about this. I *will* be smart about this. Because I'm no longer gonna let a man control me, even if it costs me everything.

If I can't have me, no one can.

CHAPTER TWENTY-SEVEN

AXEL

Raven falls asleep somewhere around six in the morning. She was so fucking jumpy and terrified.

Christ, I wasn't trying to hurt her. This was literally supposed to just...snap her out of her nonsensical hatred of me. And save her from the cold.

She looks so stressed, even when she sleeps. Her head is barely slumped forward, and her hands are wrapped around her knees.

It's making me feel uncomfortable, so I go downstairs to make myself some coffee.

This is for her own good. I tell myself that over and over as I stare at my coffee pot, unblinking. I can make her feel good.

A noise outside makes me jump. It's footsteps.

Oh fuck. Gage is coming over for the glasses. I open the

door before he can knock and wake Raven. The thought sends conflicting emotions through me, but the biggest one is that I wouldn't mind Gage knowing that she's in *my* home.

"Fuck, it's cold." Gage brushes past me to come inside, and I shut the door softly after him. He has a pristine black suit on, and his hair is styled, but he has an old pair of square-rimmed glasses on. He scowls at me.

I raise an eyebrow. "You look cute."

"Just give me the glasses."

"Okay, grumpy." I roll my eyes, taking them off. "Give me the green ones."

"They aren't green, they're black."

"Oh, Jesus Christ." I take his old pair, looking through them. "Goddamn! How do you even see in these?" I have to blink a few times to refocus, and still, the fridge is blurry around the edges.

"I don't." Gage turns on his heel.

"Okay, grumpy." I follow after him into the cold. "You're welcome! And don't lose."

"I won't," he snaps.

I roll my eyes, but it makes me dizzy. "You're a cocky asshole, you know that?"

"That's all you. I'm just prepared." Gage's voice softens slightly at the end, just enough to make me pay attention. He's prepared because Raven helped him.

A pang of jealousy flashes across my chest.

My Raven. The woman who was mine from the beginning, and he stole to hire her on.

My chest gets tight.

"Careful, brother." I cross my arms. "You know what happened with the last one." It's a low blow, and I know it.

"Shut up," Gage bites back too quickly.

Gage better understand that Raven is *my* girl. She may not know it yet, but she's fucking mine. I can't keep the words back. "You wouldn't care then that she spent the night with me."

Gage freezes. I can't fully see his glare, but I can feel it in the way he's stopped breathing. There's a tense moment where I'm not sure if we're going to fight or not, then Gage laughs.

"Sure, whatever." He turns on his heel and marches out of the house.

This fucker doesn't believe me.

I follow him out. "Don't be mad that I can pull more pussy than you."

Gage just flips me off as he's walking to Mom's waiting car. At least, I think that's what the aggressive hand raise was.

"Bring my glasses back as soon as you're done!"

Gage gets in his car, slams his door, then they leave, and I'm left standing in my doorway, somehow even more pissed off.

I found Raven first. If he thinks he can keep her with his broody ways, he's sadly mistaken. I'll get her to open up to me.

I start to stomp upstairs, then pause.

Food. People are pissy when they're hungry.

I stomp back downstairs, throwing together a quick turkey, spinach, and pesto sandwich on sourdough. Something quick so she doesn't have time to, I don't know, break the bathroom mirror and stab me with it. Then, I march back upstairs.

When I open the door, Raven is up and standing on the other side of the bed. I can't see her as well with these glasses, but I can still clock the tense way she's holding her body. Despite that, I already feel better being in her presence. It's like the tight band around my chest loosens.

"Morning." I throw her my best blinding grin.

Silence.

"Made you breakfast."

Raven ignores me. "Who was that?"

Instantly, my mood sours.

"Eat." I shove the plate on the bed.

She's silent again and doesn't move. I perch on the edge of the bed slowly. "You know, most women would kill for a chance in my bed."

"I'd kill for a chance to get out of it."

The sass immediately goes to my dick, and I feel myself stiffening. Fuck, I want to shove it down her throat and teach her some manners. Instead, I clutch my chest. "Jesus, am I really that bad?"

I hear Raven open her mouth, then nothing comes out. Then her voice tones low, "You really want me to answer that?"

I snort. I mean, kind of. I just grunt, "You have to be hungry. Eat."

"Hell no."

I stare at her for a second. She's still stiff. Okay, so she's still afraid. Slowly, I reach out and grab the sandwich, taking a bite. "You can't be one of those people who only eat 'breakfast' food for breakfast."

The woman is quiet as hell, probably wondering how to choke me from afar, which only makes my dick problem worse. I try to shift so she can't see it, putting one half of the sandwich down and then taking a bite of the other.

It's silent for a while, just me chewing and Raven wondering how she can kill me. Then, I sense movement and watch as Raven slowly drags the plate toward her.

Elation moves through me. Fuck yes. A victory!

I feel that victory for about one second before I sense movement again. Then, the food whirls toward my head.

CHAPTER TWENTY-EIGHT

AXEL

The plate hits me with a crack, food flinging onto me. For a second, all I can do is sit there.

Did she really just throw her sandwich at me? Disbelief runs through me, and I stare at her. I have pesto on my face. The oily splotches smear on my glasses. Little chunks of pine nuts and mushy spinach are also in my hair.

Then, reality hits. All I can picture is throwing her over my knee and spanking some respect into her.

Raven moves before I do. She jumps on the bed, trying to use it to get around me. I dart toward her, grabbing her before she can get out the door.

"Help!" she screams.

There's a glancing blow to my head, and I laugh, lifting her up and throwing her on the bed. "Oh, you've done it now."

I drop down on top of the struggling blur of movement. This close, I see Raven's face, and for a second, it's twisted in hate.

"I'll teach you some respect," I say playfully as I try to pin her arms down. We fight for a second, and then I get her small body restrained under me.

Instantly, Raven's eyes widen, the whites showing, and her body stills. She stops fighting, and her body is like stone. She looks through me like I'm not even there. Slowly, the look fades from fear to glassy. Her body relaxes, and her eyelids drop, but she's still not looking at me.

The look is haunting. It's like she's there, but she's not. It's a familiar look.

That look. It's like she's seeing everything and nothing.

My stomach twists, and I let her go.

"Raven?" I back off the bed. My stomach doesn't feel right.

Suddenly, I'm a child again.

"What's wrong?"

Gage's voice sounds like it's coming from behind a shower curtain.

My knee is jostled, and I blink. We're in the car going to school.

"What's going on?" Gage whispers.

What's wrong? Nothing's wrong. I was just thinking about... nothing. My mind was finally a blank wall.

"Nothing." I fold my arms and look out the window. The outside moves by in flashes of dirty white. It snowed last night, on Halloween, and the snow is dirty from the roads.

And now I can't stop thinking. About last night. About how Rich and I had a special night. About how he told me how much more mature I am than Gage. My body hurts today, but Gage wouldn't understand. No one would.

I blink back into the present, realizing I've been staring at the bed. Raven has now backed to the far edge of the bed, legs curled up to her chest.

Raven looks just like I felt.

The rage that starts to wash over me comes in a warm tingle. That rage that I try so hard to keep down every year.

The rage I try to drink and fuck away. The rage that makes me murderous.

I open my mouth to demand who the fuck hurt her, but then snap it closed.

I have the foresight to snatch the plate off the floor and stalk from the room. I make it to the top of the stairs, where I catch a glimpse of the attic landing. It looks just like the one at Rich's house.

Suddenly, I just stand there and stare. All the emotions are roaring around in my head. They all scream for attention, the betrayal, numbness, and fucking sadness like a smothering blanket I'm stuck under, unable to move.

It takes me a long time to snap out of it. When I do, it's because I hear a soft thump from the room behind me.

Then, the rage starts roaring up again.

Someone made Raven feel like this, too.

And suddenly, all the emotions have a place to go. Someone fucked with Raven. So I'll fuck with them.

For a second, a wild idea fills my mind. I *could* find them. Could hunt them down and make them pay. I feel elated at the idea. I could kill them for her. I'm not a kid anymore. I could make it right. She could be my girl for real. Like, I could date her and get to know her and fucking do all the nice things for her.

Then, I hear Rich's voice. *"You're my boy. I love you."*

Suddenly, I feel sick. The nausea rolls through me, and I dart to the bathroom just in time. Then, I hurl into the toilet. I wretch, getting everything in my stomach out. Then, I drop my head on the toilet seat.

What am I thinking? I can't love anyone. I'm not built for that shit. That was always Gage's job. Why the hell am I over here acting like Gage?

My heart twists, but I force myself to flush the toilet. Look at Axel, playing Captain Save-a-Hoe. Fucking can-get-whatever-pussy-he-wants Axel over here simping for someone he hasn't even fucked.

I wash the food from my face.

Raven will never fuck me. Plus, I think I just entered a game that is so far out of my league. I just need to let her go.

My skin prickles, and for some reason, I fucking *hate* that idea.

Fuck. No, I'm not going to get attached. What's the rule? Never fuck the same girl twice.

But I haven't fucked her yet, so I'm not breaking the rule...

Fuck. I splash my face, then rip the hand towel away and dry my face. It's scratchy and smells stale.

I can't just leave Raven like this.

I could go to her apartment and lock the door since I left it unlocked when I carted her out. Maybe while I'm there, I can see what I can find, and if there's nothing there, then there's nothing there, and we call it quits.

Yeah. I owe it to her to at least keep her stuff safe.

I straighten, smelling like a mix of lavender soap, stale towel, and pesto.

This doesn't mean anything. Just a decent thing to do after keeping a stubborn woman warm.

Fuck, if this woman won't be the death of me. I won't allow her to be. I can't.

CHAPTER TWENTY-NINE

GAGE

7 Years Old

Mom is crying. She doesn't usually cry.

I'm staring at Mom as the tears track down her face. It's all red, not smiley like it usually is. My hands feel stuck.

"I'm okay." Mom waves her hand at me, standing up. "It was just an accident, don't worry."

Mom stands up, pushing at her hair.

An accident? "Did you fall again?"

"Huh?" Mom looks at me quickly, wiping away tears.

Mom falls a lot. Dad always gets mad at her for it, and there's a lot of yelling. He gets mad a lot. This time, I'm glad he's not mad about us. He yells about our glasses and how much money they cost, and it makes me want to cry. I offer to give the glasses back to Mom, but she never lets me. I can never do anything when he yells about that.

But I can do something when Mom falls. I always get her a bag of peas from the freezer. They make her feel better.

"Oh, yeah." Mom smiles at me. "Please don't be scared."

I'm already moving to the freezer and pulling out the peas. This will make her feel better. Giving them to Mom, my stomach still feels twisted.

Mom is *sad*.

And that makes me sad.

Later that night, I can't sleep. I think... there's something in my closet. It looks like a man peeking out from the shadows.

I'm stuck. My legs won't move.

"Mom?"

The room is silent. I heard Mom and Dad earlier. They were yelling again, but they're quiet now. Maybe Mom's sleeping. Sleep is good for when you don't feel good.

I stare at the man in the closet, and he stares back.

Squeezing my eyes shut, I hope he goes away. He'll go away if I don't look at him. I know he will.

All I can see is Mom's sad face.

And I wonder—animals don't cry. Do they get sad? They must not get sad if they don't cry, right?

I'll start bringing them peas, just in case.

CHAPTER THIRTY

GAGE

It's a shit-ass day. I do everything right; I present all my arguments in a clear and compelling way. I outmaster the defense. But as the day goes on, my client gets more and more pale. She keeps glancing at the defendant. She can't keep her eyes off him, and I know what's coming. I try everything I can to avoid it.

But by the end of the day, she tells me she wants to drop the case. And for a second, all I can see is my mom.

My hands shake. She wants to drop it after everything he did?

But my client is almost frantic about it, and I'm paid to serve my client, not take a personal side in cases.

When I walk out of the courthouse, my vision tunnels. Just get to the car. Just get to the car, tell Mom everything went well, and get home. Don't think about anything else.

Like the fact that Raven is with my brother. When I'd shuffle papers, I imagined I could smell her. Even though I knew it was just in my head, I'd still look up and around the room every once in a while just to make sure she wasn't there.

Because she's with my brother.

That thought makes another wave of rage rip through me.

Of course, she's with my brother. That's where they always go.

Everything is spiraling. I get in my car, and it takes everything I have not to slam the door.

"Hey, honey, how'd it go?" Mom asks in that kind voice of hers. It makes my eyes prickle unexpectedly.

Damn Mom and her compassion. I don't need compassion. I need berating. I failed. I failed my case, and Raven played me. For a second there, I thought Raven really hated Axel. And yet, here we fucking are.

The drive home is a blur, but it's not because I can't see. All those emotions that I typically ball up so tightly are trying to break free.

Once I get home, I thank Mom for the ride and practically fall out of the car. When I push open the front door, Buddy is there on the other side, sniffing to greet me. She jumps up and down like a puppy, and I admire her soft gray color. Fuck, it's good to see again. Buddy's paws thud on the floor, and her nails make little clicks.

I wonder what color Raven's eyes are? It was dark when I dropped her off that one night. I remember the silence from her side of the car. Only it wasn't pure silence. She sucked in quick, tiny breaths.

I wonder what she sounds like when she *isn't* afraid.

I jerk those thoughts to a halt.

I don't care about Raven. She fucked with me, then fucked with my brother. That's unforgivable.

Buddy looks past me, out into the front yard.

"What?" I turn, looking outside. There's no one there.

I try to shut the door, but she just stands stiffly, her tail up and wagging slightly.

"It's just me." I gently move my dog enough to shut the door. Buddy hangs her head and lets her tail drop.

I crouch down to check on her. It's so unusual for her to act like this. Is she feeling okay?

Buddy snuffles at my bag, sniffing my papers, and her tail starts wagging again.

Is she... Did she think Raven was coming?

I stand up quickly, some part of me upset. But just as quickly as I think that, I realize I've also been catching whiffs of Raven all day, like some kind of goddamn addict.

Fucking hell.

This is obsessive. I'm done thinking about her. About what she's doing. About the possibility that she might be fucking my brother...

Fucking Christ! I let Buddy out the back door to do her business. I see that the sunflower seeds I've set out are gone. I refill the tray and check the quarters.

They're still there.

I sigh.

Poe, the raven I nursed back to health so many years ago, still returns to my mom's house every once in a while. Mom says she doesn't come around a lot, but I wish she could find me again. She was always the most gentle soul—with me anyway. She'd never come around anyone else. Looking into her eyes, I knew she could understand far more than I had originally thought. Because I was fourteen and dumb, I brought her shiny things, only realizing later that ravens like them because they think we like them. She brought me a thimble once, and I still have it.

I think about throwing it away. What does it matter anymore? Why the hell do I even bother?

Like a robot, I feed Buddy, who wolfs down her food quickly.

"No, eat slow!" I roll my eyes. Can't get this dog to slow down to save my life. I wonder if Raven's ever had a dog? She has had to. Buddy loves her.

A knock at my door interrupts my plans, and Buddy and I turn to the door. The knock is violent, and I rush to open it.

Axel pushes his way inside, breathing heavily.

"What?" I step back, taking him in. His face is red, and his fists are bunched at his sides.

"She had no food."

"What?"

Axel storms into my living room, throwing up his hands. "She had no food! No food, no money, and someone named Max who's sending her love letters?"

My first instinct is to punch Axel. He's been fucking Raven. But something isn't right. I notice something's off about his hair. "Slow down. Why do you smell like pesto?" And how the fuck did he get here? Did he drive while blind?

"Raven!" Axel turns on me. "He's fucking stalking her."

Unease rips through me. "Who?"

"Fucking Max! Are you listening?"

I haven't seen Axel this upset since Mom announced she was marrying Rich. Since then, he's shut down and put on a mask. He tries to act unbothered, but he's my twin. I know him. And now he's really upset.

Slowly, Axel's words sink in. Raven's being stalked?

"Who's Max?" I ask, my voice dropping.

Axel stalks back and forth, ripping out his hair. "I think he's Raven's ex."

Raven has an ex? Well, of course she does. She's hot and smart, so why wouldn't she?

"How do you know?" I ask.

"Because he sent her a letter!" Axel reaches into his pocket, shoving a piece of paper at me.

I scan it, a sense of dread filling me. "Did you ask Raven about it?"

"No, I just found it at her place."

"Then why didn't you ask her about it?"

"Because she's at my place!"

Those words send a bolt of white-hot rage through me, and I remember how I was picturing ripping Axel's head off all day. I can't help the next words, but they sneer out of me, "Oh, right. Because you're fucking her."

"What?" Axel stops, frowns, then throws his hands up. "No."

I snort.

He continues to keep up his farce with a scowl.

"Sure." I shake my head, the day overflowing. "Sure you aren't. Because you've never fucked my girl before." I don't mean to say it, but it comes out. And now that it's out in the open, I can't take it back.

Axel freezes. He stares at me, and neither of us says anything. Buddy moves up to nuzzle Axel, and almost robotically, he reaches down to pet her.

The room is quiet, and horror starts to creep through me. I just showed my cards and embarrassed myself.

"Listen, man." Axel's jaw twitches. "Back then, I wasn't trying to... I know you really liked Jess–"

"Doesn't matter." I wave him off. Because it doesn't. And the pity that's lacing his tone? I can't stop the shame from heating my cheeks, and I don't know why. I'm not the one who did anything wrong.

Buddy continues to beg for pets, and Axel bends down to pet her. He sucks in a few breaths, visibly calming.

It's then that Buddy pukes all over his pants and shoes.

For a second, I just stare.

Axel scrambles back, holding up his hands. "What the..."

I try to hold the laugh in, but I can't. Axel's pants are covered in slime and softened kibble. Buddy's a real one, even if I know it's just her inability to eat slowly.

"Goddamn it, dude." Axel's moaning, but his voice has less of the panic that it had earlier. He starts stripping, peeling off the wet clothes.

"No, don't–"

Too late. Fucking hell, Axel's bringing his clothes back to my washroom. He's going to drip vomit all over my house.

Once Axel leaves the room, I feel like I can breathe again, and I think about what he said.

First of all, he's not fucking Raven.

What the hell? I can't unpack all of that right now because I'm not entirely sure I believe him. Axel fucks any and every willing woman. The only thing that makes me think he might be slightly telling the truth is that Raven seems to hate his guts.

Also, Raven's being stalked?

It seems like a wild fucking story. She's being stalked, and she doesn't have any money. Although, that part might be true. She didn't pack lunch, and she did ask for an advance.

Fuck. The teeny, tiny part of me that still feels things cringes.

Axel comes back into the room, clothed in *my* pants.

"Why did you come here?" I ask, a little lost. Axel hasn't come to me for help in... years. Since we were kids. Part of me misses it, and part of me remembers that even though I see the best in people, they don't always have my best interests in mind. Axel included. If he's here, he wants something from me, and I'm sure there's nothing in it for me.

Axel runs a hand down his face. "I don't know, man. I guess I wanted..." he pauses for so long I'm not sure he's going to finish what he was saying. Finally, his words come out soft, "I just wanted advice."

I swallow.

"Listen." Axel shakes his hands out. "I think... I don't know, man; there's something different about her."

I register the vulnerability in his voice and eye him up and down. Is he manipulating me? Since when does Axel like anyone? Like... anyone? I've been convinced for a while that he doesn't even like me. That thought makes an uncomfortable lump form in my throat, and I clear it.

"Please." Axel looks at me. "I'm coming to you as a brother. You're always the smarter one."

I stare at him. He meets my gaze straight on, and for the life of me, all I can picture is little Axel. The one I'd do anything to cover for. The one I still do anything to cover for.

Only now, he wants my... He wants Raven.

And there's the catch. Once again, it's all about Axel, leaving Gage in the dust.

I cross my arms. Axel knows I'm a sucker for helping. He always pretended he didn't see me leave leftovers in the fridge for Mom to eat. I knew he did, though, because he'd always save a few bites, too, and put them in when he thought I wasn't looking.

I clench my jaw, and then the soft word that comes out of my mouth surprises me. "No."

"No?" Axel blinks at me.

"No," I say with more confidence. Axel looks crushed for a second, but for once, I don't care. I'm done letting Axel get all the things that I want.

It's not that I want Raven. Why would I want the devil in disguise, even if she's witty and smart and smells like heaven? No, it's just 'cause I want to stop being a doormat to everything my brother wants.

"No."

I turn on my heel and walk away.

If he wants Raven, he can get her fair and square. But for once in my life, I'm not fucking helping.

CHAPTER THIRTY-ONE

AXEL

Dave drops me off at my house with much less chatter than usual. I suspect he's beginning to think I'm crazy.

"Take care of yourself, yeah?" he says uncertainly.

"Sure." I wave him off. I'm not crazy. I'm just... unbalanced.

The hum of the car gets quieter as he drives off.

I was stupid to go to Gage. I'm not sure why I did. We used to be inseparable, but ever since we were teens and that night at the party, things have been different between Gage and me. Before, it was like we were a team, and then after? I'm not sure what happened after. After is when the rage started having nowhere to go. Where it started building and building until I couldn't stop it.

I push my blunt fingernails into my palms, wishing they were sharper. Wishing they would draw blood.

I'll just do this by myself because letting Raven go is no longer an option. That went out the window as soon as I saw Max's letter. I put it so close to my face I could almost taste the cologne he must have sprayed on it. Fucking nasty. His handwriting was so sloppy I almost couldn't read it, even with it at my face.

Max seems like someone who can't use a pair of scissors. He writes like he'd yell at food service employees. Like he's never lived a day where he's afraid because of the actions of another.

He acts like Rich.

My stomach twists in unease. Max doesn't get to make Raven afraid.

This won't be easy. I'm going to have to sweep up someone's mess because some goddamn stupid motherfucker made Raven afraid without also making her obsessed. Fear is *so* much better. They gravitate toward you like a moth to the flame. So much better when they're just out of reach but not far enough that they're unattainable. Makes the chase fun.

So now I have to get Celeste Raven to trust me. Just enough that I can draw her back into my flame again and again and again. I'll burn the tips of those broken wings if I have to, so that even if they heal, she'll never be able to fly far from me. Because my wings are broken too, and I need her to stay close. Once I have her, she can never leave.

My pretty, broken obsession.

CHAPTER THIRTY-TWO

RAVEN

Axel handcuffed me to the bed. He fucking handcuffed me to the fucking bed. He said he'd be back as soon as he could, but it got dark out, and I screamed myself hoarse, letting the self-pity overtake me.

It didn't work. I fought, and nothing changed.

How in the fuck do I have such bad luck? Like how did I fuck up so bad to be handcuffed to a man's bed while being stalked by my ex?

At this point, it's not bad luck. At this point, it's gotta be something I'm doing wrong. My ancestors have to be looking down and shaking their heads. I'll never have kids. This generational trauma ends here.

I'm exhausted, and my hand throbs. Earlier in the day, when I was alone, I punched the window trying to get out, and it popped something in my thumb. Then I tried throwing the dresser drawer at the window, but it split into pieces. Who the fuck knew glass was that strong? And, of course, the noise brought Axel into the room. I tried to hit him with the broken dresser, but he just wrestled me down and handcuffed me to the bed.

Instead of beating me, Axel just offered me food and water and then left. He didn't yell at me, either. He didn't even try to touch me other than to tie me down.

Clearly, Axel's playing some kind of game that I don't have the rule book for. But I'm gonna learn. Oh boy, am I going to learn.

I'm pretty sure Axel left the house because I heard a car door and then the sound of an engine pulling away.

That's when I started screaming. No one came to help me, so I spent my time imagining ways I'm going to torture Axel once I get free. Tying him down and sticking toothpicks under his nails as he cries is my favorite idea so far.

I must have fallen asleep because I'm woken by the sound of the doorknob turning. I jerk up, straightening, blinking my dry eyes.

"Hey, little bird." Axel raises his hands.

I struggle to prop myself up with my hands above my head. Axel stops in the doorway, watching me.

"Can I take those off?" He raises his eyebrow and nods at my hands.

I narrow my eyes on him. He approaches slowly, and I watch him, scanning him. He's in a tight, button-down white shirt tucked into his slim waist. As he leans over me, I smell him now. He smells like...bacon?

It's then that I smell the bacon coming from downstairs, and my stomach grumbles.

"There you go." Axel removes the cuffs and backs away.

I sit up warily.

"C'mon." Axel starts walking to the stairs. "I have breakfast."

I blink. I slept all night? He's going to let me leave the room?

We've reached a new checkpoint in the game.

I weigh my options. If he's asking me to do it, I probably don't want to. But I won't accomplish much staying here either.

When I stand up, a wave of blackness rolls over me, and I have to catch myself on the doorframe. It causes pain to fill my wrist, but I latch onto it to keep me awake.

When I recover, Axel's moved up a step, looking like he's going to try and help me.

Fuck no.

I straighten. Axel nods, then leads the way down the stairs.

I follow, taking in the house now that I'm not over Axel's shoulder. It seems older, with little dents in the paint, and the handrail is scratched. The stairs open up to the kitchen on the left and the living room straight ahead.

I look around. The furniture is nice, not unlike Gage's house. There's a front door in the living room and a back door attached to the kitchen. I wonder if they're locked?

Axel is waiting by the kitchen, where there's a small table. He has a chair pulled out. "Where would you go?"

I snap my gaze to his. He looks at the front door and then back to me.

Did he clock me looking at the exits? Okay, so he's prepared for me to run. Clearly, I'm playing right into his hands.

"Sit. I made breakfast."

I'm starving. I'm used to the feeling, so I know that it's only downhill from here. I need to eat so I have more energy to get away.

So, I sit.

Axel says thank you so softly, I wonder if I heard him right. He acts like nothing's happened, dishing me out bacon, eggs, and fresh fruit. My mouth waters, but I wait until he's served himself and starts eating before I start, too.

"Breakfast food." He nods. "Noted."

The food is good. I mean, salty, buttery, sweet goodness. The flavors explode, and I hold myself back from groaning, stuffing my face as fast as I can. I don't have anything against certain kinds of food for breakfast, not that he needs to know that. I'm just grateful for any food at this point.

Once I finish my plate, I want to load myself another, but I force myself to wait. I know if I eat too much now, I'll end up puking it up in the next few minutes. So, I grab a strawberry, forcing myself to nibble on it slowly.

I realize that Axel's watching me.

I glare back at him. His glasses are slightly more boxy than I remember them being. These are different glasses. They look like the old pair Gage has.

Axel says nothing, so I don't either. I take my time to take in the house, noting all the areas of escape and all the pieces of furniture I could potentially push into his path. I need to figure out how well he can see.

I reach out to grab the glass of water, downing it too fast, but I can't help myself. It tastes too damn good. As soon as I put it down, I slide my hand along the table, grabbing the butter knife and slipping it down to my lap.

"More water?"

I nod.

Axel gets it for me, and I take the opportunity to slip the knife into my waistband.

"I feel like I should tell you that stabbing me will only turn me on." Axel turns back to me. "But you should know that already."

I lift my chin, crossing my arms.

Axel just smiles, flashing his white teeth, then shakes his head, dropping back into his chair. Then he goes back to watching me.

The attention makes me uncomfortable. "What are you looking at?"

"You."

I shift in my seat, but he doesn't stop watching me. The

silence sinks into my skin, making me want to run. I look around. "So, now what?"

"What do you mean?"

"I mean, are you going to let me go?"

"No." The statement is quiet.

Figures. But he's not mad at me for asking, so I push my luck further, "What if I walked out of that door anyway?"

"I wouldn't let you." He raises an eyebrow. "But feel free to test it if you don't believe me."

"Why?" I can't help the bite of exasperation. "I'm my own person, Axel. You can't just... keep me."

He shrugs.

"Are you hearing me?"

Axel leans forward. "I hear you, little bird."

"So you just don't care? And don't call me that."

He shakes his head. "Oh, I care. That's the problem."

"Then let me go!"

"Tell me about Max."

The name fills me with dread. Followed quickly by fear. How the hell does Axel know Max? Does this... Did he take me for Max? Dread fills my stomach. "I don't..." Maybe it was a lucky guess? Surely, he's not working with him.

"Is he stalking you?" There's an edge to Axel's voice.

I open my mouth, then close it. That's an odd thing to ask if he's working with Max. Or maybe he's trying to throw me off.

Trying to swallow down my panic, I manage, "I don't think that's any of your business."

Axel stares at me. "Do you have feelings for him?"

"What?" I sputter. Anger rises in me, and I almost spit out the word no, but I force myself to slow down. Axel's asking this for a reason. My answer means something. The question is: what's the right one?

I eye Axel, and he looks like he's trying to hide how tense he is, reaching out for a piece of pineapple but not eating it.

If I say yes and he's working with Max, they might not hurt

me as badly. But even the idea of saying I have feelings for Max makes me feel sick. I have to make a choice.

"No," I say, holding my breath and watching Axel closely. He lets out a breath, then his eyelids flutter. When he opens them again, he smiles at me. "So, what do you do for fun?"

For a second, all I can do is stare at him. Was that the right answer? I breathe, "What?"

"Like, what kinds of things make you happy?" He's leaned back now, the lines of tension gone from his body.

I passed. The rush of relief is instant, and for a second, I feel lightheaded. I get the urge to laugh, which is odd because nothing is funny right now. "I uh... read?"

Axel grins. "Okay, nerd."

He's smiling. I've done something right again. Elation soars through me as Axel watches. We sit there in silence for a bit. Slowly, the silence becomes unbearable, and tension starts creeping back in. What am I supposed to do now? Does he want me to keep talking?

"What about you?" I ask, having to clear my throat.

"What about me?"

"What do you do for fun?" Asking the question makes me feel like I'm trying to make him feel better. Like I've forgiven him for what he's done.

Instantly, I frown.

Axel watches me. "I cook. My mom taught me to cook early on, and I don't know, I've just liked it ever since."

I don't even want to respond to that. I don't give a flying fuck what he likes. It takes a second for the disgust to roll through me before I remember I'm playing a game. I don't care, but it has to look like I care. And that fucking sucks. But I'll do anything to survive.

CHAPTER THIRTY-THREE

AXEL

As I start cleaning the dishes, Raven looks around. She does it in quick, sharp movements like she's trying to figure this out.

Funny. I know she's going to try to run again. I'm not sure what she's trying to hide.

A flutter of pure excitement turns in my stomach. Raven is going to try to *run*.

This shouldn't excite me. I tried to get it not to. I tried to go to Gage for advice.

On the outside, I keep my cool, drizzling soap over our dishes while Raven taps her finger against the table, trying not to look like she's checking out the living room.

"There are books in there."

She jumps, snapping her gaze back to me. I nod at the bookshelf.

Slowly, Raven gets up and moves to the living room, but not before she slips the butter knife back on the table, which I find fascinating. It means she's given up the idea of stabbing me with it.

Boo.

The further Raven gets from me, the more relaxed she looks.

I kick myself for letting some of that tension relax. I like when she looks like she's seconds away from exploding. I've never seen that in all the women I've fucked. Raven *hates* me.

I grin. This game is already so fucking fun.

CHAPTER THIRTY-FOUR

RAVEN

I wonder if there's a phone in the living room. I wander over, trying not to look like I'm looking for something, keeping an eye on Axel. I don't find a phone, but Axel does have nice furniture and a big bookshelf up near the front door. A front door that looks locked. When I get close to it, Axel dries his hands on a towel, walking up to sit on one of the couches.

"My mom used to read to us every night." He nods at the bookshelf. "Even when we were older. Our eyes would be tired by the end of the day, so she'd read aloud before we went to bed."

I stare at the books. They look like fantasy stories and books about knights, kingdoms, and dragons.

"I kinda hated it back then," Axel says, pulling a stick of gum out of his pocket. "It was more Gage's thing, but now I'm kinda glad she did. Helps me beat the stupid Playboy stereotype."

I shoot a glance at him. He winks at me.

He fucking winks.

I hate him.

I turn stiffly, then move to the edge of the room, testing how far I can go before Axel shifts to keep me in his line of vision. It's only about ten feet.

Axel stays quiet. I think he expects me to try to run.

So I don't.

"What are we doing?" I ask calmly like we're friends.

"Chilling." Axel has his foot propped up on his knee. He clasps his hands behind his head.

Oh my god, the way he's all comfortable when I feel like jumping out of my skin makes me rage. I want to hurt him. Tie him down and beat him with my bat.

The image of Axel tied down and at my mercy pops into my head without my permission. All those muscles and no way to protect himself. They'd pop out as he'd fight the ties. His veins would too, tracing paths up his muscled forearms.

My skin gets hot.

I shake my head to clear my thoughts, then suck in a calming breath. Then I ask, "What do you want from me, Axel?"

He's silent for a while. Then he blows out a breath of air. "We're already doing it."

A mixture of reactions fills me—impatience, disbelief, and confusion. But I don't let it show. "We are?"

"Yeah."

I stare at him in silence. He just wants to hang out with me? Bullshit. What's behind the lines? Maybe he wants me to stroke his ego or make him feel like he's a good person. I try to think about why Dad did what he did. Or even Max.

Even thinking about them makes my cheeks hot. They did it because they're small-dicked men and get off having power over others. It makes them feel powerful.

Does Axel want to feel powerful?

I stare at him. He chews his gum quietly.

If he wants to feel powerful, then he wants me to cower. To cry and fight him. Which is exactly what I did up in the room. But down here, I'm not playing his game anymore.

Axel breaks the silence. "So, your stalker."

I swallow around a lump in my throat. What is his obsession with Max? Does he feel... threatened?

The thought is so absurd that I almost snort. Almost. Two men fighting over someone who doesn't want either of them.

"I won't let you put yourself at risk. You'll stay with me until I know that's not an issue."

His words take a second to register, and I squeeze my hands into fists. He thinks he's the knight in shining armor, rescuing me from Max?

I press my nails into my palms to feel anything other than the suffocating need to bash Axel's head in.

"Cool. Now that that's settled." Axel gets up, moves to the kitchen, and grabs some things from a bag on the counter. He lays them out on the table, one looking like... a tattoo machine or some sort of tool.

I freeze. He sets out more items. I'm not sure what it is until I see him dump out a bunch of... nail polish?

"Come over," he says.

I absolutely will not.

Axel takes a deep breath, letting it out. "C'mon. I won't bite. I'm going to do your nails."

I blink. The fuck did he just say?

He sets everything up carefully. It looks like he has all the professional equipment a nail salon would. I used to get my nails done a lot. I liked the way they made my hands look, and Max liked them done. Needless to say, I don't do them anymore.

"Raven," there's a note of warning in Axel's voice.

Power, Raven. He wants to feel like he has power. Controlling the way I look is one way he'll do that.

Only I don't want to give him that power. I'd rather rip my nails off than give him that power.

"Do you even know how to do nails?" I hope that reason will make him stop. Logic.

Axel shrugs. "Mom gets them done a lot. I've gone with her to a few appointments."

"That's not what I asked." Like fuck do I want to let him get anywhere near me.

Axel just gets up slowly. "I take it you don't like to be manhandled, Raven. So come over here so I don't have to do that."

No. *No, no, no.* The monster is peeking around the corner.

"Listen, I paid a good amount of money yesterday to figure out how to do this right. I'm sure they won't be perfect, but I'll practice." Axel holds his hand out.

Play the game, Raven. Play the fucking game.

Axel takes a step toward me. He approaches slowly like I'm a wild animal.

"Sit." His voice is soft, and he steps behind me, gently pushing me to the chair. I drop into it, and Axel pulls his chair close to mine, facing me. I only snap out of it when his thighs settle on either side of my knees.

"What are you doing?" I jump, trying to shift back.

"Getting ready?" He shifts slightly so his legs aren't touching mine and looks at me, then goes back to arranging the stuff on the table. I pick at my fingers, keeping them on my lap.

If I let him have the control he wants, will he let down his guard? I both love and hate that idea. I don't want to have to play into his delusions. I thought the chapter on 'pleasing a man so he doesn't hurt me' was over. But I also want something, *anything*, to go my way.

Then, a disturbing thought fills my head. If I flirt with him, will he fold?

Axel leans over the table to grab something, and my eyes are drawn to the muscles I can see under his shirt and his trim waist.

Fucking hell.

My right thumb still hurts. I glance down at it. It's swollen up since yesterday at the joint where my thumb meets my hand.

"What do you want?" Axel pushes some muted colors my way. "I can't do crazy designs yet, but I'll try."

My throat feels dry. He's picked an array of dark jewel tones and blacks. Almost like he knows I always used to do my nails black.

"Black?" he asks.

I can barely swallow.

Axel squints and pulls a black polish toward himself. "Black would look nice on you." Then he motions at me. "Hands?"

It feels like my hand is encased in cement when I try to move it. I battle with my own muscles, feeling the loss of control like it's being yanked from my body.

Axel just reaches across the table and grabs my left hand gently, pulling it toward him, his fingers warm and soft on my skin. He leans in, squinting, then gets to work clipping the nails down.

He's close, much closer than anyone in a salon, and I can feel his breath puff across my skin as he chews his gum and focuses on my hand.

I don't say anything. I refuse to talk. Axel doesn't seem to notice though, and his brows are furrowed in concentration. I watch carefully as he takes each tool, buffing down my nails and then matching the acrylic nails to the ends of my fingers. Instead of asking for my other hand, he fixates on the one he has, some-times muttering to himself. He's surprisingly gentle, holding each finger with just enough pressure to position it the way he wants.

Axel looks up at me. "How long do you want them?"

I shift. "Doesn't matter."

"Sure it does." He looks at me like I'm crazy. "I may be a man, but I know length matters."

I stare at him. Did he just make a dick joke?

Axel just winks at me. "How long, sugar?"

I don't know how to answer without picking a fight. I notice his thighs have started pressing against mine again, and it's sending warmth through my whole body.

"My mom used to love to get her nails done," Axel says softly. "We couldn't afford it for the longest time, but when R—when things changed, she'd get them done every three weeks and would always make us admire the designs she got."

I stare at him. I wouldn't have guessed he grew up in a low-income household from the way he and his brother live now, but things can change.

Axel trims my nails to the length I normally get them with a rounded point at the end. Either he has a really good intuition, or he's been watching me.

Goosebumps run down my arms.

Axel grabs the powder, applying it to a few of my nails before he puts my hand down, laughing slightly. "Oh yeah, the other hand." He motions for it.

I don't want to give it over. It hurts.

Axel makes an impatient motion with his hand.

He hasn't hurt me so far, but I've also just given in to him with no fight.

"Say please," I say, intending for it to come out mean, but my voice is dry, and it comes out husky.

Axel's gaze snaps to mine, and my face flushes, realizing it sounded like I was flirting with him. I almost back down, but his pupils dilate. Axel's eyes bounce between mine, and then he huffs out a laugh, looking down at my hand. That gaze flicks back up at me, arresting me from behind his glasses. *"Please?"*

Axel's gaze pulls me in like a magnetic force. He looks at me like he sees me with more than his eyes. He's also unfairly attractive. If I didn't realize what an ass he is, in another life, I'd actually flirt with him.

Slowly, I give Axel my hand.

When he touches it, electricity buzzes up my skin. Then, he

brushes my thumb, and the slight motion makes a bolt of pain hit me. I hiss, pulling my hand back.

Axel lets my hand slide out of his. "What?"

It's too late, and I realize that I've shown weakness. "Uh, sorry." I give my hand back. "You shocked me."

Axel narrows his eyes at me, sliding his hand down mine and grasping my wrist. He pulls me closer to him, his grip gentle but firm, and his legs tighten around me. I try to pull away, but it's like pulling against a wall.

"You're hurt." He flips my hand over, looking at it. "What happened?"

"It's fine." I try to yank back again, but Axel holds me firm.

"It's swollen."

"It's seriously fine." The attention makes me uncomfortable. Why the hell is he pretending to care? Does it make him feel better about himself?

"It's not fine; it looks pretty bad." Axel frowns. "Was this from the dresser?"

I didn't tell him I punched the window. "Yeah," I say.

"Jesus, did you get your thumb caught in it?"

I just shrug.

"We need to put ice on it." I watch him for signs of dishonesty, but I don't see any. There's no slight smirk or excited glint in his eye.

Dad only cared if I got visibly hurt because he was afraid he'd get caught. That must be why Axel's upset.

But ice does sound nice. The skin is swollen and throbbing.

Axel moves to the fridge, and immediately, I feel the loss of his warmth. He comes back with a pack and holds it to my skin.

Axel runs his hand through his hair. "Fuck. I didn't know you were hurt."

I wait for him to beg for my forgiveness. To tell me he forgave *me* for losing my shit. To ask me to be friends with him again.

Only he doesn't. He just stands there, running his hands through his hair. "How bad is it? Do we need to get it looked at?"

I start to brush it off like I've always done, then pause.

Did he just... ask if I need to get it looked at?

"I, uh..."

I wait for him to say sike. To change his mind.

But he doesn't.

"It, uh... actually does hurt pretty bad." I pull my hand down into my lap for effect.

"Do you think it's broken?" Axel's gaze tightens.

"No!" If it's broken, he'll be more mad. I have to play this just right. "No, I mean, I don't think so."

Axel lets out a breath, visibly relaxing. "Okay, then. Sprains heal on their own."

Oh shit. Is he going to rescind his offer to get help? I quickly say, "It's just... I felt something snap."

Axel runs a hand down his face. "Snap?" He lets out a deep sigh. "Okay. Okay. You have your shoes on?" He looks down at my feet. I haven't actually taken them off yet. Or any of my clothes.

"Okay. It's cold." He moves to the living room, grabbing two coats. I watch him numbly. Is this really going to work?

"Bring the ice." He motions at the pack on the table. I grab it, and Axel throws the coat over my shoulders. It's a pink women's coat, and I frown at it.

Axel gets red. "Sometimes women... leave things here." He darts to the couch to grab his.

Oh, awesome. I didn't need to know that, and it kinda pisses me off.

I glare at him, but he just ushers me outside to the car. To *my* car.

A feeling of freedom fills my chest. My car. I can drive. Then, when he steps away, I can tell the doctor what's going on. That Axel's been keeping me against my will.

Axel gets in on the other side, and I clutch the ice pack to my hand with my half-done nails. Fuck, this is actually going to work! For once, I get my hopes up.

Axel gives me directions, and I follow them. I'm almost out of gas, but I think I'll have enough to get to the hospital. Maybe? I've never had to go to the hospital here. Never needed it, plus it's too expensive even if I did.

We drive through neighborhoods for longer than I thought we did to get here. But maybe Axel's taking me the back way.

Then, things start to look familiar, and my heart starts to pick up.

No way. He isn't...

I look around and realize we're not at a hospital. We're on Gage's street.

CHAPTER THIRTY-FIVE

RAVEN

He directed me to Gage's house. It takes a second to process.

In that second, Axel leans over, pulls the emergency brake, and slams the gear shift into park. The car grinds, slides, and lurches to a stop sideways on the road.

"If you run, I'll chase you." Axel's voice is dark, and suddenly, he's getting out of the car.

Fight or flight kicks in, and I rip my door open, flinging my seat belt off and darting into the street.

I make it three steps before strong arms wrap around my middle.

"Help!" I scream. "Someone help!"

Axel hoists me over his shoulder, and I struggle, clawing at his clothes and beating on his back. He just stalks up to Gage's door.

"Stop making a scene."

He knocks as I straighten, throwing him off balance. I feel myself fall backwards, bracing myself to hit the door. But instead, I fall back, hitting a warm body.

"What the–"

I scramble to my feet as Axel shoves inside, shutting the door behind us. "Hey, brother!"

Gage stares at us both, and Buddy is there at our feet, jumping up and down and licking my hands.

"What the hell?" Gage sputters.

I scramble to get around Axel and back out the door. Axel plasters himself to the door, blocking my escape.

I'm trapped. I can't go anywhere with both men caging me in.

Fighting didn't help. It didn't help, and I ruined any trust I built with Axel.

"What's going on?" Gage looks between us.

I swallow harshly, staring at Gage. I'm not sure what he knows or if he'll be on his brother's side. He mostly just looks confused, with a furrow between his brows. Buddy sits on my right foot, panting up at me.

"He kidnapped me." I don't break eye contact with Gage.

"What?"

Axel growls, "Raven might have broken her thumb." He takes a step toward me, and I tense, stepping back.

Gage looks confused. "What is going on?"

"Look at her thumb; she might have broken it." Axel steps forward again, and Buddy stiffens under me. She gives a low growl.

Axel stops, looking stumped.

"Raven?" Gage growls my name.

I suck in a breath, trying to calm my racing heart. Buddy pressing into my foot grounds me.

"Axel handcuffed me to his bed."

"What?" Gage's nostrils flare.

There's a second of silence, and then Gage turns to Axel. "What the hell?"

"He threw me over his shoulder and took me to his house. He kidnapped me."

"You handcuffed her to your bed?"

Axel squares his shoulders. "I was trying to keep her from hurting herself. Which she clearly did." Axel waves at me. "I brought her here so you could check her."

Their voices are loud, and both men are so tense they might start throwing punches. Great, fight each other so I can run. I look around behind me to the back door, but as I do, Gage turns back to me.

"What's wrong with your hand?"

"Nothing!" I try to pull my sleeve down further. "It would have been fine if he hadn't *kidnapped* me."

Gage's eyes flash with anger, and Buddy whines. Gage then whirls on Axel, who raises his hands.

"Beat my ass later. Take care of her first. She said it might be broken."

Gage turns again, throwing his hands up. "Fucking show me."

I hate that I flinch. Muscle memory, I suppose, but I do. Gage sees it, pausing, and his face gets even more red. He stands there, frozen for a second, sucking in deep breaths. When he speaks, his voice is lower. "I'm gonna kill him in a second, but can you please let me look at your hand?"

Axel makes steady eye contact with me from behind his glasses. His eyes flick to the door. He knows I'm thinking about running. There's the tiniest smirk.

I straighten, pointing at Gage. "No. You're going to let me go. If you don't, I'm going straight to the police, and I'm telling them every single thing."

Silence. Gage processes what I'm saying. The silence feels so long, and for some stupid reason, I have hope that he'll help me. That he'll see how scared I am and fucking help.

Gage talks over his shoulder, "Tell me you didn't *kidnap* her, Axel."

"She was starving to death, Gage, and she has a stalker! He knows where she lives, and she wants to keep putting herself at risk. I'm protecting her."

"Raven," Gage's voice is strained. "Can we sit on the couch and talk about this?"

I want to scream. What does he not understand about this?

"No." I reach for the door handle. "I'm fucking leaving."

A few things happen at once. Axel lunges for me, and Buddy jumps at him, snarling and snapping her teeth. The movement of turning the handle hurts more than I expect, shooting white-hot pain up my arm. I let out a cry, cradling my arm.

Then Gage is beside me. He snatches my arm, holding it up so he can see my hand.

"Let go of me!" I try to pull away, stumbling back into the door.

"This isn't what we talked about, brother," Gage hisses, bending down and scooping me up into his arms, bridal style.

It takes my brain a solid second to figure out that Gage isn't helping me. That he's walking me further into the house.

And that's when I start screaming. Because fuck them. Fuck them, fuck this, fuck it all. I struggle, striking Gage's face. He stumbles, putting me down, and I run. Axel blocks my path to the back door, so I dart down the hallway. There's a shout and scrambling behind me, but I don't care.

There are multiple open doorways. I can see light coming into the room on the right, so I run into it. It's a bedroom with a window, but the window is thin and high up on the ceiling.

There's scrambling in the hallway. I jump farther into the room, facing them, when Buddy bursts into the bedroom. She stands still for a second, head swiveling. Then, she runs to me, crashing into my body, then turning to face the door. As the men fill the doorway, Buddy gives a dark, rumbly growl that makes the hair on my arms stand on end.

Gage steps into the room first.

I stiffen, and Buddy barks, the sound loud and harsh.

Gage stops, looking at the dog, frowning. Axel stands in the doorway behind him.

"Get away from me." My voice shakes.

Buddy stares at her owner with the hair on her back raised.

"Buddy?" Gage's voice cracks a bit.

"Please, just go away."

Gage looks at me. "Raven, I—we can make this right—"

"No. Get the fuck out." My voice is high-pitched, but I don't care. The adrenaline is rushing through me, and I don't want to look at either of them. I don't want to hear their bullshit manipulation or them telling me why this is all my fault. All men are the same.

"Get out!" I shout, feeling the tears creep up in my vision.

Buddy growls. I see Gage wince, and then he takes a step back.

"What—" Axel starts, but Gage whirls on him.

"Shut the fuck up." He shoves Axel in the chest, pushing him back. "Just shut the fuck up!" Then he reaches back and slams the bedroom door closed.

I collapse against the wall, dropping my head into my hands. Buddy turns, licking my hands, the warm swipes of her tongue sneaking between my fingers and getting my face.

Then, the tears come. There's nothing I can do to stop them, and I hate myself for that. Why the fuck am I being so weak? I shouldn't have expected Gage to help me. I really shouldn't have. But the fact that he didn't still makes my chest ache.

Buddy brushes my thumb, and it hurts like a bitch, but I welcome the throb. It keeps me grounded. The wash of emotions is overwhelming.

"I hate men. I hate them, I hate them, I hate them." I sob into my hands. Buddy aggressively nuzzles my hands, dislodging them, then dives in for my face. She gets one slobbery lick in before I dodge her. She's persistent, though, and lunges her whole body at me, which just makes me laugh and cry. The laughing gets worse when I realize I have half a set of half-finished nails on, and one of them has torn. It looks ridiculous. Then, I start hiccuping, which makes things worse.

We sit on the floor for a long time, just me and the girl who stuck up for me. And it strikes me that, once again, a man hurt me and made me cry. Only this time, I have more than just a stuffed dog.

"Onyx?" I whisper.

Buddy licks my face. She whimpers, and I get a sudden wash of guilt.

She's probably scared. I made her that way.

History is repeating itself, only this time, I'm hurting something real.

And that makes me cry harder.

CHAPTER THIRTY-SIX

GAGE

14 Years Old

"Axel showed his penis to a teacher," Mom's voice hisses. I freeze in the hallway, just able to see Mom's head. She's talking with Rich in the kitchen.

I duck back just a little so she can't see me.

Rich laughs, and I hear something shifting on the counter.

"This isn't funny." Mom's trying to keep her voice quiet, but I hear it shake.

My gut twists. I never understand why Axel does the inappropriate things that he does. It's like he fucking wants to get in trouble. He thinks it's funny. Just like Rich does.

"It's funny as hell."

"He's fourteen! It's not safe. He could get in serious trouble!"

"You need to learn to relax. It was just a joke."

Mom's voice gets sharp. "Relax? You want me to relax about my son's safety?"

"It was *funny*," Rich emphasizes. "But if you want, I'll talk to him..."

"Please."

"You need to learn how to take a joke." There's a pause, and then I hear movement. I catch a glimpse of Rich coming up to Mom, smiling. He snatches her up, starting to tickle her.

Mom squirms.

"Laugh, honey. It's not going to kill you to laugh."

"Let me go." I watch Mom squirm. Rich starts throwing fake punches into her stomach.

It makes me uncomfortable. I'm taking a step back down the hallway when I hear Rich say, "How funny would it be if I hit you as hard as I could?"

For a second, I process what he just said. Did I hear what I thought I heard?

Did he just... threaten to hit my mom?

Before I realize what I'm doing, I stride into the kitchen. I may not be big, but I'm bigger than I used to be.

Rich makes eye contact with me and lets Mom go. Then, Mom turns, smoothing down her shirt. "Oh, hey, Gage." She tries to play it off like nothing's wrong, but the corners of her eyes are tight, and her hands start gripping her arms so tightly I can see her manicured nails digging into her skin.

"We'll discuss this later." Rich shrugs and grabs an apple from the counter.

After he walks out, I turn to Mom. It feels like the bones inside my body are vibrating, even though I know they aren't.

"He threatened you."

"Oh, honey." Mom glances back to where I was standing. "How long were you there?"

I grit my teeth. "He threatened you, Mom."

"He was just making a joke," Mom says the words like they're a script, with no emotion. She grabs my shoulders.

I shake her off. "You don't have to baby me anymore, Mom."

"Gage, I..." She shakes her head. "It's not like before, baby. It's fine. Please don't worry."

"Leave him." The words are out of my mouth before I can stop them. And once they're out, I feel so much relief. "Leave him," I say again, looking towards the living room.

"Gage, sweetie..."

"Mom, please." I can't keep the desperation out of my voice. I can't see this happen to my mom again.

She pulls me into a hug, and I just stand there stiffly. She strokes my hair, muttering things about how we have a house and food now, and how she's happy, and on and on. I tune her out because I know Mom isn't going to leave him. She'll stay, and Rich will continue to take advantage of her because Mom wants to stay, and I can't figure out why.

I love her. I know Axel loves her. Shouldn't that be enough?

But it isn't. Because I'm learning that you can't love someone enough to keep them safe.

CHAPTER THIRTY-SEVEN

GAGE

"Not the face!" Axel throws his hands up when he sees me coming for him. "Mom will cry if she knows we've been fighting."

I punch Axel in the stomach. He bows over, coughing. I hit him again in the ribs, rage flowing through me.

He fucked this up. He fucked everything up!

"She's scared of us." I knee him. Axel drops to the ground but does nothing to fight back.

"She's fucking *scared of us*!" I can't keep the rage from taking over my body. I saw that look in Raven's eye. She thought I was going to hit her. Even Buddy thought I was going to hit her, which makes my already blurry vision a foggy mess. Normally, I like to heal things. But now, I want to destroy Axel. I want to rip him limb from limb.

And that's what makes me stop. I have to hold myself back, shaking.

I will *not* become our father.

Axel groans from the floor, coughing, getting to his knees. "Damn, bro, you been working out?"

"This isn't a game," I hiss.

"I know." He pulls to his feet.

"No, I don't think you know." I want to knock him back down. Beat him till the rage leaves my body, but instead, I just tremble. "You fucking kidnapped her?"

"Dude, she's being stalked."

"Yeah, by you!" I pace, needing the rage to go into something. How the fuck am I going to protect him this time? This is a serious offense. Like, this is thirty-years-in-prison serious. And he hurt her? Goddamn it, fucking hell, he'd never get parole.

No, I'm not going to protect him. He did this.

I launch my fist into the wall.

The only problem is, now she's in my house. Which makes me complicit.

I want to yell. Scream. Punch Axel some more.

He scared Raven off. She'll never trust us now.

"It'll be okay," Axel says. "She's just scared."

I don't even reply. I'm afraid I'll actually rip his hair out if I do.

"Get the fuck out of my face," I say quietly.

Axel is silent for a minute.

He took the confidence out of Raven's voice. He made her scream. He hurt her. Just like Dad and Rich did to Mom. And he did all of that while wearing *my* face.

Axel must realize how serious I am because he leaves me to figure out how the hell to fix this.

CHAPTER THIRTY-EIGHT

GAGE

I give Raven as long as I can to come out. It feels like she's been in the master spare room for hours, but in reality, the clock only says about an hour. The more time ticks on, the more my shoulders feel heavy, the kidnapping charge falling on me as well.

Finally, I stride up to the room, raising my hand to knock on the door. It feels weird knocking in my own house.

When I knock, she doesn't answer. I try again.

Nothing.

Fear rocks through me, and I open the door, immediately spotting her just where I left her, sitting on the floor with Buddy spread out over her lap.

Buddy's tail starts thumping, and the relief that rushes through me almost makes my knees weak. I was afraid my dog was scared of me, too.

"Hey." I clear my throat. "You can come out." I wince. It sounds like I just gave her permission, like I would a small child. Or a captive.

Raven narrows her eyes at me. "Axel?"

"Gage."

My heart twists. She just continues glaring at me like she doesn't believe me. I glance down at my shirt, which is the same one I was wearing when she came in, but she's right not to trust us. And that pisses me off.

"We talked about my clock," I grumble. "You didn't think it could keep time accurately."

There's a pause, and then she lets out the tiniest breath. I don't think I would have caught it if I weren't paying such close attention.

"Let me go." It's not a question, but it's not a demand, either.

"We need to talk." The words come out brisk, and I hate how demanding they sound. But the adrenaline is flowing, and I can't seem to get it to stop.

Raven shakes her head but says nothing.

I go back and forth between guilt and hate. Guilt, because Raven looks genuinely terrified, and hate, because if she didn't try to play us, none of this would have happened.

"Buddy needs to go outside." It comes out gruff again, and I clear my throat.

Buddy cracks an eye open to look at me, then huffs. She knows I'm bullshitting, but I want to get Raven close enough so I can look at her hand. It's currently buried under Buddy's body.

"Buddy, c'mon." I whistle, patting my leg.

My dog ignores me.

"Buddy." My voice is stern.

Still, nothing.

"Food? Are you hungry?" My dog just grunts. I glare at her, then pitch my voice high like I usually do when I'm feeding her. "Does someone want dinner?"

That perks Buddy's ears up. I don't look at Raven to see if

she's judging me for my dog-dad voice. I keep my gaze locked on my dog, who hauls herself dramatically off Raven's body and ambles over to me.

As predicted, Raven gets up, too. She sticks to my dog like she's her lifeline, and it's not lost on me that she probably is.

I step back into the hall and wait there, then I decide against it and lead the way so Raven doesn't have to walk with me behind her back.

Buddy trots out, going right to her food bowl, and I try to feed her quickly before Raven can go anywhere. Axel's lurking, and I'm sure he'll stop her, but I don't want that to happen. We need to talk.

Raven's frozen by the clock in the hall, holding her arm. I try to see what her hand looks like. It's swollen but not super red; from what I can tell, her thumbnail doesn't look black.

I hold in my sigh of relief, but it's mixed with anger. Her hand is swollen to hell. If it's not broken, it's definitely sprained, or she tore a ligament.

Moving to the freezer, I check for the ice pack I used to pack with my lunches, but I don't see it. I root around, feeling the urgency clawing at my back till finally, I give up, snatching up a bag of frozen food. Frozen peas.

I stare at them for a second, and at that moment, a horrible feeling sifts through my gut.

There's a sharp coughing sound that makes me blink. Buddy's wagging her tail, going back to the food she almost choked on.

"Here." I shove the peas at Raven a little more roughly than I intended.

She sucks in a breath, catching the bag. There's a sudden stiffness in her posture, and I'm not sure if she's going to run or throw them back at me. Instead, she does nothing. And that almost feels worse.

My whole body feels hot. This isn't going the way it should be. Nothing is going right. I'm fucking this up.

Raven isn't safe, and this nagging feeling scratches the back of my mind, saying I can help make her feel safe.

I fight it. I've been fighting it ever since Axel told me about her situation. She'll never want *me* to make her safe. Not when I look like Axel. Not when she hates my guts. Not when I'm her boss.

But the more I try to run from it, the more I realize that if I don't step up for Raven, no one else will. She'll be running for the foreseeable future.

And I can't allow that.

My hands start sweating, and I shove them in my pockets so hard it hikes my jeans down, baring a strip of skin along my stomach and hips. Raven catches the movement, and I feel heat flush across my cheeks.

I have a plan. Raven's going to hate it, but I have a plan.

I yank my pants back up. "You can go, but you can't say anything."

There's a beat of silence, and then Raven throws an angry look at me.

I keep talking, the words spilling out. "I'll pay you." I rattle off the amount I calculated, pulling from both Axel's and my combined accounts. It's a healthy amount. Enough to buy a house or at least rent for years.

There's a stunned silence.

"But you have to keep the fact that Axel was a goddamn idiot between us. You can beat his ass in private for all I care, but legal action would be off the table."

The bag of food crinkles as she shifts it, but I won't look at her. I can't until the last words are out of my mouth.

"But if you stay and help me until my glasses come in," I suck in a breath, then rattle off a number that would not only buy her a house but also a car, a new identity, and fuck, even a trip out of the country.

I hold my breath for a second. I tell myself it doesn't matter what she picks.

It doesn't matter, right?
So why can't I get my heart to stop racing?

CHAPTER THIRTY-NINE

AXEL

I hear my brother's offer from my spot in the living room, and it makes me tense. Every muscle is locked up tight, and it feels like the whole world is suspended for her response. The only sound is Buddy's panting and the *tick, tick, tick* of the clock.

Gage offered her an insane amount of money. A huge portion of our life savings.

She'll take it, right?

My stomach twists. She refused when I offered her job back.

I want her to take the money. Not because I'm worried about her going to the cops. Fuck those pigs. Everyone knows charges don't stick to money.

No, not for that reason. But because I want her here, with us. Under my brother's roof. Where we can keep an eye on her and weasel our way into her very psyche. Give me a few weeks, and she won't remember what her life was like without me. And if she tries to, I'll love-bomb her with so many good memories that she'll begin to wonder if the past was just a dream.

Maybe one day she'll realize what I did, and she'll hate me, but I'm okay with that. She'll be mine.

Finally, I hear her pretty, raspy voice. "Gage?"

"Yeah?"

"Go fuck yourself."

Then, Raven stomps down the hall. I can't see much, but I can tell by the motion that she passes me on the couch. I dart to my feet.

Gage comes beside me, grabbing my arm and holding me tight. "Wait," he mutters.

"She's leaving–"

I hear the jingle of the keys, and Buddy's claws scrape as she runs for the door. Then, the front door slams, and Raven is gone.

I rip away from him. "You're just going to let her walk away?"

"Yes." Gage grinds out the word like it pains him.

"You can't just let her get away." I shake his arm off. Gage doesn't let me go, and this time, I swing on him. He ducks, and I reach for his glasses. With his hand holding me, he can't keep me from snatching them off his face.

"You can't stop her," Gage hisses. "You want to add another kidnapping charge?"

"If I have one, what's two?" I put the glasses on my face.

"I won't fucking help you."

"I don't need your help." I yank my arm away from him. "She's going to run." I take a few steps toward the door. Raven's getting away; I don't have time for this.

"Leave her alone." Suddenly, Gage is beside me.

I yank the front door open, and then he's standing in front of me, shoving me back. "Her car's out of gas. Fucking control your caveman for two fucking seconds."

"Get out of my way."

"No." There's a sneer on Gage's face, and he's looking down

on me in the way he always used to when he got better grades than me.

Ah, finally. He hates me the way he should.

"You don't get to win this one by cheating your way through."

"Cheating?" Rage starts pulsing through my blood.

"Yes, cheating." Gage is snarling now. "If the only reason she's with you is you're bigger than her, and you scare her, then you're no better than any other man out there."

He squares up like he's going to hit me. I don't even brace for it. Let him hit me. I'm watching my obsession walk away, and I'm going to stop her.

But instead, Gage just steps out of my way with an odd look on his face. It's one of... love.

And somehow, that hurts more.

"She can't go far. Just give her a minute, and she'll be back."

RAVEN

My hands shake as I try to work my keys into the lock. Someone must have moved my car out of the street 'cause now it's parked in Gage's driveway. My thumb throbs, and my left hand is clumsy with the half-manicure.

Finally, the door unlocks, and then I'm inside, cranking the ignition and reversing out of the driveway so fast that the car bumps violently as I make it into the street. The tires screech as I pull away, driving anywhere but here.

My heart is racing. I got away. I fucking got away.

"Fuck!" I hit the steering wheel. Adrenaline feels like a wash of heat under my skin, and it takes a hot second for me to pay attention to where I'm going.

Where am I going?

I realize that I've automatically headed toward my apartment. But do I really want to go there?

Where else would I go?

I take my foot off the gas and let the car coast to a normal speed. Okay. Where am I going to go?

I could just drive until I find somewhere. Sleep in the car.

I can't believe they just... let me go. I mean, they can't legally keep me. It's literally kidnapping. There has to be a catch. What's the catch?

I play through the scene in my head step by step, and it's then that I register that Buddy watched me as I left. Or at least, she looked like she did, and I could swear her eyes were sad.

Suddenly, I'm a whole lot less thrilled.

I should have taken her.

I almost whip the wheel around to go back. But then I remember that I have nothing. How am I going to take care of her if I have no plan and nowhere to go?

A deep emptiness settles into my chest. It's time to plan. I glance at the gas gauge and curse.

It's on empty. Of course it's on fucking empty.

Frantically, I sift through the glove box for cash or a card that I know isn't there while also trying to keep my eyes on the road.

Nothing.

Okay. This is fine, Raven; you just have to think.

Could I bum a tank of gas off someone? Surely, someone will take pity on me.

But the more I think about it, the more I know that won't happen. What am I going to say? Your rich, handsome business owners, who everyone respects, kidnapped me? But don't call the cops 'cause they'll tell my ex?

Fuck no. Max hangs out with law enforcement on a daily basis. I used to also, so I know just how much "help" they can be. Plus, Gage is a fucking lawyer. He's going to argue his way out of this one, and the only way I'll come out of this one is looking crazy. My thumb? He'll say I did it to myself to make them look bad. These are the Newman twins. They'd never do anything wrong.

For a fleeting second, I think about the guy who drives Axel around. He'd tell them, right?

But my stomach sinks. Tell them what? That I've been around the twins? Of course, I have. Both of them were, at one point or another, my boss.

I slow even more, realizing that I've gotten to the street my apartment is on. Slowly, I pull around back in the same spot I always park in.

What the hell am I *doing*? Even if I was able to bum a tank of gas, then what? Bum a tank of gas all the way to... where? I have no money. I can't buy food.

I let my head fall against the steering wheel. I should have taken Gage's hush money before I left. The offer he made would set me up in some cheap motel for a long ass time. I could even move from place to place so they couldn't track me.

I should have taken it.

Could I go back and get it?

Yeah. And walk right back into their clutches.

Then I think about Buddy. She wouldn't let them touch me. She was so loyal, and she barely even knew me.

The thought brings tears to my eyes. I left her. I just left her without even saying goodbye.

I don't even hold it back. I sit there, and I cry big, ugly tears. The snot runs down my face, my shoulders heave, and I just sob. I sob because I don't know where I'm going to go or what the hell has happened to my life. I sob because this is the second time I've stood up for myself, and it worked. The first was when I left Max. I slunk out in the middle of the night, but I still left. And the second was now.

I got away.

I got away, and I still failed. I have no money and nowhere to go. Only this time, it's worse.

What the hell am I doing wrong?

I let the self-pity sink in for a while. I cry until I feel numb and stare out at the darkness. I think about my entire life, trying to pinpoint what the problem is and how to fix it.

The pity morphs into anger at myself.

So, I failed. Sort of. Is this it? Am I going to give up in the back parking lot of some fucking odd-ass, stupid town?

I want to. But honestly, that would be embarrassing.

So I don't.

Because I'll be damned if I let a man ruin my life.

CHAPTER FORTY-ONE

RAVEN

I spend the night in an exhausted state of sleep and wakefulness.

Part of me expects them to come knocking at my door. To break it down and force me to come back with them.

But they don't.

It's cold as hell in my place. I spend the night tossing and turning, but by the end of the night, I have a plan.

I'm going to Alaska. One of my friends from college was from there. I don't keep in touch with her, but I'm going to try. I'm going to disappear. I'll find a local job at a library or book-store, get rid of my phone, and just disappear.

In the morning, I pack some clothes into a bag, as well as some toiletries. I don't have much, but I fit what little I can into the trunk of my car. I also grab the few books I have, including my favorite from the nightstand.

Then, when I feel armed with my life packed up into the small trunk of my car, I do what I'm absolutely dreading, and I drive on fumes back to Gage's house.

Marching up to the front door, I try not to think about what I'm doing. I'm getting the money I deserve, and then I'll disappear. I'll disappear and never let another human into my life.

The door opens, and suddenly, Buddy is there with wet sniffles and excited whines. Gage is there, too, standing in the doorway with lines around his eyes.

"I came for my money." I cross my arms against the cold.

Gage just nods once, then steps back.

I frown. I expected more of a fight. Is he just going to... agree?

It's freezing, but I won't go inside. Buddy jumps up and down, crushing my toes and licking my hands, which just makes them colder.

Suddenly, Gage is back, and he's also stepping outside.

"What the—"

"Lead the way." Gage motions at the house, where I see the garage door opening.

"I came for the money," I grit. Here's the catch. Here's where he doesn't work with me.

"I know. I have to go to the bank." Gage grabs Buddy, trying to shove her back inside. She whines and scrambles to get out of his grip, but he closes her inside with a click.

"The car is out of gas."

Gage just steps off the porch and moves slowly across the grass, disappearing into the garage. He comes back out with a gas tank.

This motherfucker.

I trot up to him. "You said you'd pay me."

"I don't know how much cash you carry around in your pockets, princess." Gage tops off the gas tank, then moves to the passenger side. "But I keep mine in the bank." He slides inside the car.

I seethe for a second, then tell myself I just need to do this one thing. I'll get my money, and then I'll go. I can spare an hour.

I slide into the driver's side, eyeballing Gage. He just looks straight ahead. He has the boxy glasses on—the old ones.

Fine. The quieter, the better.

Once again, I jerk the car into gear and floor it out of the driveway. Gage grabs for the oh-shit handle but otherwise says nothing.

Once we get to town, Gage directs me to the bank he uses. For a minute, I freak out, wondering where exactly he's telling me to go. But I see a real bank, and he directs me to stop and goes inside. I'm left sitting in the car, ready to scream. Ready to drive off without him.

But I don't. I wait for the money, glaring at Gage as he comes back out of the building, holding the door for an older lady going inside. He flashes her a handsome smile, which makes me seethe.

Gage gets back in the car, his weight making it bounce, then shoves an envelope in my hands.

I grasp it, realizing it feels a little thin. Opening it, I thumb through the cash.

"I can only get so much out at a time."

This isn't the amount he promised. It's not anywhere close. I feel the panic starting to rise. "But you said–"

"And then you ran. The new deal is you stay and help me until my glasses come in, and every day, I'll pay you as much as the bank will let me take out."

There's a moment of blankness as I try to process what he just said.

"Sorry, princess. Banks don't just have that much money on hand." If I didn't know better, I'd say Gage's tone is soft. Kind, even.

No. This isn't how it was supposed to work. I was supposed to get my cash and go.

"If I tried for more, they'd flag me for fraud, and it would take even longer. This is the best I can do. And you're going to sign this." He pulls a folded paper out of his pocket.

"Fuck no."

"Read it."

I narrow my eyes, then read what looks like a contract. It's short and simple. It's a non-disclosure agreement that begins from the first day I was hired at Newmans and lasts for a month from now. It says I won't talk about my relationship with either brother to anyone for any reason unless a future agreement is made. The amount of money he promised me is there, standing out in absurd numbers.

I try to find the loophole. He's a lawyer. There has to be a loophole.

"Not signing this."

Gage plucks the envelope of cash out of my hand. I growl, trying to snatch it back.

"Then no money."

"No." I reach across the seat, but Gage just tucks it under his thigh, and I snatch my hand back to avoid touching him.

I hate him. I hate him so much. My hands are sweating, and I rub them on my skirt. I don't know what to do. Do I steal the car and leave? That'll put me in the same spot I was before. I want to be gone. To disappear. To get a private place with my books and shut out the world.

Gage doesn't say anything else. He just lets me process. Although, I'm not really processing. I start to feel my brain go fuzzy and just... check out. Just like I did before. I feel the self-hatred rolling through me, but then it's drowned out by blissful, amazing numbness. I try to fight it, but what's the use? I don't know how to fix this shit show. I don't have the money or the power to fix it. Once again, I'm helpless.

"Can you take me to the grocery store?" Gage asks.

I stare out the front windshield.

"Tomorrow morning, eight AM. You'll sign the contract, and I'll bring you more."

His voice is annoying. It's breaking through the fog. All I gather from what he's saying is that I can get more money tomorrow. I just have to make it through today.

For freedom, Raven. You'll do anything. Play the goddamn game.

So, just for now, I put the car in drive.

CHAPTER FORTY-TWO

GAGE

I can't let Raven suffer like this.

I knew that before I offered her my savings, and I really know it now.

That doesn't change the fact that my plan to help her involves me making the girl who wants to kill me—or Axel, to her, there's no difference—comfortable.

I haven't been anything but cold to something that's not an animal in... a long fucking time. I'm not entirely sure I can do it. But the fear and anger in Raven's voice remind me so much of when I first met Poe, and she clawed at me and bit my finger open. Poe was just angry. Scared. Hurt.

And so, here I am.

Raven parks in the grocery store lot, and I find it hard to get out of the car. Her presence is smothering in a way that both hurts and is intoxicating. She doesn't say a word, and yet I can feel her anger clinging to every bit of exposed skin.

Slowly, I crack the door.

The cool air outside helps me focus. I have my old glasses on that give me a headache, but I can see enough to realize that she's parked as far away from the doors as possible.

Maybe she doesn't want to get out first.

I step out of the car, waiting to hear her door open, but it doesn't. A bolt of anxiety kicks through me. Is she going to drive off? Take the small amount of money I gave her and run?

I consider jumping in front of the car, then shake my head. I value my life. Plus, I don't want to make her feel more trapped than she already feels.

After waiting a few minutes that feel like an eternity, I circle the car, using my hand to brush along the outside until I meet the crease of the driver's door. I knock on the window.

Nothing.

I knock again. "It's cold out here."

There's a muffled response, and it sounds a lot like 'go fuck yourself.'

A flood of heat washes over my body. Why is she mad at *me*? It's Axel she should be pissed at. I'm pissed at him. I still might wring his neck for that fucking stunt he decided to pull.

But I'm not my brother. And I fucking hate that she treats me like I am.

I let the cool wind wash over my warm skin, listening to the sounds of the parking lot. The slamming doors, the locks beeping, the carts rattling. I could go inside alone. My glasses are shit, but I could try and fumble around for what I need.

But that wouldn't help the terrified woman in the car.

Raven hasn't driven away yet, which means she wants more of my money. So that's something.

I pull in a deep breath and let it out, the tip of my nose getting cold. I know how I can get Raven out of the car.

"Buddy needs more food."

There's silence, then a huff. Suddenly, I hear the handle releasing, and I step back just in time. Raven steps out, slamming the door and shoving past me. She doesn't wait, and I have to scramble to keep up with her moving form. Once we start walking, there's a lot of other movement, and I work hard to keep her as my only focus.

It's easy to keep up—Raven's legs are a lot shorter than mine—but she's hugging the backs of the cars. I'm not sure if that's out of habit or if she's trying to get me to run into them. After she leads me through a freezing puddle and I get my right foot wet, I'm going to guess it's on purpose.

That anger that isn't always far off boils. The wetness creeps down my ankle and onto the arch of my foot. Raven's long hair swishes as she walks, and I think about grabbing it and wrapping it around my fist, pulling her into me. Putting her lips to my neck and demanding she bite it.

No. Fuck. What is wrong with me?

When we make it to the doors, there are a lot of other moving bodies, and Raven ducks around them. I grab hold of the back of Raven's blazer so I don't lose her, and the woman jerks out of my grip. She knows I can't see, and she tries to take advantage of that.

I dart my hand out, gripping Raven's elbow and yanking her back into me. Only, she's so light I accidentally pull her back into my chest, where I hold her softly. I'm about to rip into her. Tell her just what I think of her petulant behavior. But having Raven this close is a shockwave to my system. I feel every bit of her pressed against me, and it makes me feel alive.

She trembles slightly, and immediately, I realize she's afraid. I push her away so she isn't pressed up against my chest and suck in a heaving breath.

The dark outline that is Raven stands there for a second.

Then, her gravelly voice says, "Fuck you, Gage. Don't touch me."

I open my mouth to respond, then shut it again. I miss the electric current that ran through me when we touched.

"I fucking hate you." She's still spewing anger, and for a second, all I can picture is her as her name's sake—a raven, flaring her broken wings and scratching at me. Raven gets closer, and suddenly all I can smell is her—a mixture of Fiji and sweat. "You touch me again, and I'll kill you."

She's standing right in front of me, finger in my face. Suddenly, my dick is hard. All I can picture is her yelling at me, degrading me, while I'm on my knees in front of her.

I shove back those thoughts. Her sweat smell is sour with fear, and I hate that.

Slowly, I raise my hands. "I am not my brother," I say the words softly. I want to say that I'm also not Max or anyone else. But I don't.

For a second, it's just me and her. Then, the sounds of the grocery store flood back in. The music, the carts, the beeps of the registers.

Raven's form moves. Her steps are choppy, and I assume she's grabbing a cart. That, or leaving me stranded and never coming back.

I hate how much I dislike that idea.

Suddenly, a harsh voice breaks out. "Watch it."

I jerk my eyes open, wishing I could see.

"*You* watch it," Raven's voice comes, then there's a rattling of carts and an intake of breath.

"You fucking cunt."

Who the *fuck* is talking to Raven like that?

Argument forgotten, I stride forward, zeroing in on the dark shape that I think is Raven. As soon as my fingers feel the brush of her hair, a part of me calms.

"Your bitch assaulted me." The voice comes from another form, this one large—a man. I don't recognize his voice. He must not be a regular.

I shove Raven behind me. I don't think twice before my

voice comes out low and quiet, "Call her that again, and I'll fuck you up."

Raven sucks in a breath behind me.

There's a stunned silence from the man in front of me, and I'm already putting the weight on my back leg to throw a punch.

"You're fucking crazy!" The man's voice is pitched higher. "I'll call the cops!"

"I'll tell them you pushed me." Raven's voice is no longer directly behind me. What the hell? Why did she move? She needs to stay behind me so I can keep him away from her.

"You're a fucking liar!"

Did he touch her? I hear rushing in my ears.

"And you're an asshole!" Raven's yelling now, and suddenly, I feel the shift. She's gonna beat this guy's ass, and I won't be able to see to protect her from any of his punches.

Nope.

I herd Raven back into the store. "Let's go." I know she doesn't want me touching her, but there's about to be a whole lot more touching if I don't get her away.

"You're a fucking cowardly waste of space!" Raven's still yelling, pushing back against me.

"Easy." I grab her shoulders and push her into what I know is the produce section.

"Get off me!"

"What does he look like?" I ask her.

"Like an entitled piece of shit!" Raven's breathing is heavy, and I hear her breath hitch.

It's that little hitch of breath that drives me crazy. I'm ready to whirl and beat the man's ass now. But if I do, she'll follow and get hurt.

I force myself to take a breath. "What did he look like?" I'm going to need details if I'm going to track him down and beat his ass later.

Raven yanks out of my grip. "I don't need you to fight my battles for me."

"Are you okay?"

Raven ignores me. For another few beats, she paces like a caged animal, and it's all I can do to keep her with me without stepping on her boundaries.

Finally, she gives an infuriated huff. "You threatened him. You're a lawyer; you can't do that."

It was a conditional threat, but whatever. "Allegedly," I tell her. "Are you hurt?"

"No, the fucker just shoved past me."

Okay, maybe instead of beating his ass, I'll bury him instead.

For a minute, I think both of us are thinking about killing him. And then, Raven lets out a long breath. "I got a basket; what do you need?"

Right. Grocery shopping.

Fuck.

How can I focus on something like grocery shopping when my hands are still humming with energy?

Then, I feel Raven moving around me, and immediately, I follow her like she has her own gravitational pull. She's walking further into the store.

Right. 'Cause we're shopping.

For a bit, I tell her what we need while I try to calm my body down. I must black out because soon we're at the dog food section, and Raven's telling me the bag won't fit in the basket.

I heave it over my shoulder. For a brief second, I wonder if Raven will be impressed. Then, I shake my head. What the fuck is wrong with me?

As I calm down, all I can feel is massive relief that she didn't get hurt.

I am absolutely a glutton for punishment. In the end, it doesn't matter that Raven hates my guts and thinks that I'm my brother; I'll still protect her with everything I have.

CHAPTER FORTY-THREE

RAVEN

Gage and I finish out the trip in an awkward silence. I'm not sure what got into me with that douche. I'm not usually a fighter, but I feel like I've completely lost it. Despite that, I felt a sense of... safety that goes beyond any logic. I've never had someone back me up in a fight before.

And, of course, it had to be the fucking asshole who's trying to blackmail me into keeping his brother out of jail.

Still, I can't get rid of the annoying warmth in my chest.

Going back into Gage's house with Buddy makes me feel this sense of familiarity. The sunken living room with the flower couches looks the same as it always has. The clock is still ticking loudly in the hall. Buddy still mouth-breathes and follows me to the fridge.

It's the same, but it's not. Because somewhere between the

car and the shopping, I decided I have a plan. And that plan is to survive until I have enough money to leave. Start my life afresh.

I start to put groceries away, then realize I have no idea where anything goes. Gage takes over quietly, putting things away in practiced motions. Sometimes, he feels a bag up and asks me what it is.

There are a few items that I blush and take from him.

I grabbed those. Those are mine. I throw one in the freezer and take the other. It's too big to fit in my waistband, where my envelope of cash is. Will Gage question me?

He doesn't.

Once the groceries are put away, I put my item in my room, but I keep the cash with me. I won't be letting that out of my sight. I float, unsure of what to do. The house is warm, so warm, and I realize I'm exhausted. And hungry and thirsty and fucking smelly.

Gage doesn't allow that for long though, knocking on my door with some snacks and water. Then he tells me he has a few files he wants to go over, as if everything is normal and it's just another workday.

It's not. It's anything but that. But for now, I don't argue. I just sit down and dig into the snacks, patting Buddy as we get to work.

We fall into a quiet kind of rhythm, pretending like nothing else has happened. Like I don't smell like days' worth of BO. Like one of my hands isn't swollen to hell, and the other isn't covered in a half-done acrylic set. Like Axel didn't fucking kidnap me, and his brother didn't bribe me to keep my mouth shut.

It's all too much to think about.

So I don't. In this moment where I don't have to fight for basic rights, I allow myself to zone out. To let that blessed fog descend over my brain. Every time I finish a snack, Gage shoves another at me.

In the evening, I stand to go to the door to go home.

"Please stay here," Gage says.

I grip my keys so hard they cut into my hands. If this idiot thinks I'm staying, then he's dumber than I originally thought.

Gage's voice softens. "I can't promise Axel won't...show up."

I stiffen, and my heartbeat stutters. I didn't think about Axel trying to track me down. But of course, he would. It makes total sense.

"Well, I'm not... I can't stay..." I look around. I can't stay here.

Buddy whines from her place on the couch, tail thumping. I didn't tell Gage she hopped up there, but I'm sure he heard it.

I don't want to spend my money on a hotel if I'm staying here to get another payment tomorrow. Plus, what's to say Axel won't find me there too? Probably owns half of them anyway.

I hate my life.

Slowly, I move back to the couch, and for a second, I think I see relief on Gage's face. Just as quickly, it's gone.

"I got you shampoo."

CHAPTER FORTY-FOUR

GAGE

Having Raven in my house feels like being in a cage with a wild animal. She's unpredictable, her moods swinging from one end of the spectrum to the other. I never know what she's going to do next. But there's an odd sense of familiarity in it. All my animals were like this until they realized I was there to help them.

There's one thing I won't back down on, though. I'm going to take care of that damn hand. And I'm going to feed her more so she gains some damn weight.

Okay, so two things.

After Raven's shower, I knock on the spare bedroom door. There's a long period of time where I don't think she's going to answer, but then I hear her feet on the other side, and it sends an odd relief soaring through me.

The door rips open. "What?"

I hold out a roll of tape. "For your thumb." Internally, I'm crossing my fingers that she lets me treat it. I don't want to get pushy with her right now. I will, but it'll set us back a few steps.

I hold my breath.

Raven huffs, and then there's an awkward silence. I sense movement as she reaches for my hand.

I pull it back toward my stomach. "Let me show you." I swallow. "You're gonna want to wrap it well enough to restrict movement but not so tight that you cut off blood flow."

There's a pause, then Raven steps away from the door. I'm not sure if that's a yes, so I step inside slowly.

Nothing comes hurtling at my head. But I hear Buddy's heavy breathing.

"Is she on the bed?"

There's a startled pause, and then Raven says, "Uh, no."

I'm blind, but I'm not stupid. Raven is a shit liar. It almost makes me want to smile.

No. No smiling. Raven will probably smack it off my face.

And now I'm hard.

"Can I have your hand?"

Silence.

I know this is pushing it for the first night, but knowing she's in pain and I'm not doing anything to help will bother me more than anything else.

Suddenly, Raven's right next to me. I hold my breath. Raven stands there, stiff. I'm pretty sure she's staring daggers at me, but I can smell her—the Fiji shampoo I got for her wrapping both of us up in a glorious, warm fog. I wish I could see her wet hair. I know she's in my clothes too. I gave her a smaller pair of sweatpants and a shirt so she could wash her clothes. And the knowledge of that kicks in some caveman part of my brain. Raven is in *my* clothes. It feels vulnerable, and I guarantee this is the only concept of vulnerability I'll get.

"Where's Axel?"

Immediately, I stiffen. Axel. The thought of what he did to

her makes anger heat my veins. "Who the fuck knows?" I bark, sharper than I intend. Then, I suck in a breath, softening my voice. "Sorry. I don't know. He can go fuck himself."

There's another silence. It stretches on so long that I just know she's watching me. I can feel her gaze on my face. Does she like what she sees?

My cheeks heat.

Shit, she'll notice. My hands start sweating.

Then, there's movement, and Raven's hands are on mine. Her touch sends a jolt of awareness through me, and I struggle to keep my face neutral.

She did it. She trusted me.

I stamp down the way my chest is trying to puff up, then slowly, gently orient my hands on hers till I find her injured one. I can't see very well, so I accidentally grab beyond her wrist. Sliding my hand down to the joint of her thumb, I can feel the hot swelling. It's puffy and firm.

"Gonna move it."

Raven doesn't respond, but she doesn't pull away either. Thrills run up my arms. She's letting me touch her. Gently, I maneuver her thumb upwards. It moves. When I try to press it down into her palm, she hisses, and both hands are on me. She tries to rip the injured one from my grip, and I feel an uneven prickling of nails. Some are longer than others. I want to snatch her fingers up and pull them to my face to see what the hell is wrong with her nails. I could force it easily, but in a monumental effort, I keep my hands steady. Instead, I ask, "Any numbness?"

There's a movement. I think Raven is shaking her head, and then she says, "No."

She probably ripped a tendon. There's not a ton to do about that without surgery, but at least it moves.

"Okay, I'm gonna wrap it." I tuck her thumb up to the side of her index finger and begin wrapping. I try not to get distracted by everything that is Raven. I can hear her soft breaths, and I can almost feel her concentration rolling across my skin. It's a heady feeling, and my hands are sweating more now than before.

I shouldn't let this get to me. Raven doesn't see me as more than my brother. I look just like the person who hurt her, and with how defensive and angry she is, she'll probably never be able to get past that.

Suddenly, it's like a stone sinks in my stomach, weighing me back down to earth. All good feelings are gone, and a coldness creeps through me.

As soon as I'm done wrapping, I let her go. "There's food in the fridge."

Raven says nothing. Just waits for me to leave the room. Doing so feels like ripping off velcro.

After I leave her and Buddy alone, I putter around my room. I feel... oddly empty. It's like I can feel all of Raven's wild, angry, terrified energy through the wall. She's like a jolt of adrenaline, all bundled up into a small, angry body.

I don't sleep a wink. I keep thinking she's going to come out and need something. Every creak of the floor and hum of the heater has me sitting upright.

I'm up early. I want to make breakfast, but I don't want everything to be cold by the time she gets up. But what time will she get up?

I shouldn't care. I should protect myself from more pain.

I'm prepping an egg bake when I hear a car door shut outside. Then another. I peek out the window and see... Who is that? I squint hard at the fuzzy, moving shapes. Is that... Axel? And who the hell is he with? It looks like a woman. They're walking up to my front door.

Oh no. *Oh no.* Not while Raven's here! What is Axel thinking?

I should have been suspicious when he stopped blowing up my phone yesterday. I should have known something was coming.

Darting to the door, I open it before they can knock and wake Raven up.

"You don't need me to hold your hand." I can hear the smile in Mom's voice.

Mom. He brought *Mom?*

I snap my glare at Axel, and he just laughs softly. "Of course I do, Mom. Thanks for dropping me off."

"Oh, well, of course. Hey, Gage." There's a pause. "Where are your glasses?"

For a second, I can't answer because I'm thinking about decking Axel right in front of Mom.

"Broke them," I grit.

"Oh, well, that's a shame. They're so expensive." I can picture Mom's concerned look and the furrow between her brows.

"It's okay." It's anything but okay. I'm blind with one of the hottest women I've ever met in my house. And she hates me. Nothing is okay.

"Okay, well, I love you boys. You can always stay with me if you need to, Axel."

"Nah, Gage said I could stay here. You know, it's a twin thing." Axel takes the opportunity to step up into my house.

Mom laughs softly. "You two were always inseparable. Anyway, call if you need anything."

"Love you!" Axel's chipper as he shuts the door.

I open my mouth, but he just snarks. "Don't hit me yet, brother; she can still hear it."

"What are you doing?" I hiss.

"Waterline break. My basement flooded." He moves into the kitchen.

"The fuck it did." I chase after him.

"You would have known had you answered your goddamn phone. Oh, are these muffins?"

"You can't stay here!"

"Ow, fuck, they're hot!" He hisses.

"Get out." There's a deep anger settling into my soul. I just got Raven to trust me. At least enough not to stab me with any of my kitchen knives. And now he wants to come back and ruin that? Typical fucking Axel.

I hear Axel chewing on the hot muffins, and rage floods my system. "She's scared of you." He better burn the roof of his mouth.

"Us," he corrects. "She's scared of us. And she won't trust me if I'm not here."

White hot rage sends a shock of anger right through my system. I stalk up to where Axel is, shoving him back into the counter.

"Oh yeah, hit me! That solves everything." Axel's laughing.

I shove him again.

"You're just like Dad, you know that?" Axel's laughter has turned to anger. "Using your fists to run from your feelings."

Suddenly, everything is hot. I want to punch him. Scream at him that I'm nothing like our Dad and I never will be. And it's that anger that lets the next words slip out of my mouth, "And you're exactly like Rich," I sneer, "whoring it up with anyone who will give you the time of day."

As soon as the words are out, I regret them. Axel's face turns so still that he looks like a statue. He barely even breathes, and it makes my stomach turn.

Then, he punches me.

"Don't ever call me that." Axel hits me again as I stagger back. "I swear to god, I'll beat your ass so hard Dad's beatings will look like child's play."

Throwing my hands up to protect my face, I sneer, "Look who's acting like Dad now."

Axel lunges forward, and then there's a scrabble of nails on the hardwood, and suddenly, Buddy barks between us.

I should register that Buddy is *out*, but I don't. The hatred is running hot through my veins, and I can't fucking stop it. "I don't give a *fuck* what you think. But if Raven doesn't want to talk to you, she doesn't have to. You have to earn that, and if she tells you to go fuck yourself with a pinecone, I expect you to ask her how big and for how long."

It takes me too long to realize that Axel isn't hitting me anymore. I focus on the sounds around me and hear a soft breath.

I turn to see a blur of movement in the hallway, and then it's gone.

CHAPTER FORTY-FIVE

RAVEN

The boys started fighting right as I got to the hallway. I stand there, frozen, listening. I honestly can't tell which one is which, as they've both changed clothes. I think Axel has the glasses on today, based on how they're acting.

Gage lands a shove on Axel. Their voices get snarly, and Axel starts beating on Gage, and suddenly, I'm a kid again, afraid as Dad beats my ass. Buddy scrambles to the kitchen.

"No!" I try to stop her, but it's too late. She jumps between the men with no worry for her own safety.

Then, Axel notices me. His eyebrows jump up for the quickest second. Then Gage turns around.

I stare at him for a second. Just long enough that he knows I heard and saw them. The confrontation scares me, but for some odd reason, I stand there and take the gamble that they won't hurt me.

Both men just look at me, then Gage says, "Raven..."

I turn on my heel and stalk away.

I'm gone. I dart back to my room, Buddy scrambling behind. My limbs feel numb, and I'm amped up. What are they doing? Not chasing me. Not hurting me. Not threatening me.

It feels odd.

My dad would have beat my ass if he caught me overhearing a conversation like that.

But they don't come storming after me. They also don't come in trying to whine their way back into my good graces, like Max would.

I stare at the door in confusion all day.

How the fuck am I supposed to play this game if I don't know the rules?

There's no lashing out for snooping?

Come to think of it, neither of them lashed out when I fought them either. Just moved me from one place to another.

And Axel never touched me, even when I was under him on his bed.

All day, I roll their fight around in my head. I realize I don't know anything about these men. Who's their dad? And who's Rich? What the hell happened to them?

I think about it all day, and all day, I don't get answers. I also try not to think about how Gage defended me. Why would he do that? What does he want from me? Is it just my silence?

I'm so tired trying to figure it out that I pass out for a little while on the floor. When I wake up, Buddy is there next to me, tail thumping. For a second, my heart races, and I scan the room.

I'm alone.

Nothing bad has happened.

Yet. It's only a matter of time, right?

As the shadows trace across the room, I get antsy waiting for the bad thing to happen. I know it's waiting around the corner.

I jump when I hear the clatter of pots in the kitchen, then shake out my hands. I'm tired of waiting. Tired of wondering what they're doing to sabotage me. I'll make an excuse to go out and see.

I call Buddy with me and open the hallway door.

I don't see either of them.

So I stalk down the hall, head high, with Buddy beside me. Axel's in the living room, lounging on one of the couches, and Gage is in the kitchen. Both turn to look at me.

I just glare, moving to the bookshelf under the grandfather clock. I snatch up a book, then stalk back to my room, heart thumping.

When my door shuts, I watch it.

But neither of them comes to bother me.

"What the fuck," I hiss, pacing the room.

I hear the men moving around, their low voices grumbling occasionally. I hear the grandfather clock chime every fifteen minutes.

The house doesn't get quiet until around ten in the evening.

It's the longest day of my life. I'm simultaneously tired and jacked up. The longer I wait for something bad to happen, the more pissed I get.

How dare they put me in this position? How *dare* they?

The clock goes off twice—once for each fifteen-minute interval, and I still haven't heard movement.

I'm boiling over with rage. This isn't fair. None of this is fair. I want them to pay.

I've been turning an idea over in my head all evening. It's a stupid idea, but it eases the rage inside me.

I have a way I can make them pay.

Finally, I can't stand the silence any longer, so I grab the spray bottle I got from the grocery store and creep to the door. Opening it, I check the hallway. Gage's door is closed. There's one more door at the end of the hall. I assume it's another bedroom. There's no sound from it. Buddy follows me, and I thank whatever gods there are that the hallway is carpeted. Still, I want to shush her loud breathing.

There's also no one in the living room.

A mixture of fear and victory turns my stomach.

I grip the bottle, pain tweaking through my hand. If Gage asked, I was going to tell him it was for my hair. But he didn't ask.

When I move to the kitchen, Buddy huffs excitedly.

"Shhh," I hush her, opening the fridge and getting out the milk. I pour it into the bottle while Buddy dances on my toes. She must think she's getting a snack.

Then, I move to the living room—the living room full of carpets and plush couches. And I start spraying. I have to use my left hand because my right thumb is still out of operation, but I spray the misted milk over every soft surface I can find, including on the velvet curtains hanging over the big glass windows. When I'm done with that, I move to the kitchen again.

Buddy yips, going to her food bowl.

I stop and listen. The house stays quiet.

Slowly, I slide the freezer open and grab the bag of shrimp that I got from the store.

Is this petty? Yes. But *god,* it feels so good.

The curtain rods are too high for me to reach, so I have to carefully drag one of the ottomans over. Standing on that and on my tiptoes, I can just reach the end of the curtains. Gage has the rich-person curtain rods, the hollow ones with a fancy bulb screwed on at the end.

I unscrew it, then rip open the bag and start stuffing as many shrimp in as possible. Frozen shrimp juice drips off the edge of the curtain rod, and that just makes me want to laugh.

Slowly, the stress rolls off me in waves. I won't be taken advantage of. I'm not a victim. Well, I guess technically I am, but I'm not helpless. I'm gonna get my money and get out. Then

I'm going to leave the country. Or at least, maybe go somewhere remote like Alaska.

Fuck, Alaska? I don't know if I can handle the dark winters...

Rustling plastic breaks me out of my thoughts. I glance down, and Buddy is rooting around inside the shrimp bag.

"No!" I jump down, yanking her head away. She still tries to wolf it down, and I have to wrestle the food away from her.

Good god.

I try to put the bag up on the top of the couch, but Buddy just jumps up to get it.

"No! Down," I hiss, bringing the shrimp back to the freezer.

That's when Buddy starts hacking. It's a deep, throaty sound that echoes in the quiet and sends a shiver of fear through me.

"Are you okay?" I rush over. Buddy's now vomiting onto the carpet.

"Ugh, no, I'm sorry, girl." I rub her back as she vomits up shrimp and mushy dog food.

Once she's done, she wags her tail and tries to eat it again.

"No!" I pull her away.

"What's going on?"

The light flips on, and I yelp, jumping and turning to see one of the twins in the living room. He rubs sleep from his eyes, and he has no glasses on. And no shirt on.

My mouth dries up looking at his chest. It's muscled and trim, and his skin is damn near glowing. My gut instinct says this is Gage, but I'm not sure. They look so goddamn similar.

"Uh, nothing."

Buddy keeps trying to lunge behind me to eat the puke.

He frowns.

"Buddy got sick," I say, looking behind me to see if the evidence is still out. Other than the ottoman being moved, the end of the curtain rod is on the back of one of the chairs.

The flash of concern on his face convinces me this is Gage. He pushes forward, feeling around for Buddy.

"Hold her; she's trying to eat it. I'll get towels." I rush into the kitchen. I don't want Gage to see the barely chewed shrimp in her vomit. That'll raise more questions than I have time for. When I get back, Gage has pulled Buddy outside. While he's distracted, I grab the bulb of the curtain rod and shove it as far into the crack of the seat as I can. Then, I start cleaning up.

"You don't have to do that," Gage says.

"It's fine." It's not. The vomit reeks, but I don't want to get caught.

"No, seriously." Gage leans in, hands brushing mine. "I'll do it." He grabs my left hand, stilling my motions. His grip is firm, and instantly, I lose control of my movements. I suck in a breath, and automatically, fear rushes in. Then, Gage gives me a gentle squeeze and lets me go. He actually lets me go.

Then common sense rolls out the window, and instead of just fear, arousal also hits me. I turn to look at the man crouched beside me to find he's already looking at me, too. He's close enough that our faces are almost touching.

His face gets pink.

I find myself staring at his lips. His lips that are so fucking close. His slightly puffy, blush lips.

Gage's breath brushes across my face, and I realize I've stopped breathing. What is wrong with me?

I scramble back, trying to get my wits about me again. I motion at him. "Your, uh... your knee is in vomit."

"Shit." Gage pulls back. He tries to wipe the vomit with paper towels and only succeeds in smearing it. Then his face twitches, and I see him trying to hold back a smile.

"You gonna let me do it now, or are you just gonna make it worse?" I try to sound gruff. Because why did I think about kissing him earlier? Something is certifiably wrong with me.

Gage laughs then. A full-blown laugh comes from his chest, and he shakes his head. "Probably just gonna make it worse, princess." He throws a look at me that, for some unknown reason, makes me blush.

I get to work cleaning again to avoid the feeling. When I'm

scooping up the last of the paper towels, Gage asks, "Couldn't sleep?"

My mind blanks for a second until I can get it working enough to say, "Buddy had to go out."

"Oh." Gage stands in the living room, staring at me again. He's looking serious, and it makes me uncomfortable.

"Look, for my part, I'm sorry."

My immediate reaction is to scoff and back away. But after I do those things, Gage is still standing there. He looks genuine. Genuine and fucking hot. Why the hell did he have to take his shirt off?

I don't have time to respond when a voice cuts in, "Well, well, well. What are you guys doing?"

I jump and look past Gage. Axel stalks into the living room.

Nope. This is my cue to leave. "Actually, I was just going to bed."

I try to brush past Gage, but he reaches out and grabs my arm, gently pulling me back to him. "You don't have to leave just because of this asshole." He raises his voice, looking beyond us. "Fuck off, Ax."

"Ax?" Axel looks confused for a second. Then his brows draw down in anger. "What are you trying to pull?"

There's a confused silence for a bit, then Axel says, "I'm Gage."

I blink, looking between them. Did I mix them up? Again?

The one holding my arm stiffens, his nostrils flaring. "Cut it the fuck out, Axel."

"You know what, you're a dick trying to confuse her like this." The newcomer stalks across the room, reaching us. "Sorry, Raven. He's an asshole."

I blink, confused, trying to grab onto any defining character-istic. The newcomer has a shirt on, but otherwise, they both have the same white hair, handsome faces, and pale eyes.

I thought the one holding my arm was Gage. I was convinced it was, but Axel has fooled me before. In the library.

The library.

I glance at the chest of the one I thought was Gage. There's nothing there. Shaking my arm out of his grip, I whirl on the newcomer and point my finger in his face. "Take your shirt off."

There's a flash of something in his gaze. Surprise, maybe?

"Take it off," I grind.

He hesitates, then shrugs and pulls his shirt off with one hand. I stare at his chest, trying to ignore the ripped abs and muscled chest that is now right in front of me. And there, on his sternum, is a small cut. It's almost healed, but it's still there from when I cut him in the library.

The newcomer is Axel.

I shove him back. Hard. Anger hits me in a hot wave. How dare he? How fucking dare he, after all he's done?

Axel grins then, looking like a Cheshire cat. "What's the matter, little bird?"

"Fuck you! I fucking hate you."

A hand grabs me and gently pulls me back. "I'll take care of this." Gage's face looks angry, with a line between his brows.

"No." I try to pull away from Gage. I'm tired of being fought over in some kind of pissing contest. This is just a game to Axel. He just wants to keep me away from his brother. To get control over the one woman who doesn't want him.

And I'm so sick and fucking tired of men taking control over me.

Suddenly, a plan flashes through my head. It's a stupid plan, really. A horrible one. One I should definitely run the other way from.

Instead of overthinking it, I whirl on Gage and kiss him.

I have to get on my tiptoes to reach his face, and I wrap my arms around his neck to pull him lower. At first, he's stiff, then he melts into me, ducking his head so I can reach him and letting me have his mouth. I know Axel can't see well, so I kiss him loudly, going at him hard and forcefully, biting down on his bottom lip until Gage opens with a gasp. He lets me, submitting to what I want to take from him. I kiss him to prove a point, but I find myself drawn to him like a magnet. He feels fucking *good*.

I force myself to rip away, looking at Axel, and what I see there makes everything worth it. There's a mix of rage and shock on Axel's face. His skin is red, and his nostrils are flared.

"Now, if you'll get out of the way." I slide my hands down Gage's chest and down his arm, grabbing his hand with my left hand. "*We're* going back to bed."

Then, I pull Gage past Axel, pulling him down the hall to his bedroom.

CHAPTER FORTY-SIX

GAGE

I think I'm dreaming. I have to be dreaming, right? There's no way Raven—angry, distrustful Raven—kissed me. Kissed me, then claimed me in front of my brother. She tastes like sin and heaven and fucking addiction all rolled up in one. I let her take the lead, afraid to scare her off, but goddamn, I want more.

Raven drags me back to my room and then slams the door. As soon as it's shut, she drops my hand.

"Don't touch me."

Her words are cold, and the whiplash makes me question what's going on. I just stand still so I don't scare her.

Raven's in my room.

Her hands are on me, and she's shoving me back, away from the door. I let her, but my hands are shaking again. What is she doing?

My knees hit the back of my bed.

"*Don't. Touch me*," Raven hisses again. Then she's on me, and I must be dreaming again because she has me pinned against the bed, and she's kissing the hell out of me. My instinct is to grab the back of her head and pull her into me. To get more. To plunder her mouth and suck the soul out of her body. I find my hands moving up, and then Raven stiffens. Immediately, I drop them back down.

But the magic is broken. Raven pulls away from me, and I can hear her panting for breath. I want nothing more than to jump up and spin us around, pinning her against the bed so she can't keep running from me. I want to grind into her and get some relief for my throbbing dick.

But Raven's quick breaths sound an awful lot like fear, and that puts a stop to my crashing thoughts.

She's still afraid of me. She's still fucking afraid.

There's the pound of footsteps past our door, and then Axel's door slams.

Then, the puzzle pieces slowly fall together, and I know why Raven kissed me. She kissed me to get back at Axel. To make him angry.

She didn't kiss me for me. She kissed me for him.

My chest feels tight.

"This means nothing." Raven's voice is tight.

The knife drives in further.

I try to find my voice, but I can still taste her on my lips.

"I'm going to stay here tonight, and you aren't going to touch me. Do you understand?"

I can't say anything around the hurt in my chest.

There's a bolt of movement; something is ripped off my bed, and then I see the bathroom light flick on.

"If you try to come in here, I'll kill you."

Then, she slams the door.

CHAPTER FORTY-SEVEN

RAVEN

It's a long fucking night curled up on Gage's bathroom floor with only a comforter. After hours of restless tossing and picking at my uneven nails, I give up and search through the vanity drawers.

Who the fuck doesn't have fingernail clippers? I search through the bathroom again. Everything hurts. I even used the towels and rugs as a makeshift bed, but the floor was cold and unforgiving. My head throbs, too. The only thing that kept me going was hearing Axel stomp down the hallway and slam the door.

I pissed him off. Finally. It makes a buzz run under my skin.

Finally, I find a pair of nail clippers buried under hair clippers.

I kissed Gage.

Fuck. My hands shake as I try to flip the clip around on the clippers with my bad hand. It's harder than I expected.

I kissed the man I swore to hate, and I can still feel his lips on mine. His body against mine, all hot and hard. The way I wanted fucking more.

This is it. I'm certifiable. Men do nothing but hurt me, and here I am, fucking throwing myself at yet another one. Kissing Gage was basically waving the come-hurt-me-I'm-available white flag. My hands shake as I try to get the clippers angled right to clip through the thick acrylic nails on my left hand. Only, without the use of my thumb, it's hard as hell. I try to position them on my thigh and press with the meat of my hand, which works until the clippers slip, sending pain through my finger and clattering to the floor.

"Shit."

After a minute, there's a knock at the door. "Raven?"

Shit! *Shit, shit.* I collect myself, making sure I'm not bleeding, then stand straight. Only Gage doesn't barrel through.

"You okay?" His voice is deep, and he actually sounds concerned. Oh god. Is he concerned? I doubt it. Probably wants to get his dick wet.

"Fine." My voice is clipped. Did he like the kiss?

There's silence, and I think I hear him walking away from the door. I grab up the clippers again. Maybe I should ask him to help.

No. No way. I'm going to remove this unpainted reminder of Axel by myself. I don't need part of the problem helping.

After a few more attempts, I'm nowhere near the power I need to cut through the nails. Sweat has built up around the base of my neck, my palms are sweaty, and my breaths are shaky. I can't do it, and it's enraging.

The bathroom is hot and stuffy, and the bedroom is quiet. I need to get out. I'll try again in a minute, but I need to get out.

I burst out of the door, only to see Gage sitting on the bed, the morning sun streaming down on him, sans shirt. All of his muscles are on display.

I suck in a breath. Was he there the whole time? Did he hear me struggling? My cheeks flame at the idea.

"Raven." He sits up straighter, regarding me with a cold look. The look is enough to douse me in a bucket of ice water.

Oh, so he didn't like it.

Cool. That's fine. Why would I care? I don't. But my whole chest feels tight.

Throwing my shoulders back, I stalk to the doorway.

"Bed or bathroom?"

I stop, refusing to turn around.

"Where did we fuck?"

I whirl, and Gage only mildly raises an eyebrow. I'm about to lay into him before I realize he's talking about keeping up the ruse. Some odd part of my chest jumps.

I meet his blank expression. Do I let him help me with the lie? Letting him help feels like a concession. But, as I stare at his masked expression, I remember that Gage hasn't actually hurt me.

"The bathroom," I grind. Then, I step out of the room.

Once I'm out of Gage's presence, there's an odd sense of... emptiness, but also a lack of that stifling energy, and I can suck in a breath again.

I consider changing, but I'd love for Axel to see me in Gage's rumpled clothes. I'm getting breakfast out of the fridge when Gage stalks into the kitchen. He's thrown on a light blue shirt, and I breathe out a sigh of relief that he's covered up.

The relief is short-lived. Axel also comes striding into the room in a black shirt, wearing the glasses. At least, I think that's who's who. I confirm it when Axel looks me up and down with a tweak to his eyebrow. "You two were awfully quiet last night."

For a second, I freeze. Axel just called us on our bullshit first thing.

"Gage isn't a screamer." I busy myself with opening the yogurt.

Someone snorts. "Damn, bro. Just as boring as ever, hmmm?"

I let out a tiny breath. Gage doesn't respond, then I hear him ask, "Did you need help with these?"

I turn, and Gage holds the clippers. He gives me a small smile, but it doesn't reach his eyes. It's like he's trying to look like he's happy.

Before I can respond, Axel gasps. "You stay away from my work with those shears."

I arch an eyebrow and turn to look at him. "I'm missing a pinky nail, and the others aren't even painted."

"I'll fix it, little bird." Axel's voice is cheerful.

"No," Gage and I answer at the same time, and my gaze flashes to his. He's looking in my general direction, and his lips are in a hard line before he settles back into that impassive state. His kissable lips.

"No?" Axel moves over to me, a furrow between his brows. "Aren't you missing one?"

His nearness starts to make my heart pound, and at first, it's because I'm not sure what he's doing, but then it's because he looks just like Gage. And suddenly, I'm remembering the way Gage kissed me.

I straighten, trying to keep the blush off my cheeks. As Axel towers over me, I wish I had my bat. I remember how Axel bowed before me and my bat, and a stupid plan fills my head. I raise my left hand to his chest, then trace the nails down his shirt.

Axel freezes, watching my hand's movement.

"Must have ripped off in the shower, huh, Gage?" I throw Axel a wink, then point my nails in and shove.

Axel steps back, and I stalk past him. My adrenaline is racing, and I can't figure out if this aggressive route is the best or the stupidest idea I've ever had. Instead of second-guessing, I plow forward, stepping right into Gage's space. "Will you fix them?"

Just like with Axel, I put my hand on his chest, but I don't dig. Gage looks down at me, and his lips part just slightly. He looks like he's sucking in a breath, and his pupils widen. I find myself lost in his gaze, and I can feel his heart pounding.

I know Axel's watching.

Gage's voice is rough. "I don't know how."

"Ax will teach you." I turn to look at him, raising a challenging eyebrow.

There's a flash of something on Axel's face before it settles back into his flirty look. "I'll do anything for you if you call me Ax again."

I called him Ax without even thinking. A sinking feeling hits my stomach.

"I'll get the stuff right now!" Axel moves out of the kitchen with too much cheerfulness. "Don't start fucking on the counters, lovebirds. Or do. Just wait till I can watch."

My face flushes, and I'm immediately thankful that Gage can't see it. I take a step away from him.

"I don't know how to do nails," Gage says in a low voice.

"I just want them off."

Gage gives a tight nod, and when Axel comes back, I'm standing at an awkward distance from Gage. Not close, but not far.

"Leave room for Jesus, damn." Axel elbows me in the side, and immediately, I snap mine out, catching him hard enough to feel like hitting a wall. He doesn't even take a step back. Fucking abs.

Axel laughs, "Where to, bitches? I need an outlet."

We settle on the dining room table, Gage and I occupying the corner and Axel leaning across the table.

I wipe my sweaty palm on my pants before handing it over to Gage.

"Glasses," he demands.

Axel smiles, "Sure! In exchange for a kiss from the lady. Since she's handing them out willy-nilly." Axel throws me a look that tells me he sees right through me.

"Fuck you."

"Don't be an ass." Gage takes the glasses, then blinks as he tries to refocus on my hand. He pulls it up to his face, pulling my fingers this way and that to look at them.

"I may be an ass, but at least I'm not a liar. What color?" Axel gives me a look with eyebrows raised.

I grit my teeth. "No color. I want them off."

"Sure more passionate shower sex won't do that for you?"

I try to keep the anger off my face. "You know," I pretend to consider. "On second thought, maybe just sharpen them to points."

Axel wiggles his eyebrows. "Already blind, babe. Poking my eyes out isn't going to help much."

"How do you get them off?" Gage is still rolling my fingers around, then picks at my nails.

"You have to grind them down." Axel reaches over, grabbing my hands.

"Don't touch me," I snarl, ripping my hand away.

Axel raises his in surrender, then starts explaining the process to Gage, talking while pointing at different parts of my nails. As soon as I put my hand back in Gage's, I feel the sweatiness of his fingers, and there's a slight tremble. He asks, "Won't it hurt?"

"Not unless you're a dick about it."

Gage clears his throat, and I'd be upset about all this, except Gage seems more nervous than I am. He keeps having to dry his hand on his pants. And for some reason, that calms me. Although I'm concerned Axel is going to start calling Gage out on it, so when Axel isn't looking, I slide my right hand under the table and pat Gage's knee. His gaze shoots up to mine, then the look calms, and he continues with a little more coolness.

During the entire session, Axel sends me secret little smiles, and when we're done and my fingers finally feel normal again, I escape the table as fast as I can.

Axel follows me. "Such a shame."

"What is?" I try to play it cool, stalking toward the laundry room to get my clothes from the dryer.

He just chuckles. "You're both such bad liars."

I refuse to look at him.

I can still hear the smile, his voice a dash of confidence. "Come to my room if you want a real dicking down." Then, he's gone.

CHAPTER FORTY-EIGHT

RAVEN

I slam the car door. Axel is insufferable. Quite possibly the worst person to ever exist. He's been harassing me all day long, eventually prompting me to practically beg Gage to go to the bank with me.

When he agrees, I fly to the car, and once Gage gets in on the other side, I start driving before he's fully shut the door. I need to get this money and go. Just get the damn money and get out of here.

Gage is quiet for some time, not even commenting when I blow a stop sign. I know he sees it because he still has the glasses.

Then, his voice breaks through my steaming thoughts. "We fought a lot as kids."

We're at a red light, and I glance briefly over at him, but Gage doesn't look at me.

"You and Axel?"

"Yeah."

"Oh, so he's always been this unbearable." I can barely keep the tremble out of my voice.

Gage huffs. "Oh yeah."

When the light turns green, we go, and I turn right. I enjoy the feeling of not having uneven acrylics. It feels like I shed an old skin.

"We could stop by your place if you want. Get anything you need." Gage's voice is quiet.

Get anything I need. Almost like I'm moving in with him.

Because I kind of did.

My chest tightens. Little does Gage know that I already have everything I need. All packed up and ready to go. The more I move, the less I have.

We drive in silence for a little bit longer before Gage says, "You know, if you really want to get under his skin, call him Garret."

"What?" I glance over at Gage again. His big hand rests on his thigh, and his long fingers look graceful and powerful. I have to rip my gaze back to the road.

"Garret. It's his real name."

"It's not Axel?"

"That's his middle name. Mom named us both G names, you know, the whole twin thing. Axel hated it, so he goes by his middle name."

I glance over at Gage again, but he's still watching the road. His hand gives a tiny squeeze on his thigh.

Garret, huh?

"Thanks," I say hesitantly.

Gage shrugs. "We're a team. Anti-Axel team."

A team? For a second, I feel relief. Then, distrust washes over me. A team with Gage? There are so many things that could go wrong. Like the biggest thing: What if he's playing me?

But Gage just leans back, finger-tapping slightly now. "He puked all over our table at the cafeteria once. Someone wiped a booger on him." Then, Gage chuckles. He actually laughs. "He begged me to say I was the one who puked. Said he had to keep up his image."

Gage is *laughing*. I snap my gaze over to him. He has smile lines around his eyes and in the corners of his cheeks, almost like dimples. His laugh is deep and unhurried and wraps around me like a hug. It feels like...comfort.

I swallow. "Did you?"

Gage's face drops, the humor fading from it. The car goes silent again, and it feels like I asked the wrong thing, although I'm not sure why or how.

"Sure did," Gage says, although his voice is quiet now.

I have this odd urge to make it better. To tell Gage about how I also go by my middle name. To tell him how Mom was a hippie before Dad met her, and that's how I ended up with a name like Celeste. About how I loved the name until a kid made fun of it every time he saw me at a camp, and I've wanted to change it ever since. About how I secretly liked switching to Raven after I had to run from Max.

But I don't say any of that. It feels locked up inside of me, and we just sit in silence until we get to the bank.

On the drive back, all I can think about is how I was almost friendly with Gage. But it's good I wasn't. The less I tell him, the better. The less Gage knows, the less he can use against me.

Although Gage doesn't seem like he wants to use anything against me, which is a dangerous concept because I thought the same about Max.

CHAPTER FORTY-NINE

GAGE

Being in a confined space with Raven makes me feel like I'm going to combust. I sit in a puddle of sweat.

Raven has an intoxicating way of just listening. I know she's storing up every detail in that sharp brain of hers. Fuck, after the kiss, holding her hand to do her nails, then being forced into the car with her, I'm going crazy.

I take a cold shower as soon as we get back. It helps a little bit, but I still find myself wondering if Axel was doing anything to mess with Raven.

But when I sit down to start prepping for my next case, Raven comes in looking unharassed. She doesn't mention that I have my glasses, so I don't either. We just fall into an easy rhythm working side by side.

Although it looks like I'm working, my brain refuses to think of anything legal and just wonders about everything about Raven. What's her favorite food? Why is it her favorite food? Will she tell me? It's almost lunchtime. Will she let me cook it for her? Why is she so distrustful? What happened with Max?

In the afternoon, Axel slides into the room. Immediately, I notice Raven's posture change. She stiffens, tucking some hair behind her ear and refusing to let her gaze leave the papers, and I hate it. I want Raven to be able to relax.

"Can't have you working for free, can we, baby girl?" Axel waves his hand at me. "Glasses."

At this moment, I hate him more than I've ever hated anyone. I want to scream at him. To tell him he's scaring her, and if he'd just stop being such a dickhead things would go okay.

But I don't. Sometimes, it's best not to fight with Axel. Especially right now when he looks like a dog with a bone. If he knows you want something, he'll go after it ten times harder.

I hand the glasses over.

"I like the jeans." Axel motions at Raven's change into her own clothes. Although I can't lie, I loved having her in mine.

Raven just continues on like he didn't speak.

Axel continues to pick at Raven. After a bit, I tell him to go the fuck home, which is a mistake because it just makes Axel grin and dig in more, getting more and more flirty. I don't want to fight him in front of her because the last time I did that, Raven ran. I'm guessing violence is a trigger for her.

But for all Axel's flirting, Raven ignores him. She just nods or brushes him off, remaining stiff. Until Axel sits next to her and brushes her thigh. "Shower sex isn't my favorite. I prefer–"

Raven shoots up, and before I realize it, her warm hand is on mine. "Kiss me."

Her fingers close around my hand, and she tugs. Kiss her? Like, right now?

Suddenly, her face is by my ear, and her gravelly voice is saying, "Take me."

The world stops spinning. For a single second, everything is wrapped up in that one question. Then Axel moves, and for a flash, his face holds anger, and I realize what this is. This is the game. She's coming to me to play the game.

Raven pulls on my hand, and I get up automatically. It's like part of my brain hasn't checked in, and that part is stuck in the past. Stuck with Jess.

And yet, inexplicably, I let Raven move me. I move like there's a collar attached to my neck, and Raven has the leash. Because that's what it feels like. Where Raven goes, I follow.

She pulls me into the room and shuts the door. Immediately, I hold my hands up, remembering her hissed command the first time she did this. I won't touch her.

There's a blur of movement, and suddenly, I'm slamming back against the door. Raven's there. She's pressing me into the door, then her hand is up in my hair, and she yanks harshly. There's a jolt of pain, followed very quickly by a tingling that runs through my entire body, and I let out a little moan. Every nerve ending comes to life, and then Raven's mouth is right there. She's so fucking close. It's like she's going to kiss me.

The blood shoots to my dick, and I lick my lips, then she disappears. There's a flurry of movement, and the bed creaks slightly.

Right. She doesn't need to kiss me. She just needs to slam me into the door to make it sound like she is.

I swallow around the hurt. I get the urge to run far, far away. Get in my car and disappear.

But then, a sound comes from the bed. It's a moan, low and throaty, full of pleasure. Immediately, I lock onto the sound, feet drawing me closer.

"Don't watch," Raven demands.

I snap my head toward the door. It's not like I can see, but who am I to refuse this stunning woman? The only woman who can put my brother in his place?

There's the sound of shifting fabric, then a methodical

bouncing of the springs. Is she... Is she fucking herself on my bed?

I'm stunned to silence, my dick hard as stone. Then, I realize there's too much rustling.

My dick is throbbing painfully. The methodical bouncing continues, and Raven lets out a tiny, awkward laugh. Only, it's half laugh, half grunt of frustration. The bouncing continues more violently, and now the springs are engaged, but it's not very loud.

If she's trying to get Axel to be able to hear, it's not loud enough.

"Fuck, this is stupid." Raven sounds livid.

I'm not sure if talking will make this worse or better, but I hate how frantic Axel's made her.

"My bad." I clear my throat. "I got the flat pillows. Better for my neck."

There's a silence where I feel myself cringe. I meant to encourage her. Flat pillows equal less resistance to hump into and, therefore, less noise. Only I'm an idiot, and I just made things worse. So I keep my head pointed at the door and raise my hands. "Want me to do it?"

Silence, then there's a defensive huff. "I'm not... I can... It's..."

I know both of us are thinking about Axel's incessant hinting that he knows we didn't fuck. It makes me angry.

"Let me help piss Axel off." I stand, but I don't face Raven. If there's anything I've learned about working with hurt creatures, it's not to lay the pressure on like a dickhead. Let them go at their own pace.

"Fucking fine," Raven hisses. There's a scramble, and I hear her get off the bed. I get on the bed, realizing I just signed up to hump my pillows in front of the hottest woman I've ever met.

I understand now why Raven asked me to look away.

But I can still feel her tension from beside the bed. Can practically smell the way she's sweating. I'm already making a fool of myself, so why not a little more?

I gather the pillows under my crotch and give a test hump. The bed moves, but not as much as it would if I had a real body under me. A real body like Raven.

Fuck.

I still feel her stiffness from here. She's miserable. I've spent my whole life trying to keep people from being miserable. So, I dig my own proverbial grave and double down. "Pillow humping, out of ten. Ratings for form, passion, and..." I trail off as I adjust the pillows so they're closer to the headboard. I grab the headboard as I thrust, giving a satisfying creak. "And volume."

"Are you... making a joke?"

I want to snort. I haven't joked in so long that I clearly don't know how to do it. This is going very badly. Everything is going very badly. This is not the image I had in mind when I thought about doing things with Raven.

There's a moment where I hesitate. Raven's using me to get back at Axel. Just like Jess did.

The hurt makes my chest clench so hard I have to pull in a breath. I should definitely stop. I should definitely run the other way as fast as I can.

"A rating, huh?"

I shudder out a breath. "Yeah."

It's not like I'm fucking her. It's not like Jess. This is fake.

I start humping the pillows in front of Raven. I grip the headboard and slam it forward every time I thrust, making the bed creak. I try harder, seeing if I can make it hit the wall.

I can.

I find that I don't even need to hump as much as I do just thrust the headboard into the wall.

Besides the creaks, it's silent. Awkwardly silent.

"Do you think he can hear?" Raven asks.

I slam the bedframe back harder. I'm sure he followed us,

and I'm sure he can, but I want to get Axel off her back. To make it absolutely clear that a boning is happening in here.

So, I commit the ultimate suicide in front of Raven.

I moan.

I moan like there's really someone under me. Like I'm sliding my dick into a hot, wet pussy. Like I'm sliding into Raven.

That is not an image I needed because now I'm fucking hard while I'm supposed to be pretending. Every little movement sends a brush of sensation to my dick, and I stiffen my hips, leaning all my energy into my forearms.

Fuck, she'd feel so good beneath me. Or on top of me. Or anywhere she wanted.

No.

Stop.

Fuck.

The groan I let out this time is real. It just makes my cheeks flush more. Despite the fact that I'm keeping my hips stiff, the movement up top is still brushing the pillows under me, stroking my dick where it's pressed against my leg.

Don't come. Don't fucking come.

I think about anything I can to distract me. Work. The upcoming case. The one Raven's helping with. Her soft, gentle hands. What they'd feel like tracing down my back for real, and not just in a shower fantasy.

Fuck.

If I don't stop, I'll come.

I freeze, trying to keep my breathing under control.

There's an awkward silence.

Does Raven know? Can she tell I was about to blow in my fucking pants? I sneak a glance at her, but I can't see much.

"You know," Raven drones. "In all my pillow-humping days... I've seen better."

The tension breaks.

"Your hips are stiff as fuck. Let me guess, you also can't dance?"

"Hey," I stifle an outraged laugh. "I can line dance."

"That's what I thought." Raven sounds looser than she did before. Less stressed. And I feel a familiar rush of relief. It's odd feeling it right now. It feels like... like I felt after I could help my animals feel better. It was what I always fought for with Mom, but never fully got.

Which makes me remember that Raven is, in fact, a thousand times more complicated than an animal. And my success rating with humans is not very high.

"You done?" Raven asks.

"Huh?" I glance at her.

"Well, you're making yourself look like a one-pump chump." I hear the laughter in her voice this time. She's actually teasing me.

I'm grabbing the pillow under me to throw at her when her voice sobers up. "Do you think he'll buy it?"

I pause. I hate to admit that I'm not sure. I'm not sure that Axel would believe anything short of fucking in front of him, and Raven would never do that. I feel unbelievable disappointment for all the wrong reasons.

"We need something that he can see." Raven's pacing. That nervous energy is back, and I hate it.

I think it at the same time that she says, "A hickey."

My dick springs back to life. I would love to give her a hickey.

"Give me a hickey." Raven's voice is uncertain.

I want to lunge at her and take the opportunity before she changes her mind. But it's the hesitation in her voice that makes me pause. It's not uncertainty, it's fear. Anytime sex is brought up, Raven is afraid.

Of me? Or of sex?

I know she has a stalker. That would be enough to justify her constant fear. But she seems afraid of sex.

"Do it to me," I say on impulse. I clear my throat. "Give me the hickey."

Raven's still there, by the edge of the bed, but she's stopped pacing. I can practically hear her thinking through my offer.

I lay on my back on the bed so I'm lower than her. "Give him a reason to believe it."

She's still hesitating. I take my hands and put them under my ass so they're pinned beneath me.

Do it. Take me. I don't say the words 'cause I don't want to scare her off. But my dick thinks they're fantastic, and I'm hard again. Hard with nothing but my slacks to hide my raging boner.

I hope she doesn't look. Please don't fucking look.

"Don't touch me," she says, almost whispering it. Almost like she doesn't realize she's saying it. There's such a depth of apathy in her words that it's like it's not even Raven saying them. It makes my chest tighten painfully.

Then her fingers are on my chin, and she's angling my face away and baring my neck to her. My heart starts racing. Raven could do whatever she wanted to me in this instant, and I'd let her. Fuck my life, I'd let her.

Her lips are at my neck, her hot breath brushing along my skin before she latches onto me. She sucks gently at first, and I feel her soft tongue against my skin, and it sends shivers racing down my neck. Her fingers are still on my jawline, holding me down, keeping me laid out so she can mark me.

I'm so hard I feel my dick pulsing against my pants.

Then, Raven sucks harder, and there's a bite of pain that shocks me and makes my head spin. I suck in a breath and hold it, trying to keep the moan back.

Then, Raven releases me with a pop.

Immediately, I want her back. I want her lips all over me. I want her to mark me as hers all over my fucking body.

"Did you make it dark enough?" I ask, feeling her fingers on my chin as I talk. She jerks her hand back.

"It's pretty fucking red."

I bite back the groan that wants to come out. Partially 'cause

I wanted her to say no and do it again, and partially because it's hot as hell that she marked me, and I'm a chump for thinking so.

I hear Raven back away.

I sit up and grab a pillow to cover my dick.

Raven disappears into the bathroom, and it gives me time to settle my hard-on. I settle it by telling myself that this isn't real. It isn't real, and if I make it real, I'm just going to repeat history. That sobers me a bit.

When Raven comes back out, she's back to her brisk self.

"Anti-Axel is a stupid name."

It takes me a second, then I raise an eyebrow. "Do you have a better one?"

"How about Garret Crusher? Ball Busters? Team Fuck All Men?"

I put a hand to my chest like I'm insulted.

"Oh, get over yourself," Raven says, but there's no bite to her tone.

I laugh softly, and I swear she turns to look at me. My face flushes. I shouldn't have laughed. God, I'm a sucker for fucking punishment. It's just... easy around her, and I need to fucking stop that.

"Gage?"

"Yeah?" I pretend I didn't catch on to the tension in her tone again. Both of us are awkward again.

"It's Celeste."

"Huh?"

"My name. It's Celeste. My middle name is Raven." Her voice is soft, and for a second, I feel like I'm talking to the real Raven. Or *Celeste*, I guess.

Fuck, I like that name.

Then, her tone changes. "Axel knows, so I figured you should, too."

Then, she's gone, stalking out of my room.

CHAPTER FIFTY

AXEL

The music pounds against my chest, and the lights flash. I lean into the sticky bar at Trick or Treat, staring blankly at my empty drink.

I was fine until I saw the hickey on Gage's neck.

The bartender pours me another shot, and I take it before it stops moving across the counter.

I'm mad. I'm more than mad. I'm murderous. Even though I have no right to be. I dug my grave while Gage swept in and wooed her off her feet.

Raven. Wooed. I didn't think that was possible. It shouldn't have been possible.

She's faking it. I grip my drink so hard my fingers ache.

So what if she's faking it, Axel? She hates you so much that she'll actually fall in love with him just to spite you.

Raven and I have the same hate burning in our bones. I know for a fact she'd rather love my brother than ever fall for my advances.

I pound a drink, embracing the burning sting as it goes down. I revel in it. But as soon as the sting is there, it's gone. This is where Raven came after I got her fired. I came here to feel something. Anything. Even if it's guilt.

Someone slides up next to me, talking between song sets. "Burrito night is weird for a club, yeah?"

I glance over to see a pretty blonde woman in her thirties motioning at a menu. I didn't even know they had menus here. I think I recognize the woman from around, but I'm not sure. She's probably one of the ones I left hanging just because it's fun to watch them get frantic. She has to be desperate if she's at a strip club.

The woman eyes me up and down with a hungry look. Like she's hungry for the kind of meat that doesn't come on a menu.

My body has no reaction. I look away.

"Bad day?" she yells over the music and waves the bartender over.

I go back to staring at the wall.

"Is it a woman?"

I blink slowly. The woman beside me is pretty with petite features and blue eyes. Something I'd normally like. But there's no interest. She just looks like another wall decoration.

I think I'm drunk already.

"That bad, huh?" The woman takes her shot.

I frown. What is she talking about? All I can think about is Raven. At home with my brother. The pretty sounds coming out of her lips as my brother fucks her.

Gage was always the better one between us. He always got good grades, always loved Mom, was polite to Rich, and saved animals. He never seemed to get angry like I did.

The alcohol rolls in my head, making my thoughts jumbled and emotional. I'm not sure why I'm so angry. I can't stop. But I can cover it up well. Boy, can I cover it up. A smile here, a flirt there. And people fall for it. They love it. They walk away, never knowing the real me. I get all the pussy I want, and I go home alone. And I have risky sex, too. I get high off the danger—the possibility of an STD, the possibility of a pregnancy, the handprints, the ropes, the blood.

And yet, it all feels the same at the end of the day. Adrenaline, orgasm, crash.

Hate.

Hate, hate, hate.

Sex means nothing to me, and yet, I hate myself enough to keep doing it.

I used to think that was the life. But at some point, it gets boring. Surely there's more, right?

No, it didn't just randomly get this way. This fucking bullshit started after Raven walked into my life, all soulful eyes and fucking burning hate.

She hates just like me. Only she doesn't hide it.

I curl my lip, gripping my shot glass.

"Well, my day's been shit, so I'll drink with you." The woman lifts her drink to me in a cheers.

I forgot she was there. I look at her closely. She doesn't look like she hates. She looks soft. Tired. A little dead inside.

Nothing like a good pity-fuck to get me to hate myself even more.

The concept has a tiny thrill running through me. But just as soon as it's there, it's gone again.

And that pisses me off.

So, I go through the motions out of spite. The woman is eager to take my advances. By the end of the night, I'm blackout drunk, and I don't care. I've decided I'm going home with the woman. We make it to the parking lot, the bitter cold rushing in around me, sobering me slightly.

"Where are you parked?" the woman asks.

Annoyance fills me. Raven wouldn't ask that. She'd just

snatch the keys from me and push me into the passenger seat. This bitch doesn't even know I can't drive.

"I'm blind." The words come out deadpan. Technically, I can still see, but I'm so fucking tired of explaining that.

"Whatever." She laughs like I told a joke. When I don't laugh with her, she sobers a bit. "Well, I can drive."

"Good." I just march after her.

The woman's car smells off. Not bad, just off. Just like old cloth seats and I don't like it.

"Do you want to go to a hotel or..."

No. I don't want to go to a hotel.

For some reason, I find myself rattling off the address to Raven's place.

It would be funny, right? Going to Raven's place. Fucking another woman at Raven's place.

I feel the car stop before I realize we've gotten there. The woman pulls up to the front instead of around to the back, but she's stopped the car before I can tell her that. I feel like I'm wrapped up in a fog.

There's a knocking at my door, and I shake myself out of it, trying to pull the door open. It won't move. Why won't it move?

Oh yeah. I have to push.

I chuckle to myself as I step out of the car.

The woman grabs my arm. "Careful."

Careful? I'm fine. I'm fucking fine. I shake her off.

"You got something."

I blink, focusing so the two women merge into one. She's bending down on Raven's doorstep and brings up a... present? It's a wrapped square with a package of animal crackers on top.

I frown.

The woman hands me the things, and I see a letter on top. A letter addressed to Celeste.

"Who's Celeste?" There's a cautious tone in her voice.

Rage washes over me, and my vision blacks out. Max. It's from fucking Max.

He's still after her?

Hate, hate, hate. It makes my blood so hot I feel like I could burn down the world. Burn Max down, using only matches. I'll melt his skin off his body one match at a time. How long will it take? Not long enough.

"Are… you okay?" I barely register the woman's tone.

"Take me home," I demand.

"I–"

"Take me fucking home!" I fling the passenger door open and jump inside.

The drive to Gage's house is silent, except where I bark directions. Nothing is going right. Nothing is going fucking right.

When we get there, the woman insists on grabbing my arm again. I'm not sure why, because I can walk by myself.

I trip over something and fall in slow motion, but I don't drop the present.

"Get… up."

Somehow, we make it to the steps. I'm not sure how. Then, there's an awful banging. The woman is knocking.

I try to shake the woman off, and then the door opens. Gage is there, with Raven behind him.

"Hey, brother," I sneer, handing over the items.

Then, I puke into the bushes.

CHAPTER FIFTY-ONE

RAVEN

I notice two things: Axel is drunk, and he has a hot woman on his arm. A woman I've never seen before. A woman who looks hot enough to be a movie star.

A bolt of... something shoots through my stomach.

Buddy tries to scrabble past me, growling and barking, and I barely grab her collar in time. She's angry, with deep, aggressive barks I've never heard before.

Axel barely makes it inside, even with the woman helping him in. Even though he's stumbling, he locks eyes with me. His normally pretty eyes are red and glassy, and he hits me with a cruel smile. He shrugs the woman off, movements exaggerated and rough.

The woman freezes, not backing away but not trying to help either. She just... stands there. Axel weaves, trying to catch himself on the wall. When Gage reaches out to steady him, Axel tries to push him off, squaring up.

A confusing mix of emotions fills me. Who the hell is this? And why the hell is Axel bringing his hookups here? Also, if said hookup doesn't get out of here, I think Buddy's going to bite her.

"Back up!" I keep holding Buddy, who's lunging at the group and snarling.

Axel lunges at Gage, and they start grappling. The woman doesn't move in time and catches an elbow to the face.

"Fucking go!" I yell, getting dragged forward a few steps by Buddy.

That seems to break the woman out of whatever trance she is in, and she scurries out the door.

"I'm fucking fine." Axel is slurring, and I catch a whiff of alcohol. The smell takes me right back to the pool party where Max groped me. Then Axel locks gazes with me again, his eyes glassy, and suddenly, all I see is Dad.

And then *I'm* the one locked there, unable to move. Every instinct is screaming at me to just make myself as small as possible, and he'll stop being mad at me. He won't hurt me as bad.

Then, a growling mass pushes past me and snaps at Axel.

I blink.

Buddy. Buddy's going to bite him.

I snap out of it, instinctively trying to stop her. But she's not biting; she's just standing in front of me, growling, and her tail is stiff.

Right. I'm in Gage's house. I'm not a kid anymore, and Max isn't here.

I straighten, taking a deep breath.

Axel stands, shoving past Gage to go to the kitchen. He stumbles around in there, hitting cabinets with loud bangs.

"You good?" Suddenly, Gage is in front of me. He reaches out like he's going to grab my shoulders, then stops just shy of making contact.

The earlier fear rushes through me, and my knees feel weak.

"Hey." Gage catches me, his hands gentle. Before I think about it, I grab Gage's shirt and pull myself to him, using his body to rest.

For a second, Gage doesn't move. He's like a solid wall, firm and strong. But it's not enough. I want more. Need more. Need that solid strength to feel like it's a part of me, not just something I can touch but can't have.

There's another bang in the kitchen, and I jump.

"It's okay." Gage squeezes my shoulders.

Buddy jumps around us, whining. I feel her tension like it's my own.

"Easy, girl," Gage says to Buddy, his voice deep and calming. "You're okay."

I can't help the shiver that runs across my skin.

More. I need more. More of that feeling when I kissed him in front of Axel.

Impulsively, I reach up and grab the short hairs on the back of Gage's neck and pull him down into my face. I care about nothing except calming the confusing feelings rushing through me.

Gage's breath brushes my lips, and he licks his own, accidentally getting mine in the process. I smash my face into his, kissing him with abandon. I just want to get this ugly feeling out of my chest, and my body is hot. I just want to feel something. To feel a spark of connection, of lust, of *anything*.

I kiss Gage harder, feeling the heat curl across my skin. My nipples harden, and when I press my body into his, sensation sparks in my breasts. I press against Gage, pushing him back toward the living room.

He allows it, following where I direct until I shove him back on the couch. There's a voice in the back of my head screaming that I should think about this. But there's also another voice, equally as loud if not louder, saying that this is exactly what we need.

I settle on Gage's lap, pushing him down so he's lying there.

Gage could fight me. I know he could use his weight to flip me around, pin me down, and take what he wants from me. I see his hands jerk once, then he lifts them up and puts them behind his head. He's panting, breathing heavily, and I can feel his erection pressing up against his thin PJs and my crotch.

And his eyes. He looks up at me with a look I've never seen from him before. It's like his walls have fallen away, and now I can see the naked desire there. Desire and yearning and a little bit of something I can't read.

He wants me. Gage wants me.

I suck in a breath, waiting for Gage's greedy hands to roam all over me. Waiting for him to plow forward like men do, taking what he wants from my body.

But he doesn't. He waits, pulling in a shaky breath. I feel his dick throb once, and he swallows, his Adam's apple bobbing with the effort. His hands stay behind his head, his biceps bulging.

And still, he doesn't take.

Gage groans, and it's a mix between a growl and a moan. His body jerks once, and he tips his head back, exposing his neck to me.

The rush of sensation that tingles from my clit out is insane. I wait for the contempt. The disgust I had with the man in the bathroom stall all that time ago.

But it doesn't come.

CHAPTER FIFTY-TWO

GAGE

I want her. I want her so badly, I feel my body shaking against my will. But the way she melts into me? It feels euphoric. Feels like putting on your glasses and seeing the most beautiful sunset. Seeing the details on your dog's face. It feels like comfort and home.

Just as much as pleasure is there, panic is too. What do I do? After Jess, I could never find someone who didn't know Axel too, and I always took care of my own needs. Now, I'm cursing myself. How do I take care of Raven? I've barely had sex. Jess wanted it hard. Wanted me to take her aggressively.

Raven grinds against me, and I bite back a moan. She feels so goddamn good.

There's movement off to the side, and then Axel's drunk voice says, "Did he pay you to kisss him?"

Raven stills, stiffness coming back to her body.

Immediately, I want to kill Axel. I want to kill my own brother.

"C'mon, little bird. We both know you're jussst in this for the... money." He hiccups.

"I'll get rid of him," I grind.

"Touch me."

The demand rocks through me, and I freeze. Raven wants me to... touch her?

"Fucking touch me." Raven's voice is a growl now, and she grinds into my dick so hard it makes light shoot across my blurry vision.

She's doing this because Axel's here. It hurts. It hurts a lot. But then, I steel myself. Raven's made no lies about why she's here, unlike Jess. Raven just wants me to help her get back at Axel. Nothing more, nothing less. I can do that.

I can do that.

I slip my hands out from behind my head, moving them across her shoulders and down her back. I trace her gently, figuring out where she is.

Raven just grinds into me impatiently.

What does she want? Does she want me to take control?

I swallow, my throat tight. I don't know if I can take control right here, right now. I don't know what I'm doing.

But I won't hesitate. That's what I did last time, and it wasn't enough.

So I wrap my arm around Raven, buckling her elbow enough that I can lift my hips up, flipping us so I'm on top of her.

Raven sucks in a startled breath, then she's stiff again. She's stiff under me, all through her torso and legs. Her breathing is startled and choppy.

Fuck. I bury my head between the couch and her ear, muttering low so Axel can't hear it.

"You okay?"

There's a moment where Raven doesn't respond, and that

scares me. I lift some of my weight off her so I can try to look at her. She's mostly blurry, but I squint to see if I can see her face.

There's the shifting of clothes, and Axel moves across the room. Raven's head turns to watch whatever he's doing, and then she's back facing me. She kisses me fiercely, and I don't expect it. It makes me jump as Raven chases after my lips, biting and sucking on my bottom lip hard enough to hurt.

"Play with me," she demands in a frantic, husky voice.

I don't like it. Raven doesn't seem okay. She seems rushed and upset.

But then she grabs my right hand and yanks. When I let the weight off it, she pulls it down her torso and to the band of her pants.

I suck in a breath as my fingers brush her silky skin.

I shouldn't do this. But she wants me to. Team Fuck All Men, or whatever.

Then, she's pushing my hand farther, and I suck in a breath as my fingers brush silky curls. Fuck. My dick is so hard it fucking hurts.

Then her gravelly voice says, "Be a good boy and touch me."

That does it. I can't refuse anything Raven tells me to do. I slide my fingers into her curls, then farther, where I meet wetness. She's soaked, and it startles me.

I thought this was just a game?

Raven's hips arch into my touch, and she lets out a breathy moan. I can't hold back my own, pressing my fingers down, feeling her body, brushing my fingers across her, noticing when she tenses under me. So I brush that part again, what must be her clit, because she sucks in a breath of air that doesn't sound like it's for show.

I go after that spot, gently rubbing it up and down and round and round. Raven shifts her hips more when I circle it, and I'm not sure if she's trying to get away from the touch or if she's trying to get more.

Slowly, I let off the pressure. Raven chases my fingers more. So I press slightly harder, and she sucks in another breath.

Good. Okay, she wants firmer.

I continue the same pattern, and for a bit, I feel her clit stiffening. Then, it softens, and her breaths seem to come less frantically.

Fuck. I fucked it up.

Raven's hand traces down mine. She makes a frustrated sound, and I wince. I'm not doing it right.

"My thumb," she says.

Oh fuck. Her injured hand. I pull away so I'm not touching her, and she grunts at me again. "Fuck no, come back. Let me ride your fingers." As best as she can, she guides my hand down farther, curling her fingers into mine, pressing me into warm heat.

Oh fuck yes. My dick is weeping in my pants, and I grunt. I have to hold it together.

Raven presses more, and I adjust so my middle and ring fingers are the ones she's pressing on. They slip into tight, wet heat, and I shudder.

"There," Raven pushes into me, so I slide deeper, and I feel her pussy clench around me. Then, she moves her fingers up to her clit, and I feel her moving.

I want to listen to her. Hear every breath she takes and which ones she holds. To hear the tiny shudders and any hint of a moan. I want it all.

I slightly lower my palm so it brushes her hand. I can feel her fingers circling, and she moans, her pussy clenching on me again. She's circling faster than I was. Her voice is soft, and it feels like it's meant for me and me only. She says, "Good boy."

I know it's not. I know it's meant for Axel to hear, too, but it takes a monumental effort not to let it shiver through me. The words try to go up through the Fuck All Men and break it to splinters, sounding a lot more like 'fuck the game.' She's mine. She's fucking *mine*.

Once I've gathered myself enough, slowly, carefully, I move my fingers in and out of Raven's pussy. She lets out a tiny noise high in her throat, and for a moment, I almost come. I feel a gush of wetness around my fingers. I grind my hips into the air. There's not enough friction. Raven's pussy squeezes me again, and she makes another sound deep in her throat; then, she's squeezing me harder than she has been.

"Fuck," she grunts, and the sound is laced with repressed pleasure, and her cunt pulses rhythmically around me.

Then Raven's thigh jumps up and brushes the head of my dick, and I come. I explode in my pants, shooting burst after burst as I come, imagining it's my name on Raven's lips.

CHAPTER FIFTY-THREE

RAVEN

I'm stuck, panting, trying to come down from the pleasure. That orgasm was the best I've had in... a long fucking time. And Gage gave it to me.

While Axel watched.

A forbidden thrill hums under my skin, immediately followed by fear.

I yank Gage's hand out of my pants and attempt to get up, but Gage's body is in the way. I have to scoot back, looking over at Axel. His hand is wrapped around his dick, but there's a flash of an expression in his cocky look. It's there, then it's gone again. If I didn't know better, I'd say he looked... sad.

I didn't mean for him to watch. I hate that I fucking liked it.

And it's then that I see what's by the chair he's sitting in. It's a wrapped present, and on top of it is... a pack of animal crackers.

Animal crackers. The snack that Max gave me all the time.

"What is that?" My brain is processing slowly. Way too slowly.

Axel glances down. "Gift. For you." When he looks back up at me, he's sneering.

Axel got me animal crackers?

No. *No, no, fuck no*.

"You okay?" Gage's deep voice asks. I want to jump at the comfort he's offering. Want to cling to his chest and hold him so tight he never lets me go. To hide from my real life and the reality of the situation, and pretend that our little game is the only real thing.

But that's not true. It's just a game, and Axel reminded me of that in the way only he can.

I shove back away from Gage.

"Get off me." The demand comes out harsher than I intended, but I can't help it. I feel the panic creeping up in my bones.

I lost sight of the goal. The goal is to get my money and disappear somewhere safe. Somewhere alone. Somewhere no one can hurt me. Instead, I got caught up in playing a stupid game that'll get me hurt.

So I get up and run.

CHAPTER FIFTY-FOUR

GAGE

The second Raven runs, I want to chase her. And for once, instead of overthinking everything, I do.

I get up, running after Raven, praying there's nothing out of place in my house.

I catch her right before she slams the door to the guest room.

"Get away." She sounds scared.

"Raven, I—"

"I said not right now. What the hell do you not understand about that?" The high pitch of her voice makes me want to fight the thing that scared her. Make her feel better.

"Are you okay? What happened?"

I hear Raven suck in a breath. Then another, and another, until her breathing has slowed. Finally, when she talks, it's clinical and detached. "Thanks for your help, but I don't need you anymore."

"For my... help?"

"Yes, Gage. Now get out of the door before I shut it."

The game. She's talking about the game.

And yet, I know it was more than just the game. Or if it wasn't, it could be more. I've seen glimpses of the strong, funny, sassy woman she works so hard to hide.

"Move, Gage." Raven's hands are on me, and she shoves me back.

I don't want to get out of the doorway. I want to fight for her, for this, tooth and nail.

Then, Raven slams the door in my face.

Over the next few days, Raven is distant despite my best efforts at communication. She only appears to get food, go to the bank with me, and let Buddy out. Axel's distant too, although he can go fuck himself. It's a miracle I don't kill him. I tell myself I won't because I don't want to go to prison. Who would be here for Raven?

I try to get Raven to talk to me, but she refuses. It's like a door has closed, and the person I'm talking to isn't Raven; it's some disconnected robot.

While the clock ticks endlessly in the hallway and I re-wash the same dishes, I'm reminded of all the times I should have fought for something and didn't. I never fought when Mom was being abused. Not really. I just said a few things here and there. I never fought for her.

I never fought to be more outgoing like Axel. I just slid into self-pity, wondering why people didn't like me.

I never fought when Jess left. In fact, I let her. I never called her again. I didn't even fight for my client who backed out. I just... took it.

Why the hell didn't I fight?

I throw the bowl I've washed three times back into the sink.

It clatters around, that goddamn crack still stained from Buddy's food.

I'm done not getting what I want and having an angry pity party over it. Raven is what I want. She's hurt, afraid, and so very complex, and it's gonna take a hell of a lot of work, but I'm going to get her.

But I have to be smart about it. She can't know how much I want her, or she'll treat me the same way she does Axel.

She comes down later that day for the lunch I've cooked up. I made chili and cornbread with extra beans and all kinds of sugar in the bread. I want her to get as many calories in every bite as she can. It brings me a special kind of pleasure knowing she's eating the food I've provided and that she's no longer hungry.

After Raven has settled in and started eating, I mention offhand that Mom's Halloween party is tomorrow. I tell her that she doesn't have to go, but it would be nice to have her to help get me there.

And in her dry, lifeless way, she agrees.

I hold myself back from celebrating.

"We'll have to get costumes."

"What?" For a second, there's a flicker of something in Raven's voice. It's anger, but it's still life.

I shrug. "Mom's super big on costumes. It's kinda like our thing."

Okay, maybe I'm exaggerating a bit. Mom is big on costumes, but I've refused to dress up since I was eighteen. But costume shopping means more time with Raven, specifically without Axel.

When we finish eating, I grab the car keys. I hear a huff, but Raven follows.

"You'll have to pay me double for this," she mutters as she brushes past me and out the front door.

I have Raven take us to the only Halloween store in town—it's the one that always pops up this season in the empty warehouse that was once a craft store and, before that, a department store.

When we get in, the place smells industrial, with a hint of polyester and plastic. I have Raven show me to the adult section, and I'm super tempted to reach out and grab her elbow. Not because I can't see her fuzzy form, but because I want an excuse to connect with her. But I also don't want to scare her.

We walk for a bit, then Raven stops abruptly, and I almost bump into her. "What are you looking for?"

"I don't know." I pretend to look at the aisle of outfits. "Knight costume."

She mutters something that I don't catch. Then, she pushes an outfit into my hands.

"What is it?"

"Knight costume."

I feel around, expecting to feel hard plastic armor. I just feel a lot of fabric and... tulle? I bring it up to my face, and the costume is pink.

Oh. Oh? So she wants to be like that.

But I'm not mad. If anything, it makes me excited. Raven's still there, even under her unaffected exterior.

"What are you going to wear?" I ask.

"Me? Nothing?"

"Nah, if I'm dressing up, you have to also."

"Hard pass."

"Fine, I'll pick for you."

"You can suck my dick."

The way she says it, I picture her giving a sweet smile. I snort, running my hand along the selection, feeling plastic hangers, hard sequins, rough tulle, and my favorite—silk. I can't help but think it feels like the inside of Raven's pussy. Little does Raven know that if she had a dick, I'd drop to my knees right now and suck it till she begged me to stop.

Up close, I can see colors. I find something black with what I think are wings, if I'm feeling the feathers correctly.

"Here! You can be a Raven." I hand the costume out.

There's a pause. "That's a demon."

I frown. "Right? You can be Raven. 'Cause only a demon would give her *blind* team member a princess costume and say it's a knight costume."

There's a snort, and it brings me more joy than I've had in the last few days. Suddenly, the costume is being yanked from my hands, and I stifle a smile.

"You're kind of an asshole," I tell her.

"Likewise."

But the tension falls away as we shop. She fights with me a little more about the costume, but finally gives in when I tell her I'll pay her enough for a hundred costumes. She refuses to tell me what costume she picks, although I know she grabs something.

I walk away feeling lighter than I have in days.

CHAPTER FIFTY-FIVE

AXEL

"You look like an idiot." I stare at Gage, who's folding into the backseat of the car. He's wearing a cheap knight costume, complete with a hollow plastic sword that's bent in the middle. That, paired with his old glasses, makes him look like a dork.

"Good thing I can't see." Gage grins in a cheery way that makes me want to knock the smile off his face.

"Well, *I* can, and you're an embarrassment."

It's then that Raven walks into the light cast by the garage, and I suck in a breath. She's in a baseball uniform with tight white pants that cling to her thighs and ass. There are pink socks that hug her legs up to her knees, and she carries that pink aluminum bat.

"What?"

"Nothing." I collect myself, even though my dick involuntarily stiffened. There's something about the form-fitting uniform that does it for me, and that pisses me off.

"How does she look?"

"Like a gold digger," I mutter, just before Raven moves to the driver's seat. She sees that I'm in the front, then throws a smile back at Gage. A beautiful smile that I'm close enough to see crinkles the edges of her eyes. Then, she hammers the nail in the coffin by reaching back and squeezing his thigh.

Gage lets out a tiny groan.

Awesome. So wonderful. I get to witness them act like fucking teenagers and pretend I'm not here.

The drive to Mom's is silent. I try not to look at the two lovebirds, but I can imagine what they're doing every time Raven throws a glance backwards. She's giving him sex eyes. The half-lidded, pupils blown, come-fuck-me-now eyes.

Someone honks, and Raven cusses. I glance around, seeing a car swerve out of the way. We must be in an intersection.

"Fucking watch it!" I flip the other car the bird. "Learn how to drive."

"Jesus," Gage mutters. "Easy, dude."

Oh yeah, he's gotta get his dick wet a few more times before he dies of a broken heart. I grouse until we pull into Mom's driveway. Correction, Rich's driveway. Mom never had money before meeting Rich. I'm convinced that's why she stayed with his insufferable ass all these years.

Their yard is full of Halloween decorations, complete with light-up plastic pumpkins, ghosts, and gravestones. Fake bats hang from the tree, and black cats with their backs arched line the walkway. Even with my lack of vision, I know it looks like shit. It's all old and sun-washed and doesn't look a bit scary. And yet, Rich doesn't make Mom change them out. Probably because that would be more money he has to spend.

I climb out of the car, slamming the door and not even waiting to see if the lovebirds follow.

I was going to flake out on tonight. Tell Mom I went to the

Fright Night Carnival. I make it a point to avoid Rich at all costs. However, Gage was insistent on going with my girl on his arm, and I've seen how this ends. Not good for Gage.

I need a drink. I need a goddamn fucking drink.

CHAPTER FIFTY-SIX

GAGE

Introducing Raven to Mom went well. And by well, I mean Raven and Axel sat so tense it felt like they had cactuses up their asses, and all the while, Rich threw snide comments at Axel. I'm the only one with a weapon on my costume, but everyone else feels much more lethal.

Axel gets drunk, rip-roaring drunk, while Mom tries to talk with Raven, and Rich makes tone-deaf comments.

I'm about to rip my hair out.

I interrupt before things can get worse. "Mom, where's Mason?" There were supposed to be other friends and family at this party, and it's well past start time. I'm painfully aware of how Raven keeps shifting in her seat and looking at the door.

She's probably thinking about running, and I kinda want to

run with her. Why the hell did I think introducing her to Mom this way would go well?

"I think he decided to go to the carnival instead," Mom says.

I frown as Axel heaves off the couch. He makes a shuffle step, almost trips on my sword, then stumbles to the bathroom; Raven tells me she's going to grab a drink and asks if I want one.

Yes. I want anything that keeps me close to her.

I bump into something on the way to the kitchen, tripping over it and cursing a little. Fucking glasses. I'm acting just as drunk as Axel.

When the fluorescent light of the kitchen lightens my vision, warm hands pull me to the side. "Careful, table."

Fuck. Why would Mom move the table? It was probably Rich. He likes to keep us off balance.

"I think Axel's puking." Raven keeps her voice low.

Oh, for fuck's sake. "Let him. Are you okay?" I want to reach out and grab her face. Feel if there's a crease between her eyebrows. See how tense she's holding her lips.

But I hold myself back.

"Fine." Her answer is clipped.

Then, the sound of violent hurling comes from the bathroom. Axel was always a loud puker.

"Oh god, is he okay?" Mom's voice comes from the living room.

"I'm sure he's fine," Rich reassures.

The sound comes again, and it grates on my nerves. Axel's been a royal pain in the dick, and even now, he's still getting all the attention.

"I'll check on him, but you good?" I ask Raven.

"Fine," she says again, but this time there's less venom. "Kick his ass for me, yeah?"

More than okay with that.

I stalk down the hall to the bathroom, where the door is open and the light is off. I flick it on and off a few times. "Wakey, wakey."

Axel groans.

"You did this to yourself, you know."

There's a pause, then Axel moans. "Come to gloat?"

"Yep." I lean on the doorframe.

I hear Axel shift, and then he screams into the toilet again. When he's done, I hear him thump back down. "That checks out. You were always the good one."

I snort.

"Goody-two-shoes." Axel's voice is sing-songy. "Run to tell Mom anytime Axel looked at him wrong."

I cross my arms.

"That's why it wasn't you, you know." There's a hollow thump, and I think Axel has dropped his head against the bathtub.

I shake my head. He's so drunk that the puking hasn't even sobered him up. We're definitely going to have to leave him here tonight. Oh no. I roll my eyes.

"It's why Rich didn't pick you."

"What?" I wonder if I can take away the key Axel has to my house.

"Why Rich didn't pick you. Because you'd tell Mom."

"What are you talking about?"

"About the..." Axel's voice lowers like he's telling a secret. "You know. Hiding the pickle. Gloving the popsicle." He giggles like he's telling a joke.

Oh my god, he's drunk as fuck. He's definitely going to choke on his vomit tonight. "Let's get you to bed." I lean down, trying to get my arm around his. "Don't puke on me."

"You know what, I'm glad it wasn't you, though."

I try to pull Axel up, but he's a dead weight.

"I'm glad because you were always the good one." Axel's voice tightens. "You wouldn't have been good if it happened. You would have been like me."

No. *No, no, no.*

The reality of what Axel's saying slams into me like a brick wall. And for a moment, all I can do is hang there, not breathing.

No. This can't be true. Because I don't *want* it to be true.

"You know, I thought about killing him for what he did." Axel hiccups, then giggles. "I know he touched her. He's just like Rich."

I can't say anything. I can't even breathe.

"I don't know if Max likes kids like Rich, but I know he touched *her*."

The words rip through me like a blast of cold air.

Axel laughs. "Something about them... you jussst know."

Breathe. I have to breathe. I force a ragged breath in, then another and another. I feel like I can't exhale... like I'm the one who's going to get sick.

Axel settles himself against me, and I stagger to keep him upright. Even as the anger fills me, the things Axel says are rushing through my head.

Axel is just drunk, right? He's just talking nonsense like all drunk people?

Like I'm being controlled by a remote, I walk Axel to his room. Mom kept them for us if we ever wanted to visit. Axel follows without a fight. When I drop him to his bed, I pull the glasses from his face so he doesn't crush them. He doesn't even argue when I switch them out. I grab a trash can and make sure the pillows are piled up behind him so he isn't lying on his back.

"Do you think it's true?"

"What?" I can barely breathe enough to get the word out.

"That it doesn't mean anything."

I stare at my brother. He has a dopey smile on his face. "Sex. That it doesn't mean anything?"

I can't answer. It's like all words are stuck in my throat.

Axel just smiles wistfully. "It doesn't, you know. It's just... fucking." He blinks once. "But I kinda wish it did."

I hate the vulnerability in my brother's voice. It scares me more than anything.

"But then, if it means something, it's the scariest thing in the world." Axel closes his eyes, and his breathing gets heavy. Then, he passes out.

CHAPTER FIFTY-SEVEN

RAVEN

Gage has been gone for a few minutes, and I'm doing everything I can so as not to have to go back to the living room with their parents. I'm not one for small talk, and the atmosphere is off. And that's not just because Gage's mom is a sexy gingerbread man, and Rich won't stop talking about the hunting trip he has planned at his lake house. I don't like Rich. There's something about him that immediately made me tense. Also, every time Axel wasn't looking, Rich sent him the most disgusted looks.

The boys call Rich by his first name, although they call their mom "Mom." I can see the resemblance to her. She has the same fairy-like features, though they look more masculine on the boys.

I down my drink, then pour another, keeping my bat tucked up under my arm. I didn't want to leave it in the living room, but now it feels weird to be holding it. It's stupid, and I hate that

Gage made us dress up. His mom is the only other one who participated, and now I feel duped.

I think about the way Gage smiled when I finally agreed and dug his elbow into my ribs. I smacked him for it, which only made him laugh. Then he wrapped his arms around me, scuffing his fist into my hair while I half-heartedly fought him off.

"He okay in there?"

I jump, face hot at the memory I was jolted out of. Rich stands in the kitchen, filling up a solo cup with some pink punch that I think is supposed to look like blood.

"I think so." I stopped hearing the puking, as well as a door opening and their low voices, so that's a good thing, I guess.

Rich's gaze is either on my own drink or my chest. It drops down my body, then back up again. Immediately, he gives a throaty chuckle. "Kids. Can't hold their alcohol." His eyes are glassy, although he doesn't slur. I recognize it well.

I just nod, looking back at the hallway. I need Gage to come back so we can go.

"Can I get you something else to drink?" Rich walks toward me. "We have some juice in here to mix."

"No, I'm good." I move the bat into my hand and point it at the floor.

Rich gives me another once-over with his glassy eyes. "So, both of them, huh?"

I frown.

"Kinky." Rich winks. "Although, if you want my opinion, Axel's an idiot. You're better off with Gage."

My mouth drops open, and for some reason, anger fills my chest like a balloon. These are his boys? How dare he talk about his own kids like this?

Before I can say something, Rich opens the fridge. In doing so, he bumps my arm with the drink and spills it all down my jersey.

I sputter, both from the cold and the accusation.

"Oh my god! I'm sorry!" Immediately, Rich grabs the towel

from the oven, and then he's there, pressing it to my chest. I feel his hand squeeze around my breast.

I see red. Before I can think twice, I take the baseball bat that's pointed at the ground and jerk it upwards, right between Rich's legs.

Rich crumples, dropping to the ground, and I yank the bat away, my hand shaking.

It's at that moment that Axel appears, looking shaken.

I blink. Only, it's not Axel; it's Gage in his knight costume, but he's put the glasses on, and he looks more pale than usual.

"Ready to go?" he asks, then frowns at Rich on the floor. There's a look of disgust for a second, and then it's gone.

"He tripped." I find myself grabbing onto Gage's arm. It's just to direct him and has nothing to do with the way my hands are shaking or the slight spin the alcohol has given me. He has the glasses, so he doesn't need me to lead him.

Still, I don't let him go.

Gage doesn't leave right away. Instead, he leans down to where Rich is struggling to stand. Then, in a lethal voice, he says, "Go to your lake house for the night."

Rich tries to catch his breath, waving us off.

Gage waits for a second, then leans in. "Did you hear me, old man?"

Rich snaps his gaze up to Gage's. "Who the fuck are you talking to?"

Taking a step closer, I realize again just how big Gage is. His voice is quiet and sends a shiver down my spine. "Go to your lake house, or I'll rip your balls off and stuff them down your throat until you choke."

Does Gage know what Rich just did? Did he see it?

For a second, Rich is still. His eyes widen, then he raises his hands. "Jesus, okay. No need to be like that."

"You'll stay for a while. If I hear you've come back here..."

Rich raises his hands.

Gage stands there until Rich backs off, and when he does, I feel an odd sense of victory.

With some grumbling to Gage's mom, Rich leaves. Gage then kisses his mom's forehead and asks her to look out for Axel. She's confused, but Gage just says Axel threatened to beat Rich's ass, and he's too drunk to move him.

When he says that, I get the most unreasonable wash of disappointment. Did Gage not see what Rich did to me?

"Axel okay?" I ask as Gage gets in the car, and I put the keys in the ignition. It's a question I shouldn't even be asking. I shouldn't care how that asshole is doing. I blame it on the small buzz I have going.

Gage's fake sword bunches up as he folds into the seat. He cusses and pulls it out of his belt, then runs his hands through his hair. "Uh, yeah. He's just drunk, he'll be fine." There's a long pause, and I almost ask if we should stay, but then I stop.

Axel's a big boy. He can live with the consequences of his actions.

Discomfort shifts through me. I can still feel Rich's grip on my breast, filling me with a familiar defeat and disgust. Men are disgusting pigs.

Gage's hand shifts, and I jump, having gotten so wrapped up in my thoughts that I forgot he was there.

"You okay?"

I glance at him briefly, unsettled that he noticed. There's a crease between his eyebrows, and his gaze looks soft. But the alcohol-warmed part of my brain gets excited that he noticed. He cares.

I have the insane urge to reach across the console and put my hand on his clenched one.

The thought makes fear jackknife in my chest. Have I learned nothing?

Apparently not, because Gage is upset about something. And the alcohol in my system insists that deep down, he's a good guy, and I can trust him.

I drive in silence that feels so loaded and yet so...lonely. Nothing feels okay right now. I just want...something to ground me.

Movement makes me glance over. Gage's hand twitches, and I rip my gaze away from the veins tracing over his hand. I focus on driving.

Then, there's movement again. When I glance over, Gage's hand has moved an inch towards me. As we drive, his hand gets closer.

I'm driving with my left hand, my right clasped in a tight fist on my thigh. I should move my hand. Should pull away screaming.

But, for some insane reason, I don't.

His pinky brushes mine, and an electric zap runs up my arm and down my spine. We sit there for a minute, not moving. My body hums with energy from just that single touch. It's not a selfish or demanding touch. It's gentle and hesitant, a lot like Gage.

And for a glorious moment, I feel *him* through it.

Then, his finger is gone, and my hand is there alone. Gone is the warmth and the comfort, and I want it back.

Ignoring the screaming in my head, I push my hand closer to Gage's, brushing up over his pinky so my palm sits on his. Just so in this moment, I'm not alone with my thoughts.

Then, he reaches his pinky out and grips mine in a firm touch that isn't an accident.

I brake for a stop sign a little too hard, jerking myself and him forward.

"Fuck," I mutter.

Gage turns to me, voice deep with concern. "Are you okay?"

I look at him, seeing his handsome gaze fully focused on me. All I can do is make a choking noise. "Yeah."

Gage must think I'm choking cause of the seatbelt. "Fuck." His hands are all over me. All over my shoulders, patting me down, brushing my neck, causing heat to tingle all the way up to my face. "Can you breathe?"

No. But not for the reason he's thinking. I clear my throat, making a show of brushing those big hands off. "I'm fine."

Gage looks stricken for a second, and seeing him look like that makes me feel bad. Makes me wish I could take that look off his face. I clear my throat and ease off the brake. "So, uh, the costumes were an attempt to publicly humiliate me, huh?"

Gage lets out a soft breath of air, and then one hand pulls away. I clench my fist in my lap this time, hiding it between my thighs. What the fuck is my problem?

To get the attention off my mortifying reaction, I mutter, "You didn't tell me this was team Fuck Axel, Embarrass Raven."

There's a pause, and I'm not sure if he's going to answer me. Then, Gage says in a gruff voice, "Yep. That was the plan all along. Get you dressed as a sexy baseball player to embarrass you in front of my parents."

But my hormones and my buzzed mind scream. Gage called me sexy.

"I don't mean–I, uh…" Gage stutters. "Sorry, uh. I meant your costume was perfect."

I stifle back a smile. A prickle of fear and excitement runs across my skin and up the back of my neck. What is going on right now?

Bad things, my anxiety screams. *When you trust people, bad things happen.*

When we pull into the driveway, I feel Gage's hand tighten once on mine, and then he's gone. I feel the loss, and then I see him coming around the car to my side.

Is he… He's going to open my door.

I open it before he can get there. "I can do it."

Gage stands there, eyebrow up. "Couldn't let me get at least one 'knight in shining armor' joke in?"

"You've had all night." I stalk around the car to go inside the house, keeping the smile off my face.

Buddy's excited to see us, jumping around, stepping on toes, and panting with her disgusting breath.

"Okay, okay," Gage says as he flips on some lights, but there's no real anger behind his fake annoyance. I move around him to get to the kitchen where the water is, but Gage bumps into me.

"Sorry," I say automatically.

"Yeah, I don't think you are." Gage pops an eyebrow with a slight smirk on his face.

I freeze. He's... flirting with me. Openly. My heart races.

"You're right. I'm not." I move to step around him, but Gage crowds me back against the counter. Immediately, my breathing hitches, and I look up at him. Gage looks down at me with a soft look in his eyes. Then, he raises his hands. "No touching. Just wanted to look at your neck."

"Huh?"

He bends down to squint at it.

Oh. The seatbelt.

"It's literally fine." I try to duck past him, but Gage just shifts so he's in the way again. Alarm bells ring in my head while excitement fills my veins. His closeness makes me want to scream and run, but also reach out and grab him to pull him closer.

"Don't bullshit me. Did you feel anything pop?"

Oh, right. He's talking about my neck. But all I can think about is how I can feel his breath on my skin.

"I was driving, like, five miles per hour." I cross my arms mostly to keep them from reaching out and tracing the strong torso in front of me. Then I look up at Gage, and his face is intense.

"Answer the question." It's a demand.

Fear, intoxication, and lust hit me all at once. Then, doubt and uncertainty. I don't usually like men to take control, so why in the hell is his bossiness doing something for me?

I realize it's been too long since he asked the question, and I scoff. "You're not the boss of me."

For a heartbeat, Gage stands there. Then he leans back the tiniest bit, and I have the insane urge to flip our positions and pin him against the counter. To see what he'd do. To see if I can get that rush of power from pushing men around.

So, because I'm stupid and a little buzzed, I lean forward and test the limits. "You can't tell me what to do, Gage Newman."

Gage's nostrils flare, and he sucks in a breath while taking the tiniest step back. It's like a shot of adrenaline in my veins. I put my hand on his chest and push. Then I grab his arm, pulling it so his back is to the counter, and our positions are flipped. I lean in, breasts brushing the fake plastic armor he has on instead of his warm skin.

Both of us are breathing hard. I expect Gage to try and control me. To grump at me and demand I do exactly what he says. But, just like every time we've played the game, he doesn't. He just waits for me to take the lead.

It's fucking intoxicating. I suck in a breath, enjoying the moment of total control. Then, fear creeps in. Is this for real? Or is he just manipulating me to trust him so he can take advantage of me? Get me drunk and off my game enough to do what he wants to me, like bathroom guy? To get me incapacitated like Max?

My thoughts spin round and round, and I'm not sure what to think or do.

"Celeste?" Gage says my name softly, like a question, and it startles me back into reality. He's looking down at me with a gaze that almost looks... adoring. He looks at my lips like he's going to kiss me. Like he's going to take me right here without the game.

And I want him to.

That scares me.

"I, uh, my neck is fine." I take a step back, heat flushing across my face. I need something, anything to distract from what's going on right now. I motion at his glasses. "Plus, you should be able to see now that you stole these back."

Gage's smile falters.

I keep talking, needing to fill the space. "The glasses are the true victims in this custody exchange."

I try to move around Gage, and this time he lets me. I grab a glass and fill it with water. I need to sober up, or I'm going to do something really stupid. I wait for it to fill, then swallow down three gulps before I hear Gage moving.

"Speaking of my brother... he, uh... said something about Max tonight."

I wince, then freeze. Why the fuck was Axel talking about Max?

"Oh yeah?" I play it cool, taking another drink, but this time, it's hard to swallow. It's like there's a rock in my throat. When Gage doesn't respond right away, the hairs start prickling on the back of my neck.

"I just... he said, was he, uh..."

I turn, and Gage tries to offer me a fake smile.

"What?" The fake smile isn't helping. In fact, now I feel unease creeping into my gut. I don't want to know what he's going to ask, but I also *need* to know what he's going to ask.

"You know what, nevermind." Gage turns away.

"What were you going to say?"

"Nothing. Axel was just drunk."

"What did he say?" He's not going to drop Max's name and then not tell me. I want to know what they think they know. How can I make a plan to stay safe if anything has changed?

"It was nothing. He was just being an idiot." Gage sounds mad now, which only ups my fear. Why the hell is he mad? For a brief second, I let Gage hear the fear in my voice. He'll talk to me if he knows I'm afraid.

Then Gage drops his gaze and stares at the floor. He says nothing.

"Fine," I say. I slam my cup down on the counter and stalk out of the kitchen.

Gage's frustrated growl follows me, and I stalk to my room and slam the door, still riled up from the closeness of Gage's body.

CHAPTER FIFTY-EIGHT

GAGE

"Would you just hold still?" Buddy thrashes beneath me, refusing to open her mouth for her dewormer. "It's for your own good."

She doesn't listen. In fact, she squirms right out of my grip for the third time in a row. I let out a little half-grunt.

All morning, I've been having flashbacks. I remember the times Axel made inappropriate jokes when we were kids. Rich would laugh while Mom scolded. I remember the time Axel fucked his first girl without using a condom, then the next day fucked her best friend, and how he was so cocky about it. I couldn't for the life of me understand why he was so fucking thoughtless.

"It doesn't mean anything," he said as he clapped me on the shoulder. "Stop being such a prude."

He didn't spend any extra time with Rich that I remember. They never went on trips together.

I try to justify what Axel said with any other possible meaning.

I try to pin Buddy down again, this time standing over her and tilting her head back to me.

Axel did have his own room.

Against my will, my eyes fill with tears.

No. It's not possible. Because if it is, that means I spent my whole childhood trying to protect my mom when it was my brother who needed it all along.

"What are you doing?" Raven's gravelly voice sounds alarmed. I glance up to see her standing in the hallway. A second later, she's striding over to me with anger in her eyes.

"Giving Buddy her dewormer." I try to clear my throat.

Buddy struggles again.

"You're being rough with her." Raven kneels in front of Buddy.

"She won't take it!"

"Give it to me," Raven hisses, hand grappling to get my fingers uncurled from the pill. I let her, and she pries Buddy's mouth open at the corners. Then she drops the pill in, clamping her hand around her muzzle and stroking Buddy's neck. After a second, she releases her.

I stand there, waiting to see if Buddy will drop the pill. She doesn't.

"Let her go," Raven demands.

"She's gonna spit it out," I growl, but I let her go reluctantly. I expect Buddy to race down the hall so we can't see her and drop it, but she doesn't. She just moves to her food bowl and looks back expectantly.

"Stroke her neck, and she'll swallow." Raven stands. I can feel her shrewd look on me.

Suddenly, all I can think about is last night. How we were so close to kissing. How Raven stood there in front of me; for a second, she was unguarded. Her mouth was open, and her pupils dilated. She looked like she wanted me. My arm tingles from where she grabbed it to pin me against the counter, and all I wanted was for her to trust me enough to touch me more. To let me show her that I didn't want to hurt her.

I don't want to hurt her. I just want her to feel safe.

Then something happened last night. Her eyes changed, and her lips snapped shut. I watched her fade away in front of me, and I did nothing.

I did nothing.

Just like I saw all the signs with Axel, and I did nothing.

I take a step back, heart clenching in my chest.

"Uh, thanks," I grind, eyes starting to well up. Fuck! I can't cry in front of her.

Then, the worst thing happens. The front door opens, and Axel's voice comes through. "Honey, I'm home."

CHAPTER FIFTY-NINE

AXEL

My head is pounding so hard as I stumble into Gage's house.

Oh my god, why did I drink so much?

I know I embarrassed myself last night. I don't remember everything exactly; I just have pictures in my head. Gage with his hand on Raven's thigh. Gage jumping to make her comfortable. Rich looking like a smug motherfucker. I definitely puked my guts out.

I'm hungover as fuck, and I know I'm not welcome here, but I couldn't spend another minute in that house. Not in that bedroom. I begged Mom to drop me off here.

I know I'll get hatred and disdain from Raven and Gage.

But hey, they can't hate me more than I hate myself.

Gotta look at the bright side.

There's a bolt of movement down the hall, and I'd bet

anything it's Raven. I grin, even though I don't feel happy. "Did I interrupt something?"

Gage is silent.

I let the fake smile fall away, too tired to keep it up. I stink, my head is screaming, and I need to sleep for fucking... forever, probably.

"Love you too." I blow him a kiss, then stumble down the hall. I'm tempted to crash in Raven's room, but I just don't have the energy for that fight right now. Instead, I find my way to the other spare room by the laundry and pass out.

When I wake up, I first realize how dry my mouth is and how bad I stink.

Fuck. What fucking day is it?

It seems light outside, and after I stumble to the bathroom to guzzle water from the faucet, I find myself unsettled.

I definitely embarrassed myself last night. Last night? Two days ago? Fuck, I remember the anger hitting me so hard I shook. Then Gage was helping me.

I want to go back to being unconscious.

Unfortunately, that doesn't work. I smell like shit. I stalk to the laundry room to see if Gage has any clean clothes in the washer, and as I do, I bump into someone. Someone small that smells like men's shampoo.

Involuntarily, I suck in a breath.

"Watch where you're going," Raven's voice curls around me with a familiar bitterness.

I love that bitterness. Lean into it. At least it's not apathy.

I raise my hands. "Would it be the wrong time to say I can't 'watch' anything?"

I don't have my glasses. I don't know where they went. I toss Raven my signature smile, although I don't feel it in my soul.

"Whatever, *Garret*." Then, she tries to shove past me.

There's a flicker of something in my chest. I snap my hand out at her, and I grab her arm. It's small and delicate. "What did you just call me?"

"Get the fuck off me!" Raven writhes in my grip. "Don't think I won't hit you in the balls too."

I let go of her writhing form but stay in the doorway. "What?"

She's seething, and I can tell she moves away from me. "I hit Rich in the nuts with my bat, and I'll do the same to you."

A flash of something like… relief rolls through me, and I bark out a laugh. Raven hit Rich in the nuts? Oh god. The image is a dream. The laughter takes over and becomes somewhat of a manic thing, making me laugh until my stomach hurts.

God. Her hatred is intoxicating. It breathes a tiny bit of life into my dead soul. I kinda want to kiss her.

No. I *really* want to kiss her.

"Get the fuck out of the way," Raven demands.

Right. I'm still in the doorway.

I think about making a show of keeping her here. Flirting with her just to see her anger boil over. But then I just… stop.

I'm too tired for that shit. Plus, for an odd reason I can't explain, the thought of pissing Raven off right now makes me feel… guilty.

Fucking alcohol. I need to stop drinking. Such a fucking buzzkill.

I take a step back, and when Raven storms past me, the guilt churns in my stomach, and I mutter, "Sorry about the animal crackers. I found them on your doorstep."

I sense Raven freeze for a second. Then, she's gone, disappearing down the hall.

Oh yeah. Definitely need to stop drinking. Who the hell did I just become? Gage?

Shaking myself out of it, I change, realizing that my stomach is growling, and I move to the kitchen for a snack. Once my head is in the fridge, I hear dishes clinking. I glance over to see a form that's larger than Raven's standing there.

I groan, "Cool. First tongue lashing by Tweedledee out of the way, now it's time for Tweedledum."

Only Gage doesn't say anything. I stand there, waiting, but still nothing.

I arch an eyebrow. "Thanks for telling Raven my name, by the way. Real big brother of you."

Gage doesn't say anything, and I imagine that pinched look on his face. I shake my head, returning to the fridge and popping open a soda can, guzzling it down.

"Axel..."

There's something off about Gage's tone, and I stiffen. He sounds... torn.

"If I punched you last night, I'm not sorry." I feel for the container of yogurt I know is in here, but suddenly, I'm not hungry anymore. "I'm sure you deserved it."

Gage still doesn't say anything. Then, he asks, "What the hell happened with Rich?"

Rich? Nothing happened with Rich besides him sitting on the couch like an asshole. Oh, and Raven hitting him in the nuts.

I snort. "Raven and that bat are deadly. It's only a matter of time before your nuts are next."

"What?" Gage sounds genuinely confused for a second.

"You know. Raven. Rich. Bat. Nuts."

"What in the fuck are you—" Gage pauses. "Wait, no. That's not what I was talking about."

So what in the hell—

Oh god. Oh... Oh fuck. My stomach sinks. He can't know about that, right? I didn't tell him. No way I'd tell him something like that. Right?

I grab the closest thing in the fridge and then shut the door. "Just needed a snack; see ya."

"Axel."

It's the pity in his voice that makes my stomach sink.

He knows.

"That's lemon juice."

I pause, feeling the item in my hand. I pop the top, and a puff of lemon-scented air escapes. Embarrassment heats my cheeks. I never knew how to tell Gage about everything. Even thinking about it makes shame heat my cheeks. Immediately, I shake it off.

"Axel I—"

I hold up my hand, still facing away from him. "Don't do the pity thing, Gage. I don't need your pity."

Silence.

My chest hurts. I don't want him to feel bad for me. Never have. What the hell is feeling bad going to do? It won't change the past.

"Why the fuck didn't you tell me?" Gage's voice is small. Like he's a kid again.

A rush of heartbreak, anger, and fear rushes through me. I should walk away. I should just keep walking and not even respond. But I feel that self-hatred creeping in. The part I can never truly escape washes over me.

"Why, Gage?" I whirl on him. "Because I was seven? Because at the end of the day, it doesn't mean anything? It doesn't change who I am, Gage. I'm still me." The words rush out of me in a boiling-hot spew of hatred.

"Axel, I—"

"Why don't you not make this about you for five fucking minutes!" I can't keep the word vomit down. It's like years of pressure are breaking down a barrier, and I'm helpless to stop it. "You know you'd be a lot more bearable if you didn't fucking try to be so goddamn perfect all the time."

My hands are shaking, and I'm fully ready for his rebuttal. Let him fight me. I've been waiting years to fucking tell him off.

Only, it doesn't come. He says nothing, and that just makes me angrier.

"You know what? Fuck off, Gage."

I turn to leave and stalk away.

CHAPTER SIXTY

GAGE

I don't let Axel get far. I have absolutely no idea what to say or what to do in this situation. This is different from my job, where I can spout a law or argue a point. Axel would just fight me, and we'd be nowhere closer to where we need to be.

Where do we need to be? What the hell am I supposed to say? But I'll be damned if I do nothing. I'll be fucking *damned*.

I stalk after Axel, following him to his bedroom.

"What the fuck do you want?" Axel whirls on me, throwing his hands in the air. He's angry, but behind all that anger, I hear the fear in his voice. The way it strains and is pitched higher than normal. He sounds lost.

"Here," I say gruffly, holding out the glasses. I both don't want to see for this conversation, and want him to feel less panicked.

Axel snatches them from me, breathing heavily.

I'm scared to say the wrong thing, so I open and close my mouth a few times. Nothing is right. Because the whole situation is wrong, and he doesn't want pity.

So, I cross my arms. "So, the bat?"

There's a moment of silence. Then, Axel lets out a hissed breath.

I can't tell if it's a good thing or not, but I keep going. I remember seeing Rich on the floor, and now that I think about it, I realize that Raven did have the bat in her hands.

"It wasn't just a prop," I say, but it's not a question.

"Was it ever?"

I picture Rich, the person I most want to kill, curled up on the floor after my tiny woman gave him what he deserved. And that image makes me let out a small burst of air.

"Fucking hell." I run a hand through my hair.

We settle into silence for a minute until Axel says, "You like her."

Instantly, I bristle. Why the hell does he care? But as soon as that reaction rushes through me, I stamp it down. So I like her. So what?

"I do." As I say it, my cheeks flame. And instantly, I feel bad. Because I remember Axel likes her, too.

"Damn." Axel chuckles, but his voice is tight. "When's the wedding?"

"You're an idiot."

Axel starts making kissing noises, but behind the teasing, there's a note of frantic energy.

"It's okay. Pretty sure she's mad at me, so..." I motion uselessly. "Not going anywhere."

"Again? Damn, what'd you do?"

"Nothing," I mutter.

"Did you try to take her bat?"

I don't answer.

"Whatever." I hear Axel move, and it scares me. I don't want him to stop talking to me. I want it to be like when we were kids again. Back when he was scheming to sell poems in school for pieces of gum.

"I... She just stopped talking to me."

"Did you tell her she should date me since I have a bigger dick?" Axel's voice is deadpan.

"What? No!" I sputter. "We're twins; it's the same—" I cut myself off. "No, everything was going fine, and I thought we were going to kiss, and then she pulled away, and I... let her."

The room gets silent. It is awkward talking to my brother like this. We haven't done this in... years. But it also feels familiar. Like coming home after a long, long fucking time. So, instead of running, I keep talking.

"I did nothing, Ax." I swallow harshly. "I let her get away."

Axel is silent for so long that I think he's going to make fun of me.

Then I feel his hand clap my shoulder. "Okay, so you didn't pressure her into a kiss. Congrats, you're not a fucking dickwad."

I snort.

"I'm being serious. You're not a Max. Congrats."

I stiffen. "Max?"

Axel lets out a breath.

"She hasn't told me about Max," I say.

"Me either." Axel's voice falls back into that emotionless tone. "But she doesn't have to. You see how she gets. He either beat her ass or..." he trails off. We both know what he's talking about. I desperately hope he does say it. Like saying it will make it a reality.

Not that it would make me view her any differently. But because it's making me murderous. Both options. And I don't recognize this feeling in me.

But maybe I do. It's the feeling I've been having since the party.

"He'll never touch her again," Axel says, voice low. "And we're not gonna ask her about it."

I swallow. I want to ask her about it. I want to know every detail so I know how to protect her.

"We're not gonna ask," Axel says again, this time harsher.

I just nod.

"Good." His tone softens. "Good. We won't make her relive it unless she's ready."

I get it. I understand. I don't like it, but I understand.

Axel claps my shoulder. "You good?"

I choke, feeling stupid. Axel's the one going through it, and I'm over here drowning. It's then that I register the liquid slosh, and I realize he's still holding the lemon juice.

To ease the tension, I ask, "You gonna drink that, or?"

"Fuck you," Axel says, but this time, it has no bite to it. "I am kinda hungry, though. Fetch me some food, why don't you."

"Get your own food, you lazy fuck," I say, but there's no bite to my words. I start moving to the doorway.

"Oh, and Gage?"

I stop.

Axel's voice drops. "It wasn't your fault." And then, with a shuffle of socked feet, he's gone.

CHAPTER SIXTY-ONE

RAVEN

I help Gage with his work, and neither of us mentions the almost-kiss in the kitchen. There's an odd tension between us that I've determined to ignore. This is my job. I've saved up a nice amount of cash, stashing it in different places so Gage can't steal it from me as easily. It's going to set me up nicely. The thought is both comforting and unsettling.

I'm going to have to start over. Like, completely over. I won't know anyone, and that thought freaks me out.

Buddy adjusts her head where she has it on my lap. Whenever we work, she's here, touching or drooling on me in some way. My chest tightens. I'll have to leave Buddy.

"Does it... smell in here to you?" Gage wrinkles his nose, looking around.

"Oh, uh... no?" It definitely does. There's a hint of spoiled milk.

"I changed the trash," Gage mutters.

I wait for the satisfaction that I expected, but it feels a little hollow. Gage has been nice to me, and I feel guilty that I fucked with his things. Axel's? Sure. Not Gage's.

Then, Gage shrugs, and I see his shoulders tense. He starts to wipe his hands on his pants—grey sweatpants that I've been trying so fucking hard to keep my eyes off—and clears his throat.

"Uh, I was wondering if... Do you want to go to the bookstore later?"

I blink.

"It's okay if not," Gage says quickly. "I just wanted to get something. You don't have to." He grabs the pile of papers in front of him and then picks them up to straighten them.

Why the fuck is he nervous? It's odd to see such a big, grumpy man look so uncomfortable. It's almost... cute. And now I definitely feel guilty about his living room.

I immediately stifle that thought and say, "Sure, whatever you want." I'm getting paid to help him, so I may as well get paid to go to the bookstore. Plus, I wouldn't mind getting out of the house for a bit. The smell is kinda giving me a headache.

"Cool." For a second, Gage's face lights up. "I'll get changed."

I stare at him as he walks away like his ass is on fire. Why the hell is he acting so weird? This is just an errand, right?

What if it's not just an errand?

My stupid, dumbass heart kicks up a beat. He asked if I wanted to go. Like it was optional. Like... he asked me to hang out with him.

Now, my heart is flying.

No. It's not optional. I'm here to help him.

I get up to get ready and find myself in front of the mirror, studying how I look. I haven't put makeup on in a long time, and my hair is slightly tangled. I get it brushed out and debate throwing some makeup on.

Wait, why am I even thinking about that? I didn't even consider mascara with the Halloween costume. Plus, it's not like he can really see it anyway.

It's just because he made a show about getting dressed. Fuck, I should have asked him what he was going to wear. Should I now? It's just a bookstore, right?

I go back and forth for a second, then throw some quick makeup on and step out into the hallway. I find Gage in the kitchen, and he is in a light blue suit.

I stop in my tracks. The clothes fit his muscled form perfectly and bring out the lightness of his eyelashes and hair, giving them a frosted look.

Fuck. He looks stunning. And I'm underdressed.

Gage must hear me 'cause he turns. "Ready?" The question is gruff.

"I uh... I need to change."

"I'm sure it's fine."

I glance down at my pleated skirt and pantyhose. It's nothing fancy, just the same stuff I've been wearing. "I didn't realize it was fancy." My face burns.

"You're fine." Gage motions at me.

"I'll just go—"

"Raven," his voice softens. "If you're wearing what you usually wear, then you look amazing."

My face burns. Was that... Did he just...?

Then Gage turns on his heel and heads toward the door. I scurry after, trying not to look at the way his ass fills out his dress pants.

By the time we get to the car, Gage opens the driver's door for me.

I hesitate, looking at his slightly tense body language.

Whatever. I'll be fine, right? I'm driving. It's not like I'm driving us to murder central. If I don't like it, I can just turn around.

Unless he has a weapon.

I'll wreck us both into a tree if he does.

"You okay?" Gage asks softly.

"Uh, yeah." I silently slide into the car. He shuts the door softly behind me and then goes around to the other side.

My hands are sweating.

Gage gives me directions on the way to the bookstore. It's awkward. I'm expecting some knife to come out and for him to gut me. Dead bitches can't be snitches.

But then why did he get dressed up? Plus, he hasn't looked at me once on the trip. He grips his thigh again like his life depends on it, and I wonder if he'll bruise.

I should have brought my bat.

"Cold today," Gage says, breaking me out of my spiral.

"Yeah," I say. The sky is the kind of pale blue only winter can bring. It's not unlike the color of Gage's eyes.

When we get to the store, it looks like a normal store. No murder vibes. Plus, it's in the middle of town, and there are people around. I suck in a breath.

The parking is on the street. Gage heaves out of the car like he's on fire. He moves around the front, tracing a hand along the hood to my side.

I open the door before he can get there.

"I got it," Gage says.

I stand up beside him, having to brush past his form to get out of the car. "It's fine."

Gage grabs my arm gently, pulling me back and away from the street. "Careful."

I huff, pulling my arm away. "I'm fine. Isn't that my job?"

Then Gage almost walks into a decorative planter, and I grab his arm, pulling him to the side just in time.

"Careful," I say.

Gage huffs. "Now you're just fucking with me."

"If you want to faceplant in the planter, be my guest."

Gage snorts. There's a second where I'm not sure if he's gonna get pissed. Then, he shakes his head, muttering something under his breath that sounds a lot like "humped pillows already, can't get any worse."

Then he holds his arm out to me. "Walk me inside?"

I pause. The arm is definitely so he doesn't run into anything else. But when I take it, Gage softly places his hand over mine and leads me to the store.

My heart races again. What the hell is going on here? If I didn't know better, this would feel like a... date.

My heart races so hard I think it's gonna beat out of my chest.

Oh, god no. I'd rather get murdered. At least with murder, things are pretty cut and dry. Romance? Relationships? That's turned out like shit for me before.

I turn to look back at the car, trying to plot my escape. While I do, Gage gently guides me into the store, and the smell of books surrounds us.

No, don't panic, Raven. Don't panic. I suck in deep breaths of the store, the smell of musty pages calming me slightly. There are books on floor-to-ceiling shelves everywhere.

"Hey there." The older man behind the register doesn't even look up.

"Hey," Gage greets, his voice deep and even friendly sounding.

It looks like we're in the pop culture section, with history further down, and then the path veers to the right. Then, Gage just stops. He glances down at me, and I do everything I can to avoid his gaze. Why is he looking at me? Can he see how hot my face is?

"Do you see the action section?"

I blink. Right. Action. We're in a bookstore. He just came for a book.

Relief fills me, tinged with another emotion that I can't quite pin down. If I didn't know better, I'd say it was disappointment.

Which would be crazy.

I take a second to look and see if there are any signs hanging from the ceiling, but the store looks like a maze of bookshelves with no clear map. Despite my earlier anxiety, even being around so many books makes me feel like things are going to be okay. It's quiet and peaceful.

"Are you looking for a specific book?" I ask as I peer down the rows of books, spotting a sign for action.

"Uh, no. Just whatever."

Wait, he came here with no plan? But I don't ask him. Because it's none of my business. My job is just to get him where he needs to be and to get out.

We browse the action section for a bit, but it feels weird without Gage knowing what he wants.

"What do you read?" I ask.

"Superheroes. Used to read about knights when I was younger." Gage runs his fingers along the spines.

That explains the costume.

"Wanted to be a knight so damn bad." Gage laughs softly. "Then, a firefighter. Then, a superhero. Pretty much anything cool. Oh!" He pauses on a book, pulling it out. "I love it when the covers are like this."

The book is wrapped in a cellophane dust jacket and crinkles softly when he opens it. He puts it to his nose and smells. He lets out a little groan that makes a tingle run down my skin. "Smells so good."

I eye the book. I love the way old books smell.

"What did you want to be?" Gage asks, handing the book to me.

I look at him.

"When you grew up? What did you want to be?"

I shrug, taking the book and giving it a quick sniff. It smells amazing. Then I turn back to the books, staring at them so I don't have to look at Gage.

I wanted to be a princess when I was really young. Then, a badass superhero. Then, a librarian. I just say, "Oh, you know. The normal girl stuff."

Gage grabs another book, opening and closing it to get the crinkle. "What's normal girl stuff?"

Oh god. He's going to make me say it, isn't he?

"Princesses and shit." My face burns. "It's stupid." Princesses are a fairytale, and an even bigger fairytale is the princes who save them. It's just not how the world works, as much as my fucking childhood self wanted it to.

"Not more stupid than wanting to ride a rhinorse into battle."

I glance at Gage. "A what?"

Gage looks my way, an eyebrow raised. "Princesses don't have rhinorses?"

I'm about to cross my arms when Gage waves a hand in the air, "Half-rhino, half-horse. It's kinda a staple for badasses. At least, it was in my mind." Gage sighs dramatically. "Imagine my distress when I found out they weren't real."

I snort, then look at him when he's facing the books again. He looks hot, combing along the spines gently. This is such a different side to him than the grumpy asshole who hired me.

I turn back to the books, breathing in a deep breath, and realize that, at this moment, I'm comfortable. For a minute, the fear and panic that follow me everywhere just... disappears. I look for it, but I feel nothing but peace among the pages and the man beside me.

It's then that I see something on the shelf that makes me suck in a breath.

CHAPTER SIXTY-TWO

GAGE

Raven makes a sound that makes all the blood rush to my dick. It's a little gasp for air that I want her to do over and over. Then, I hear a book sliding off the shelf.

"Oh my god."

"What?"

"Is it…" Raven trails off, and pages feather against her fingers. "No way."

"What is it?" What in the hell has her making that sound? Whatever it is, I'm going to buy a million of them.

"A collector's edition." Raven's voice is full of unrestrained wonder, and it makes my heart beat faster.

"What book?"

"The Unseen Hand. It was my favorite book as a kid."

Her favorite book? I lock onto that detail like it's food and

I'm starving to death. I've been dying to ask Raven everything about herself, but I don't want to scare her off. I try to play it cool. "What's it about?"

"A girl who acts like a boy back when women had no power, and that wasn't allowed. Because she wasn't raised like society wanted, she was sassy and aggressive and got what she wanted." There's so much passion in Raven's voice that it's like the book has unlocked a portal to her soul. She sounds so goddamn beautiful right now.

"It sounds amazing."

"And the cool thing is, it's old as fuck." I can practically see the sparkle in her eyes. "There's a lot of religion in it, but in the end, it was a story about a girl who found her power and never let it go, even when they tried to take it from her."

"It sounds really good. Get it."

"It really is." She's smiling. I can't see it, but I can hear it, and fuck if I don't want to kiss the hell out of her right now.

Then, her voice drops. "Uh, no, it's okay. I didn't bring my purse."

Outrage fills me, and I catch it a second before I blurt out something stupid that'll make Raven run for the hills. Instead, I say mildly, "I want it. I want to hear the story."

There's an uncertain pause. I hate that. I want the joyful Raven back.

"You might not like it. I was just a kid; it's probably stupid now."

Wait, why is she backing off? It clearly makes her happy. Oh my god, am I coming on too strong? Fuck. I need to chill.

So, I pretend like I don't care about the book even though it's the most interesting thing in the store besides her. "Stupid, huh?"

"The main character jumps on the back of her enemy," Raven says, and I sense the motion of her putting it back. "Since when does that ever work?"

"Hmmm," I make a thoughtful noise. It would work with me.

If Raven jumped on my back, I'd run off with her. But I don't say any of that. Instead, I just take a meandering step away. "That does sound stupid. How will I ever look at you the same?"

There's a small pause, and I'm pretty sure I have Raven's full attention, so I give a tiny sigh as if I'm disappointed. "If you insist on getting it, I'm afraid I'd have to fire you. I specifically put in the paperwork that anyone who reads about back-jumping heroes is out."

I turn away from her. For a heart-racing second, I think she's going to shrink away. To be too afraid to sass me.

Then, I feel her tiny hand thump on my back. "You're an asshole."

I laugh, and this time, it's a real laugh. Real joy fills me, and for a second, I feel better than I have in weeks. Months, even. Maybe years.

We keep browsing, and some of that earlier tension is gone. I continue to tell Raven I'm going to fire her, and Raven gives it back as good as I dish it out. I make Raven hand me the book before we go. I've gotten past one tiny wall, and it feels like I've won a huge battle.

Maybe the rhinorse wasn't such a bad idea after all.

CHAPTER SIXTY-THREE

RAVEN

"No. Absolutely not."

"Why not?" Gage stands at the edge of the couch, arms folded, muscles straining against his suit.

"Because!" Anxiety churns in my gut.

"I want to hear the story."

"I am not reading that to you." I motion at the special edition we brought back from the store. I was secretly so excited when he got it, and I haven't been able to take my eyes off of it. Buddy sniffs it like it might be a treat. Although I'm not sure how she can stand to use her nose. If it's bad in here for us, how bad must it be for her?

"Are you afraid you're going to mess up?"

"No. I just, I don't want to." Now, I'm crossing my arms like a child. There's a slew of emotions churning inside me. What if the book isn't as good as I remember? What if it's too slow, and he hates it? What if he judges me for what's inside? No. This is far too intimate.

"Good. 'Cause I charge a fee for every word you fuck up." Gage sits down on the couch, patting the spot next to him with a haughty expression.

"You what?" I sputter. Is he serious right now?

"You heard me. Every fumbled word comes out of your paycheck."

I see the corner of Gage's mouth twitch, then he goes back to his mask.

He's playing.

"How much?" I ask, bending down to grab something.

Gage purses his lips. "I don't know, I think maybe five—"

He doesn't see the pillow coming as I whap it into his head. Gage gives a startled 'oomph', and Buddy dances between us, tail wagging. It takes Gage a second to recover, and he straightens his glasses. His face breaks into a smile an instant before he lunges off the couch.

I squeal, trying to run before strong arms wrap around my middle and yank me back to a hard chest. Then he drops us both back so we're sitting on the couch, pinning me to him.

"Let me go." I struggle, trying to keep the laugh out of my voice.

"No."

"Gage!" I squeal as Buddy sticks her face in mine, licking. My arms are pinned at my sides, and I'm unable to stop her, so I just thrash back and forth, gagging. "It stinks!"

Gage chuckles. "What was that? Sorry, I can't hear you over the ringing in my head."

"I didn't hit you that hard."

"Huh?"

I fight Gage's iron grip, but he's relentless. He keeps me

pinned against his body without an inch of wiggle space, and soon, I'm panting and out of breath, trying to keep Buddy away with my feet.

"Get her, Buddy." Gage leans me down, right into her face.

"Stop!" I see the mouth of unending bad breath descend.

"You going to read to me?"

"Yes! Yes, just let me go!" I'll say whatever I need to just get away.

Gage hauls me up effortlessly. "See? How hard was that?"

"Now let me go."

There's a second where he doesn't. A second where I feel how hard he is under my ass. A second where I realize he could do whatever he wanted with me.

Then, Gage releases me, and I scramble up and away from him. Gage arches an eyebrow and smirks.

I have an odd moment of relief, embarrassment, and... disappointment. Disappointment? What the hell is wrong with me?

"Get to reading." Gage kicks his feet up on the coffee table, grabs the book, and hands it to me.

"I'm under duress," I grump, but I take it.

Gage just grins.

"And I'm not paying you."

He just closes his eyes, that smile still on his face.

I try not to focus on anything besides just reading the words on the page. Soon, I get caught up in the story that I remember so well. Gage sits there quietly, listening with his eyes closed. After a while, I'm not sure if he's gone to sleep; he's so still. But when I pause, he shifts his head in my direction. "Need water?"

"No, I just thought... you were asleep."

"You're the one who sounds tired."

I shrug. There's something about reading that puts me into a trance.

"Do you want to move to the bedroom?"

My stomach drops at the same time my heart leaps. It does

this weird pitter-patter, and I feel like my whole body is racing to catch up.

Gage's voice is gentle. "Just in case you pass out. More comfortable. Stinks less."

He's inviting me to his room. At night. For sleeping. And anything else.

So, I'm not reading into this. This was a date. My emotions tangle, but above all that, I feel a thrill of excitement.

"I, uh..."

The silence stretches on so long it gets uncomfortable, but I'm frozen. I'm not sure what I want to do. I think... I might want to go, but I'm also scared.

Gage stands up. "You got me, I lied. I just don't want to carry you to your room after you pass out in here. Don't want you drooling on my shoulder." He fake shudders.

He's joking, but I catch the tension around his eyes, and I hate it. I want that happiness back. But he's inviting me to his room. After Max...

"I don't uh... I can't share a room with anyone." As I say it, fear washes over me. I feel a hole get bigger in my chest, and it aches. That ache is mixed with a fucking insane desire for him to understand.

Instead of pressing, Gage just nods. But not before I see a flash of hurt on his face.

Fuck. *Fuck, fuck, fuck.*

"Plus, I'm pretty sure your pillows hate me." I try to smile. "Don't think I could show my face there anymore."

Gage laughs, breaking the tension. "You? I'm pretty sure they've filed a formal complaint against me. I've been sleeping with them at the end of my bed. Can't look at them."

"Oh yeah, you'll be paying for their therapy for the rest of your life." I laugh and follow Gage as he gets up. We both walk back to our rooms, and I tense, waiting for him to pressure me. Instead, Gage just tips his head at me. "You read pretty well today. I won't be exacting any fines. I'm a lenient master."

"You ass." I shove at him, and he just smiles gently.

"Hey, Raven?"

I stop. I shouldn't have turned him down. My whole body is riled up from where he touched me. He's hot and kind, and why the hell did I turn him down?

"You have the prettiest voice I've ever heard."

Then he disappears into his room and shuts the door.

CHAPTER SIXTY-FOUR

GAGE

The next morning, neither of us says anything about last night. Even though it threw my world upside down. I need more of her. More... everything. Now that I've seen what makes her happy, I want to do it for the rest of forever.

Raven trusted me with a boundary last night, and my chest feels tight. I feel honored. I want her to know I'll guard that boundary with my life. Even if it means I never get to share a room with her. Which hurts like a bitch, but that hurt doesn't even compare with the feeling of making Raven feel safe. Earning and keeping her trust will be my highest honor.

But at the same time, I'm scared. I don't want to hurt her. But that doesn't mean I won't. I'm human, and I probably will at some point. Raven doesn't need promises. She needs action.

So when she comes into the kitchen for breakfast, I motion

at a bowl of yogurt and berries I've prepped for her. She moves to it, staying in the kitchen. We've taken to eating in here. I'm not sure what the smell is, and sometimes it's worse, but it's definitely bad in the dining room and living room. I cracked a window, but I heard Raven's teeth clattering and immediately shut it. She hasn't gained enough weight for that yet. I'm going to get a professional cleaner to come in, but in the meantime, we'll eat in the kitchen.

"Sleep well?" I ask.

Raven makes an 'mhmm' sound, the spoon clinking in the bowl.

I swallow, nerves filling me.

I'm going to ask Raven on a date. Another date. A real date. And this time, I won't chicken out, and I'll actually call it what it is. And even as I think it, my mouth dries up.

Oh god. I can't do this. My heart races like I'm about to get in a fight.

"Raven?"

"Hmmm?"

"Go out with me?" The words rush out of me, and I clear my throat. "I mean, will you? Tonight. On a date."

The clinking stops.

Oh my god. I feel sick to my stomach. Why the hell did I go so aggressively? First thing in the morning, and I couldn't even let her wake up.

I almost offer to pay her.

I'm opening my mouth when she says, "Uh... shouldn't I be asking?"

I freeze. "What?"

"I mean, I'll be driving. So technically, *I'd* be the one taking *you* on a date." The bowl scrapes across the counter.

Oh my god. She's not turning me down. She's making a joke. Relief hits me so hard that I think I'm going to pass out.

Then, there's a laugh from the hall, and I stiffen. It's Axel.

"Shut up, Axel." Suddenly, Raven is there in front of me,

patting my arm. "Of course, I'll take you on a date. Where to, princess?"

"Tom's Steakhouse." My brain hasn't caught up with my mouth because it's taking me a whole two extra seconds to realize that she said yes. She said yes.

I catch a snicker, and then Raven brushes past me, and I sense her leaving the kitchen. There's a muffled 'ow' from my brother, and then her footsteps disappear down the hall.

Yes. She said yes.

Elation pulses through me like helium, and I'm pretty sure I'm going to lift off the ground. I don't think I'll ever come down.

It takes me some time to realize that Axel hasn't moved. He's still standing there, and then, with a flicker of movement, he's gone.

CHAPTER SIXTY-FIVE

AXEL

I never thought sadness and pride and jealousy could mix together until right fucking now.

Gage is happy. I can hear it in his voice. And not just the happiness he gets from winning an argument. This seems real. Peaceful. Like he's in love.

Awww. It's so cute I could puke.

I stalk back to my bedroom, shutting the door. I never thought I could feel such blinding jealousy.

Gage has always had everything I want.

Suddenly, my chest is tight, and it feels like my heart is going to beat out of it. Pain lances through me, making me catch my breath as I bend over.

I'll never know what it's like to feel love like that.

It's hard to catch a breath.

I'll never know love like that because I'm literally unable to put down the act. I winked at Raven in the hallway—winked—and I'm not even sure why I did it. Maybe I didn't want her to see the pain on my face as she passed.

I've gotta get out of here. It's too painful to keep watching these two have something that I want.

I spin around, thinking about grabbing my things, but everything here is Gage's.

Right. 'Cause I didn't belong here in the first place. I forced my way in like I do with everything in my life.

This is what I get. I deserve this.

Even as I nod to myself, the pain in my chest remains.

I'll go. Disappear. Start my life over where no one knows me as 'the player,' and maybe down the road, I can change. Find some inkling of the same thing that Gage and Raven have.

My body physically reacts to the thought of leaving the two of them, rooting me to the spot. I fucking love my brother, even though sometimes, I fucking hate him. And Raven... I'm obsessed. I want to harness some of the strength she has and learn how to have it myself.

One more day. I just want one more day.

No.

I can't watch them on their little date as they fall in love. My stomach twists at the thought.

I want that to be me.

Maybe it can be. A voice whispers.

No. It can't.

One time. Just once. Then you can leave and never see them again.

What in the fuck? How can that be possible?

Switch places with Gage.

Fuck. My stomach twists as the thought takes root. That's horrible. It would be so wrong. Plus, he'd never allow that. I shake my head, moving toward the door.

He doesn't have to allow it. You're identical. Figure out a way to get him out of the house. Tell him Mom's hurt, and he has to go right away.

No! I hit my hands against my head, even as the plan sinks its claws into my chest.

Take it. Take one night where you feel love. Then you can disappear, and they'll move on with their happy little lives.

I fight with the thought, pacing back and forth, back and forth.

No, I won't.

Yes, I will.

Fuck! I rip at my hair. But the longer I think about it, the more I know I won't be able to resist.

I can't stop myself. I'll take one date. One time where I feel something other than hatred. And then I'll go.

CHAPTER SIXTY-SIX

RAVEN

What the hell is taking Gage so long?

I glance out the window. Gage told me he'd be out in a second and to get the car started, and that was, like, five minutes ago.

I shift, feeling stupid in my ripped jeans and jean jacket. The only nice clothes I have are my work clothes, and he's already seen me in them. Does it matter? It doesn't matter. I wish I had perfume to wear so he could tell I at least put some effort into it.

I wasn't going to agree, even though deep down, I wanted to. I wanted to blush and jump up and down and act all stupid. But then, I saw Axel standing in the hallway.

Plus, I can always pull out. When this contract is done, I'm gone. I'll start my life fresh. What's keeping me from at least enjoying while I'm here? He can't hurt me if I leave soon anyway.

The thoughts should be comforting. But for some reason, I feel all shifty, like I can't get comfortable.

Finally, Gage steps out of the house, tucking a teal shirt into his pressed slacks. At first, I think he has the glasses, but then I see they're the old pair. He moves around to the passenger side, shooting me a small smile. "Sorry about that."

I arch an eyebrow. "That'll cost you."

Gage blinks, then laughs softly. "Damn. Bleeding me dry over here."

The words are said jokingly, but I can't help but wince. I've seen the amount of money he gives me every day. It's more than I've ever seen in my life. And a tiny part of me feels bad.

No. I deserve this.

As we pull out of the driveway, Gage's fist is clenched on his thigh again. But as we drive, it loosens up until he's leaning back in his seat, fully relaxed.

When we get there, I dart out of my seat before he can get the door. But this time, Gage just waits for me on his side, arm held out with eyebrow raised.

"No knight in shining armor today?" I grab his arm and walk him up to the doors.

Gage stares at me for a second, then a smile crosses his face. "You're quite the gentleman for both of us."

I can't keep the small laugh out of my tone. "Gentleman is a step down from knight. I suppose I'll have to try harder."

He pats my hand. "We don't all start off perfect."

The place is fancy. Not suit and tie, but still fancy with muted lighting, slow classical music, and a wait to be seated. Suddenly, I feel extremely out of place in my old clothes and unstyled hair.

Then, Gage pulls me toward the hostess, who seats us in the back, away from other people. It's a booth table, and I slide into the bench. I'm grateful to have something solid at my back so I don't feel like people are staring at me. Gage slides in beside me, which only makes my heart pound more. I'm so out of my element right now.

"Raven?" Gage asks.

I blink. The hostess is staring at me expectantly. Oh. Drinks.

"Just water is fine. Thank you."

She smiles at us and disappears.

"You okay?"

I clear my throat. "Oh, yeah. Fine." My voice sounds a little off, and I pray he doesn't call me out on it.

Gage just nods. He's so big that he takes up almost all the space on the bench. It feels weird not to have him seated across from me. If I want to see him, I have to crane my neck to the side.

"I can move," I offer. Maybe bench seats are always his.

"No." I sense his arm sliding across the back of the bench, although he doesn't touch me.

I squirm. This feels different than the bookstore. I'm not sure what I'm supposed to be doing.

"Oh, you didn't know? You're going to be feeding me like a baby bird."

I snap my gaze over to him.

There's the tiniest arch of his eyebrow and twitch of the corner of his mouth.

"You're so stupid." I shake my head, turning back to see that the lady has returned with our drinks. She slides a pink, fruity-looking drink Gage's way and a water mine. As soon as she leaves, Gage switches our drinks.

"I didn't order—"

"A sword. For the lady knight." He waves his hand at the drink, where a garnish of fruit is speared by a tiny, fluorescent pink plastic sword.

I feel my defenses crumble. Jesus. Can he be at least a little less thoughtful so I can keep him at arm's length?

"Hmmm. What do I want to eat?" Gage grabs a menu and opens it. Only he's holding it upside down.

Gently, I pull it from his hands and flip it over.

He gasps in minor outrage. "You trying to make me look stupid?"

"No, just—"

He tries to flip it again, and I take it. "This is the right way, I promise."

"What are you getting?"

I look at the menu for the first time. I see steaks and pasta bowls and fish, and fuck, my mouth starts watering.

And then I see the prices.

Fuck.

I hastily scan the menu, trying to find the cheapest option and pretending like I just can't decide.

"You?"

"I always get the steak dinner meal." Gage leans back. "Axel always gets the pizza."

The prices on both are more than I could ever imagine paying for food. Jesus Christ. Finally, I scan to the bottom and find something that's at least a little more reasonable.

"You come here with Axel?" I ask, a little surprised. I thought they hated each other.

"When Mom forces us to on birthdays." Gage shakes his head, then settles into a thoughtful silence.

I couldn't imagine what it would be like to hate my brother. Or to have Axel as a brother. I always wanted siblings growing up, but I guess not like this.

When the hostess returns, Gage orders a steak, and I ask for the grilled cheese. After she leaves, Gage turns to me. "I fucking love grilled cheese."

It looks weird to see Gage, all pressed shirt and styled hair, completely comfortable in this environment, cussing like that.

"Me too."

"We used to make fancy grilled cheese when times were tight." Gage leans back in his seat, exposing his strong torso.

Jesus. I've never seen him work out. How the hell does he look like this?

I'm entirely grateful he can't see me ogling him 'cause I snap my gaze up to his. His eyes are locked on mine. Oh shit. Maybe he can see it.

"Fancy grilled cheese?" I manage to say.

"Yep. You caramelize onions and butter both sides of the bread with bacon fat before frying."

My mouth waters at the thought.

"If you had bacon fat. Sometimes, we just used margarine."

"You know the best kind of struggle meal is cinnamon sugar toast," I say.

"Oh my god!" Gage's eyes light up, and he sits up straight. "The best!"

We fall into easy conversation after that. Occasionally, Gage's hand slides down to brush my back. It makes me shiver every time, and the wild part of me wishes he'd touch me more.

But he doesn't. By the end of the night, I'm twitching with all the small touches. I wish I'd had a glass of wine with my meal to relax my body's reaction to Gage, but I didn't, and now I'm stuck feeling his touch like a live wire to my skin. It makes me hot and flushed and fucking turned on.

I'm not sure if Gage feels the same way. He's his normal stoic self, although he laughs a lot more than he ever did.

When we get through with the meal, Gage grabs the bill faster than I thought he could. I hesitate, expecting a joke about how he's paying me to be here.

But it never comes.

When we walk back out to the car in the cold wind, Gage pushes me to the driver's side and opens the door. Then he pulls something out of his pocket. "You forgot something, m'lady." It's the sword.

I laugh, taking it.

"A true warrior never leaves her weapon behind. You could skewer an eyeball or testicles with this."

My face twists. "Get in. Your lady is getting cold."

Gage's face changes, a dark smile creeping across his face. "I'll warm her up."

I'm caught up in that smile for a second, imagining what he'd do to warm me up, all the places he'd put his body, until another burst of icy wind comes in.

I poke his stomach with the sword. "Get in already."

Gage laughs, moving around the car. When he settles in, an energy fills the car. It's a loaded silence.

What is he thinking? Is he just as turned on as I am, or am I misreading the situation?

I jump as Gage's hand settles on my thigh. His thumb strokes up and down on my jeans, brushing the part with a rip. Every time I feel his skin on mine, it's like fire. Okay, so not misreading.

When we get back to the house, I'm barely breathing. I stop in the driveway, but Gage doesn't take his hand off my thigh. I sit there, unsure of what to do, until Gage turns toward me. My gaze locks on his lips, which he licks.

"Raven."

I suck in a breath.

"You know you can tell me no at any point, right?" His gaze is firm, gentle, and full of restrained power.

"Yes," I can barely get the word out.

"And you know that I'll listen, right?"

I can barely nod.

"Words, Raven."

"Yes."

"Good." His hand leaves my thigh for a second, then it's back, and he's closing something into my fist. It's the sword.

"Slice my nuts off if you must."

Then his lips crash down on mine, and suddenly, I'm wrapped in *him*. His scent, his strength, and his desire. He kisses me like he's been wanting to all night. Like it's something he needs desperately.

Suddenly, he's gone. I'm gasping for air before I realize he's on my side of the car, unstrapping me and lifting me out.

"Gage!" I gasp in surprise.

"You've impaled me with your lancet!" Gage holds me closer, and I realize I accidentally stuck him in the chest. I laugh as he walks us to the door.

We reach the steps, and I wonder if Gage can see them.

"Don't drop me." I struggle to see where we're going.

Gage stumbles a step, and I half-scream. He snatches me back up to his chest. "Whoops." But there's a smirk in his voice.

"That... You're a dick!" I shove his chest.

"So you've said."

As soon as we're inside, Buddy yips in excitement. Gage puts me down, only to press his body into mine, smashing me against the wall, bending down to kiss me. It makes heat surge to my pussy.

He wants me. I want him. What's one little fuck? It won't hurt anything.

So I kiss him back, nipping at his lips and chasing him with a desperate energy.

Gage groans. The delicious kind of groan that I love. It's a plea for more. A needy little sound.

Then, he's dragging me toward the bedroom. I don't put up a fight until I remember something that lights a spark of adrenaline.

"What about Axel?"

Gage slows. There's a weird look on his face before it disappears. "What about him?"

"What if he's... here?" I look around, but the house seems quiet.

Gage stops fully. "He won't do anything. If that's what you're wondering."

I'm not sure what I'm wondering. Is he here? Will he hear us? Would he beat his dick like he did while we were on the couch?

For some reason, my pussy pulses at the thought. Then, I shake my head. Why do I care?

"Let's go." I move toward the bedroom, thinking we're going to go to Gage's, but then he pulls me toward the spare room I've been staying in.

"You're the one who took me on the date," Gage says, a teasing arch to his eyebrows. He looks so different like this. Not the stuffed-up Gage I first met. Actually, he's a lot more like Axel. I'm not sure how that makes me feel.

"You're right. Time to give up your holes as payment." I motion at the doorway with my sword.

I expect a teasing response, but Gage's pupils grow. He takes a step closer, his voice going low and husky. "Yeah?"

Suddenly, I imagine what Gage would look like tied to the bed, spread out for me to do whatever I wanted to. Or on his knees so I could straddle his face and make him eat me until I came.

I feel myself grow wet, and I shove Gage into the room. "Take your clothes off."

Gage does, stripping out of his shirt so quickly I would have missed it if I blinked. Then his pants go, and I'm staring at his gloriously naked body. I realize I've never seen him fully naked. But he is, in fact, hot as hell, and his dick is already hard.

Then he's stalking toward me, grasping my arms and lifting me up effortlessly.

I squeak, and then Gage throws me on the bed. I just have a chance to scramble up before he's there, pulling down my pants. All kinds of thoughts rush through me: lust, anticipation, fear, condoms.

"Just a taste. Please?" There's a desperate look in Gage's eyes. The desperation makes me feel hot all over.

"You can ask nicer than that."

There's a moment where Gage just watches me, and his gaze softens. "Please. I'll... I'll do anything."

"Anything?"

He swallows, and his Adam's apple bobs. "I just, I want to… to make you…"

I watch him struggle. It gives me a rush all the way up my body. I grab his hair, pulling his head down to my crotch. "Make me feel good."

That's all the permission he needs. Gage pulls my pants the rest of the way down and off before diving back down, spreading my thighs with his massive hands. I brace myself for the aggressive assault, yanking his hair up and away from me. Gage listens, slowing his movements, then his hot tongue meets my pussy in a slow, sensual lick. He lets out a sound that's a mix between a rush of air and a moan that makes my clit tingle. I loosen my grip, and Gage immediately drops his head, moving his hands up to spread me open. Then, his tongue is there, hot and firm, stroking my clit in small circles.

The sensation that hits me is immediate. I'm already turned on, and this is like a shock to the system. I arch into him, but Gage just lays one heavy arm across my waist and pins me down. In response, I yank his hair again.

He glances up at me once, but he doesn't stop tonguing my clit or holding me. The eye contact shoots a bolt down my spine. He looks like he's looking into my soul. The look is passionate and hungry, and… affectionate.

I suck in a breath and look away, the eye contact too intense. This is just a hookup. Just a hookup, Raven.

Then, Gage moves his other hand down, and I feel his fingers against my opening, pressing in slightly.

"Fuck." I arch my back, waiting for him to push them in. Only he just lets them sit just inside me, not going any further.

"More," I gasp.

When he doesn't do anything, I look down, and there's a teasing look in his eye.

"Gage," I growl.

He pulls away from me for a second. "As you wish." Then his

fingers press into me and brush against my G-spot. Sparks flash across my vision, and I squeeze my eyes shut.

He presses into me and eats, getting me so close to my orgasm. Every time I'm almost there, he backs off just the slightest bit. After the third time, I realize he's doing it on purpose.

I sit up. "Get up here."

Gage looks up at me, his gaze hazy.

I pat the bed beside me. "Hurry."

Gage hesitates but does as I ask.

"Flip," I demand, so he's lying on his back. His eyes widen as he realizes I'm about to straddle his face. Then, I settle down on his tongue, and he lets out a vibrating groan. I lean into it, feeling the groan get me right up to the edge of an orgasm again.

I lean forward toward where his dick is hard and throbbing against his stomach. "Were you being a tease?"

Gage can't answer 'cause I'm on his mouth, but then I grab his dick, and he grunts. He stiffens in my hold, hot and throbbing.

"Couldn't be you, right?" I stroke him up and down, smirking at the way his dick jumps in my hand.

Then Gage attacks my clit harder, sucking on it and pulsing his mouth. I hiss, frozen in pleasure for a second.

No. I renew my efforts on his dick, stroking it up and down, cupping my hand over the tip, and spitting on it. Then, I take him into my mouth.

Gage's whole body locks up, and his mouth freezes on me.

I let go of him with a pop. "I'll teach you to edge me."

I set to do just that. I suck Gage with a fervor I've never sucked before, enjoying every slight movement that he gives. Every sound, every gasp for air around my pussy. I hold myself over his face longer and longer, cutting off his air while I stroke his dick with my mouth. Every time I feel his balls draw up, I back away.

After the third time, Gage is sputtering.

"Please," he says, but it's muffled.

I snort. Please is so uncreative. Boring, almost. I just tickle my finger down the underside of his shaft, feeling goosebumps perk up on his thighs.

"Make me come, and this wouldn't have to happen."

Then he brings all his attention to my clit, licking and sucking it until I'm right at the edge, shivering. Then, with one powerful pulse of his mouth, I fall over the edge, coming on his face.

Gage groans into me, vibrating my orgasm higher, longer. I shake with pleasure, exploding on his tongue, stomach clenching in waves.

Finally, when I come down, I pant onto his dick, which is throbbing in my hand. When I stroke him, Gage whimpers, "Raven, please," he pants.

"Please?" I'm still trying to catch my breath.

"Fuck, I—fuck!" His voice changes as I stroke all the way to his tip.

I place my lips on him. "Hmmm."

His hips shift. "I'm gonna..."

"What? You're gonna come?" Immediately, I freeze all of my movements. Gage groans, body trembling.

"You haven't gotten permission yet."

His plea is immediate. "Please. I need to."

I lean down to breathe on his dick, hoping it's enough to keep him right on the edge.

"Oh god," his fingers are in my thighs, and they're digging in. I shiver with the bite of pain.

"Don't move. If you move, I won't let you come."

I wait for him to acknowledge what I said. I hear blankets rustle and feel him nodding against my pussy. Then, I drop my mouth onto his dick and hold it steady.

Gage jerks the tiniest bit, then stays still, just like I asked. I wait for him to move. To shove up into me and take what he wants from my mouth. But he doesn't. He obeys with a fine trembling in his thighs.

I suck as a reward, holding suction and massaging my tongue along him.

"Oh fuck, oh my god, fuck, fuck, fuck, I'm going to come." There's a constant stream of words behind me, but I ignore them. I just wait for the throbbing to pass, then slowly move my head up and down. It's too slow, and I know it. Again, I wait for Gage to disobey.

He doesn't. He holds still just like I asked, even though I feel he's a stroke or two away from coming, his balls up tight.

I feel like I'm going to come myself, reveling in Gage's restraint.

Then, I let loose. I suck him, running my mouth up and down his dick. I feel the throb and keep going.

With a shout, Gage comes in my mouth. I suck his cum down, pulsing my mouth around him. His hips make little jerks, but he holds himself still.

When I pop off his dick, both of us are panting. The only sounds in the quiet room are our breaths. Then, I crawl off Gage. For a brief moment, I want to lie next to him. Snuggle up, close my eyes, and just soak in the feeling.

Then I remember that this is just temporary. I remember how much it'll hurt later if I do that.

But I want to. I want to so badly I can feel it like a pressure in my chest.

What will it hurt?

But if I stay here, I'll fall asleep, and I absolutely cannot fall asleep next to Gage. So, in a motion that makes physical pain fill my chest, I slip off the bed, grabbing my clothes.

"Raven?"

I make a noise.

Gage rolls to his side. He looks handsome and sated, and he is stunning lying there. Curse him.

"You good?"

"Yep." I hold my shirt to my chest. "Just, uh… gotta pee. You know. UTI." Then I walk to the bathroom.

The little moment of hurt in his eyes is almost enough to get me to go back. To crawl into bed with him and lay there until we both fall asleep.

Almost.

It'll be easier this way in the long run.

CHAPTER SIXTY-SEVEN

AXEL

I've never hated myself more for not sticking to the goddamn plan.

I didn't take Gage's date. In fact, I left the house before they finished getting ready.

And that's where I found the letter. It was a plain white letter addressed to Celeste, slipped into the crack of the door.

Celeste,
I know your feelings may have changed, but mine haven't, and you haven't given me a chance to explain.
I just wanted love. You got so distant. You wouldn't hug me, kiss me, or hold my hand. I know you told me

not to do it, but that was just my way to feel intimacy. I fucked you because I cared, and I wasn't going to let anything ruin us.

I miss you. Please. We can still fix this. A rebound is not the option. It means nothing.

Come home. I love you,

Max

I crumple the letter in my fist. The first time I read it, I could barely focus through the rage. Rich would come get me when he felt lonely. After, he would stroke my hair and tell me what a good son I was. About how he loved me. Then, he'd leave again until he needed his next fix.

But I felt lonely, too. And I was the most lonely when he was there.

And Max did that to Raven.

I'm standing outside his house. The idiot left a return address on it. So I called Dave up, offered him a promotion, and asked him to drive me to Raven's old town. I had him drop me off a few blocks away, then told him to go.

Kill, kill, kill.

The hatred is boiling over in my chest. I don't think I've felt more angry and helpless and fucking reckless. But someone else made Raven feel like this, too, and I absolutely won't let that slide.

I drop the bag I brought in the front yard, lift the pink aluminum bat over my shoulder, and stride to the front door.

Knock knock, motherfucker.

CHAPTER SIXTY-EIGHT

AXEL

"Who the fuck are you?" Max scrambles back into his living room, which is lit by the glow of the TV. The dim light makes it harder for me to see. That's good. Every kill is a ten out of ten if you can't see it exactly.

"You're shorter than I thought you'd be." I stalk after Max. Short and bald. Jesus, Raven. Swinging way below your caliber.

"Get the fuck out of my house!" He shuffles in his pocket for his phone, I presume.

"Hmm," I muse. "How about no? Is that a word you understand?" I yank down my mask, a black piece that goes over my nose and mouth.

"What the—back off!" Max backs into the kitchen, hiding behind the island.

He's a coward, but I didn't expect anything less.

"Do I need to spell it out for you? N - O. Nope. Hell nah." I tap the bat in my palm, enjoying the thrill of power that Max's cowering gives me. He's a lot like Rich—brave until there's someone bigger in the room. And I am bigger. A hell of a lot bigger. I almost feel bad.

"It's your turn, Max."

To his credit, he grabs something off the island and hurls it at me. It hits my chest with a thud that pounds through my chest cavity. I glance down. An apple.

Slowly, a grin traces across my face. Damn. If I weren't damn near blind, I could have hit that sucker right back at him with the bat.

I shrug, flipping the bat, praying I catch it and make it look cool.

I do.

Laughing, I stalk around the island.

"Fire!" Max yells, trying to dart to the living room where the open front door stands. "Someone help, fire!"

Oh, hell no. I spring after him, catching up right before he gets outside. Yanking him back by the collar, I slam the door shut.

Max scrambles to run the other way, but I've had enough. I slam the bat down into his moving form and make contact, the shock vibrating all the way up my hand and into my bones.

Max screams, and I groan, the sound and the pain jarring my brain up to a buzz. It feels like the first time I kidnapped Raven, only better this time. 'Cause she's not scared. Only he is.

He's still on his feet, stumbling away.

Damn. I need better form. I'll ask Raven to give me pointers.

With a pang of sadness, I realize I'm leaving. Immediately, that sadness hardens into anger.

"Come back here, you fuck." I chase after his form, raising the bat above my head. It hits the ceiling with a crack.

"Fuck," I hiss, using all of my strength to whip the bat down into Max's form. It connects, sending the jolt of impact up both my arms. Both of us groan, and Max goes down.

"Don't understand no, huh?" I pant, stepping over Max's body. In the lighting, I can't quite see what damage has been done. I imagine it though. In my head, he has a nice dent in that bald head of his. Blood is splattered across his face where there's fear there. The same fear he made Raven feel. The same fear Rich made me feel.

I swing the bat again, and this time, there's a wet crunch. I know there's blood now.

I grin. I'm in control now.

Max hacks, and there's a splattering sound.

"Not so big anymore, huh?" I step over where his legs are, then stomp down, aiming for his knee. I must not hit it 'cause my foot rolls off muscle. Still, he gives a satisfying scream.

"Too bad she's not here to see you like this." I wish she were here. I wish with every fiber in my body that she were here.

Then, I shake myself out of it. She's busy with Gage. On a *date*.

Everything feels hot. I swing the bat again. This time, it hits him and then glides off and hits the floor with a loud crack.

Fucking hell.

I swing again. And again. And again, until I'm lost in the motion of it. Over and over and over until my arms are numb. At one point, I hear Rich's entitled laugh, and I swing harder and harder. It's not until the bat bounces back and almost hits me that I come back to the present.

It's quiet, other than the hum of the TV and the haggard sucking of my breath. There's an ad on TV. I recognize it. It's an ad we're running for Newman's to try and expand.

Suddenly, I'm full of shame. I treated Raven like shit.

I raise the bat again, laying into Max. Or, what's left of him. The soft, wet thuds are way more neutral than they should be. And I realize I'm wet.

No, not wet. Bloody.

I suck in a few more breaths. This probably looks like a murder scene. Well, it kinda is.

Gage is gonna kill me.

Gage. On a date with Raven.

Good. Let him kill me.

I rack my brain to remember if I touched anything. Left any evidence.

I did. The door handle. Striding over to it, I swing the bat into it. The aluminum clinks off the metal. I hit it again and again and again until it cracks off. Grabbing both pieces, I stalk out of the house into the cold night air.

This should have made me feel better. I want to feel better.

So why do I feel... empty?

Raven should have been here. I did this for her, and she'll never know.

I yank my mask back up, standing on the front porch for a minute, just breathing in the air through the mask. It smells... coppery.

I don't feel bad. At all. Raven deserved to have someone wipe this shitstain from the earth.

But I wish she knew.

I grab my bag and go back inside. Stripping out of the bloody clothes I was wearing, I change into clean ones. I use the mask to wipe the blood from my bat. I sent Dave home after he dropped me off. I'll walk as far as I can go and then hitch a ride home.

The walk serves to numb me beautifully. Somewhere, some trucker picks me up and drops me off at the edge of Hollows Grove. It's a long walk back to my place, but also short at the same time. All I can think about is Raven.

When I'm back home, I light my clothes on fire in the bath-tub, which sets the fire alarm off. Once I get that calmed down, I shower, scrubbing every last fleck of blood off me and down the drain. Then, I fill the tub with water and bleach, throw the bat into it, and let it sit. As I stare at the bat, I feel a wash of overwhelming exhaustion. The hatred is gone for the first time in... forever. My chest feels empty. Numb. Fuzzy.

It's a weird feeling. I must just be too exhausted to feel anything.

I need to go. To go start another life before I kidnap Raven again and go down a path that there's truly no coming back from.

Before I go, I need to drop Raven's bat off with her again. Kinda a sentimental touch. It's her security, and I don't mean to take it from her.

Or maybe I can buy her a new one.

I will. Tomorrow.

For now, I crawl into the same bed I tied Raven to, imagining I can still smell her scent. And then I drift off.

The next morning, my arms hurt. I search for that hatred, that ever-present rage. But it's not there. Or if it is, it's lurking somewhere in the background.

Fuck. I should have started killing creeps a lot sooner.

The bat is still in the tub, and I fish it out of the cold water. I don't want to buy her another. I want her to have this one. It's a trophy. She deserves to have the trophy. Now that it's clear of DNA, it won't get her in any trouble. Maybe I can ask Gage?

No. I most definitely cannot ask Gage. I'm supposed to be leaving.

Jesus. I don't want to go. Where will I go? Everything I know is here. But staying here and watching Gage and Raven?

Nope. I'd go to prison. For sure, no questions asked. I'd force Raven to live with me, and this time, I wouldn't let her go. Because Gage makes her happy, he could stay. As long as he doesn't try to keep her from me.

Sharing?

I turn the idea around in my head.

Raven is happy with Gage. They can be sweet and insufferable together. But she's not all sweetness. She has a nasty side to her that wants out. I just know it. And that side is for me.

Nope. Dangerous thoughts. Not for me, but for her.

I'll just drop the bat off and figure it out from there. Just one step at a time. Mom drives me to Gage's house, and the drive goes by in a blur. I think she's talking to me, telling me about how Rich has gone hunting, and it's nice to have the house to herself. Then, we're there.

"Are you okay?" Mom asks quietly.

I blink. No. I'm not okay. The woman I can't keep my thoughts away from hates me, and rightfully so. But instead of saying that, I turn and give Mom the same look she used to give us when we'd ask her the same thing as kids. "I'm okay. Just tired."

For a second, I think Mom is going to call me on my bullshit. Surely she knows I'm lying to her. She used to do the same to me.

But instead, she just says, "Okay. Tell Raven I said hi."

I won't be doing anything of the sort. But I step out of the car, saying, "Love you."

I wait till Mom pulls away. I can't go in the front door. I'll snatch her up if I see her.

So I go to the back door, slip the bat inside, then step away. That step feels like I'm ripping velcro away. It feels wrong.

Fuck. I force myself to go, and as I do, I sense movement on the porch.

Looking up, I see a massive black raven sitting on the railing, only feet away. I freeze, staring at it. What the hell? Was it there when I walked up? My heart races, and the bird just stares at me with its beady, black eyes. Is this Poe?

I can't move. Fear holds me still. I can't move, or it'll claw my eyes out.

It's gotta be Poe. Poe always hated me, and this one looks like it'd eat my heart out and laugh.

The sliding door opens behind me, and I jump.

"What are you doing?" A voice—Raven—asks.

Poe hops a little, and I jump. "Shhh."

"What are you—oh shit." I hear her step outside.

"Don't—"

She closes the door.

"What are you doing?" I hiss.

"Looking. What are you doing?"

I swallow. At any minute, Poe will have had enough and will come swooping at either of our faces. I inch to angle in front of Raven.

"I'm waiting for it to go so I can leave," I grit.

Raven is silent for a second. "Are you... scared of it?"

"No," I spit, but Poe ruffles her feathers and cocks her head. I freeze.

"Oookay," Raven drags out the word.

"What are you doing?" I swallow. Why the fuck isn't she scared of an animal that's clearly bigger than her head and can move fast as fuck?

"Other than discovering you have ornithophobia, I'm getting some air."

"Arith—whatever. Why aren't you sucking loverboy's air?" I can't keep the bitterness out of my tone.

She says nothing. I risk a glance back at her, and her lips are tight. And fuck, she's just as beautiful as I remembered.

But she looks pissed with a sort of haunted look. Like she's been fighting.

"Are you fighting? Again?" Jesus, these two need a fucking therapist on standby.

"No!"

I angle so I can see her while still keeping Poe in my periphery. "Then why are you hiding?"

"I'm not hiding."

I snort the tiniest bit, and it makes the bird jump. It hops down the railing, and I back up, getting in front of Raven again.

"It's not going to hurt you." Raven steps out around me, and I grab at her, but she just shakes off my hold. "Ravens are smart. If it wanted to hurt you, it would have done it already."

"That does not help."

She just laughs.

"This is Poe. Gage raised it." I glare at the animal that has followed me like a specter throughout my childhood.

"What?" She turns to me sharply, making the bird jump again. She asks again in a quieter tone, "What?"

I just raise my eyebrows at her. "Gage is basically a grouchy Snow White. He used to help all kinds of animals when we were growing up. Nursed them back to health. You know, stupid princess shit."

Raven's eyes are suspicious at first, narrowed at me. Like I would make up a lie to make her like my brother more.

Although, he's the only person I'd ever lie for.

"Yep, he's practically perfect." I wave my hand lightly at her in a shooing motion. "Go back in there and live your happily ever after."

Because I'm thinking about how easy it would be to throw her over my shoulder again, and the longer I'm with her, the harder it is to remember why that's a bad idea.

"He's sweet." Raven says it like it's a bad thing. And damn, I can't help but latch onto that. Is that a bad thing?

"That's not what you wanted?" I keep my voice blank.

Raven doesn't respond for a long time. I think I see the panic warring in her eyes.

Fuck. Satan is really testing me right now. Why the hell did I have this change of heart?

Oh yeah. 'Cause I can't fucking stand myself.

I grind my teeth. "Gage is nice. Disgustingly nice. He'll take care of you."

"Are you being sarcastic?"

I grind my teeth harder. "No."

She considers that for a long moment, dark hair tossing in the wind. Then, she raises her head. "Well, it doesn't matter anyway. I'm leaving."

For a second, I don't register what she's saying. Then, her

words sink in. She's... leaving? What the hell does she mean she's leaving? Gage will be heartbroken. Again.

I open my mouth to lay into her, then stop. Raven's just like me. No amount of railing at her will get her to change her mind. In fact, it'll only make it worse.

"You can't tell me not to. You guys kidnapped me."

I drone, "Don't give the credit to my brother; that was all me."

"Well, I can't stay. Max knows what town I'm in."

He knows a whole lot more than that. Well, knew. Suddenly, my mood improves.

"I just... I can't..." Raven's words trail off.

"Are you trying to convince you or me?"

"Fuck you."

Automatically, I say, "If you're offering."

Suddenly, Raven turns on me, shoving me back.

Instinctually, I whirl on her, grabbing her upper arms and pushing her back into the glass. Maybe it's my imagination, but I catch a whiff of Gage's cinnamon on her. All the pent-up adrenaline and wanting and longing are too far gone, and I lean into her, heaving for breath. "If you think watching you with my brother hasn't been the biggest form of torture... If you think I'm not a hair's breadth away from taking you with me and making you hate me for the rest of your life," I shake her a little, "You're sorely mistaken."

I force myself away from her, sucking in breath after breath. I expect her to be afraid. To be frozen like she was on the bed. Only this time, Raven's pupils are blown, and her chest is heaving.

"How... fucking dare you!"

She comes at me again, and this time, I snap my hand up to her throat, pinning her again. "Was I not fucking clear?" Her proximity is seeping into my bones. I want her. I *need* her. I want to see every last emotion on her face as I fuck into her. "I'll do anything I want to you, and you'll like it."

Raven just glares at me, fingers gripping my wrist as if that would stop me. "I don't think you will."

Disbelief and adrenaline fill me. Is she really daring me right now?

Suddenly, there's a prick in my side, and then Raven arches an eyebrow. "You won't do anything because you care too much about what Gage thinks. If he found out you forced me, he'd never forgive you."

I stare into her light eyes, defensive anger raging under my skin. How the hell does she know that? If she can read me that easily, then she'll also know I won't touch her against her will because I know what that feels like.

And that's not something I'm prepared for Raven to know.

Raven smirks, and then the jabbing in my side continues. I glance down, and she jabs one more time before she slips out of my hold.

"What is that?"

Raven waves a small pink needle at me. Only it's not a needle. It's a cocktail sword.

"I need your help." She turns back inside. "You owe me. And you owe Gage." And with that, she disappears inside.

CHAPTER SIXTY-NINE

RAVEN

I'm gambling that my dare will get Axel to come inside, and I'm praying it doesn't. What the hell is wrong with me?

Being around Axel is intoxicating in a dangerous way. He's always one step away from doing something insane, and now that I know he won't do anything that'll piss Gage off, I feel safer. Because he loves Gage. Truly, deep down, he loves his brother.

Also, guilt is eating at me, and the living room smells unbearable. You can smell it in the bedrooms now. Cleaners will never find the source, and Gage doesn't deserve this.

You know who does? Fucking Axel. Infuriating, dickish, hot Axel.

Hot? I hate that I think he's hot. But of course I do. He's handsome in exactly the same way his brother is, only Axel has a hint of danger that I find, against all logic, intoxicating. I know he won't touch me, no matter how much he wants to, and *that* makes heat run through me. Which confirms that I am, in fact, incredibly fucked up. Also, I was just in bed with Gage, and now I'm drooling over his brother? Fuck me.

I grab the spray bottle I've filled with cleaning products and start spritzing the couch before I hear the sliding glass door open.

A mix of elation and fear fills me. Axel comes inside and stands silently behind me. The skin on the back of my neck tingles, but I just say in a bored tone. "I need the curtain rod."

"Where's Gage?"

"Sleeping." At least, I think he is. I didn't check. I wanted to. Wanted to see how he's doing. Find something to make fun of him for.

I can feel the blood tingling through my thighs. That monster is back chasing me. This can only end one way for me: heartbreak. My job is up soon, and even if he likes me, Gage will eventually grow tired of me. I'll become just another hole to use when he feels like it.

I just want to scream at the monster to shut up. To shut the fuck up and let me live in peace.

Axel doesn't move.

"Curtain rod." I motion at it, grabbing a wad of paper towels.

For a second, I think Axel is going to argue with me. Then, he lifts a delicate eyebrow and shakes his head, muttering as he grabs the rod.

"Careful! Don't tip it." I'm sure the shrimp has rotted to a nice juice at this point. Although maybe I could get him to dump it all over himself...

"What the fuck?" Axel hisses as the smell explodes, and I jump to catch the wad of grey goo that falls out of the end of the rod.

I try to hold in a gag. Then Buddy comes jumping at me, trying to lick the end of the rod.

"No!" I try to hold the towels away while I hold Buddy by her collar. She can lunge too close, and I hiss, handing the wadded-up shrimp towels to Axel.

"Fucking—" He grabs at them, but not before they topple to the ground.

I yank Buddy back. "Throw it away! Outside."

Axel looks pale for a second. Then I see the thoughts rolling in and recognize the second he thinks about turning this on me.

Oh god. Instead of scaring me, his challenging look just makes me want to fight harder. I'm going to poke the bear. Because I can. Because he deserves it.

I raise an eyebrow. "You're going to fucking throw it away." I may be shorter than Axel, bending low to hold Buddy, but I still do my best to look down my nose at him.

A mean smirk crosses Axel's face, making goosebumps run across my arms.

Then, Axel drops to his knees beside me. He lifts a hand, and I flinch, but he only brushes away hair that had fallen into my face. Gently. Then he runs a finger down my cheek, and god, if I'm not turned on by it.

Axel talks low, leaning in, "At a certain point, I'll think you're asking for it, brother or not." His breath brushes my neck. "Don't tempt me, little bird."

Goosebumps run up and down my arms. He looks at them and smirks. Then, gently, he runs his hands across them. "Your lust feels so pretty."

Then he gets up and stalks out of the house.

I have a second to catch my breath.

Fuck. I got caught up in... him. Just like I do with Gage. Just as soon as I think that though, I realize it doesn't matter. I'm leaving. None of this matters.

That sobers me. I try to get my body to calm down because I'm not done with my task. I'll be damned if I leave the house without at least cleaning up the mess I made.

When Axel comes back in, I throw a rag at him. "I'll spray, you wipe." My thumb is getting better. Still sore, but I have a lot more movement now. I spray enough cleaner on the couch that it'll be wet to sit on. But I need to get as much milk out as I can.

I expect Axel to say something. To keep flirting. But he doesn't. He just gets to work beside me, silently cleaning.

"You're leaving today," Axel says. It's not a question.

I glance at him, a little startled. How the hell did he know that? Is he going to try and stop me?

There's a glint of mania in Axel's eyes, then he goes back to the couch.

"You're a coward for leaving."

The accusation cuts deep. I jerk back. "Excuse me?"

"You heard me, little bird." His voice is quiet. Soft.

Anger fills me, and my cheeks get hot. How dare he? I'm my own person. I'm allowed to go and do whatever I want, especially if that means leaving a place I was forced to stay in.

Slowly, I suck in a breath. "You know, you act like some meathead who only wants to get his dick wet, but I think, deep down, you're just a scared little boy."

Axel freezes, and I know I've hit something sensitive. He watches me, and I see his tongue moving along his teeth behind his closed lips. "Makes two of us, huh?" Then he drops his rag and steps away. Just in time for Gage to walk in, sans shirt.

"Oh. Hey." He narrows his eyes at Axel, who tenses.

Axel's trying to throw on his mask with a joking smile, but I see how thin it is. He doesn't want Gage to see the real him.

Too bad. If he's gonna call me out on leaving, I'm gonna call him out on his bullshit. I throw a blinding smile at Gage.

"Axel was just offering to stay. He's gonna help clean, then have lunch with us."

I hear Axel make a sound of disagreement. Gage frowns for a second but then says, "Oh. Okay. Sounds good."

And Axel shuts up. Like I knew he would.

"I'll get something started." Gage moves to the kitchen.

I throw a triumphant grin at Axel, who glares at me in return. Then, I send him a wink and get back to cleaning.

CHAPTER SEVENTY

AXEL

"Help me with the quesadillas?"

I hate the look Gage gives me. It's like this grumpy dog that's trying not to beg for food, but it can't help the hopeful tail wag.

Gage doesn't need the help. He may act helpless to get Raven's attention, but he can make fucking melted cheese between two tortillas. He's asking 'cause he wants to talk. He's not subtle.

And yet, I can't refuse. It's Gage.

I groan, casting one last look at the back door where the bat is. I'll stay for lunch. That's it.

When I get to the kitchen, Gage rubs the back of his neck, throwing a tiny glance at me before motioning at the food. He has the old glasses on, so I shoo him away from the burner. "You trying to light that towel on fire?"

I whip the towel away that got a little too close. "You fuck one time, and your head is in the clouds."

Gage grunts. Then he glances at me again, and his shoulders are tense. I can tell he wants to ask what Raven and I were doing. If she told me about them.

"Poe was out back," I say. "Said she was here for your soul."

"Really?" Gage jerks his head up. "She found me? I hope there was food for her." I hear him walk out of the room.

"Yeah, souls," I mutter, the butter sizzling and smelling amazing.

When Gage comes back, he grabs a bag of tortillas and throws it at me.

Instead, he asks, "Where were you last night?"

Is that what he really wants to know? I butter the pan. "Frolicking in the buttercup fields."

"Axel."

I consider telling him I didn't want to listen to them fuck without being invited. Instead, I go the safer route. "I was braining Max."

Gage snorts. Then, when I don't say anything, there's a pause. It's a long pause as if Gage is running every option through that analytical brain of his.

"For real?" The question is hesitant.

"Yep." I sprinkle cheese on. Cheese is good. The more, the better, although Gage disagrees. He likes a thin snap. I wonder what Raven thinks?

"Braining how?"

"Bat."

Silence again. It goes on for so long that I consider giving him a justification and telling him about the letter. However, the last time I tried that, he still lost his shit. May as well just get the shit-losing over with.

"You're putting too much cheese on."

I snap my gaze over to him. Gage's arms are crossed.

"You're not going to freak out?"

Gage narrows his eyes. "Is that going to undo the braining?"

"No."

He lets out a long breath. "Did anyone see it?"

I blink. Is he really just going to accept this?

"Do you think I'm stupid?"

"No, but I do think you're rash," Gage snaps. "Did anyone see it?"

"No."

"Tell me everything."

So I do. I leave out the part about leaving town after. He'd try to stop me if he knew. He's already going to have to stop Raven. I expect him to lecture me. Tell me where I slipped up. Where I could get caught. All the normal Gage things.

But he doesn't. He just asks, "Why?"

"Why? Because he's a piece of shit." I frown, that classic anger back from just talking about it.

"There are pieces of shit all around you, and you let them live."

I bite my lip, flipping a quesadilla. What is in the air? These two fuck, and suddenly it's a call-Axel-out day?

I'm quiet. I don't want to talk about it.

"Well, whatever your plans for Rich are... I want in."

It takes a second to digest that, and I blink a few times before turning to him. Gage looks *pissed*. His lips are turned down, and his eyes are a mask of anger.

There's a moment where we do nothing but look at each other. Then, I let out a short laugh. "Damn. Whatever's in that pussy is magical."

Gage snorts, grabbing the plate of quesadillas. "I think she's gonna run."

"I know she's gonna."

Gage stops, staring at the food. He has... darkness in his eyes, and I can't help but be struck by how much he looks like me at this moment. And despite the fact that it should make me scared, all I feel is satisfaction.

Despite all our differences, we're both still brothers, and we'll both fight for what we want. And what we want is Raven.

CHAPTER SEVENTY-ONE

RAVEN

Lunch is silent. Both men sit at the other end of the table, right next to each other. Both eat while watching me with unnerving intensity. I would have a hard time telling them apart, but I've been around them for long enough to recognize the slightly withdrawn look in Axel's eyes. Despite that, they look like twin images of each other, and something has changed. I'm not sure what, but something during their hushed conversation in the kitchen.

It sends a thrill through my body. I'm not sure if I should run or stay as still as fucking possible.

I don't eat much, which Gage notices. He demands I have another serving. It goes down like dust.

Finally, when Gage thinks I've had enough, he wipes his

mouth with a napkin, meeting my gaze behind his glasses. "I hear you're thinking of running."

Oh shit. I shoot an accusatory look at Axel. And that's when I realize what the difference is. The animosity between them is lower. They're sitting on the same side, and neither of them has fought the entire meal. They've both been focused on me.

That sends an unexpected mix of dread and anticipation through me.

Axel just shrugs his shoulders. "Whoops."

I snap my gaze back to Gage. "It's not running. I've done what we agreed I'd do."

A look flashes across Gage's face before he shutters it. "I want you to stay."

I swallow, the declaration hanging heavy over the table.

"I, uh..." A rush of thoughts runs through my head. My plan to run to Alaska and open a bookstore. Max. The feelings I've started to have for Gage. This push and pull Axel and I have.

My fingertips get cold.

"She's scared," Axel volunteers.

I cut him a harsh glance, which he pretends not to see.

"Of what?" Gage asks.

I frown. "I'm not scared. I just... can't. I'm going to start over."

Gage's gaze shutters even more.

"I'm a free woman. I can do what I want." Why the hell do I feel defensive right now?

"Poe is free, but she comes back." Axel's look is positively evil. He knows he's poking me where it hurts.

I stand. "Thanks for lunch. We need groceries. I'll get them."

Axel and Gage stand with me. Axel has a slight smirk on his lips. "Awww, don't go flying off now."

"Don't tell me what to do."

"I won't." Axel points at Gage. "I want you to tell him what to do."

I glance between them. Gage looks confused.

him and shuddering when his lips feather across my skin. Gage stops talking, and it's the most intoxicating feeling. He's listening to me. Obeying.

"That's a good boy."

Gage's lashes flutter. The fine lashes that look like they're frosted over, hooding over his light eyes. He's into it. He loves it. There's one final moment of hesitation before I grab the rope. "Put your hands behind your back."

Gage looks up at me, not doing what I asked. I grab him under the chin, forcing him to look up at me, feeling the strong beat of his heart. I wait for him to tell me no. To tell me to stop.

"Do it. Now."

Gage swallows against my grip but does as I ask. The chair has no armrests and a wooden back, but Gage is big enough that he has no problem.

"Good." I step over him so I'm straddling him.

Axel steps behind the chair with rope, grabbing Gage's wrists. Beneath me, Gage tenses a little.

I arch an eyebrow at him, and immediately, Gage loosens. The power he's giving me is intoxicating. I suck in a breath, feeling a shiver run down my spine. Then, I wrap my own rope around Gage's torso. I want him fully under my control, unable to even lean forward.

His broad chest heaves with breath, but he just watches me. "Fuck, Raven..."

"Yes?"

Gage squirms, but Axel is done securing his hands.

"What?"

"God, you're so..." He struggles for words.

I wait for him, unbuttoning my shirt. His eyes go wide, staring at me as I strip down to my bra.

"Gage?" I say, leaning into him.

"Huh?" he asks, eyes locked on my tits in my bra.

I lean into him, whispering into his ear. "You can touch me."

I feel his body respond, pulling against the ropes, but he can only move the smallest bit. He makes a sound of distress. A whimper, really. And it shoots straight down to my clit.

Then, Gage's lips are on my neck, kissing and nipping until I pull away. He tries to clear the stricken look from his face when a sound pulls my focus away.

"Damn, you're cold." Axel nods at me with an approving look in his eye. And suddenly, I feel awkward again. I'm sitting on his brother with my shirt off for both of them to see. Are they going to get mad? Jealous?

I glance back at Gage, but he's only focused on me, and his eyes look hungry. I'm too scared to look at Axel, although I can feel his smoldering gaze all over my skin.

"Come here," Gage says in a low voice.

"I'm right here," I say, reaching around to unclip my bra. When it falls away, both men pull in a breath. Then my tits are there in Gage's face, but not quite close enough for him to lean his head forward to touch.

He tries though.

"Raven," he strains at the ropes.

"Hmmm?"

Gage fights the restraints, his large body twisting and bucking. For a second, I worry he'll get out, and that just makes me get even wetter. But the ties hold, and he remains where he is, chest heaving.

"Raven, please." There's a note of desperation in his tone. A pretty sound. One I've been aching to hear this whole time.

"I want your pants off." I start to try to take them down, but it's difficult with him secured in the chair. He can get some clearance off the seat, but not enough to clear the thick band.

Axel moves beside me, leaving the room and coming back with a pair of scissors. I eye the sweatpants sadly. I like these. Gage will have to get more.

I move to the band, and Gage stills, eyes on mine.

"I won't cut you," I promise.

"Booo," Axel says. I glare at him. He just winks. "You can cut me anytime you want."

"Not happening," I mutter, slicing through Gage's pants after some considerable sawing. As soon as I'm done, I clear his underwear too. Gage's dick pops out, hard and bobbing. My mouth waters at the sight of it, remembering how it felt, throbbing in my throat last night. I slide my own pants down, pointedly ignoring Axel right beside us. My cheeks heat, and I try to focus just on Gage. I shimmy out of my pants.

"Damn," Axel says, all traces of joking gone from his voice. I risk a look at him, and he swallows hard, the mask he usually wears gone. Instead, he's looking at me with unfiltered lust.

I sit on Gage's lap, feeling his warmth against my now naked body.

"Condom," he gasps.

I glance down at him. I'm clean, but I'm not on birth control. I haven't needed it since I left Max.

"I'm clean." He bucks his hips as much as he can. "Axel, top drawer in my bedroom."

As Axel leaves, I lean into Gage while he's gone, embarrassment curling up my spine.

"God, Raven, you make me so fucking hot." There's a throaty sound in Gage's voice. "Fuck, Axel, hurry up!"

"Easy." Axel returns, laughing. He drops a packet between our chests, the packaging scratching as it falls between us.

I glance over at Axel while unwrapping the condom. He just lifts an eyebrow.

I get back to the man in front of me, grabbing his dick and rolling the condom over it. Gage swallows audibly. "I want to be inside you. Please."

"Please?" I taunt, but having Gage's dick in my hand makes me want it too. I want to feel him grind against my G-spot until it's all I can think about.

"Please, oh fuck." His dick jerks in my hand. He grinds his

hips up as much as he can. "Oh fuck, I can't–" He gasps for breath. "I can't think; I need it so bad. Please, just–"

I pull him to my entrance and press just the tip inside. Then, slowly, inch by inch, I sink down.

Gage throws his head back and moans, the veins in his neck sticking out. The stretch is delicious, sending pleasurable thrills through me. I shake with the effort to hold myself up, and Gage strains at his ropes.

Finally, I sit all the way down, settling onto his lap, pleasure racing through me.

Gage pants, his breath heavy. I start to move, wanting to grind up on him.

"Wait," Gage tenses, "Wait, fuck! Just wait."

I freeze, then start slowly rolling my hips. "I didn't hear a please."

"Please," Gage whimpers. "I'm going to come."

I stop. Gage swallows heavily, squeezing his eyes shut. I glance over at Axel, expecting to see him stroking his dick. Only, he's fully clothed, staring at me with hooded eyes. There's an expression there that I can't quite make out.

Then Gage shifts, making my pussy clench, and I moan. I slip my hand between us, playing with my clit. I'm already so wound up that immediately, my pussy flutters. Gage sucks in a breath and holds it, his body still.

"Do you want to feel me come on your dick?" I ask, feeling close already.

Gage nods, then quickly answers, "Yes, yes, please."

Since he answered so sweetly. I rub myself in tight circles, my body already on the edge. I build and build until I come, body exploding with pleasure. I curl into Gage, pussy pulsing around him. I feel his arms try to move, and then he stops. The pleasure holds me captive for a few beats, and I start to relax around him, breathing heavily.

After a few beats, I start to grind on Gage, but Axel says, sounding bored, "Just one?"

My eyebrows shoot up, and I glance over at him.

"You can do more. Come around him until he can't hold out any longer."

I look at Gage, who has a hungry look on his face.

"See how many it takes him." Axel leans back in his chair, getting a mocking tone. "How many can you last, big bro?"

I take him up on the dare, rubbing myself again, already on the edge from the last orgasm. This one tips me over even more powerfully, and I can't help but groan into Gage's neck.

Then, I do it again and again until it becomes painful. The more sound I make, the more Gage's breathing picks up and his body tenses. Finally, when I'm circling my clit, not sure if it's hurting more than it feels good, Gage grunts, body tensing, and I can tell he's about to come. I rise up and down, riding his dick until Gage grunts in a stuttered way, dick jerking, coming so hard I can feel the spurts of cum through the condom. It pushes me over the edge one last time, and we both come together, locked in pleasure.

Even once the pulsing pleasure stops, I find myself locked in a haze of pleasure, everything looking fuzzy. Closing my eyes, I lay my head on Gage's shoulder, just breathing. He nuzzles his head into mine. For a second, I freak out and feel for the monster that's usually around the corner. I stiffen, waiting for it to pounce when I've let my guard down. But there's nothing. For some odd reason, I feel nothing but safety. And I can't get up the energy to freak out about that.

CHAPTER SEVENTY-TWO

AXEL

Good god.

That was... fuck.

I stare at the stunning woman draped over Gage's chest. Watching them was the most intoxicating thing I've done in a long time, and I wasn't even the one fucking.

My chest is tight, and my pants are tight, too. There's an ache in both places, but my chest hurts more. It's a bittersweet ache. Gage deserves this. I'm not so much of an asshole that I can't admit that. But... I can't help but feel... lonely. I rub at it.

Gage shifts, looking down at the woman in his arms. It's then that I notice her shoulders are moving. They're hitching.

Is she... crying?

"Raven?" Gage asks.

She doesn't answer, just burrows in further, her shoulders shaking harder.

"Raven?" This time, Gage tries to move to see her face, but he's still tied down. He throws a look my way. "Untie me."

I frown, moving to do as he asks, trying to see Raven's face. She won't let me look at it.

Gage strains impatiently.

"Hold still, fucker," I hiss, the ropes getting jerked out of my hands.

"Are you hurt?"

More silent crying.

Alarm rips through me as I undo the knot. Then I look Raven over, looking for any injury. She doesn't seem hurt.

Gage tries to get up, but the ropes Raven tied around his chest are still there. He cusses as the chair jolts, then scrambles to untangle them under Raven's body. She just brings her hands up to her face.

"Ax," Gage says, and it's panicked.

"Easy," I mutter. "Just... get her to her room."

Gage does, finally standing and carrying her down the hall and into her room. Then he puts her down. "Are you hurt?"

Raven shakes her head, throwing her hands in front of her face. "Don't look at me."

I do, scanning her for injuries on her front or blood between her legs. Nothing. I feel helpless, and it makes panic send adrenaline through my body.

Gage is panicking, running his hands all over her. I grab his shoulder and pull him back. This could be something like 'sub drop.' I've seen it happen to the women I've messed with in the past. Even felt it myself after inflicting something particularly violent or bloody. It feels like the cocktail of emotions and hormones all spill over, and you're left... empty.

"I'm fine." Raven dashes away the tears, and now that I can see her face, I see the numbness creeping in. The disconnect.

"You're not fine. What's wrong?" Gage is all up in her face, brushing her hair away, looking intently at her as if he just looks hard enough, he'll be able to see her. She swats at him numbly, but he doesn't back off. "Tell me."

She crosses her arms over her chest.

"Raven, I swear to god—"

"It was too much," she blurts. "I... I made you. I made you do it."

There's a stunned silence. Gage looks back at me, and I just frown.

"Yeah, that was... kinda the point."

"No! I mean, I *made* you. And now I'm using you." Her eyes well with tears again, and she dashes them away. Then I see that detached look come back in her eye. "I'm tired. I'm going to sleep."

"Made me? You didn't make me do anything."

But Raven has turned and is headed to bed.

With a snarl, Gage grabs her arm and whirls her to face him. Then, he shoves her back on the bed so she's lying back, then steps over her. "You didn't make me do shit." Then he presses his body over her, pinning her to the mattress.

"Gage." She struggles weakly.

"No, Raven. You really think you could make me do something I don't want to do?" He drops his face in hers, and he's angry. I see it in the tense lines of his body. "Make me get off you."

"Gage!" She's still trying to hide her face.

"*Make me,*" Gage hisses, angry.

"Gage," I say.

"Make me, Raven."

She thrashes now, completely unable to move his big body. There's a flash of fear in her eyes.

"That's enough." I grab Gage's shoulder roughly and rip it back. It throws him off balance for a second, then he's back on top of her.

"You proved your point." I try to rip him off again, but Gage is fucking strong.

"Fine!" Raven spits. "You want to know what's wrong so bad?" Her face twists in hate. "I forced you, and I liked it."

There's a moment of stunned silence.

"What?" Gage growls.

"I did exactly what Max did to me." Suddenly, the hate is gone, covered by a blank look that scares me a lot more.

"Get the fuck off her." This time, I put the palm of my hand under Gage's nose and shove back violently. It has the intended result. Gage clutches at his face, tears welling in his eyes.

Raven immediately curls up, covering her face.

"Look at her," I hiss.

Gage's eyes go from angry to watery and scared.

"Fucking oaf." I shove him back. "Get out."

"Raven, I didn't mean—"

"Get out. You can talk about it later." I push him until he's almost out of the room, and this time, he lets me.

"Wait, I need—"

"Give her a goddamn second." I shove him out and shut the door. For a second, I stand there, unsure if I should leave as well.

There's a rustle behind me, then I hear Raven flick on the bathroom light. The shower turns on, and I wait for the bathroom door to shut, but it doesn't.

I should go. I should definitely go. Run for the hills. Get the fuck out of here like I originally planned.

But that tiny part of me that knows how isolating it is to push people away because of what you've been through wants me to stay.

I shouldn't stay. This is just going to hurt me.

And yet, I find myself being drawn, step by step, to the bathroom.

Raven didn't shut the door. She knew I was in here and didn't shut me out.

I stand there, fists clenching and unclenching. This isn't me. I'm not the comforter. I'm not Gage.

But Gage doesn't understand. I do.

I knock on the doorframe. "It's Axel."

I hear nothing. Just the water hitting the floor.

Totally stupid. I should go now.

What if she's not okay? What if she's hurting herself?

Concern fills me, and I peek around the corner. Raven is sitting on the floor next to the sink, legs curled up to her chest.

Fuck.

Slowly, so I don't scare her, I move into the bathroom. She doesn't tell me to go. Doesn't make any indication that she sees me. Slowly, very slowly, I lower myself to the floor beside her. For a long while, I don't say anything. We just sit there while the room fills with steam.

Finally, I say, "I also find the bathroom floor to be the superior seating. Often after too many drinks. It cools the asscheeks."

Nothing.

Okay. Fine. I just let my head fall back against the sink.

I should go. I really should. Shouldn't get myself messed up in these emotions. Especially since I know she's about to leave.

But my body feels like lead. I can't just leave her without trying something.

"You know," I say. "Wanting to recreate experiences is the brain's way of processing trauma."

Raven doesn't move. So I keep going. "You get stuck in this... loop. I don't know. It's like you can't get out of it until your brain has solved every last piece."

Silence.

I close my eyes. "Like, maybe if I hadn't said this or done that, it would have been different." *Maybe if I had been more grown up, I would have known what was happening.*

Finally, Raven huffs, "That sounds fake."

The relief from hearing her voice makes me crack my eyes

open. "It could be. I went to some sex therapy camp a long time ago, so it could be total bullshit."

"You? Therapy?"

I shake my head. "I know. Wild, huh?" I went to try to figure out what was wrong with me. Why I couldn't stop fucking every woman that crossed my path. Why I was terrified of intimacy. "I got kicked out," I say.

"Why?"

"I fucked one of the teachers."

Raven laughs a real laugh, but it quickly disappears.

My tone sombers. "You're not like Max, Raven."

"How do you know?" Her voice is full of so much sorrow, it hurts something in my chest. Because she's like me. That's how I know. Raven wouldn't inflict the same pain on other people that's been inflicted on her.

"If Gage was scared, would you have kept going?"

Silence.

"Answer me. If you saw fear, would you have kept going?"

"No."

That's what I thought.

The water continues to pound down. Finally, Raven huffs. "Guess I should turn that off."

"Or get in."

She glances at me.

I pretend to pull my glasses off. "I won't look." We both ignore the fact that she's totally naked in front of me as we speak, and I just watched her fuck my brother.

"You're so stupid."

I know I am. I'm stupid, so no one sees the real me. Although with Raven, it feels different sometimes. Like it becomes less about hiding and more about making her laugh. "Well, Mr. Stupid is telling you to get in. Gage is a bit of a hot water monster. After he hit thirty, he obsessively checks the thermostat and water usage like an old man."

She gives a tiny smile. And it makes *me* want to smile. Not a fake smile. A real one. Then she gets up, and I have to physically rip my gaze away from her ass.

No. Be a gentleman.

Fuck. When did I sign up to be a gentleman? Oh god. I'm getting soft. I'm becoming Gage.

"Ax?"

I shudder at my nickname. "Hmm?"

"You're not as big a dick as I thought you were."

I bark out a laugh, unable to help myself. "You wound me."

Raven smiles, and it's the prettiest thing I've ever seen. It makes me want to see it more. I stand there while she showers, then realize that she's okay now. I can go.

I don't want to go.

Fuck, I don't want to go. But this is my brother's girl. As much as I like her, I won't repeat that mistake twice. It broke Gage, and he wasn't the same after that. We weren't the same.

So I force myself out of the bathroom.

Once out, I keep walking despite the fact that I want to walk straight back in there and tell Raven how obsessed I am with her. How I'm not gonna let her run from us. And I'm going to keep her. Forever.

But I don't. I keep walking into the hall.

Then I trip over something.

CHAPTER SEVENTY-THREE

GAGE

Coming out of the bedroom, Axel trips over me and Buddy.

I scramble to my feet. "Is Raven okay?"

"Yeah, dude, she's fine." Axel waves me off, walking away.

Wait. Why is he walking away? What's going on?

"Where are you going?"

"Walking away so I don't fuck your girlfriend."

That stops me in my tracks, but Axel doesn't stop. He keeps going. I stride up to him, snatching his arm. "Just wait."

"Did you not hear what I just said?" Axel looks at me, and I hear the anger in his tone. But it's not just anger. It's pain.

"I heard you." Honestly, I assumed that's what he was doing anyway. And for the first time, the thought didn't fill me with heartbreaking pain. There was some pain, but it felt old. Raven likes Axel. I know she tries not to, but she likes him. She's been obsessed with getting back at him the entire time I've known her. And he likes her too. A lot.

Axel squints at me. "Are you... Did you hit your head or something?"

I wish. Because I'm actually considering something crazy. Something I never in a million years would have thought I'd offer.

I swallow. "I'm an idiot."

"I'm well aware," Axel drones. I register a flicker of movement as his head looks down the hall like he's planning on walking away again.

"No, wait. I mean, I need help with her." Axel knew what to do tonight. He knew how to take care of her. I was the one being a dickhead. The one hurting her.

"Get a therapist," Axel says, "Now get off me."

"No! I'm saying... she likes you. Us. She likes both of us."

He tries to shove me off.

"Listen." I dig my fingers into his shoulders. "I see the way she looks at you. The way she fights." I close my eyes but keep going. "She wants you, Axel. Not just me. You too."

It's silent, and I'm too afraid to open my eyes. But the words are true. Axel and I are different people, and for some reason, she likes both of us. She likes taking control of me, and she likes it even better when Axel directs her.

"What are you saying?" Axel's voice is cautious.

"I'm offering to share, you stupid asshole." As soon as the words are out, I feel an odd relief. Like the tension I've been holding for so long just... dissipates.

I open my eyes, wishing I could really look at my brother. I want to see what he thinks. Instead, I feel the way his muscles tense like rocks under my fingers. They hold that position for so long that I know he's actually thinking about what I said. Then, there's a tiny intake of breath. One that I'm sure he didn't mean for me to hear.

Then, he stiffens again. "I'm not relationship material." He tries to shove past me.

Is he... trying to walk away from this?

I stride after him with newfound confidence, stopping him again. "You're just gonna walk away?"

"Yep." Axel keeps going.

"Who's the one running now?"

Axel doesn't stop.

"If you leave, you're the coward. Raven needs you. Needs both of us."

There's a pause so silent only the ticking of the grandfather clock can be heard.

Axel's shoulders are tense. "I..."

I know he's afraid. Fuck, I am too. But I'm tired of sitting back in fear and letting life pass me by. I just cross my arms. "You'll cut the bullshit act, and you'll do exactly what you did tonight. You'll be you. The real you."

I wish I could see what's going on in his head. If Axel runs now, I know Raven will run too. She'll pack up with the money I gave her and head... wherever she was going to head. Because as much as she'd deny it, she'd see Axel leaving as a rejection. Hell, *I'll* see it as a rejection.

"I can't... love her like you can." Axel's voice cracks, and his voice comes out so quiet, I can hardly hear it. "I'm broken, Gage."

My chest hurts, and I stride up to him, spinning him around. Instead of saying anything, I wrap him in my arms. Much like Raven did, Axel crumples. He doesn't cry, but I want to.

"We're all a little broken, Ax. Doesn't make us any less worthy of love."

CHAPTER SEVENTY-FOUR

RAVEN

After Axel leaves, I wash my hair thoroughly, thinking about all that has happened. For a minute, I thought Axel was going to get in the shower with me, and that thought had me more turned on than I wanted.

No. I'm with Gage. This is so wrong of me.

I wash off quickly, stepping into the steamy room. As I do, there's a shape against the doorway.

I jump. It's Axel. Or is it Gage? No, it's Axel. He's fully clothed in the same outfit he watched me fuck his brother in.

"Fuck! I thought you left." My cheeks burn, and I grab for a towel.

"Would it change anything if you knew I killed your ex?"

"What?" I start to dry off, then Axel's words register. I blink, looking up. "What?"

"Would it change anything," Axel raises an eyebrow, face deadpan, "if you knew I took a bat to Max's head last night?"

I'm stuck, staring at him. There's no way he's serious... right?

He looks fucking serious. A multitude of emotions rush through me. Axel killed someone? Killed Max?

No way. No fucking way?

Axel's expression doesn't change. He doesn't say, 'gotcha' or 'kidding.' Just stares at me.

I laugh. And as I laugh, Axel just stares, which makes me laugh harder.

"That's what I thought." Axel turns away.

"Wait." I take a step towards him, then stop. This man says he killed someone. He's dangerous. That thought makes a forbidden thrill rush through me. If what he's saying isn't a joke, it wasn't just someone. It was Max. Fear, shock, and disbelief roll through me, but there's something else. It almost feels like... relief.

"A bat?" I ask.

Axel looks at me like he wasn't expecting that response.

"My bat?" I ask.

"Yes." There's the tiniest eyebrow raise.

"Oh my god." I'm trying to process the information. Max. Max is dead? He used *my* bat? A feeling of rightness fills me.

Axel turns to leave again, and I grab his arm this time. "Don't go."

Axel stares at me, his gaze conflicted. His eyes dance between mine, then drop down to my lips. He licks his. "Don't make me say it."

My heart is racing. "Say what?"

Axel steps into me. Just a tiny step, and I find myself sucking in a breath, heat rushing over me. Axel is hot, just like his brother, but it's more than that. He's an asshole. But I've seen under that mask. And now... he killed Max? For me? To... protect me?

I'm fucked, but among the conflicting emotions that brings me, it also makes me want to kiss him.

Axel takes another step, brushing my chest.

"What about Gage?" I ask breathlessly.

"Who do you think sent me in here?"

I've become a broken record of 'no way.' I've seen the way they bicker. No way Gage wants to just... share.

Then I remember the change in Gage. How the brothers seemed more at peace with each other.

Axel's gaze is locked on me, and his entire body is tense. "I'm not a gentle person, Raven. I can't be. I—" His voice locks up, then the mask falls back over his face. "That's Gage. It's not me."

My heart is racing. This is crazy. Is this happening? Could I have both of them? What about my plan to run?

While I'm frozen, Axel drops his gaze and then turns back to the door. Oh my god. He's going to leave, and this chance will be over. Axel is like me, and he'll never offer twice.

"Wait," I croak. "Wait."

Axel freezes.

"I'm not gentle either." I clear my throat.

In a terrifying moment, I think Axel's going to walk away. But finally, slowly, he turns back around. His gaze is shrewd.

I narrow my eyes. I'm a little unstable but not gentle.

Axel takes a tiny step toward me like he's stalking me. Tracking every move I make.

"So you don't want me to lay you down and make sweet, sweet love to you?" His gaze never leaves me.

The idea makes me scared.

Axel must see something he likes 'cause his eyes light up. "Do you want me to make you scared, Raven?"

A delicious fear rolls through me, and I realize that I do want that. I must be certifiably insane. This man kidnapped me and says he killed my ex. And I want to let him make me scared?

But he also never once hurt me. He hasn't touched me against my will. He even kind of protected me.

It makes my heart race.

Axel takes another step closer. "That first time when you said you fucked Gage in the shower? Truth or lie."

I swallow and take a step back.

Axel cocks his head, talking slowly. "Truth? Or lie?"

"Lie." My back hits the shower door.

A slow grin creeps over Axel's face. "Good girl." Then, he pounces on me. His hard body slams into mine, and then his mouth is on my neck, biting so hard that pain explodes.

Fear also explodes. Deep, bone-gripping fear. Axel is all over me. He's stronger than I am, and I couldn't stop him if I wanted to. I shove back against him, only to realize I can barely move my arms.

Axel pushes into me again, slamming my body into the shower door. I tense, but there's something soft behind my head. His hand.

My chest heaves.

Not safe. Not safe.

Then Axel stops. His whole body pressed against mine, frozen. All I can do is heave in breaths while my chest feels tight. No. I wanted to enjoy this. Why the hell can't I enjoy this?

Then, Axel moves. I stiffen even more, but then he's pressing something into my hand. It's hard. He pulls away from me just enough so I can look at what it is.

A knife.

My knife. The one I pulled on him back in the library. And the blade is open.

"Breathe," Axel's voice is soft.

He just gave me a knife. I could stab him with it.

"I've had passionate, nail-dragging shower sex on my mind ever since you talked about it with Gage. And seeing as you're already wet..." He ducks his head down, shoving the towel aside and nipping at my breast. I gasp, but his tongue is there soothing the sting.

He says nothing about the knife. Then, he yanks me toward him, and the shower door opens, and he lifts me inside.

"Axel—"

Then the water's on, and I gasp as the spray turns cold. "Axel!"

"I love it when you say my name." His head is in my neck, biting along the underside of my jaw.

The water gets warm quickly, and soon, I'm melting into his touch. It's rough and aggressive and so fucking needy. For a second, I worry that he won't stop if I ask him to. But the hardness of the knife in my grip soothes me. And with that, I realize I don't want him to stop. I'm choosing this. I fucking want this.

I grab Axel's torso with my free hand, yanking him back into me. "Your clothes," I gasp.

He grins, and instead of pulling his shirt off, rips the soggy thing off with a loud tear. His glasses clatter to the shower floor.

Then I can see the water dripping down his sculpted torso, and it makes my mouth water. Shimmying out of the pants takes a little longer, and as soon as they're around his ankles, he snaps a hand out, grabbing my neck and pinning me to the shower wall.

"See something you like, little bird?"

His grip makes me cough, but I grin. The power behind his grip should be terrifying. It is.

"Know why I call you that?" He's on me, rubbing his hard dick against my pussy.

"Condom," I gasp, dragging my fingers down his shoulders.

Axel laughs, and it's a cruel sound. "Oh, but you didn't say please."

His grip doesn't ease, and I have to cough out the word. Then he's ducking down for an instant, and the pressure is gone.

I suck in a breath.

"It's not because of your name." Axel rips into a packet that he must have pulled from his pocket.

I narrow my gaze at him, and he makes a show of rolling the condom onto his throbbing length.

"It's 'cause you remind me of Poe. With your pretty broken wings. And your ability to claw my soul straight from my body." Then Axel's on me again, this time lifting me up under my arms.

I squeal, kicking my feet, but then he's there, pressing between my legs. He slows when he lines his dick up with my entrance, gaze meeting mine. His glasses are gone, and his pale eyes are blinking away the water. I tremble.

"Ready, little bird?"

I sneer at him, and then he's shoving into me, stuffing me so full I gasp. It doesn't hurt, the fucking from earlier readying me. But it's sudden, and it's full. I wrap my arms and legs around him to gain some stability, careful not to cut either of us.

"That's a good girl. Cut me with those pretty little nails." Then Axel pounds into me, groaning. "Make me bleed, vicious little thing."

"Are you telling me what to do?" The stimulation of Axel's dick quickly brings me right back to the arousal I had just an hour ago.

Axel grunts, "Be a good girl and hurt me."

So I do. I rake the nails of my free hand down his back, which just results in him shuddering and pressing in closer to me. He grinds his pelvis into me, rubbing on my clit in the process and making me gasp.

"Harder," Axel groans.

At first, I hesitate. Then, I dig my nails into him so hard there's no way I'm not ripping his skin open. I feel the way he locks up in pleasure, and it makes a rush of pleasure fill me. Oh god, I want to see him bleed. For me.

"Vicious," he pounds into me, "little thing."

Then he's slipping his hand between us, fingers pressing down to find my clit. I'm already so stimulated that when he brushes it, I tighten my legs around him.

"Ah, gonna come already? Couldn't take it?" Axel's voice is

mocking. In response, I wrap tighter around him, bouncing on his dick. The movement just builds up my own orgasm, though.

Axel laughs. "Poor little Raven. Couldn't handle five minutes with this dick before she needs to cream all over it."

Tracing my hands up, I fist them in his hair and yank his head back, exposing his neck to me. Then, I take the knife and put it to his throat. Not close enough to touch it because I'm afraid I'll actually cut him, but close enough to see if I can get his eyes to hood. To see if he'll submit to me. I say, "You like to run your mouth."

Axel laughs into the spray, then turns his head to the side.

I yank it back. "What. Having a hard time breathing?"

Axel's smiling wider than I've seen him smile before. It's a crazy smile, and I know he has to be getting water in his mouth.

I hold him there till his body jerks, and then I let him go. Immediately, he drops his head to my face, and suddenly, a warm wash of water floods my mouth. I hack, but Axel chases me, warm lips sealing against mine. I breathe through my nose, then bite Axel's lip. Hard.

He yanks away, hissing.

I grin at him.

"Fuck," Axel licks his lip. "You're the hottest thing I've ever touched." Then he's pumping into me again. Harder, but he keeps his hand on my clit, rolling and pinching and pulling. He's good at it, working me up into a frenzy despite my trying not to come.

But finally, I can't hold it back anymore, and I come. I explode all over his dick, pulsing in rhythmic ecstasy. The feeling rushes through my body as Axel laughs into my neck, muttering mocking things. Then he works me up again and again and again. Finally, he comes too, burying himself in my pussy and pinning me to the shower wall. He bites my neck and kisses it. He kisses all up my neck, then back down.

While I'm coming down, he pulls out of me, washing me off, turning the water off, and wrapping me in a towel. After both sessions, it's all I can do but lean into him, relying on him to keep me up. Carefully, I put the knife on the counter so I don't cut either of us. Axel holds me, carefully guiding me out of the shower and to the bedroom.

He hesitates when he lays me down on the bed, then lifts my hand to his mouth. I think he's going to kiss me, but he just opens his mouth and gently nips at my fingers. Then, he leaves the room.

CHAPTER SEVENTY-FIVE

GAGE

Sharing Raven is going to take some getting used to. After so many years of competing with Axel, it feels strange to get back to the way things used to be. Where we were best friends and worked together, no matter what it was. There were times I'd do Axel's homework, and he'd introduce me to all his new friends at school, insisting I come along even if I didn't want to.

Jealousy still creeps in, tightening my stomach. What if she decides she doesn't like me? What if she likes Axel better?

I pace back and forth in the kitchen.

I should go in there right now. Watch them fuck. Make sure she remembers I'm still a part of this.

But then I hold myself back. If Raven decides she doesn't like me, then that's on her. If Axel's gonna get in the way of her wanting me, maybe it wasn't meant to be between us anyway.

My chest hurts at that thought.

No. That's not gonna happen. But if it does, I'd rather her be with Axel than some stranger anyway. Selfishly, I'll still get to see her.

Unless Axel goes to prison. For murder.

I keep pacing.

I should go in there.

No! Fuck.

I need to put all this energy somewhere.

I can't believe Axel killed Max. Fuck, this has to be some joke, right? Could Axel kill someone? I think about the dead look I see in his eyes, especially around Halloween. Now I realize why that's there.

Rich.

A flood of rage fills my system, and I clench and unclench my hands. If Axel thought Max had to die, I trust him.

But I don't trust his ability to stay out of trouble. I need the details. All of them.

Is Rich next?

My stomach clenches, not because I care about Rich, but because my brother is rash. Impulsive. And you know what two things don't go well with getting away with murder? Rash and impulsive.

I pace around back and forth back and forth.

I could do it.

I stop, staring at the sink I've already cleaned three times since Axel went to be with Raven.

I could kill him.

I put my forearms on the counter. The sink isn't clean enough. I can smell it. It's not clean enough.

Fuck. I grab more cleaner and scrub. I wait for the distress to hit me. The 'I can't believe I just thought about murdering a person' to sink in.

No. Not a person. A pedophile.

The guilt doesn't set in.

Okay. How long do I have before Axel decides to go after Rich, too?

Fucking Raven will calm him for a bit.

How long is a bit?

Oh my god, he's fucking Raven. I'm gonna go in there.

No. No, I'm not. She didn't invite me, and most of me is okay with that.

I'm gonna fix this. I'm gonna fix it before Axel can butt in and fuck it all up. I wasn't able to protect my brother before. But I can now.

CHAPTER SEVENTY-SIX

RAVEN

I worry that things will be awkward the next day, so I avoid coming out of my room for as long as possible. Is everything going to be different now? I mean, I've fucked both of them. Will they fight each other? Fight me?

Will they coddle me? Treat me like I'm damaged, ask me about Max, or decide I'm too much? I really don't want to talk about Max. It's clear they know. I don't want to relive it.

When I finally come out of the room, Buddy following behind me, Gage and Axel are bickering about what pizza they should order for dinner.

"Ah, good," Gage motions at his brother. "Tell this idiot that three cheese is too much cheese. Gotta break it up with some pepperoni or *something*."

"Too much cheese?" Axel groans, rubbing his forehead. "Do you hear yourself?"

They continue to bicker, tossing insults back and forth, and it makes me relax. I slide into a spot on the loveseat, patting Buddy.

Gage gets up with a dramatic sigh, then comes over to me. "Hey, princess."

"Hey, don't–" I cut off as he turns to sit on me.

"Gage!"

Too late, he's dropped his weight on me and leans back. I grunt, trying to squirm away, but his weight pins me down solidly. His back vibrates as he asks, "I thought Raven came out."

"Get off!" I half laugh, half cry.

Axel's voice is muffled. "I didn't hear her defend cheese. She must not be here."

"You guys aren't *that* blind."

I continue struggling, and then Gage shifts. "Oh! There you are! Why didn't you say anything?"

I gasp for air, wiggling my torso around his back. "Get off you fucking... giant... fucking..."

"Hmmm. Not unless you pay the tax."

My legs are fully pressed into the bottom of the cushion, and they're getting wet from the last bit of the cleaner that hasn't dried. "Okay! Fuck, get off!"

"Good." Suddenly, Gage's weight is gone. Then, I'm being whisked up and plopped back down in his lap.

Axel watches us with a bored expression.

"Help," I gasp, trying to claw my way out of Gage's grip.

Axel winks at me. "Why? Watching you struggle is way more fun."

I growl, making Gage chuckle behind me. "Okay, time to pay the tax." He reaches to the side table where the book lies.

"The tax for existing?" I struggle now that he's only holding me with one arm, but it's like fighting with a large, meaty seatbelt.

"The tax for having such a sexy voice," Gage says into my ear.

Heat crawls across my skin, and I huff, but I stop struggling.

"Atta girl." He drops the book in my lap. "Read."

I glance at Axel, who just watches with a mildly curious look.

"You deserved the milk in your couch," I mutter. "You're insufferable."

"Milk? In my couch?"

I freeze. Oh fuck. I forgot Axel knew and kinda assumed he told Gage.

"Did you spill something?" Gage asks. He doesn't sound mad, just curious.

"Yeah. On purpose," Axel laughs.

When I don't respond, Gage grips me harder. Then his nose hits my neck, and he pulls in a breath. "Fuck, princess," he grumbles out in a dark laugh.

I squirm, but it only serves to make me feel just how hard Gage is under me. That sends a rush of blood to my pussy.

"Read," Gage demands in my ear.

As much as I hate being told what to do, coming from Gage, it doesn't feel scary. Plus, it's hard to argue with the seatbelt tucked firmly around my body. So, reluctantly, I start reading.

There's a comfort that settles into the room. Axel stays even though he must be lost. I read more until my eyes get heavy. A few times, we shuffle around, Gage brings me a blanket, and Axel brings me a drink. I read until I'm pretty sure Axel passes out, and my eyes grow heavy.

Then, I'm woken by a jostle of movement. It's Gage, lifting me into his arms.

"What are you doing?" I mutter.

"Shhh. Just drool on my shoulder and go back to sleep."

I should wake up more, but I don't want to. Instead, I settle into his shoulder. Feeling something drop away, I realize my blanket has fallen off.

Distantly, I hear Gage say, "Ax, bring that?"

Gage is warm. He's like a furnace. A comfortable, muscly

furnace. And when he tries to drop me off in my bed and take that heat away, I reach my arms out.

For a second, I think he's gonna go, and I wake up a little more, clutching him to me. I don't want him to go, and I'm afraid he will.

There's a pause, and then he settles in next to me. I burrow down, creating a new cocoon of warmth.

I feel movement on my other side, and then Gage's voice says, "Ax is here too. You okay?"

Why the hell is he trying to wake me up? I just mutter. Something tells me I should be scared. That they could hurt me.

But Gage asked if I was okay. I'm in control here. They aren't doing anything I haven't asked them not to do.

Then, I shove those thoughts back down. I'm comfortable, and I just want to sleep. Gage and Axel will protect me from anything that wants to hurt me. Oh, and Buddy.

I sit up, trying to look for Buddy.

"She's here," Gage says; then I feel something jump up on the bed. It's her.

With a contented sigh, I settle back down into the warmth. And then I pass out.

CHAPTER SEVENTY-SEVEN

RAVEN

I wake up late the next day feeling like I got the best sleep of my life. I'm warm and comfortable and... safe.

Yawning, I stretch out slowly. I'm in the spare room, and the bed is empty.

I start to remember yesterday. The fucking. The orgasms. The... bed sharing?

I sit up straight. Was that real? Frantically, I search my mind for dreams of being touched. But nothing comes. I feel more rested than I have in a long time.

I relax a little.

Oh my god. I'm starting to... trust them.

The thought makes me both scared and relieved. The kind of relief that washes over my entire body and makes me sink down on the bed.

I'm not sure how I feel about all that. But I do know in this moment, I'm happy.

That happiness doesn't last long. I go to the kitchen to find a note from Gage saying he has a work thing and he'll be back. I heard the shower running in the bedroom, so Axel must be cleaning up.

Suddenly, there's a knock at the front door.

Buddy barks, running to it. I check the peephole and see a mailman walking away. A package.

Holding Buddy back, I open the door and grab the package. It's addressed to Gage from someplace called Optic Connections.

It takes me a second before I realize what it is.

It's Gage's glasses.

For a second, one blissful second, I'm excited for him. Then, everything crashes underneath me.

I'm no longer needed.

I stand frozen, staring at the box.

Gage doesn't need me anymore.

He has his glasses. He doesn't need me anymore.

I'm stuck, staring at the box for a while, until Buddy's cold nose brushes my hand.

I rip my hand up to my chest. The peaceful numbness that I'm so used to is creeping back in.

Buddy boops my leg, brushing aside some of the numbness. I take a step back, trying to get back into that world.

She chases me, stepping on my feet.

I'm no longer needed. Because at its root, being here was a job.

Buddy's jumping up and down now, thinking the package is for her.

I just... lost my job. I got paid. I can leave now. Go chase my dreams. I look for that feeling of elation. Freedom. I can finally do what I want.

But there is no elation. And for one wild second, I consider throwing the glasses in the trash outside, pretending like they had never come in.

Then Axel comes into the kitchen. I hide the package behind me on the counter as Axel says in a serious tone, "Hey, something happened. We need to talk."

CHAPTER SEVENTY-EIGHT

GAGE

5 Hours Earlier

I didn't become a lawyer to figure out how to kill people and get away with it.

So how the fuck am I here? Asking my mom to drive me to go murder her husband?

Well, I didn't tell her that. I told her he and I had some things to discuss from the night of the party.

Which isn't technically a lie.

Mom drops me off, and I tell her to head to the one and only coffee shop in this area. She's happy to give us some privacy. Mom always was a sucker for everyone getting along.

I'm counting on the fact that we're out in the middle of nowhere, and the sheriff's department is small and underfunded. Underfunded means very little training for specialty cases, AKA telling the difference between a suicide and a murder. Mom would never suspect I had done anything. Hell, a few weeks ago, I would never have suspected I could do anything either.

But it was like meeting Raven got me unstuck. Like she breathed oxygen into my crushed lungs, and now, finally, I can do what needs to be done.

My hands shake. There are still so many things that could go wrong.

There's a slight moment where I'm standing in the long driveway, and my brain screams at me to turn around, but immediately, I shut it down and walk toward the house.

Each step I take sends a calm through me. The birds sing, and my steps are crisp. Even though it's mid-day, it's still cold.

Rich touched my brother.

A wave of heat washes under my skin. It's the same feeling I had when Dad was hitting Mom. Helpless anger.

Only this time, every step that takes me closer to Rich's place drains the helplessness and fuels the anger. Before I realize it, my leather-gloved hand is knocking on the door to the small, one-story cabin with the attached garage.

It takes Rich a long time to come to the door, but I know he's home. I know he was up early hunting and came back mid-day to eat and drink or dress whatever he caught.

Finally, I hear shuffling behind the door, and I adopt Axel's lazy stance. Then it opens, and Rich is there, blinking in the bright light. For a second, his face twists into a smirk.

"Axel."

I shove inside with a cocky grin on my face, just like Axel would. Rich steps back.

"Finally decided to take me up?" Rich asks.

I grunt, pulling up my shirt and slipping the pistol from my waistband. I got it from the town crazy lady. The kids all say she's a witch. She does have all kinds of odd things in her store, including guns. This pistol has been bought and 'gifted' so many times that it would have no way of being traced back to me.

Unless she talks. Which she won't. Some of my clients have known her to give the 'abuser special.' Never thought I'd need it too.

Rich glances at me, then at the gun, then turns away. "Gonna take more than a pistol to take down a deer, son."

"What about a person?" I ask, voice lowering as a deadly calm creeps across my body. I've played this out in my head so many times that it feels like I've already been here before.

Rich tosses a look over his shoulder, then does a double-take, seeing I'm pointing the gun in his direction. I'm not aiming it. I'm too close. Don't want him reaching out and grabbing it. That would force me to shoot him, and that's harder to dress up. But also, I can't aim with the small sights, even with the glasses.

"What are you doing?" Rich asks. He puts on his hard voice, but I hear a slight rasp.

"Giving you a choice."

"Gage?"

"I can shoot you in the heart and leave you to bleed out, or you can write a suicide note, and I'll let you go to sleep the easy way. Carbon monoxide."

"What is going on?" A hint of anger creeps into Rich's tone.

Anger. As if he's the one who has the right to be angry. My own anger is hard to access. It's like all that anger is finally channeled into calm action.

"How often did you touch him?" I ask.

"What?" I hear Rich shuffling back, probably to get his own gun. I swing my own to where I know the couch is and then pull the trigger. There's an explosion of sound, and I point the gun right back at Rich. Gunshots aren't unusual in this area, and a bullet hole in a soft surface isn't easy to find. This is also a hunting cabin with guns everywhere.

"I don't know what you're talking about." The rasp is so much throatier now.

"I'm sure you don't. Now choose."

"Gage, whatever's going on, I'm sure we can make it right." His voice is high, like a child's.

He's a coward, but I didn't expect anything less.

"A choice, or I'll make it for you." There's a power that comes from finally doing something. I'm finally protecting my family, and it's never felt more right.

I expect him to fight. To try to get a gun or throw something at me. Instead, all I hear is his fast panting for breath. I hear his mouth open and close a few times like he's trying to say something but can't.

"Go." I step into him, pushing him backwards until we reach the garage. "Where are the keys?"

More gasping. He must be frozen.

I feel along the wall. We came up here a few times as kids, and sure enough, my gloves brush something, and keys jingle.

"Please," Rich finally gasps. "I'll leave."

"That wasn't an option. Get in the garage."

Rich starts blubbering in full-blown panic, his adrenaline fully taking over. But still, he doesn't fight me. Because he's a coward and always has been. Only cowards do things to children.

I fire another round to get Rich to write the letter. This time, it's into the ceiling, and it's much louder in the garage. I have him turn the car on while he writes. I'm not convinced he's able to write anything legibly. Whatever. I wasn't going to give him the easy route anyway.

I planned for this. The easy route was Plan B. And then, if that doesn't work, plan C, D, and E. I don't care what goes down today. I'm taking back what he stole—safety.

Permanently.

For a moment, I stand there, listening to Rich blubber and the car run. Then, I lean into the car, putting my pistol up under his chin.

"Please," he says, and all I can hear is Axel saying that. I hear it in his voice when we were kids and still trading gum for poems.

I pull in a breath, preparing my ears, and then pull the trigger. The force jerks my hand back.

There's a boom, then nothing but ringing.

Warmth splatters down on my jacket and gloves with little plops despite my efforts to keep out of the spray.

For a second, I hear ringing, the car, and Rich's clothes as he twitches against the seat. Then, he stops moving.

As he stops, all I can think is it's too bad Axel isn't here to hear him die. But if anyone goes down for this, I don't want it to be him. I'm the detail-oriented one. I can make sure none of my DNA, and therefore his, gets on the scene. I know what to say and what not to say.

It's my way to protect him, even though I couldn't do it before.

Once the ringing slows down a bit, I wrap Rich's finger in the trigger and lay his hand and the gun in his lap, like it fell there.

I'm wet.

No, not wet. Bloody.

I suck in a breath. This will look like a suicide.

And I'll look like the hero who came in at the last minute to save him.

I yank Rich's body out of the car and onto the floor, starting chest compressions. I do them hard enough to break some ribs so they know I was trying to help.

I dial 911 on my phone, working my body up. I give a panicked relay about blood and death and CPR. I've read enough 911 transcripts to know how real callers act.

I do CPR on Rich's body for fifteen minutes until the fire department arrives.

Then I step away, sweaty and covered in his blood, while they try uselessly to save him.

I don't feel bad. At all. Axel deserved to have someone wipe this shitstain from the earth. Mom might be sad at first. In fact, I know she will be. But we'll be there for her. Axel and me, and —my heart jumps at the thought—maybe even Raven.

CHAPTER SEVENTY-NINE

GAGE

Numb chaos ensues as I break the news to Mom and then call Axel. On the phone, Axel sounds skeptical, but he doesn't question me. Mom loses her shit and insists on staying while the Sheriff's Department does their investigation. I should be surprised, but I'm not. I knew some part of her loved Rich, no matter how he treated her. She was blind to everything but the companionship he offered.

After a few hours, the shock sets in for Mom. She doesn't want to talk or do anything. I offer to stay with her, but she asks to be alone.

At first, I balk. I don't want to leave her alone after she just lost her husband. Instead, I call her book club friends. The first one I get a hold of tells me she'll get in touch with everyone, and they'll be over.

They pick Mom up from my driveway.

Axel meets me in the driveway. He waits until Mom drives away, then there's a silence between us. Then, he clasps my hand, gripping it so hard I suck in a breath. He clasps me on the back. There's unspoken emotion in his grip, and for the first time today, I almost lose it. I don't know what to say to him. And what if he's mad at me? Rich was in our lives for a long time. Also, I wouldn't put it past Axel to have had a hit out on Rich already. But I couldn't let him take the fall for that. It's time I protected him, even if it doesn't erase the past.

Then, Axel speaks, his voice tight. "Are you gonna need a lawyer, brother?"

I step back to look at him. His gaze is flinty, and there's no sadness.

I let out a breath. "You offering?"

He chuckles and runs a hand through his hair. "I mean, I'm not certified, but my annoying ass brother has taught me enough. It can't be that hard, can it?"

I laugh. Then, there's silence. He says nothing but everything at the same time.

It's okay. We're going to be okay. Everything is going to be better now. It feels like something that was missing fills my chest again.

Now, we just need Raven, and everything will feel complete.

When we get inside, I strain my ears to hear her voice. It's changed since she first got here. It's still raspy and hot, but there's a warmer sound to it. She's faster to smile and even laugh. I like to think it's because she's not hungry anymore and maybe even feels safe.

My chest warms. It lights my heart up in ways I didn't think it could. I feel happy. Content. Like I can face anything as long as Raven and Axel are here.

I don't hear her in the kitchen. I look around the corner into the living room.

"I briefed her on what happened," Axel says.

I peek down the hallway, wishing I had the glasses so I could see Raven in detail. I want to see her sleep-mussed hair. Her hesitant eyes. Her loose body language that's saying she might be scared, but not of us. But I don't see that. In fact, I don't see any movement from Raven or Buddy.

Suddenly, Raven appears in a flurry of movement. Something in my chest loosens, and I grin, "Hey, princess."

"Hey," she says, sounding rushed, pushing past us.

"Sorry about the blood, I'll–"

Raven moves to the front door. "It's okay. I'll be back."

I frown.

"Where are you going?" Axel asks.

"Out. I'll be back."

Then she shuts the door, and she's gone.

My gut twists. That was odd. Was the blood triggering for her?

I stride for the front door, pull the door open, and squint in the bright light outside. I can barely see the movement of her car pulling away.

"Where the hell is she going?" Axel asks.

I don't answer him. Because I don't know.

CHAPTER EIGHTY

AXEL

It's been thirty-eight minutes since Raven left. I pace back and forth. Something isn't right. She ran out of here like someone was chasing her.

Like she was running.

I rip at my hair. What could have made her run?

I know. It was the intimacy. We slept in the same bed as her. Gage explained later that she said she never shares a room. We pushed her too hard. Now she's running scared.

How do I know? 'Cause I'm scared as balls, too. It's what I would have done.

Fuck. She's running with so much money it'll be damn near impossible to track her back down.

I realize that I'm terrified in a way I can't laugh off. Every second that she's away, my chest feels tighter. Like it's solidifying into a solid block of rock. Like I'll never feel again. Like I'll become the old me before I knew her.

"Why the fuck did I not put a tracker on her?" I kick the couch, sending pain up my toe.

"She's coming back." Gage's voice is weak.

No. *No, no, no.* If Raven runs, she'll always be afraid. She'll never let herself feel. She'll become me.

And I refuse to let her do that to herself.

I'm going to find her. And when I do, I'm going to plant a tracker on her car so she can never get away from us. I storm to the front door when it bursts open.

CHAPTER EIGHTY-ONE

RAVEN

I was a coward and ran. Not away, but to the store. I don't know how to deal with death. Especially the death of an asshole like Rich. I figured maybe they needed a little space?

I stare at the flower section. Rich was awful, but I'm sure his death means something to the twins, especially to their mom.

I pick out a dozen red roses for her, then put them back. Is that too romantic? What if they remind her of him?

I work myself into a mess over the flowers, not sure which ones to get. And deep down, the fear that I'm not needed anymore beats a steady pulse in my brain.

Not needed. Not wanted. No longer useful.

I'm sure they found the glasses by now.

I'm not sure which flowers I end up picking. Somehow, I end

up back in the car, staring at the dash. Old habits scream at me to run. To leave before they can reject me.

But then I remember Gage's gentle touches. Axel's controlled power. The way that they both made me feel safe for the first time in… forever.

I can't run. I won't leave them alone right now.

So I drive back to the house, sucking in breath after breath, trying to collect myself. I know this is the right choice. I feel it deep down in my bones.

Doesn't stop me from shaking a little.

When I step back into the house with my flowers, the door opens while I'm pushing it. I bump into someone – Axel – as he tries to leave.

Axel fixes me with a wild look, and suddenly, his hand is around my throat, and he's spinning me, shoving me backwards. His hand comes between my head and the wall, and then he's pushing me into it, demanding, "Where the hell did you go?"

"I–" The flowers are getting crushed, but Axel just presses me in harder. Then Gage appears, hair messy and a panicked look in his eyes.

"Get off me!" I try to push Axel's hand away enough to breathe. He's strong. He isn't hurting me, but spots are starting to form in my vision.

"You can't run from us." Axel's voice is panicked.

I try to argue, but I can't breathe.

Then, Axel smashes his lips into mine. He kisses me in a crushing, brutal way, pressing into me until all I can focus on is him. Axel. The smell of mint and the feel of his strong body up against me. For a second, I relax into him.

"Let go of her."

There's a flash of movement, and then Axel is ripped off me. I suck in a breath. There's an immediate emptiness.

"Raven! No one's going to hurt you." Gage is right there, eyes wild. He's so close that I can feel his breath on my skin while he holds Axel back.

I slide along the wall, getting out of Axel's reach. Once I've stepped into the living room and neither of them gets any closer, I feel the wash of adrenaline sweep over me.

I glance back at the back door, then force myself to take a breath.

"Princess." Gage's voice is sad. I snap my gaze up, realizing both he and Axel watched me look at the back door. Gage is sad, and Axel is...afraid. Buddy is standing there, looking conflicted.

"Are you okay?" Gage asks.

No? And shouldn't I be asking them that question?

"Raven," Axel's fists are clenched, but Gage no longer has to hold him back. "Fuck, I'm sorry. You scared me, and I freaked out."

Wait. That came from Axel? It sounds like something Gage would say.

I look between the two men. Did I mix them up?

"Please don't run." It's Axel. Again. He's asking nicely?

His eyes are tense, and his whole body is vibrating. "Fuck, you scared me so bad."

"Both of us." Gage runs a hand through his hair. His sleeve is covered in dried, flaky blood.

"Are you okay?" I ask, suddenly sucking in a breath. Blood. Gage is bloody.

I dart forward, examining his arm.

"I'm fine." Gage grabs my exploring hands, gripping them tightly. "Are you okay? Where did you go?"

I suck in a breath. "I went to get flowers..." I glance around, seeing the crushed bouquet on the floor.

"Flowers?" Gage frowns.

"Yeah, for... 'cause of Rich..."

There's a pregnant pause, and then suddenly, Axel reaches out and grabs me. He pulls me to him in a crushing hug, squeezing the breath out of me. "Fuck, Raven."

Did I do something wrong? Oh my god, I did something wrong.

Then Gage is there, also wrapping us in his arms while Buddy shuffles around the three of us, prodding us with her nose and trying to get in the middle. It feels...complete. Whole. We stand there for a while, and then Axel's deep voice says, "That's not why you ran, is it?"

I wince, pulling away. Of course, he can see right through me, and he can't even see. I'm officially the world's most transparent person. My cheeks burn.

"I, uh..."

"I have something to show you." Axel steps back. I can't even look at him. If he's giving me an out and not forcing me to answer the question, I'll take it.

"Do you have your keys?" he asks as he steps out the front door.

"Yeah." We're leaving? But my face is on fire, and walking outside helps cool it.

Outside, Axel waits for me to catch up, then his hand is around my elbow. He pulls me to him, muttering in a low voice, "Get in the car, Raven."

"Where are we going?"

"You don't want to watch me embarrass myself?" He's so close we barely have an inch between us. I glance back to see Gage in the doorway. Buddy stands there, tail wagging and mouth breathing.

"Where?" I ask again.

"Car, little bird. You want to ruin the surprise?"

Axel starts herding me back towards the car, and I let him. When I drop into the driver's seat, Axel rushes around the front of the car like he's afraid I'll bolt. Then he gets in. "Seatbelt."

I huff, pulling it over my body.

Axel nods and then directs me to put the car in reverse. I do, then he gives me directions through town. It's not lost on me that the last time he did this, he tricked me into coming to Gage's house. The longer we go, the more tense I get. We pass familiar spots until, finally, we pull up in front of my studio apartment. Then, Axel slows the car and parks.

Is he… leaving me? Dropping me back off? Kicking me out? Pain and betrayal cut through my chest. "What…"

Axel shifts in his seat. "I had a whole thing planned." He thrums his finger against the center console. "It was embarrassing. A Gage thing."

He's so uncomfortable, it makes me curious. I watch the tense lines of his body, and his jaw clenches.

"Don't run, Raven." Axel's voice catches. "You'll break his heart."

My chest physically aches. So he's not going to let me get out of this conversation.

Axel clears his throat. "Don't make fun of me. I'm going to do this my way." He sucks in a deep breath. "I'm finding myself again in you. I don't know how the fuck you do it, but you're everything I'll never be. You're kind and smart and fucking brave. I need you to teach me to be fucking brave." His voice cracks, and he clears his throat. "We bought this place for you to make it into a bookstore or whatever else you want. Gage knows. If you leave, he'll never recover."

His words hit me in a wave. A multitude of emotions wash over me all at once. I don't know which one to address. The biggest one I feel is… relief. Axel *does* care. As much as he tries to pretend he doesn't, he does care. And he'll say it even when he knows I'm leaving.

The thought makes me want to cry. Relief of my own fills me. If they really want me to stay, maybe I don't have to leave.

I open my mouth, and Axel looks scared. Honest-to-god fear lines his whole body.

I smile softly. I just ask, "What was the other way?"

"What?" Axel looks my way, the whites of his eyes still visible.

"Gage's way?"

Axel snorts, his face getting pink. "A poem."

I try to picture Axel reading a poem, getting stiff with all the emotions, and a chuckle escapes me.

"Oh, you think that's funny?" Axel's whole face is rosy.

I don't think it's funny. I think it's sweet, but all the stress is rolling over me, and I can't keep from laughing. "It's sweet."

Axel looks disgusted. "Yeah, well. You owe me five packs of cinnamon gum."

I arch an eyebrow.

"Poems are expensive these days."

"I'm not paying you if I don't get to see it."

Axel crosses his arms. "I already threw it away." His eyes shift.

"No you didn't. Let me see it."

"Not a chance in hell, little bird. What's your answer?"

I get stiff again. "My answer?"

"Are you gonna break my brother's heart or not?"

There's a silence where I can see he's asking for more than just Gage. Axel is nervous. His fingers flutter on the console, and I can see tiny beads of sweat on his forehead. I don't think I've ever seen him like this. He's waiting for my answer. Waiting, not demanding. Not locking me in a room.

I swallow, then reach my hand over to cover his, squeezing once. "I can't work in a store while freezing my nuts off."

Axel blinks, then looks at me with an odd confusion.

"Does the heat work?" I ask.

There's a flash of something in his gaze. I think it's hope before he stifles it under a smirk. "And what if it does?"

"Good." I lean back. "'Cause all I can pay with is in poems, and a certain someone refuses to give me the one I'm owed."

"Fuck, Raven." Axel's tone is earnest, with so much relief in it that it makes my throat tighten. He lets his head fall back against the seat, releasing a breath. Then, he starts laughing, dropping his head to his hands.

I lightly slap his shoulder. "You said you'd embarrass yourself. You didn't even cry."

Axel just laughs more and pulls something out from under the seat. "Guess I won't have to use these."

Handcuffs. He has handcuffs.

This time, I punch him hard.

Axel leans over like I shot him, grasping his arm. "Jesus, woman!" But he's grinning.

"Be glad it wasn't the glasses this time." I stifle a smile at his antics.

Axel shoots me a look. "If it means I get to keep you, you can break my glasses all you want."

CHAPTER EIGHTY-TWO

RAVEN

Axel won't tell me what his plan is, but on the way back, he gets that spark in his eye that makes me both nervous and excited. Thinking about Gage sitting at home and thinking I don't want him makes me antsy, and I drive faster.

However, when we get back, I'm scared to go inside. I didn't mean to hurt Gage by leaving. Either of them.

Axel doesn't open my door. He just waits for me.

I suck in a few breaths, then step outside. Axel hands me something, and I glance down. It's his knife.

"Oh, now you give me this?" I ask.

There's a slight smirk on Axel's face. "I prefer my balls attached to my body, thank you very much."

"But not Gage's?"

"You wouldn't cut Gage." Axel strides toward the house with an annoying air of confidence.

When I make it inside, Gage is on the couch with Buddy. He half stands, then hesitates like he isn't sure if he should come up to me. I notice he has the new glasses on. Buddy rushes over to me.

I stop, hurt flowing through me. I hate the hesitant look in his eyes.

"Gage, I'm–"

"Read, Raven." Axel comes over to me with a bag of things. From it, he pulls a book. Not just any book. My book. The one I got with Gage.

Axel's voice drops an octave. "Read. Out loud. Now."

I want to argue, but Axel's tone tells me he'll enjoy it too much if I argue. Instead, I take the book, move to the couch, and sit down stiffly. I glance at Gage, who's looking at me with softness in his gaze.

"Sorry," I say softly, looking at the ground. "I got scared, I..."

Gage moves to sit next to me, and Buddy jumps up on the couch, too.

"Read, Raven," Axel demands loudly.

I flip the book open and start reading automatically.

"You never have to apologize for being scared, Raven." Gage's tone is soft.

I glance at him, and he looks nothing but sincere.

I read, but I'm not really comprehending what's going on. All I can think about is Gage's presence beside me, big and looming, and the way he's being so soft. They bought me a place to open a bookstore. It's so sweet, and I'm not sure how to express how much it means.

I switch from the story to say softly, "Axel didn't read me your poem–"

Axel stalks into the room, and he's carrying that bag. "Why'd you stop?"

I narrow my gaze. "What are you doing?"

"Read, and I'll answer."

I glare at him, but when he doesn't respond, reluctantly, I go back to the book.

"Here's the game," Axel says, and when I look up, he pauses. He motions back at the book. When I start reading but not comprehending, Axel keeps talking. "You're gonna peg Gage while you read that book."

My gaze snaps up.

Axel winks at me, and Gage mutters, "What?"

Axel pulls something from the bag, and it takes me a second to realize what I'm looking at. It's a harness with a hole in it. Axel pulls something from the bag. No, not something. A dildo.

And fuck, if excitement doesn't roll through me mixed with a little fear. I've never pegged someone.

"Axel," Gage grinds.

"Yes, my sugar plum?" Axel bats his eyes at him.

"What are you doing?"

"Getting you laid. Raven, please keep reading."

I slam the book shut. Axel just stares at it, then turns his bored eyes on me. "If you stop reading, you lose the right to come."

My mouth drops open.

"She can come whenever she wants," Gage growls.

"Okay. Then *you* lose the right to come." Axel shrugs. "Way to make it weird, brother."

"Wait," I say, turning to look at Gage. I expect to see anger on his face, and there is a little, but his pupils are blown, and his breathing is quick. He likes the idea.

Goosebumps run across my skin. Because I like the idea too.

"Now, Raven, please get undressed."

I narrow my gaze at Axel. "What are you going to do?"

"Fuck that sweet pussy while you peg my brother."

Oh fuck. *Oh fuck, oh fuck, oh fuck.*

Axel leans into me, breathing on my neck. "You like that idea, little bird?"

I huff, crossing my arms. "No."

He watches me for a second, then grins. "Keep reading. Gage, turn around."

Gage watches me for a second, voice low. "You okay, princess?"

He's asking about more than just this. My throat feels tight, and all I can do is drop my hand to my pocket, where I pull out the knife Axel gave me.

Gage looks at it, and then his gaze bounces up to mine.

"Axel gave it to me so I could cut his balls off."

Slowly, Gage smiles. "The lady hath upgraded her sword."

"Knight." I sniff at him.

"Read," Axel warns behind me. "And keep that thing away from my balls."

Gage winks at me, then slowly turns away from me, giving me his back. He kneels on the couch, clasping his hands behind his back.

I'm pretty sure Axel would take great joy in taking away Gage's right to come, so I rip my gaze away from Gage and try to find my place in the book again. I jump when I feel Axel's hands on my waist.

"Easy," he whispers. "Clothes first, then harness."

His hands trace softly along the hem of my pants, and then he pulls them down, taking my panties with them. I adjust to help him pull them off my legs. He then pulls off my shirt, letting me pause the reading and switch the book between my hands. I do my best to keep reading, heart pounding. I'm pretty sure they can hear the breathlessness my voice has taken.

Something wraps about my right thigh, then clicks securely behind me. Then, my other thigh. I glance down, seeing that Axel has secured the harness to my thighs, and there's already a flesh-colored dildo in it. My heart races, and I suck in a breath.

There's a soft chuckle behind me, then Axel's breath ghosts over my shoulder. "I'm gonna put some lube on your fingers so you can get him ready."

Get him ready? Fuck, I don't know how to do this.

"Read," Axel reminds gently.

I force myself to go back to the page, reading out loud while cold lube drizzles down my fingers. Anxiety tries to take over, but reading forces me to pay attention to something other than the things I don't know how to do.

"Touch him," Axel says.

I glance at Gage, whose face is pressed to the side, looking at me. He licks his lips. "You good?"

I nod, and he flashes me a grin. Then his pants are down, and he strips his shirt; his hands are clasped behind his back again. He's vulnerable and open before me, and it strikes me that I don't deserve his submission.

There's a strike of pain on my ass, and I yelp.

"Distracted?" Axel smirks.

"Jesus," I glare at him, but Gage's fingers clench and unclench, and I find myself staring at him again. And the ass he has offered up for me.

Slowly, I reach down, making sure to slide some of the lube down his crack, but then I reach between his legs and give his dick a pull. He's hard already, and he lets out a small moan. A moan that makes a shiver run down my shoulders.

I remember my task and start reading again, focusing on the words instead of wondering what Gage's ass would feel like against my fingers, about how tight he'd be if I tried to put a finger inside him.

Axel's hand traces down my ass, and I jump. He just chuckles, then I feel him bend down, and he bites the globe of my ass.

I yelp, jumping.

Gage looks back, and Axel drones, "Eyes forward, cupcake. I don't want to be gazing into your eyes while her wet cunt wraps around my dick."

The words fill me with anticipation, and I cup Gage's balls and squeeze. He closes his eyes and moans, rocking into my hand. Then slowly, ever so slowly, I trace my hand up to where I feel his asshole, rimming my fingers across it.

Gage groans this time, pressing back into me. As he does, I feel Axel's fingers drop down to my pussy, feathering across it.

I run my fingers over Gage's asshole a little firmer, and he bucks back into me again. "Fuck, princess. Both hands."

I pause and wait for him to look back over his shoulder. Then, I get back to reading the book in my other hand.

Gage groans, but I keep teasing him, emboldened. As I do, Axel teases me, fingers circling my clit just enough to get me excited before backing away. He does it a few times, and I get annoyed, putting my finger on Gage's asshole, feeling the warm lube. Then, I push, and my finger pops in. Gage lets out a full moan, clenching around me. Slowly, I piston it in and out, listening for the way his breathing flutters. It's so fucking hard to focus on the book when all I want to do is listen closer to the sounds Gage is making.

"Axel," I huff, dropping the book and handing it back to him. "That's enough."

"It's enough when I say it's enough." He leans up and bites the side of my neck. I gasp, arching my back, feeling my finger move in Gage, and his body tenses. I find myself torn between fighting Axel and just allowing him to direct the scene.

"I promise I'll let you enjoy it, pretty bird." Axel hums into my neck. "I just want to hear you come while you're trying so desperately to obey me."

The thought sends a shiver through me. He wants to hear the same sounds I want out of Gage. Axel is just like me.

For a brief second, I wrestle with the idea. Submitting means giving over an obscene amount of power. But then I look at the man submitting under me. He looks so beautiful and powerful. Not broken. Happy.

So I let out a breath and start reading the book again.

"Good girl," Axel's voice has gone growly, and he goes at my clit with renewed purpose. Slowly, I slip another finger up to where my other one is, pressing experimentally. Gage pushes back against me, so I pull out my one finger enough to slip another in. Gage's body bucks, but he lets out a soft moan.

I freeze, unsure if he's uncomfortable, but Gage glances back at me with a soft, shy look, and his pupils are blown.

His look sends pleasure shooting through me like lightning, and a small breath escapes me.

Axel soaks it up. I feel his body shiver behind me, and he attacks my clit with firm circles. As I read, I feel my body building up higher and higher. I'm close, so close, my breaths getting faster despite my effort to hide it.

Then Gage clenches hard on my fingers, and Axel tweaks my clit, and I come, moaning out my next word in a long breath, my voice getting deeper as the orgasm stretches on and on.

"Good girl. Good fucking girl. Trust me, and I'll reward you." Axel continues to play, dragging out my pleasure. Gage must be groaning, too, and the sounds are enough to stretch out the pulses in my body.

I blink, focusing fully on Gage on his knees in front of me. He looks blissed out, fine tremors going through his thighs as he leans heavily against the couch. His asshole is relaxed now, everything slippery from the lube.

I pull my fingers out and swipe the dildo along his ass, catching the loose lube and using it to prep the dick.

A shiver of something runs across my skin. I'm not sure if it's fear, anticipation, or both. But I do know that the sight of Gage spread out for me, trusting me, fills me with a warm feeling in my chest.

I don't deserve this.

I stare at him, eyes suddenly feeling prickly.

Gage glances back at me, and then something brushes my hand. I glance down, blinking. It's his hand. He grabs my finger and squeezes it once, twice. Then he says so softly I almost don't catch it, "I'll read you the poem later, princess."

Axel's fingers slow, then his lips are at the place where my neck connects to my shoulder, and he kisses it gently. "What are we whispering about?"

I have to stifle a smile, and then suddenly, my eyes burn even more. Because instead of being afraid, I feel... okay. No, more than okay. I feel happy. Safe. In control. And it's these two that made me feel that way.

A vast wave of peace washes over me, and it feels like that scary thing that's always been around the corner fades into oblivion. I don't need to be scared of it. I don't need to keep running from it. Because I'm safe.

I catch myself before I can cry, focusing on the dildo to get myself back together.

Gage is ready, his hole open and glistening with lube.

"Ready?" I ask, my voice no more than a whisper.

"Never more," Gage leans back into me softly, his legs and ass pressing into me, grounding me.

If he's ready, maybe I can be too.

Then, slowly, I bring the tip of the dildo to Gage's ass. He arches his back, and the tip disappears inside him.

The sight fills me with an erotic thrill. Gage's body accepts everything I have to give him, pushing back on the strap like he's eager for it. Like he's eager for me.

I reach a hand down to grab his dick, and it's hot and throbbing.

"No, wait, I'll come."

I grin, and then I feel something pressing against me. Axel is standing behind me, rubbing his dick along my slit.

I bend over to give him a better angle, leaning against Gage's back, feeling the rumbles in his back and the pressure of my tits pressed up against him. I take a little bite out of Gage's side, enjoying the way he tenses for a second, then relaxes back into me.

Axel presses into me, and the sudden feeling of fullness hits me all at once. His movement forces me deeper into Gage, which makes him grunt. It feels so overwhelming that my brain short-circuits.

Axel doesn't let me overthink it. He just rocks into me, dick rubbing up against my G-spot, pushing me into ecstasy. I reach around, grabbing Gage's dick and just holding. I squeeze as he pulses once, twice. Then he bucks back into me, jerking back and forth.

"Oh Raven, fuck, I think I'm gonna—"

"Come," I demand, jerking him off. With a high-pitched groan, he does, his entire body locking as pulse after pulse of cum spurts from him.

Axel groans, cupping my neck and yanking me back to his chest. Then he pounds into me, taking my body in claiming strokes that feel like he's branding me as his. The movement forces me and the dildo into Gage's body, and he groans, bracing his legs wider.

As I come, I realize that I didn't want to run from these two in the first place. I was just afraid. Afraid of things not being perfect. Afraid of getting hurt.

But you know what?

Things will never be perfect. Life will never be perfect. I will never be perfect.

But that doesn't mean I can't be happy. That I can't be safe, even when I'm scared.

And that's really all I need.

3 Months Later

"Would you... hold still?" I try to hold Buddy down to wrestle her into the costume I've prepared for her. She tries to bite at the cardboard pieces I've glued to a harness.

"No!" I giggle, only getting one side on before I hear someone at the door. I jump up, pretending like I'm messing with the food on the counter.

It's Gage and Axel's birthday today. I've spent the day decorating and preparing, nervously bustling from one task to another. They're going to think it's so stupid.

"Honey, I'm home," Axel yells from the front door. There's a silence, and then he stalks into the kitchen. "Hey, little bird. What have you been doing?"

I keep mixing the salad, and he comes up behind me, putting his chin on my shoulder.

"Happy birthday," I say.

There's a pause, then Axel bites my neck gently. "Thank you."

While he and I aren't the sappy types, we're both getting far more comfortable with expressing emotion around each other.

The front door opens again, and I hear Gage walk in. I glance over to see Buddy dancing at his feet, her costume half falling off.

"What's this?" Gage looks confused, then laughs at the dog.

I groan, slapping my hands over my cheeks. "That wasn't the whole thing. She wouldn't let me get the costume on."

"It looks... good!" Gage says, a smile creeping at the corners of his mouth. He stalks up to me in dark slacks and a button-up, turning my face to his and planting a kiss there.

"She's supposed to be a rhinorse," I mutter.

Gage's mouth parts, then his gaze softens. "Raven... that's..."

"Stupid, I know." I turn back to the salad.

"Really sweet," Gage finishes, turning my face again to kiss me. His kiss is soft at first. Almost reverent. Then, he kisses me harder, gripping my face and pulling me into him. It leaves me breathless, and I pull away, cheeks heating. "Dinner is ready if you guys want to eat."

"Dinner?" Axel sounds excited.

"Pizza." I motion at the dining room, then look at Gage. "And steak. Although I'm not sure if I did it right."

"Oh my god." Gage is grinning.

"Sit down," I hustle him to the dining room. As long as I can stay busy serving them, the burning flush on my cheeks will stay down.

Both boys settle in, and I notice they've worn the same outfit today. Fitted black shirts with dark slacks and dark glasses. The dark colors bring out their pale features in a way that makes them look frosted over. They look hot. Like they always do. I do have to do a double-take, ensuring they both sat in their respective spots.

If possible, the men have only gotten hotter over the last few months. They've both been getting to know me in their own ways, fighting over which nights are theirs to take me on dates and, sometimes, taking me out together. They both also help with my future bookstore. Axel assists with the business and sales aspects, while Gage handles the legal and accounting matters. I'm going to call it Buddy's Books. It's stressful as fuck. There are all kinds of things that go into owning a business that I had no idea about. Even today, it was tough to pull myself away to make this dinner.

The boys motion for me to sit between them, as has become our custom. Axel on the left, Gage on the right. I'm sure they decided to do that so they could both feel me up while we eat, as they both do. Often.

As the boys load up their plates, I notice the subtle attention both of them are paying me. The way their bodies lean toward me and how when I reach for a slice of pizza, their heads follow the movement.

They dig in, and I take a few bites, but I was grazing as I cooked. This meal is about them, not me.

I eye the steak. It looks dark. Did I cook it too long?

"Gonna eat that?"

I glance up to see both of them still eyeing me.

"Oh, yeah." I wave them off, then pick up the pizza and take a bite. It's mostly to appease them. I wonder if the paperwork I filed earlier went through. I haven't heard back from the state at all. I find that the stress the business brings makes me less interested in food and more interested in solving every problem right as it pops up. This is my first time being self-sufficient. It means I don't have to rely on anyone financially, even though the boys would never let me suffer. But I want this for myself.

Gage reaches out and shoves my plate towards me. I blink. I must have zoned out.

"Is the steak okay?" I ask.

"Delicious," Gage says on my right. "Now try some."

"Nah, I ate while I was cooking," I shrug.

Silence. Then, Gage's low voice drones, "Did you just 'nah' me?" His voice is unbothered, but the quiet heat behind it has me stiffening.

I glance to my right, narrowing my eyes at him.

"She definitely did." Axel's hand drops heavily onto my thigh on my other side.

"Wanna rethink that?" Gage asks, his look hooded. There's a flash of something before it's gone. That flash of something makes me want to push back. Gage is usually so submissive. Now he wants to challenge me?

I raise an eyebrow. "It's the truth."

"You need to eat dinner."

His tone brooks no argument, which surprises me further. What has gotten up his ass? "Need?" I ask, turning so I can look straight into Gage's eyes. He doesn't blink.

"Is there an echo in here?" Axel squeezes my thigh, and then his lips are at my ear. "I'd suggest you do as he says."

"And I'd suggest you don't tell me what to do." I drop my hand over the one on my thigh and squeeze back hard. "I'm not hungry."

There's a moment of stillness that's loaded with energy. It makes heat curl across my skin as I feel their undivided attention on me. Both of them feel like Axel right now, and with Axel, I usually lose control in a way that makes me feel like I'm in control, but I'm really not.

Then, Axel chuckles, and slowly, Gage stands up. His chair pushes back with a scrape, and adrenaline rushes through me. I poked the bear. The bear that's normally a dog and rolls over on its belly for me.

I stand up, but as soon as I do, Axel wraps his arms around my torso and yanks me back down onto his lap.

"Hey!" A mixture of arousal and anger flushes under my skin, and I fight his hold. But Axel's grip is firm, holding me tightly on his lap. He's firm, but his grip doesn't hurt.

"What the hell?" I sputter.

Gage sits on the table slightly in front of me, muscled thighs spread. He says nothing; he just grabs my plate and starts heaping food onto it.

"Axel," I swing my head around to glare at him.

He just raises an eyebrow.

"Please, I–" I don't know how to feel. Aroused, definitely. But there's still a hum of frustration. Usually, I'm in control. They're taking that from me.

Gage turns back to me, plate on his leg, the pieces of meat all chopped up. "Pizza or steak first?"

I let my gaze travel up his thigh to his torso, then meet his gaze. Slowly, I arch an eyebrow. "What do you think you're doing?"

If I expected him to roll over and show me his belly, he doesn't. "Feeding my woman." He motions at the plate. "Steak or pizza?"

"Is there an echo in here?" I ask. "It's your birthday. I should be doing this for you."

His gaze flashes briefly. "Right. It's our birthday. So why don't you be a good little present and give us what we want?"

I huff out a breath of air, trying to grasp any strand of control I can get. "Your ass is gonna pay for this later. You know that, right?"

Axel chuckles under me, and I feel the vibrations through my back.

Gage leans down, fixing his gaze on me. I meet it with a mixture of anger, confusion, and a bit of fear.

Slowly, Gage reaches his hand out to touch my face.

I lean my head back in silent defiance. He just follows the motion, gently cupping my jaw, then tracing his fingers down it. He then moves his fingers to my forehead, tracing them between my eyebrows, smoothing the wrinkle there.

"You haven't been eating enough."

His words settle over me. I haven't been eating enough? That's ridiculous. I've been eating. "I don't know what you're talking about, Gage. I eat."

Gage just hums, then his hand grazes down the side of my face to my neck, then down to my arm. The touch is feather-light but somehow still burns as it goes. He moves across where his brother has my arms pinned, then finds my wrist.

Prickles of pleasure run up my skin.

"You haven't been eating enough. Your skin gets dry, your hair is rougher than normal, and you're less quick to laugh. You're stressed, Raven." His fingers stop dancing across my skin, and then he grabs my wrist and squeezes. "I won't stand by while my woman doesn't take care of herself."

His attention is like a heavy weight. I feel it all over my body, and I shift under Axel's muscled arms. He doesn't ease up.

"I..."

"So Raven..." his voice softens. "Celeste." Then it softens even further, so it's just a whisper. "Princess. You're gonna eat some steak for us. Then some pizza." Gage picks up a piece of meat with his fingers and pushes it toward my face.

"Wait!" I swallow, pulling my head back, feeling heady and unbalanced. Like he just stripped me naked for both of them to see. And maybe he kind of did.

Gage pauses.

"Wait, I..." I try to come up with a suitable response. Shame washes over me, along with anger. He's right; I haven't been taking care of myself. I've been putting the business first. But it wasn't like I was trying to neglect myself. I don't like that he not only saw it, but he called me out on it. "I'll eat when you let me go. Don't tell me what to do."

There's a pregnant silence in which Axel does not let me go.

Gage takes one breath in. I see his chest expanding, filling up his shirt.

For a brief second, I look for that old fear that's followed me most of my life. Only, it's just Gage in front of me. The familiar lines of his body soften as he lets the breath out.

"I don't think you're understanding." Gage leans in. "I can and will tell you what to do. You do it for us all the time. And we love it. I'll always get off on letting you take the reins, Raven. But," he leans closer till his breath brushes my face, "that doesn't mean we won't take care of you." His hand traces back up my arm. "That we won't notice every detail you may not see your-self." He's up to my shoulder. "And what I noticed is you're not eating." Then, his hand is at my neck, and he wraps his fingers around it, gently squeezing. "You can be angry. You can fight us, but you have to eat."

I swallow, feeling my throat bob against his hand. He's not letting up on the pressure, but he's not hurting me. He's just a steady presence, one that'll just push harder if I fight. Again, I search for that old fear. I don't find it. Instead, I just find comfort.

"Do you trust us enough to take care of you, Raven?"

The question is soft. So soft in contrast to the two powerful men around me.

My heart races. Not because the answer is no. Because the answer is yes. I *do* trust them.

Gage is still holding my throat, waiting for a response. I don't say anything. Instead, I relax into Axel's hold and open my mouth. Relinquishing control. Inviting Gage to do what he wants. To take care of me.

There's silence for a beat, and then Gage makes a throaty sound. Under me, I feel Axel's crotch stiffen.

Gage tries to clear it, then offers me a bite of steak. I take it, the flavor dancing on my tongue. It's good. Really fucking good.

"That's a good girl." Gage's voice is husky. "That's a good fucking girl."

He feeds me bite by bite, alternating the steak and the pizza. As he does, I feel my grip on the business worries start to slip away. I'd love to be financially independent. And I will be one day. But that won't come at the expense of my relationship with Gage and Axel. I won't let my past build up walls between us.

Axel loosens his hold, rubbing circles on my skin. Both of them shower me with attention until it makes me dizzy.

Finally, when the food is gone, I'm not sure if I need to jump their bones or let them jump mine.

Then, I remember that it is their birthday, and I got them presents. For a second, I worry they'll think the presents are stupid. Then, I shake that off.

Gently, I wiggle my way off Axel's lap, and this time, he lets me. I go to grab the gifts, and when I return, both men are clearing off the table.

"Shit, Raven, you didn't have to do this," Gage says, but I see the flash of softness in his eyes. Axel too.

"I know I didn't *have* to." I step around Gage to hand a long, wrapped gift to Axel. Before he can grab it, I throw it at his chest.

Axel jumps in surprise. "What the—"

"It's bread. Figured it was a bit of a tradition at this point."

Axel unwraps the item, which is, in fact, a long baguette. He laughs, eyes shining.

"Shoulda hit him in the head," Gage grumbles.

I plop a bag in front of Axel. "This is the real gift."

Axel doesn't take his eyes off me, and there's a hunger there. But slowly, he pulls an item out of the bag. "Nail polish?"

"For you," I say. "And me. Figured you could get your skills up. For real this time."

Axel looks surprised, then excited. Then he frowns. "For me?"

"Yep." I pop the p. "You're gonna let me do your nails so I can tell you two apart."

Axel gasps in fake outrage.

In reality, I want to spend more time with him. More time where his legs are pressing into mine, and he's touching all over me. More time talking about nothing and everything all at once.

Gage laughs. "Oh, how perfect. Raven won't be the only princess in the house."

I expect Axel to argue, but he just smirks at me. "Okay, game on."

Gage's present is in front of him. I squirm. Axel's gifts were funny, but Gage's are more thoughtful. Gage opens his slowly, and when he sees what's inside, he stares for a minute.

"It's okay if you don't like it, I just thought—"

"Raven." Gage shuffles through the books on tape I got for him, looking through the titles. I worked with their mom to find all of Gage's favorite books from when he was a kid.

Gage looks up at me, eyes shining with tears. "It's perfect. Thank you."

I can't keep a smile back, and I kiss him.

Axel clears his throat. "Is now a good time to tell you you've gotten us mixed up?"

I laugh, pulling away from Gage, but both of them look serious.

"You're lying." I poke at Axel's chest. He just raises an eyebrow. "Am I, princess?"

I glance between the two of them. I've known them for long enough now that it's second nature to tell them apart. The way they act feels like night and day. Except right now, they're both acting the same.

"Hey," I narrow my eyes. "Not funny."

Neither of them reacts.

"Let's play a game." The one on the right stands. "You run, we'll chase."

I stiffen, a thrill running through me.

"You guess who's who correctly, and you get to pick who to peg. You guess incorrectly..." He looks down at me, a grin twitching on his lips.

The other one speaks up, "You get it wrong, and the name you guess gets to peg *you*."

The twin beneath me stands. I could swear it's Gage, but he gives me a mean smirk and that flips everything upside down.

I suck in a breath, licking my lips. I feel alive. Before, I would have run for the hills. Now, I enjoy the thrill. Because Gage shows me what it's like to love when you're scared. And Axel... Axel shows you can be broken and still loveable.

And I think that's what I was looking for all along.

The End.

ACKNOWLEDGMENTS

Thank you so much to my team, my crew, and my book family. Sarah, Alex, Taylor, and Laurelyn. You guys help SO MUCH, and I'm sooooo grateful for you. Except you, Taylor. You told me pantyhose is not spelled pantihoes, and I'd like to file a formal complaint.

An extra thank you to my sensitivity readers, Alisha, Mariah, and Kelsey, as well! You guys are the absolute best; thank you so much for helping me make this story better.

If anyone is actually still reading this, thank *you*. I love sharing my stories with you guys. I have the best job in the world.

If this is your first Alina book and you want more, please be warned that my other books are significantly darker than this one.

You can stalk me on:
    TikTok - alina_may_author
    Instagram - alina_may_author
    Facebook - Alina May's Book Babes